# THE SLEEPING DOLL

# THE SLEEPING DOLL

## Jeffery
## DEAVER

HODDER &
STOUGHTON

Copyright © 2007 by Jeffery Deaver

First published in The United States of America in 2007 by Simon & Schuster, Inc.

First published in Great Britain in 2007 by Hodder & Stoughton
A division of Hodder Headline

The right of Jeffery Deaver to be identified as the Author of the Work
has been asserted by him in accordance with the Copyright, Designs and
Patents Act 1988.

A Hodder & Stoughton Book

1

A CIP catalogue record for this title is available from the British Library

Hardback ISBN 978 0 340 83384 1
Trade paperback ISBN 978 0 340 83385 8

Typeset in Fairfield Light by
Palimpsest Book Production Limited, Grangemouth, Stirlingshire

Printed and bound by Clays Ltd, St Ives plc

Hodder Headline's policy is to use papers that are natural, renewable and
recyclable products and made from wood grown in sustainable forests.
The logging and manufacturing processes are expected to conform to the
environmental regulations of the country of origin.

Hodder & Stoughton Ltd
A division of Hodder Headline
338 Euston Road
London NW1 3BH

'The Boxer'
Copyright © 1968 Paul Simon
Used by permission of the Publisher: Paul Simon Music

*For the G Man*

*After changes upon changes, we are more or less the same.*
*After changes we are more or less the same.*

Paul Simon, 'The Boxer'

September 13, 1999

# 'Son of Manson' Found Guilty In Croyton Family Murders

Salinas, California – Daniel Raymond Pell, 35, was convicted today on four counts of first-degree murder and one count of manslaughter by a Monterey County jury after only five hours of deliberations.

'Justice has been done,' lead prosecutor James J. Reynolds told reporters after the verdict was announced. 'This is an extremely dangerous man, who committed horrendous crimes.'

Pell became known as the 'Son of Manson' because of the parallels between his life and that of convicted murderer Charles Manson, who in 1969 was responsible for the ritualistic slayings of the actress Sharon Tate and several other individuals in Southern California. Police found many books and articles about Manson in Pell's house following his arrest.

The murder convictions were for the May 7 deaths of William Croyton, his wife and two of their three children in Carmel, Calif., 120 miles south of San Francisco. The manslaughter charge arose from the death of James Newberg, 24, who lived with Pell and accompanied him to the Croyton house the night of the murders. The prosecutor asserted that Newberg initially intended to assist in the murders but was then killed by Pell after he changed his mind.

Croyton, 56, was a wealthy electrical engineer and computer innovator. His Cupertino, Calif., company, in the heart of Silicon Valley, produces state-of-the-art programs that are found in much of the world's most popular personal computer software.

Because of Pell's interest in Manson, there was speculation that the killings had ideological overtones, as did the murders for which Manson was convicted, but robbery was the most likely reason for the break-in, Reynolds said. Pell has dozens of prior convictions for shoplifting, burglary and robbery, dating back to his teens.

One child survived the attack, a daughter, Theresa, 9. Pell overlooked the girl, who was in her bed asleep and hidden by her toys. Because of this, she became known as the 'Sleeping Doll'.

Like Charles Manson, the criminal he admired, Pell exuded a dark charisma and attracted a group of devoted and fanatical followers, whom he called his 'Family' – a term borrowed from the Manson clan – and over whom he exercised absolute control. At the time of the Croyton murders this group included Newberg and three women, all living together in a shabby house in Seaside, north of Monterey, Calif. They are Rebecca Sheffield, 26, Linda Whitfield, 20, and Samantha McCoy, 19. Whitfield is the daughter of Lyman Whitfield, president and CEO of Santa Clara Bank and Trust, headquartered in Cupertino, the fourth largest banking chain in the state.

The women were not charged in the deaths of the Croytons or Newberg but were convicted of multiple counts of larceny, trespass, fraud and receiving stolen property. Whitfield was also convicted of hampering an investigation, perjury and destroying evidence. As part of a plea bargain, Sheffield and McCoy were sentenced to three years in prison, Whitfield to four and a half.

Pell's behavior at trial also echoed Charles Manson's. He would sit motionless at the defense table and stare at jurors and witnesses in apparent attempts to intimidate them. There were reports that he believed he had psychic powers. The defendant was removed once from the courtroom after a witness broke down under his gaze.

The jury begins sentencing deliberations tomorrow. Pell could get the death penalty.

## Chapter
# ONE

The interrogation began like any other.

Kathryn Dance entered the interview room and found the forty-three-year-old man sitting at a metal table, shackled, looking up at her closely. Subjects always did this, of course, though never with such astonishing eyes. Their color was a blue unlike sky or ocean or famous gems.

'Good morning,' she said, sitting down across from him.

'And to you,' replied Daniel Pell, the man who eight years ago had knifed to death four members of a family for reasons he'd never shared. His voice was soft.

A slight smile on his bearded face, the small, sinewy man sat back, relaxed. His head, covered with long, gray-black hair, was cocked to the side. While most jailhouse interrogations were accompanied by a jingling soundtrack of handcuff chains as subjects tried to prove their innocence with broad, predictable gestures, Daniel Pell sat perfectly still.

To Dance, a specialist in interrogation and kinesics – body language – Pell's demeanor and posture suggested caution, but also confidence and, curiously, amusement. He wore an orange jumpsuit, stenciled with 'Capitola Correctional Facility' on the chest and 'Inmate' unnecessarily decorating the back.

At the moment, though, Pell and Dance were not in Capitola but, rather, a secure interview room at the county courthouse in Salinas, forty miles away.

Pell continued his examination. First, he regarded Dance's own eyes – a green complementary to his blue – and framed by square, black-rimmed glasses. He then perused her French-braided, dark-blonde hair, the black jacket and beneath it the thick, unrevealing white blouse. He noted too the empty holster on her hip. He was meticulous and in no hurry; interviewers and interviewees share mutual curiosity. (She told the students in her interrogation seminars, 'They're studying you as hard as you're studying them – usually even harder, since they have more to lose.')

Dance fished in her blue Coach purse for her ID card, not reacting as she saw a tiny toy bat, from last year's Halloween, that either twelve-year-old Wes, his younger sister, Maggie, or possibly both conspirators had slipped into the bag that morning as a practical joke. She thought: How's this for a contrasting life? An hour ago she was having break-fast with her children in the kitchen of their homey Victorian house in idyllic Pacific Grove, two exuberant dogs at their feet begging for bacon, and now here she sat, across a very different table, from a convicted murderer.

She found the ID and displayed it. He stared for a long moment, easing forward. 'Dance. Interesting name. Wonder where it comes from. And the California Bureau . . . what is that?'

'Bureau of Investigation. Like an FBI for the state. Now, Mr Pell, you understand that this conversation is being recorded?'

He glanced at the mirror, behind which a video camera was humming away. 'You folks think we really believe that's there so we can fix up our hair?'

Mirrors weren't placed in interrogation rooms to hide cameras and witnesses – there are far better high-tech ways to do so – but because people are less inclined to lie when they can see themselves.

Dance gave a faint smile. 'And you understand that you can withdraw from this interview anytime you want and that you have a right to an attorney?'

'I know more criminal procedure than the entire graduating class of Hastings Law rolled up together. Which is a pretty funny image, when you think about it.'

More articulate than Dance expected. More clever too.

The previous week, Daniel Raymond Pell, serving a life sentence for the 1999 murders of William Croyton, his wife and two of their chil-dren, had approached a fellow prisoner due to be released from Capitola and tried to bribe him to run an errand after he was free. Pell told him about some evidence he'd disposed of in a Salinas well years ago and explained that he was worried the items would implicate him in the unsolved murder of a wealthy farm owner. He'd read recently that Salinas was revamping its water system. This had jogged his memory and he'd grown concerned that the evidence would be discovered. He wanted the prisoner to find and dispose of it.

Pell picked the wrong man to enlist, though. The short-timer spilled to the warden, who called the Monterey County Sheriff's Office. Investigators wondered if Pell was talking about the unsolved murder of farm owner Robert Herron, beaten to death a decade ago. The murder weapon, probably a claw hammer, was never found. The Sheriff's Office sent a team to search all the wells in that part of town. Sure enough, they found a tattered T-shirt, a claw hammer and an empty wallet with the initials *R.H.* stamped on it. Two fingerprints on the hammer were Daniel Pell's.

The Monterey County prosecutor decided to present the case to the grand jury in Salinas, and asked CBI Agent Kathryn Dance to interview him, in hopes of a confession.

Dance now began the interrogation, asking, 'How long did you live in the Monterey area?'

He seemed surprised that she didn't immediately begin to browbeat. 'A few years.'

'Where?'

'Seaside.' A town of about 30,000, north of Monterey on Highway 1, populated mostly by young working families and retirees. 'You got more for your hard-earned money there,' he explained. 'More than in your fancy Carmel.' His eyes alighted on her face.

His grammar and syntax were good, she noted, ignoring his fishing expedition for information about her residence.

Dance continued to ask about his life in Seaside and in prison, observing him the whole while: how he behaved when she asked the questions and how he behaved when he answered. She wasn't doing this to get information – she'd done her homework and knew the answers to everything she asked – but was instead establishing his behavioral baseline.

In spotting lies, interrogators consider three factors: nonverbal behavior (body language, or kinesics), verbal quality (pitch of voice or pauses before answering) and verbal content (what the suspect says). The first two are far more reliable indications of deception, since it's much easier to control *what* we say than *how* we say it and our body's natural reaction when we do.

The baseline is a catalog of those behaviors exhibited when the subject is telling the truth. This is the standard the interrogator will compare later with the subject's behavior when he might have a reason to lie. Any differences between the two suggest deception.

Finally Dance had a good profile of the truthful Daniel Pell and moved to the crux of her mission in this modern, sterile courthouse on a foggy morning in June. 'I'd like to ask you a few questions about Robert Herron.'

Eyes sweeping hers, now refining their examination: the abalone shell necklace, which her mother had made, at her throat. Then Dance's short, pink-polished nails. The gray pearl ring on the wedding-band finger got two glances.

'How did you meet Herron?'

'You're assuming I did. But, no, never met him in my life. I swear.'

The last sentence was a deception flag, though his body language wasn't giving off signals that suggested he was lying.

'But you told the prisoner in Capitola that you wanted him to go to the well and find the hammer and wallet.'

'No, that's what *he* told the warden.' Pell offered another amused smile. 'Why don't you talk to him about it? You've got sharp eyes, Officer Dance. I've seen them looking me over, deciding if I'm being straight with you. I'll bet you could tell in a flash that that boy was lying.'

She gave no reaction, but reflected that it was very rare for a suspect to realize he was being analyzed kinesically. 'But then how did he know about the evidence in the well?'

'Oh, I've got that figured out. Somebody stole a hammer of mine, killed Herron with it and planted it to blame me. They wore gloves. Those rubber ones everybody wears on *CSI*.'

Still relaxed. The body language wasn't any different from his baseline. He was showing only emblems – common gestures that tended to substitute for words, like shrugs and finger pointing. There were no adaptors, which signal tension, or affect displays – signs that he was experiencing emotion.

'But if he wanted to do that,' Dance pointed out, 'wouldn't the killer just call the police *then* and tell them where the hammer was? Why wait more than ten years?'

'Being smart, I'd guess. Better to bide his time. Then spring the trap.'

'But why would the real killer call the prisoner in Capitola? Why not just call the police directly?'

A hesitation. Then a laugh. His blue eyes shone with excitement, which seemed genuine. 'Because *they*'re involved too. The police. Sure . . . The cops realize the Herron case hasn't been solved and they want to blame somebody. Why not *me*? They've already got me in jail. I'll bet the cops planted the hammer themselves.'

'Let's work with this a little. There're two different things you're saying. First, somebody stole your hammer *before* Herron was killed, murdered him with it and now, all this time later, dimes you out. But your second version is that the police got your hammer *after* Herron was killed by someone else altogether and planted it in the well to blame you. Those're contradictory. It's either one or the other. Which do you think?'

'Hm.' Pell thought for a few seconds. 'Okay, I'll go with number two. The police. It's a set-up. I'm sure that's what happened.'

She looked him in the eyes, green on blue. Nodding agreeably. 'Let's consider that. First, where would the police have gotten the hammer?'

He thought. 'When they arrested me for that Carmel thing.'

'The Croyton murders in ninety-nine?'

'Right. All the evidence they took from my house in Seaside.'

Dance's brows furrowed. 'I doubt that. Evidence is accounted for too closely. No, I'd go for a more credible scenario: that the hammer was stolen recently. Where else could somebody find a hammer of yours? Do you have any property in the state?'

'No.'

'Any relatives or friends who could've had some tools of yours?'

'Not really.'

Which wasn't an answer to a yes-or-no question; it was even more slippery than 'I don't recall.' Dance noticed too that Pell had put his hands, tipped with long, clean nails, on the table at the word 'relatives'. This was a deviation from baseline behavior. It didn't mean lying, but he *was* feeling stress. The questions were upsetting him.

'Daniel, do you have any relations living in California?'

He hesitated, must have assessed that she was the sort to check out every comment – which she was – and said, 'The only one left's my aunt. Down in Bakersfield.'

'Is her name Pell?'

Another pause. 'Yep . . . That's good thinking, Officer Dance. I'll bet the deputies who dropped the ball on the Herron case stole that hammer from her house and planted it. They're the ones behind this whole thing. Why don't you talk to them?'

'All right. Now let's think about the wallet. Where could that've come from? . . . Here's a thought. What if it's not Robert Herron's wallet at all? What if this rogue cop we're talking about just bought a wallet, had *R.H.* stamped in the leather, then hid that and the hammer in the well? It could've been last month. Or even last week. What do you think about that, Daniel?'

Pell lowered his head – she couldn't see his eyes – and said nothing.

It was unfolding just as she'd planned.

Dance had forced him to pick the more credible of two explanations for his innocence – and proceeded to prove it *wasn't* credible at all. No sane jury would believe that the police had fabricated evidence and stolen tools from a house hundreds of miles away from the crime scene. Pell was now realizing the mistake he'd made. The trap was about to close on him.

*Checkmate* . . .

Her heart thumped a bit and she was thinking that the next words out of his mouth might be about a plea bargain.

She was wrong.

His eyes snapped open and bored into hers with pure malevolence. He lunged forward as far as he could. Only the chains hooked to the metal chair, grounded with bolts to the tile floor, stopped him from sinking his teeth into her.

She jerked back, gasping.

'You goddamn bitch! Oh, I get it now. Sure, you're part of it too! Yeah, yeah, blame Daniel. It's always my fault! I'm the easy target. And you come in here sounding like a friend, asking me a few questions. Jesus, you're just like the rest of them!'

Her heart was pounding furiously now, and she was afraid. But she noted quickly that the restraints were secure and he couldn't reach her. She turned to the mirror, behind which the officer manning the video camera was surely rising to his feet right now to help her. But she shook her head his way. It was important to see where this was going.

Then suddenly Pell's fury was replaced with a cold calm. He sat back, caught his breath and looked her over again. 'You're in your thirties, Officer Dance. You're somewhat pretty. You seem straight to me, so I guarantee there's a man in your life. Or has been.' A third glance at the pearl ring.

'If you don't like my theory, Daniel, let's come up with another one. About what really happened to Robert Herron.'

As if she hadn't even spoken. 'And you've got children, right? Sure, you do. I can see that. Tell me all about them. Tell me about the little ones. Close in age, and not too old, I'll bet.'

This unnerved her and she thought instantly of Maggie and Wes. But she struggled not to react. He *doesn't* know I have children, of course. He can't. But he acts as if he's certain. Was there something about *my* behavior he noted? Something that suggested to him that I'm a mother?

*They're studying you as hard as you're studying them . . .*

'Listen to me, Daniel,' she said smoothly, 'an outburst isn't going to help anything.'

'I've got friends on the outside, you know. They owe me. They'd love to come visit you. Or hang with your husband and children. Yeah, it's a tough life being a cop. The little ones spend a lot of time alone, don't they? They'd probably love some friends to play with.'

Dance returned his gaze, never flinching. She asked, 'Could you tell me about your relationship with that prisoner in Capitola?'

'Yes, I could. But I won't.' His emotionless words mocked her, suggesting that, for a professional interrogator, she'd phrased her question carelessly. In a soft voice he added, 'I think it's time to go back to my cell.'

# Chapter
## TWO

Alonzo 'Sandy' Sandoval, the Monterey County prosecutor, was a handsome, round man with a thick head of black hair and an ample moustache. He sat in his office, two flights above the lockup, behind a desk littered with files. 'Hi, Kathryn. So, our boy . . . Did he beat his breast and cry, *"Mea culpa"?'*

'Not exactly.' Dance sat down, peered into the coffee cup she'd left on the desk forty-five minutes ago. Non-dairy creamer scummed the surface. 'I rate it as, oh, one of the least successful interrogations of all time.'

'You look shook, boss,' said a short, wiry young man, with freckles and curly red hair, wearing jeans, a T-shirt and a plaid sports coat. TJ's outfit was unconventional for an investigative agent with the CBI – the most conservative law-enforcement agency in the Great Bear State – but so was pretty much everything else about him. Around thirty and single, TJ Scanlon lived in the hills of Carmel Valley, his house a ramshackle place that could have been a diorama in a counter-culture museum depicting California life in the 1960s. TJ tended to work solo much of the time, surveillance and undercover, rather than pairing up with another CBI agent, which was the bureau's standard procedure. But Dance's regular partner was in Mexico on an extradition and TJ had jumped at the chance to help out and see the Son of Manson.

'Not shook. Just *curious.*' She explained how the interview had been going fine when, suddenly, Pell turned on her. Under TJ's skeptical gaze, she conceded, 'Okay, I'm a *little* shook. I've been threatened before. But his were the worst kinds of threats.'

'Worst?' asked Juan Millar, a tall, dark-complexioned young detective with the Investigations Division of the MCSO – the Monterey County Sheriff's Office, which was headquartered not far from the courthouse.

'*Calm* threats,' Dance said.

TJ filled in, '*Cheerful* threats. You know you're in trouble when they stop screaming and start whispering.'

*The little ones spend a lot of time alone . . .*

'What happened?' Sandoval asked, seemingly more concerned about the state of his case than threats against Dance.

'When he denied knowing Herron, there was no stress reaction at all. It was only when I had him talking about police conspiracy that he started to exhibit aversion and negation. Some extremity movement too, deviating from his baseline.'

Kathryn Dance was often called a human lie detector, but that wasn't accurate; in reality she, like all successful kinesic analysts and inter-rogators, was a *stress* detector. This was the key to deception; once she spotted stress, she'd probe the topic that gave rise to it and dig until the subject broke.

Kinesics experts identify several different types of stress individuals experience. Some types arise primarily when someone isn't telling the whole truth. Dance called this 'deception stress'. But people also ex-perience general stress, which occurs when they are merely uneasy or nervous, and has nothing to do with lying. It's what we all feel when, say, we're late for work, have to give a speech in public or are afraid of physical harm. Dance had found that different kinesic behaviors signal the two kinds of stress.

She explained this and added, 'My sense was that he'd lost control of the interview and couldn't get it back. So he went ballistic.'

'Even though what you were saying *supported* his defense?' Lanky Juan Millar scratched his left hand absently. In the fleshy Y between the index finger and thumb was a scar, the remnant of a removed gang tat.

'Exactly.'

Then Dance's mind made one of its curious jumps. *A to B to X.* She couldn't explain how they happened. But she always paid attention. 'Where was Robert Herron murdered?' She walked to a map of Monterey County on Sandoval's wall.

'Here.' The prosecutor touched an area in the yellow trapezoid.

'And the well where they found the hammer and wallet?'

'About here, make it.'

It was a quarter mile from the crime scene, in a residential area.

Dance was staring at the map. She felt TJ's eyes on her. 'What's wrong, boss?'

'You have a picture of the well?' she asked.

Sandoval dug in the file. 'Juan's forensic people shot a lot of pics.'

'Crime scene boys love their toys,' Millar said, the rhyme sounding odd from the mouth of such a Boy Scout. He gave a shy smile. 'I heard that somewhere.'

The prosecutor produced a stack of color photographs, riffled through them until he found the ones he sought.

Gazing at them, Dance asked TJ, 'We ran a case there six, eight months ago, remember?'

'The arson, sure. In that new housing development.'

Tapping the map, the spot where the well was located, Dance continued, 'The development is still under construction. And that –' She nodded at a photograph. '– is a hard-rock well.'

Everybody in the area knew that water was at such a premium in this part of California that hard-rock wells, with their low output and unreliable supply, were never used for agricultural irrigation, only for private homes.

'Shit.' Sandoval closed his eyes briefly. 'Ten years ago, when Herron was killed, that was all farmland. The well wouldn't've been there then.'

'It wasn't there *one* year ago,' Dance muttered. '*That*'s why Pell was so stressed. I was getting close to the truth – somebody *did* get the hammer from his aunt's in Bakersfield and had a fake wallet made up, then planted them there recently. Only it wasn't to frame him.'

'Oh, no,' TJ whispered.

'What?' Millar asked, looking from one agent to the other.

'Pell set the whole thing up himself,' she said.

'Why?' Sandoval asked.

'Because he couldn't escape from Capitola.' That facility, like Pelican Bay in the north of the state, was a high-tech superprison. 'But he could from here.'

Kathryn Dance lunged for the phone.

# Chapter
# THREE

In a special holding cell – segregated from the other prisoners – Daniel Pell studied his cage and the corridor beyond, leading to the courthouse. To all appearances he was calm but his heart was in turmoil. The woman cop interviewing him had spooked him badly, with her calm green eyes behind those black-framed glasses, her unwavering voice. He hadn't expected somebody to get inside his mind so deeply or so fast. It was like she could read his thoughts.

Kathryn Dance . . .

Pell turned back to Baxter, the guard, outside the cage. He was a decent hack, not like Pell's escort from Capitola, who was a burly man, black and hard as ebony, now sitting silently at the far door, watching everything.

'What I was saying,' Pell now continued his conversation with Baxter. 'Jesus helped me. I was up to three packs a day. And He took time outta His busy schedule to help me. I quit pretty much cold.'

'Could use some of that help,' the hack confided.

'I'll tell you,' Pell confided. 'Smoking was harder to kick than the booze.'

'Tried the patch, the thing you put on your arm. Wasn't so good. Maybe I'll pray for help tomorrow. The wife and I pray every morning.'

Pell wasn't surprised. He'd seen his lapel pin. It was in the shape of a fish. 'Good for you.'

'I lost my car keys last week and we prayed for an hour. Jesus told me where they were. Now, Daniel, here's a thought: you'll be down here on trial days. You want, we could pray together.'

''Preciate that.'

Baxter's phone rang.

An instant later an alarm brayed, painful to the ears. 'The hell's going on?'

The Capitola escort leapt to his feet.

Just as a huge ball of fire filled the parking lot. The window in the back of the cell was barred but open, and a wad of flame shot through it. Black, greasy smoke streamed into the room. Pell dropped to the floor. He curled up into a ball. 'My dear Lord.'

Baxter was frozen, staring at the boiling flames, engulfing the entire lot behind the courthouse. He grabbed the phone but apparently the line was dead. He pulled his walkie-talkie off his belt and reported the fire.

Daniel Pell lowered his head and began to mutter the Lord's Prayer. 'Yo, Pell!'

The con opened his eyes.

The massive Capitola escort stood nearby, holding a Taser. He tossed leg shackles to Pell. 'Put 'em on. We're going down that corridor, out the front door and into the van. You're –' More flames streamed into the cell. The three men cringed. Another car's gas tank had exploded. 'You're going to stay right beside me. You understand?'

'Yeah, sure. Let's go! Please!' He ratcheted on the shackles good and tight.

Sweating, his voice cracking, Baxter said, 'Whatta you think it is? Terrorists?'

The Capitola escort ignored the panicked hack, eyes on Pell. 'If you don't do 'xactly what I say you'll get fifty thousand volts up your ass.' He pointed the Taser toward the prisoner. 'And if it ain't convenient to carry you I *will* leave you to burn to death. Understand?'

'Yessir. Let's go. Please. I don't want you or Mr Baxter getting hurt 'causa me. I'll do whatever you want.'

'Open it,' the escort barked to Baxter, who hit a button. With a buzz, the door eased outward. The three men started down the corridor, through another security door and then along a dim corridor, filling with smoke. The alarm was braying.

But, wait, Pell thought. It was a second alarm – the first had sounded *before* the explosions outside. Had someone figured out what he was going to do?

*Kathryn Dance* . . .

Just as they passed a fire door Pell glanced back. Thick smoke was filling the corridor around them. He cried to Baxter, 'No, it's too late. The whole building's going to go! Let's get out of here.'

'He's right.' Baxter reached toward the alarm bar of the exit.

The Capitola escort, perfectly calm, said firmly, 'No. Out the front door to the prison van.'

'You're crazy!' Pell snapped. 'For the love of God. We'll die.' He shoved the fire door open.

The men were hit with a blast of fierce heat, smoke and sparks. Outside a wall of fire consumed cars and shrubbery and trashcans. Pell dropped to his knees, covering his face. He screamed, 'My eyes! God, it hurts!'

'Pell, goddamn it –' The escort stepped forward, lifting the Taser.

'Put that down. He's not going anywhere,' Baxter said angrily. 'He's hurt.'

'I can't see,' Pell moaned. 'Somebody, help me!'

Baxter turned toward him, bent down.

'Don't!' the escort shouted.

Then the county hack staggered backward, a bewildered expression on his face, as Pell repeatedly shoved a filleting knife into his belly and chest. Bleeding in cascades, Baxter fell to his knees, trying for the pepper spray. Pell grabbed his shoulders and spun him around as the huge escort fired the Taser. It discharged but the probes went wide.

Pell shoved Baxter aside and leapt at the escort. The big man froze, staring at the knife, the useless Taser dangling from his hand. Pell's blue eyes studied his sweaty black face.

'Don't do it, Daniel.'

Pell moved in.

The escort's massive fists balled up.

No point in talking. Those who were in control didn't need to humiliate or threaten or quip. Pell charged forward, dodging the man's blows, and struck him hard a dozen times, the knife edge facing out and extending downward from the bottom of his clenched right hand. Punching was the most effective way to use a knife against a strong opponent willing to fight back.

His face contorting, the escort fell to his side, kicking. He gripped his chest and throat. A moment later he stopped moving. Pell grabbed the keys and undid the restraints.

Baxter was crawling away, still trying to get his Mace out of his holster with blood-slicked fingers. His eyes grew wide as Pell approached.

'Please. Don't do anything to me. I was just doing my job. We're both good Christians! I treated you kind. I –'

Pell grabbed him by the hair. He was tempted to say, You wasted God's time praying for your *car keys?*

But you never humiliated or threatened or quipped. Pell bent down and efficiently cut his throat.

When Baxter was dead, Pell stepped to the door again. He covered his eyes and grabbed the metallic fireproof bag, where he'd gotten the knife, just outside the door.

He was reaching inside again when he felt the gun muzzle at his neck.

'Don't move.'

Pell froze.

'Drop the knife.'

A moment of debate. The gun was steady; Pell sensed that whoever held it was ready to pull the trigger. His hissed a sigh. The knife clattered to the floor. He glanced at the man, a young Latino plainclothes officer, eyes on Pell, holding a radio.

'This's Juan Millar. Kathryn, you there?'

'Go ahead,' the woman's voice clattered.

*Kathryn* . . .

'I'm eleven-nine-nine, immediate assistance, at the fire door, ground floor, just outside the lockup. I've got two guards down. Hurt bad. Nine-four-five, requesting ambulance. Repeat, I'm eleven-nine –'

At that moment the gas tank of the car nearest the door exploded. A flare of orange flame shot through the doorway.

The officer ducked.

Pell didn't. His beard flared, flames licked his cheek, but he stood his ground.

*Hold fast* . . .

# Chapter
# FOUR

Kathryn Dance was calling on a Motorola, 'Juan, where's Pell? . . . Juan, respond. What's going on down there?'

No answer.

An eleven-nine-nine was a Highway Patrol code – though one that all California law enforcers knew. It meant an officer needed immediate assistance.

And yet no response after his transmission.

The courthouse security chief, a grizzled, crew-cut retired cop, stuck his head into the office. 'Who's running the search? Who's in charge?'

Sandoval glanced at Dance. 'You're senior.'

Dance had never encountered a situation like this – a firebomb and an escape by a killer like Daniel Pell – but, then, she didn't know of *anybody* on the Peninsula who had. She could coordinate efforts until somebody from MCSO or the Highway Patrol took over. It was vital to move fast and decisively.

'Okay,' she said. And instructed the security chief to get other guards downstairs immediately and to the doors where people were exiting.

Screams outside. People running in the corridor. Radio messages flying back and forth.

'Look,' TJ said, nodding toward the window, where black smoke obscured the view completely. 'Oh, man.'

Despite the fire, which might be raging *inside* now, Kathryn Dance decided to remain in Alonzo Sandoval's office. She wouldn't waste time by relocating or evacuating. If the building was engulfed they could jump out of the windows to the roofs of cars parked in the front lot, ten feet below. She tried Juan Millar again – there was no answer on his phone or radio – then said to the security chief, 'We need a room-by-room search of the building.'

'Yes, ma'am.' He trotted off.

'And in case he gets out, I want roadblocks,' Dance said to TJ. She pulled off her jacket, tossed it over a chair. Sweat stains were blossoming under the arms. 'Here, here, here . . .' Her short nails tapped loudly on the laminated map of Salinas. Gazing at the places she was indicating, TJ made calls to the Highway Patrol – California's state police – and the MCSO.

Sandoval, the prosecutor, stared grim and dazed at the smoky parking lot too. Flashing lights reflected in the window. He said nothing. More reports came in. No sign of Pell in the building or outside.

None of Juan Millar either.

The courthouse security chief returned a few minutes later, his face smudged. He was coughing hard. 'Fire's under control. Limited pretty much to outside.' He added shakily, 'But, Sandy . . . I've gotta tell you, Jim Baxter's dead. So's the Capitola guard. Stabbed. Pell got a knife somehow, looks like.'

'No,' Sandoval whispered. 'Oh, no.'

'And Millar?' Dance asked.

'We can't find him. Might be a hostage. We found a radio. Assume it's his. But we can't figure out where Pell went. Somebody opened the back fire door but there were flames everywhere until just a few minutes ago. He couldn't've gotten out that way. The only other choice is through the building and he'd be spotted in a minute in his prison overalls.'

'Unless he's dressed in Millar's suit,' Dance said.

TJ looked at her uneasily; they both knew the implications of that scenario.

'Get word to everybody that he might be in a dark suit, white shirt.' Millar was much taller than Pell. She added, 'The pants cuffs'd be rolled up.'

The chief hit transmit on his radio and sent out the message.

Looking up from his phone, TJ called, 'Monterey's getting cars in place.' He gestured toward the map. 'CHP's scrambled a half-dozen cruisers and cycles. They should have the main highways sealed in fifteen minutes.'

It worked to their advantage that Salinas wasn't a huge town – only about 150,000 – and was an agricultural center (its nickname was the 'Nation's Salad Bowl'). Lettuce, berry, brussels sprout, spinach and artichoke fields covered most of the surrounding area, which meant that there were limited highways and roads for escape. And on foot, Pell would be very visible in the fields of low crops.

Dance ordered TJ to have Pell's mug shots sent to the officers manning the roadblocks.

What else should she be doing? She gripped her braid, which ended in the red elastic tie that energetic Maggie had twisted around her hair that morning. It was a mother–daughter tradition; every morning the child got to pick the color of the rubber band, ribbon or scrunchie. Now, the agent recalled her daughter's sparkling brown eyes behind the wire-rimmed glasses as she told her mother about music camp that day and what kind of snacks they should have for Dance's father's birthday party tomorrow. (She realized that it was probably at that moment that Wes had planted the stuffed bat in her purse.)

She recalled, too, looking forward to interrogating a legendary criminal.

*The Son of Manson . . .*

The security chief's radio crackled. A voice called urgently, 'We've got an injury. Real bad. That Monterey County detective. Looks like Pell pushed him right into the fire. The EMS crew called for medevac. There's a chopper on its way.'

No, no . . . She and TJ shared a glance. His otherwise irrepressibly mischievous face registered dismay. Dance knew that Millar would be in terrible pain but she needed to learn if he had any suggestions as to where Pell had gone. She nodded at the radio. The chief handed it to her. 'This's Agent Dance. Is Detective Millar conscious?'

'No, ma'am. It's . . . it's pretty bad.' A pause.

'Is he wearing clothes?'

'Is he . . . Say again?'

'Did Pell take Millar's clothes?'

'Oh, that's negative. Over.'

'What about his weapon?'

'No weapon.'

Shit.

'Tell everybody that Pell's armed.'

'Roger that.'

Dance had another thought. 'I want an officer at the medevac chopper from the minute it lands. Pell might be planning to hitch a ride.'

'Roger.'

She handed the radio back, pulled out her phone, hit speed dial four.

'Cardiac Care,' Edie Dance's low, placid voice said.

'Mom, me.'

'What's the matter, Katie? The kids?' Dance pictured the stocky woman, with short gray hair and large, gray-framed round glasses, concern on her ageless face. She'd be leaning forward – her automatic response to tension. 'No, we're fine. But one of Michael's detectives is burned. Bad. There was an arson at the courthouse, part of an escape. You'll hear about it on the news. We lost two guards.'

'Oh, I'm sorry,' Edie murmured.

'The detective – Juan Millar's his name. You've met him a couple of times.'

'I don't remember. He's on his way here?'

'Will be soon. Medevac.'

'That bad?'

'You have a burn unit?'

'A small one, part of ICU. For long term we'd get him to Alta Bates, U.C.-Davis or Santa Clara as soon as we could. Maybe down to Grossman.'

'Could you check in on him from time to time? Let me know how he's doing?'

'Of course, Katie.'

'And if there's any way, I want to talk to him. Whatever he saw, it could be helpful.'

'Sure.'

'I'll be tied up for the day, even if we catch him right away. Could you have dad pick up the kids?' Stuart Dance, a retired marine biologist, worked occasionally at the famous Monterey aquarium, but was always available to chauffeur the children whenever needed.

'I'll call right now.'

'Thanks, Mom.'

Dance disconnected and glanced up to see Prosecutor Alonzo Sandoval staring numbly at the map. 'Who was helping him?' he muttered. 'And where the fuck is Pell?'

Variations of these two questions were spinning through Kathryn Dance's mind too.

Along with another: What could I have done to read him better? What could I have done to avoid this tragedy altogether?

# Chapter
# FIVE

The helicopter in the parking lot directed swirls of smoke outward in elegant patterns as the blades groaned and the aircraft lifted off, bearing Juan Millar to the hospital.

*Vaya con Dios . . .*

Dance got a call. Glanced at the phone screen. She was surprised it had taken so long for the man to get back to her. 'Charles,' she said to her boss, the agent-in-charge of the west central regional office of the CBI.

'I'm on my way to the courthouse. What've we got, Kathryn?'

She brought him up to date, including the deaths and Millar's condition.

'Sorry to hear that . . . Any leads, anything we can tell them?'

'Tell who?'

'The press.'

'I don't know, Charles. We don't have much information. He could be anywhere. I've ordered roadblocks and we're doing a room-by-room search.'

'Nothing specific? Not even a direction?'

'No.'

Overby sighed. 'Okay. By the way, you're running the operation.'

'What?'

'I want you in charge of the manhunt.'

'Me?' She was surprised. CBI certainly had jurisdiction; it was the highest-ranking law-enforcement agency in the state, and Kathryn Dance was a senior agent; she was as competent as anyone to supervise the case. Still, the CBI was an investigative operation and didn't have a large staff. The California Highway Patrol and the Sheriff's Office would have to provide the manpower for the search.

'Why not somebody from CHP or MCSO?'

'I think we need central coordination on this one. Absolutely makes sense. Besides, it's a done deal. I've cleared it with everybody.'

Already? She wondered if that was why he hadn't returned her call right away – he was roping down CBI's control of a big media case.

Well, his decision was fine with her. She had a personal stake in capturing Pell.

Seeing his bared teeth, hearing his eerie words.

*Yeah, it's a tough life being a cop. The little ones spend a lot of time alone, don't they? They'd probably love some friends to play with . . .*

'Okay, Charles. I'll take it. But I want Michael on board too.'

Michael O'Neil was the MCSO detective Dance worked with most often. She and the soft-spoken officer, a lifelong resident of Monterey, had worked together for years; in fact, he'd been a mentor when she'd joined the CBI.

'That's fine with me.'

Good, Dance thought. Because she'd already called him.

'I'll be there soon. I want another briefing before the press conference.' Overby disconnected.

Dance was heading toward the back of the courthouse when flashing lights caught her eye. She recognized one of the CBI's Tauruses, the grille pulsing red and blue.

Rey Carraneo, the most recent addition to the office, pulled up nearby and joined her. The slim man, with black eyes sunk beneath thick brows, had only two months on the job. He wasn't quite as unseasoned or naïve as he looked, though, and had been a cop in Reno for three years – a tough venue – before moving to the Peninsula so he and his wife could take care of his ill mother. There were rough edges to be worn off and experience to be tucked under his extremely narrow belt but he was a tireless, reliable law enforcer. And that counted for a lot.

Carraneo was only six or seven years younger than Dance but those were important years in the life of a cop and he couldn't bring himself to call her 'Kathryn', as she frequently offered. His usual greeting was a nod. He gave her a respectful one now.

'Come with me.' Recalling the Herron evidence and the gas bomb, she added, 'He's probably got an accomplice, and we know he's got a weapon. So, eyes open.' They continued to the back of the courthouse, where arson investigators and Monterey County crime scene officers from the Enforcement Operations Bureau were looking over the carnage. It was like a scene from a war zone. Four cars had burned to the frames, the two others were half-gutted. The back of the building was black with soot, trash cans melted. A haze of blue-gray smoke hung over the area. The place stank of burning rubber – and an odor that was far more repulsive.

She studied the parking lot. Then her eyes slipped to the open back door.

'No way he got out *there*,' Carraneo said, echoing Dance's thought. From the destroyed cars and the scorch marks on the pavement, it was clear that the fire had surrounded the door; the flames were meant to be a diversion. But where *had* he gone?

'These cars all accounted for?' she asked a fireman.

'Yeah. They're all employees'.'

'Hey, Kathryn, we have the device,' a man in a uniform said to her. He was the county's chief fire marshal.

She nodded a greeting. 'What was it?'

'Wheelie suitcase, big one, filled with plastic milk containers of gasoline. The doer planted it under that Saab there. Slow-burning fuse.'

'A pro?'

'Probably not. We found the fuse residue. You can make 'em out of clothes line and chemicals. Got instructions from the Internet, I'd say. The sort of things kids make to blow stuff up with. Including themselves a lot of times.'

'Can you trace anything?'

'Maybe. We'll have it sent to the MCSO lab and then we'll see.'

'You know when it was left?'

He nodded toward the car the bomb had been planted under. 'The driver got here about nine fifteen, so it'd be after that.'

'Any hope for prints?'

'Doubt it.'

Dance stood with her hands on her hips, surveying the battleground. Something felt wrong.

The dim corridor, blood on the concrete.

The open door.

Turning slowly, studying the area, Dance noticed behind the building something in a nearby pine and cypress grove: a tree from which dangled an orange ribbon – the sort used to mark shrubs and trees scheduled for cutting. Walking closer, she noticed that the mound of pine needles at the base was larger than those beneath the others. Dance dropped to her knees and dug into it. She unearthed a large scorched bag made of metallic cloth.

'Rey, need some gloves.' She coughed from the smoke.

The young agent got a pair from an MCSO crime-scene deputy and brought them to her. Inside the bag were Pell's orange prison uniform and a set of gray hooded overalls, which turned out to be some kind of fire suit. A label said the garment was made of PBI fibers and Kevlar and had an SFI rating of 3.2A/5. Dance had no idea what this meant, other than that the material was obviously protective enough to get Daniel Pell safely through the conflagration behind the courthouse.

Her shoulders slumped in disgust. A fire suit? What're we up against here?

'I don't get it,' Rey Carraneo said.

She explained that Pell's partner probably had set the bomb and left the fireproof bag outside the door; it had contained the fire suit and a knife. Maybe a universal cuff or shackle key too. After he'd disarmed Juan Millar, Pell had donned the garment and run through the flames to the tree marked with the orange tag, where the partner had hidden some civilian clothes. He'd changed and sprinted off.

She lifted the Motorola and reported what she'd found, then gestured an MCSO crime scene officer over and gave him the evidence.

Carraneo called her to a patch of earth not far away. 'Footprints.' Several impressions, about four feet apart – left by someone running. They were clearly Pell's; he'd left distinctive prints outside the fire door of the courthouse. The two CBI agents started jogging in the direction they led.

Pell's footsteps ended at a nearby street, San Benito Way, along which were vacant lots, a liquor store, a dingy taqueria, a quick-copy and shipping franchise, a pawn shop and a bar.

'So here's where the partner picked him up,' Carraneo said, looking up and down San Benito.

'But there's another street on the other side of the courthouse. It's two hundred feet closer. Why here?'

'More traffic there?'

'Could be.' Dance squinted as she scanned the area, coughing again. Finally she caught her breath and her eyes focused across the street. 'Come on, let's move!'

\*　　\*　　\*

The man, in his late twenties, wearing shorts and a Worldwide Express uniform shirt, drove his green panel truck through the streets of downtown Salinas. He was intensely aware of the gun barrel resting on his shoulder and he was crying. 'Look, mister, I don't know what this is about, really, but we don't carry cash. I've got about fifty on me, personal money, and you're welcome –'

'Give me your wallet.' The hijacker wore shorts, a windbreaker and an Oakland A's cap. His face was streaked with soot and part of his beard was burnt. He was middle-aged but thin and strong. His eyes were a weird light blue.

'Whatever you want, mister. Just don't hurt me. I've got a family.'

'Wal-*let?*'

It took stocky Billy a few moments to pry the billfold out of his tight shorts. 'Here.'

The man flipped through it. 'Now, William Gilmore, of three-four-three-five Rio Grande Avenue, Marina, California, father of these two fine children, if the photo gallery's up to date.'

Dread unraveled inside him.

'And husband of this lovely wife. Look at those curls. Natural, I'll bet any money. Hey, keep your eyes on the road. Swerved a bit there. And keep going where I told you.' Then the hijacker said, 'Hand me your cell phone.'

His voice was calm. Calm is good. It means he's not going to do anything sudden or stupid.

Billy heard the man punch in a number.

'Lo. It's me. Write this down.' He repeated Billy's address. 'He's got a wife and two kids. Wife's real pretty. You'll like the hair.'

Billy whispered, 'Who's that you're calling? Please, mister . . . please. Take the truck, take anything. I'll give you as much time as you want to get away. An hour. Two hours. Just don't –'

'Shhhh.' The man continued his phone conversation. 'If I don't show up, that'll mean I didn't make it through the roadblocks because William here wasn't convincing enough. You go visit his family. They're all yours.'

'No!' Billy twisted around and lunged for the phone.

The gun muzzle touched his face. 'Keep driving, son. Not a good time to run off the road.' The hijacker snapped the phone shut and put it into his own pocket.

'William . . . You go by "Bill"?'

'"Billy" mostly, sir.'

'So, Billy, here's the situation. I escaped from that jail back there.'

'Yessir. That's fine with me.'

The man laughed. 'Well, thank you. Now you heard me on the phone. You know what I want you to do. You get me through any roadblocks, I'll let you go and no harm'll come to your family.'

Face fever hot, belly churning with fear, Billy wiped his round cheeks.

'You're no threat to me. Everybody knows my name and what I look like. I'm Daniel Pell and my picture'll be all over the noon news. So I don't have any reason to hurt you, long as you do what I say. Now, summon up some calm. You've got to stay focused. If the police stop you I want a cheerful and curious deliveryman, frowning and asking about what happened back in town. All that smoke, all that mess. My, my. You get the idea?'

'Please, I'll do anything –'

'Billy, I know you were listening to me. I don't need you to do "anything". I need you to do what I asked. That's all. What could be simpler?'

# Chapter
# SIX

Kathryn Dance and Carraneo were in the You Mail It franchise on San Benito Way, where they'd just learned that a package delivery company, Worldwide Express, had made its daily morning drop-off moments after the escape.

*A to B to X . . .*

Dance realized that Pell could commandeer the truck to get past the roadblocks and called the Worldwide Express Salinas operations director, who confirmed that the driver on that route had missed all remaining scheduled deliveries. Dance got the tag number of his truck and relayed it to the MCSO.

They returned to Sandy Sandoval's office, coordinating the efforts to find the vehicle. Unfortunately there were twenty-five Worldwide trucks in the area, so Dance told the director to order the other drivers to pull over immediately at the nearest gas station. The truck that kept moving would contain Daniel Pell.

This was taking some time, though. The director had to call them on their cell phones, since a radio broadcast would alert Pell that they knew about his means of escape.

A figure walked slowly through the doorway. Dance turned to see Michael O'Neil, the Sheriff's Office chief deputy she'd called earlier. She nodded at him with a smile, greatly relieved he was here. For Dance, there was no better law enforcer in the world with whom to share this tough burden.

O'Neil had been with the MCSO for years. He'd started as a rookie deputy and worked his way up, becoming a solid, methodical investigator with a stunning arrest – and more important, *conviction* – record.

He was now a chief deputy and detective with the Enforcement Operations Bureau of the MCSO's Investigations Division.

He'd resisted offers to go into lucrative corporate security or to join bigger law-enforcement ops like the CBI or FBI. He wouldn't take a job that required relocation or extensive travel. O'Neil's home was the Monterey Peninsula and he had no desire to be anywhere else. His parents still lived there – in the ocean-view house where he and his siblings had grown up. (His father was suffering from senility, and his mother was considering selling the house and moving the man into a nursing facility; O'Neil had a plan to buy the homestead just to keep it in the family.)

With his love of the bay, fishing and his boat, Michael O'Neil could have been the unwavering, unobtrusive hero of a John Steinbeck novel, like Doc in *Cannery Row*. In fact, the detective, an avid book collector, owned first editions of everything Steinbeck had written. (His favorite was *Travels with Charley*, a nonfiction account of the writer's trip around America with his Standard poodle, and O'Neil intended to duplicate the journey at some point in his life.)

Last Friday Dance and O'Neil had jointly collared a thirty-year-old known as Ese, head of a particularly unpleasant Chicano gang operating out of Salinas. They'd marked the occasion by sharing a bottle of Piper Sonoma sparkling wine on the deck of a tourist-infested Fisherman's Wharf restaurant.

Now it seemed as if the celebration had occurred decades ago. If at all.

The MCSO's uniform was typical county sheriff's khaki, but O'Neil often dressed soft, and today he was in a navy suit, with a tie-less dark shirt, charcoal gray, matching about half the hair on his head. The brown eyes, beneath low lids, moved slowly as they examined the map of the area. His physique was columnar and his arms thick, from genes and from playing tug of war with muscular seafood in Monterey Bay when time and the weather allowed him to get out his boat.

O'Neil nodded a greeting to TJ and Sandoval.

'Any word on Juan?' Dance asked.

'He's hanging in there.' A sigh. O'Neil and Millar worked together frequently and went fishing once a month or so. Dance knew that on the drive here he'd been in constant touch with the doctors and Millar's family.

The California Bureau of Investigation has no central dispatch unit to contact radio patrol cars, emergency vehicles or boats, so O'Neil arranged for the Sheriff's Office's central communications operation to relay the information about the missing Worldwide Express truck to its own deputies and the CHP. He told them that within a few minutes the escapee's truck would be the only one not stopped at a gas station.

O'Neil took a call and nodded, walking to the map. He tucked the phone between ear and shoulder, picked up a pack of self-adhesive notes featuring butterflies and began sticking them up.

More roadblocks, Dance realized.

He hung up. 'They're on Sixty-eight, One eighty-three, the One-oh-one . . . We've got the back roads to Hollister covered, and Soledad and Greenfield. But if he gets into the Pastures of Heaven, it'll be tough to spot a truck, even with a chopper – and right now fog's a problem.'

The 'Pastures of Heaven' was the name John Steinbeck had given to a rich, orchard-filled valley off Highway 68 in a book of the same title. Much of the area around Salinas was flat, low farmland, but you didn't have to go far to get into trees. And nearby, too, was the rugged Castle Rock area, whose cliffs, bluffs and trees would be excellent hiding places.

Sandoval said, 'If Pell's partner didn't drive the getaway wheels, where is *he*?'

TJ offered, 'Rendezvous point somewhere?'

'Or staying around,' Dance said, nodding out the window.

'What?' the prosecutor asked. 'Why'd he do that?'

'To find out how we're running the case, what we know. What we *don't* know.'

'That sounds a little . . . elaborate, don't you think?'

TJ laughed, pointing toward the smoldering cars. 'I'd say that's a pretty good word for this whole shebang.'

O'Neil suggested, 'Or maybe he wants to slow us up.'

Dance said. 'That makes sense too. Pell and his partner don't know we're on to the truck. For all they know, we still think he's in the area. The partner could make it look like Pell's nearby. Maybe take a shot at somebody up the street, maybe even set off another device.'

'Shit. Another firebomb?' Sandoval grimaced.

Dance called the security chief and told him there was a possibility the partner was still around and could be a threat.

But, as it turned out, they had no time to speculate about whether or not the partner was nearby. The plan about the Worldwide Express trucks had paid off. A radio call to O'Neil from MCSO dispatch reported that two local police officers had found Daniel Pell and were presently in pursuit.

The dark green delivery truck kicked up a rooster tail of dust on the small road.

The uniformed officer who was driving the Salinas Police squad car, a former jarhead back from the war, gripped the wheel of the cruiser as if he were holding on to the rudder of a ten-foot skiff in twelve-foot seas.

His partner – a muscular Latino – gripped the dashboard in one hand and the microphone in the other. 'Salinas Police Mobile Seven. We're still with him. He turned onto a dirt road off Natividad about a mile south of Old Stage.'

'Roger . . . Central to Seven, be advised, subject is probably armed and dangerous.'

'If he's armed, of *course* he's dangerous,' the driver said and lost his sunglasses when the car caught air after a run-in with a serious bump. The two officers could hardly see the road ahead; the Worldwide truck was churning up dust like a sandstorm.

'Central to Seven, we've got all available units en route.'

'Roger that.'

Backup was a good idea. The rumors were that Daniel Pell, the crazed cult leader, this era's Charles Manson, had gunned down a dozen people at the courthouse, had set fire to a bus filled with schoolchildren, had slashed his way through a crowd of prospective jurors, killing four. Or two. Or eight. Whatever the truth, the officers wanted as much help as they could get.

The jarhead muttered, 'Where's he going? There's nothing up here.'

The road was used by farm equipment and buses transporting migrant workers to and from the fields. It led to no major streets or highways. There was no picking going on today but the road's purpose, and the fact it probably led to no major highways, could be deduced from its decrepit condition and from the drinking-water tanks and the portable toilets on trailers by the roadside.

But Daniel Pell might not know that and would assume this was a road like any other. Rather than one that ended, as this did, abruptly in the middle of an artichoke field. Ahead of them, thirty yards or so, Pell braked fast in panic and the truck began to skid. But there was no way to stop in time. The truck's front wheels dropped hard into a shallow irrigation ditch, and the rear end lifted off the ground, then slammed back with a huge crash.

The squad car braked to a stop nearby. 'This is Seven,' the Latino cop called in. 'Pell's off the road.'

'Roger, is he –'

The officers leapt out of the car with their pistols drawn.

'He's going to bail, he's going to bail!'

But nobody exited the truck.

They approached it. The back door had flown open in the crash and they could see nothing but dozens of packages and envelopes littering the floor.

'There he is, look.'

Pell lay stunned, face down, on the floor of the vehicle.

'Maybe he's hurt.'

'Who gives a shit?' The officers ran forward and cuffed and dragged him out of the space where he was wedged.

They dropped him onto his back on the ground. 'Nice try, buddy, but –'

'Fuck. It's not him.'

'What?' asked his partner.

'Excuse me, does *that* look like a forty-three-year-old white guy?'

The jarhead bent down to the groggy teenager, a gang tat teardrop on his cheek, and snapped 'Who're you?' in Spanish, a language that every law enforcer in and around Salinas could speak.

The kid avoided their eyes, muttering in English, 'I no saying nothing. You can go fuck youself.'

'Oh, man.' The Latino cop glanced into the cab, where the keys were dangling from the dash. He understood: Pell had left the truck on a city street with the engine on, knowing it'd be stolen – oh, in about sixty seconds – so the police would follow it and give Pell a chance to escape in a different direction.

Another thought. Not a good one. He turned to Jarhead. 'You don't think, when we said we had Pell and they called all availables for backup . . . I mean, you don't think they pulled 'em off the roadblocks, do you?'

'No, they wouldn't do that. That'd be fucking stupid.'

The men looked at each other.

'Christ.' The Latino officer raced to the squad car and grabbed the microphone.

# Chapter
# SEVEN

'A Honda Civic,' TJ reported, hanging up from a call with DMV. 'Five years old. Red. I've got the tags.' They knew Pell was now in the Worldwide Express driver's personal car, which was missing from the company's lot in Salinas.

TJ added, 'I'll let the roadblocks know.'

'*When* they get back on site,' Dance muttered.

To the dismay of the agents and O'Neil, some local dispatcher had ordered the nearby roadblocks abandoned for the pursuit of the Worldwide Express truck. His placid face registering what for O'Neil was disgust – a tightening of the lips – he'd sent the cars back on site immediately.

They were in a meeting room up the hall from Sandoval's office. Now that Pell was clearly not near the courthouse, Dance wanted to return to CBI headquarters, but Charles Overby had told them to remain at the courthouse until he arrived.

'Think he wants to make sure no press conferences escape either,' TJ said, to which Dance and O'Neil gave sour laughs. 'Speaking of which,' came TJ's whisper. 'Incoming! . . . Hit the decks.'

A figure strode confidently through the door. Charles Overby, a fifty-five-year-old career law enforcer. Without any greetings, he asked Dance, 'He wasn't in the truck?'

'No. Local gangbanger. Pell left the truck running. He knew somebody'd snatch it and we'd focus on that. He took off in the delivery driver's own car.'

'The driver?'

'No sign.'

'Ouch.' Brown-haired, sunburned Charles Overby was athletic in a pear-shaped way, a tennis and golf player. He was the newly appointed head of the CBI's west central office. The agent-in-charge he replaced, Stan Fishburne, had taken an early retirement on a medical, much to the CBI staff's collective dismay (because of the severe heart attack on Fishburne's account – and because of who had succeeded him on theirs).

O'Neil took a call and Dance updated Overby, adding the details of Pell's new wheels and their concern that the partner was still nearby.

'You think he's really planted another device?'

'Unlikely. But the accomplice staying around makes sense.'

O'Neil hung up. 'The roadblocks're all back in place.'

'Who took them down?' Overby asked.

'We don't know.'

'I'm sure it wasn't us or you, Michael, right?' Overby asked uneasily.

An awkward silence. Then O'Neil said, 'No, Charles.'

'Who was it?'

'We're not sure.'

'We should find that out.'

Recrimination was such a drain. O'Neil then said he'd look into it. Dance knew he'd never do anything, though, and with this comment to Overby the finger pointing came to a close.

The detective continued, 'Nobody's spotted the Civic. But the timing was just wrong. He could've gotten through on Sixty-eight or the One-oh-one. I don't think Sixty-eight, though.'

'No,' Overby agreed. The smaller Highway 68 would take Pell back to heavily populated Monterey. The 101, wide as an interstate, could get him to every major expressway in the state.

'They're setting up new checkpoints in Gilroy. And about thirty miles south.' O'Neil stuck monarch butterfly notes in the appropriate places.

'And you've got the bus terminals and airport secure?' Overby asked.

'That's right,' Dance said.

'And San Jose and Oakland PD're in the loop?'

'Yep. And Santa Cruz, San Benito, Merced, Santa Clara, Stanislaus and San Mateo.' The nearby counties.

Overby jotted a few notes. 'Good.' He glanced up and said, 'Oh, I just talked to Amy.'

'Grabe?'

'That's right.'

Amy Grabe was the SAC – the special-agent-in-charge – of the FBI's San Francisco field office. Dance knew the sharp, focused law enforcer well. The west central region of the CBI extended north to the Bay area, so she'd had a number of opportunities to work with her. Dance's late husband, an agent with the FBI's local resident agency, had too.

Overby continued, 'If we don't get Pell soon, they've got a specialist I want on board.'

'A what?'

'Somebody in the bureau who handles situations like this.'

It was a jailbreak, Dance reflected. What kind of specialist? She thought of Tommy Lee Jones in *The Fugitive*.

O'Neil, too, was curious. 'A negotiator?'

But Overby said, 'No, he's a cult expert. Deals a lot with people like Pell.'

Dance shrugged, an illustrator gesture – those that reinforce verbal content, in this case, her doubts. 'Well, I'm not sure how useful that'd be.' She had worked many joint task forces. She wasn't opposed to sharing jurisdiction with the Feds or anyone else, but involving other agencies inevitably slowed response times. Besides, she didn't see how a cult leader would flee for his life any differently than a murderer or bank robber.

But Overby had already made up his mind; she knew it from his tone and body language. 'He's a brilliant profiler, can really get into their minds. The cult mentality is a lot different from your typical perp's.'

Is it?

The agent-in-charge handed Dance a slip of paper with a name and phone number on it. 'He's in Chicago, finishing up some case, but he can be here tonight or tomorrow morning.'

'You sure about this, Charles?'

'With Pell we can use all the help we can get. Absolutely. And a big gun from Washington? More expertise, more person power.'

More places to stash the blame, Dance thought cynically, realizing now what had happened. Grabe had asked if the FBI could help out in the search for Pell, and Overby had jumped at the offer, thinking that if more innocents were injured or the escapee remained at large, there'd be two people on the podium at the press conference, not just himself alone. But she kept the smile on her face. 'All right then. I hope we get him before we need to bother anybody else.'

'Oh, and Kathryn? I just wanted you to know. Amy wondered how the escape happened, and I told him your interrogation had nothing to do with it.'

'My . . . what?'

'It's not going to be a problem. I told her there's nothing you did that would've helped Pell escape.'

She felt the heat rise to her face, which undoubtedly was turning ruddy. Emotion does that; she'd spotted plenty of deception over the years because guilt and shame trigger blood flow.

So does anger.

Amy Grabe probably hadn't even known that Dance had interrogated Pell, let alone suspected she'd done something careless that facilitated the escape. But she – and the San Francisco office of the bureau – sure had that idea now. Maybe Sacramento too, the CBI headquarters. She said stiffly, 'He escaped from the lockup, not the interrogation room.'

'I was talking about Pell maybe getting information from you that he could use to get away.'

Dance sensed O'Neil tense. The detective had a strong streak of protectiveness when it came to those who hadn't been in the business as long as he had. But he knew that Kathryn Dance was a woman who fought her own battles. He remained silent.

She was furious that Overby had said anything to Grabe. Now she understood: *That* was why he wanted CBI to run the case – if any other agency took charge, it would be an admission that the bureau was in some way responsible for the escape.

And Overby wasn't through yet. 'Now, about security . . . I'm sure it was tight. Special precautions with Pell. I told Amy you'd made sure of that.'

Since he hadn't asked a question, she simply gazed back coolly and didn't give him a crumb of reassurance.

He probably sensed he'd gone too far and, eyes ferreting away, said, 'I'm sure things were handled well.'

Again, silence.

'Okay, I've got that press conference. My turn in the barrel.' He grimaced. 'If you hear anything else, let me know. I'll be on in about ten minutes.' The man left.

TJ looked Dance over and said, in a thick southern accent, 'Damn, so you're the one forgot to lock the barn door when you were through interrogating the cows. *That's* how they got away. I was wondrin'.'

O'Neil stifled a smile.

'Don't get me started,' she muttered.

She walked to the window and looked out at the people who'd evacuated the courthouse, milling in front of the building. 'I'm worried about that partner. Where is he, what's he up to?'

'Who'd bust somebody like Daniel Pell outa the joint?' asked TJ.

Dance recalled Pell's kinesic reaction in the interrogation when the subject of his aunt in Bakersfield arose. 'I think whoever's helping him got the hammer from his aunt. Pell's her last name. Find her.' She had another thought. 'Oh, and your buddy in the resident agency, down in Chico?'

'Yup?'

'He's discreet, right?'

'We bar surf and ogle when we hang out. How discreet is that?'

'Can he check this guy out?' Dance held up the slip of paper containing the name of the FBI's cult expert.

'He'd be game, I'll bet. He says intrigue in the bureau's better than intrigue in the barrio.' TJ jotted the name.

O'Neil took a call and had a brief conversation. He hung up and explained, 'That was the warden at Capitola. I thought we should talk to the supervising guard on Pell's cell block, see if he can tell us anything. He's also bringing the contents of Pell's cell with him.'

'Good.'

'Then there's a fellow prisoner who claims to have some information about Pell. She'll round him up and call us back.'

Dance's cell phone rang, a croaking frog.

O'Neil lifted an eyebrow. 'Wes or Maggie've been hard at work.'

It was a family joke, like stuffed animals in the purse. The children would reprogram the ringer of her phone when Dance wasn't looking (any tones were fair game; the only rules: never silent, and no tunes from boy bands).

She hit the receive button. 'Hello?'

'It's me, Agent Dance.'

The background noise was loud and the 'me' ambiguous, but the phrasing of her name told her the caller was Rey Carraneo.

'What's up?'

'No sign of his partner or any other devices. Security wants to know if they can let everybody back inside. The fire marshal's okayed it.'

Dance debated the matter with O'Neil. They decided to wait a little longer.

'TJ, go outside and help them search. I don't like it that the accomplice's unaccounted for.'

She recalled what her father had told her after he'd nearly had a run-in with a great white in the waters off northern Australia: 'The shark you don't see is always more dangerous than the one you do.'

# Chapter
# EIGHT

The stocky, bearded, balding man in his hard-worn fifties stood near the courthouse, looking over the chaos, his sharp eyes checking out everyone, the police, the guards, the civilians.

'Hey, Officer, how you doing, you got a minute? Just like to ask you a few questions . . . You mind saying a few words into the tape recorder? . . . Oh, sure, I understand. I'll catch you later. Sure. Good luck.'

Morton Nagle had watched the helicopter swoop in low and ease to the ground to spirit away the injured cop.

He'd watched the men and women conducting the search, their strategy – and faces – making clear that they'd never run an escape.

He'd watched the uneasy crowds, thinking accidental fire, then thinking terrorists, then hearing the truth and looking even more scared than if al-Qaeda itself was behind the explosion.

As well they should, Nagle reflected.

'Excuse me, do you have a minute to talk? . . . Oh, sure. Not a problem. Sorry to bother you, Officer.'

Nagle milled through the crowds. Smoothing his wispy hair, then tugging up saggy tan slacks, he was studying the area carefully, the fire trucks, the squad cars, the flashing lights bursting with huge aureoles through the foggy haze. He lifted his digital camera and snapped some more pictures.

A middle-aged woman looked over his shabby vest – a fisherman's garment with two dozen pockets – and battered camera bag. She snapped, 'You people, you *journalists*, you're like vultures. Why don't you let the police do their job?'

He gave a chuckle. 'I didn't know I wasn't.'

'You're all the same.' The woman turned away and continued to stare angrily at the smoky courthouse.

A guard came up to him and asked if he'd seen anything suspicious.

Nagle thought, Now that's a strange question. Sounds like something from an old-time TV show.

*Just the facts, ma'am . . .*

He answered, 'Nope.'

Adding to himself, Nothing surprising to *me*. But maybe I'm the wrong one to ask.

Nagle caught a whiff of a terrible scent – burnt flesh and hair – and, incongruously, gave another amused laugh.

Thinking about it now – Daniel Pell had put the idea in mind – he realized he chuckled at times that most people would consider inappropriate, if not tasteless. Moments like this: when looking over carnage. Over the years he'd seen plenty of violent death, images that would repel most people.

Images that often made Morton Nagle laugh.

It was a defense mechanism probably. A device to keep violence – a subject he was intimately familiar with – from eating away at his soul, though he wondered if the chuckling wasn't an indicator that it already had.

Then an officer was making an announcement. People would soon be allowed back into the courthouse.

Nagle hitched up his pants, pulled his camera bag up higher on his shoulder and scanned the crowd. He spotted a tall, young Latino in a suit, clearly a plainclothes detective of some sort. The man was speaking to an elderly woman who wore a juror badge. They were off to the side, not many people around.

Good.

Nagle sized up the officer. Just what he wanted, young, gullible, trusting. And began moving toward him slowly.

Closing the distance.

The man moved on, oblivious to Nagle, looking for more people to interview.

When he was ten feet away, the big man slipped the camera strap around his neck, unzipped the bag, reached inside.

Five feet.

He stepped closer yet.

And felt a strong hand close around his arm. Nagle gasped and his heart gave a jolt.

'Just keep those hands where I can see them, how's that?' The man was a short, fidgety officer with the California Bureau of Investigation; Nagle read the ID dangling from his neck.

'Hey, what –'

'Shhhhh,' hissed the officer, who had curly red hair. 'And those hands? Remember where I want 'em? Nice 'n' visible . . . Hey, Rey.'

The Latino joined them. He too had a CBI ID card. He looked Nagle up and down. Together they led him to the side of the courthouse, attracting the attention of everybody nearby.

'Look, I don't know –'

'Shhhhh,' the wiry agent offered again.

The Latino frisked him carefully and nodded. Then he lifted Nagle's press pass off his chest and showed it to the shorter officer.

'Hm,' he said. 'This is a little out of date, wouldn't you say?'

'Technically, but –'

'Sir, it's four years out of date,' the Latino officer pointed out.

'That's a big bowl of technical,' his partner said.

'I must've picked up the wrong one. I've been a reporter for –'

'So, if we called this paper, they'd say you're a credentialed employee?'

If they called the paper they'd get a nonworking number. 'Look, I can explain.'

The short officer frowned. 'You know, I sure *would* like an explanation. See, I was just talking to this groundskeeper, who told me that a man fitting your description was here at eight-thirty this morning. There were no other reporters here then. And why would that be? Because there was no *escape* then . . . Getting here *before* the story breaks. That's quite a . . . whatta they call that, Rey?'

'Scoop?'

'Yeah, that's quite a scoop. So, 'fore you do any explaining, turn around and put your hands behind your back.'

In the conference room on the second floor of the courthouse, TJ handed Dance what he'd found on Morton Nagle.

No weapons, no incendiary fuse, no maps of the courthouse or escape routes.

Just money, wallet, camera, tape recorder and thick notebook. Along with three true crime books, his name on the cover and his picture on the back (appearing much younger, and hairier).

'He's a paperback writer,' TJ sang, not doing justice to the Beatles.

Nagle was described in the author bio as 'a former war correspondent and police reporter, who now writes books about crime. A resident of Scottsdale, Ariz., he is the author of thirteen works of nonfiction. He claims his other professions are gadabout, nomad and raconteur.'

'This doesn't let you off the hook,' Dance snapped. 'What're you doing here? And why were you at the courthouse before the fire?'

'I'm not covering the escape. I got here early to get some interviews.'

O'Neil said, 'With Pell? He doesn't give them.'

'No, no, not Pell. With the family of Robert Herron. I heard they were coming to testify to the grand jury.'

'What about the fake press pass?'

'Okay, it's been four years since I've been credentialed with a magazine or newspaper. I've been writing books fulltime. But without a press pass you can't get anywhere. Nobody ever looks at the date.'

'*Almost* never,' TJ corrected with a smile.

Dance flipped through one of the books. It was about the Peterson murder case in California a few years ago. It seemed well written.

TJ looked up from his laptop. 'He's clean, boss. At least no priors. DMV pic checks out too.'

'I'm writing a book. It's all legit. You can check.'

He gave them the name of his editor in Manhattan. Dance called the large publishing company and spoke to the woman, whose attitude was, Oh, hell, what's Morton got himself into now? But she confirmed that he'd signed a contract for a new book about Pell.

Dance said to TJ, 'Uncuff him.'

O'Neil turned to the author and asked, 'What's the book about?'

'It isn't like any true crime you've read before. It's not about the murders. That's been done. It's about the *victims* of Daniel Pell. What their lives were like before the murders and, the ones who survived, what they're like now. See, most nonfiction crime on TV or in books focuses on the murderer himself and the crime – the gore, the gruesome aspects. The cheap stuff. I *hate* that. My book's about Theresa Croyton – the girl who survived – and the family's relatives and friends. The title's going to be *The Sleeping Doll*. That's what they called Theresa. I'm also going to include the women who were in Pell's quote "Family", the ones he brainwashed. And all the other victims of Pell's too. There are really hundreds of them, when you think about it. I see violent crime like dropping a stone into a pond. The ripples of consequence can spread almost forever.'

There was passion in his voice; he sounded like a preacher. 'There's so much violence in the world. We're inundated with it and we get numb. My God, the war in Iraq? Gaza? Afghanistan? How many pictures of blown-up cars, how many scenes of wailing mothers did you see before you lost interest?

'When I was a war correspondent covering the Middle East and Africa and Bosnia, I got numb. And you don't have to be there in person for that to happen. It's the same thing in your own living room when you just see the news bites or watch gruesome movies – where there're no real *consequences* for the violence. But if we want peace, if we want to stop violence and fighting, *that*'s what people need to experience, the consequences. You don't do that by gawking at bloody bodies; you focus on lives changed forever by evil.

'Originally it was only going to be about the Croyton case. But then I find out that Pell killed someone else – this Robert Herron. I want to include everyone affected by *his* death too: friends, family. And now, I understand, two guards're dead.' The smile was still there but it was a sad smile and Kathryn Dance realized that his cause was one with which she, as a mother and Major Crimes agent who'd worked plenty of rape, assault and homicide cases, could empathize.

'This's added another wrinkle.' He gestured around him. 'It's much harder to track down victims and family members in a cold case. Herron was killed about ten years ago. I was thinking . . .' Nagle's voice faded and he was frowning, though inexplicably a sparkle returned to his eyes. 'Wait, wait . . . Oh my God, Pell didn't have anything to do with the Herron death, did he? He confessed to get out of Capitola so he could escape from here.'

'We don't know about that,' Dance said judiciously. 'We're still investigating.'

Nagle didn't believe her. 'Did he fake evidence? Or get somebody to come forward and lie. I'll bet he did.'

In a low, even tone Michael O'Neil said, 'We wouldn't want there to be any rumors that might interfere with the investigation.' When the chief deputy made suggestions in this voice people invariably heeded his advice.

'Fine. I won't say anything.'

'Appreciate that,' Dance said, then asked, 'Mr Nagle, do you have any information that could help us? Where Daniel Pell might be going, what he might be up to? Who's helping him?'

With his potbelly, wispy hair and genial laugh, Nagle seemed like a middle-aged elf. He hitched up his pants. 'No idea. I'm sorry. I really just got started on the project a month or so ago. I've been doing the background research.'

'You mentioned you plan to write about the women in Pell's Family too. Have you contacted them?'

'Two of them. I asked if they'd be willing to let me interview them.'

O'Neil asked, 'They're out of jail?'

'Oh, yes. They weren't involved in the Croyton murders. They got short terms, mostly for larceny-related offenses.'

O'Neil completed Dance's thought. 'Could one of them, or both, I guess, be his accomplice?'

Nagle considered this. 'I can't see it. They think Pell's the worst thing that ever happened to them.'

'Who are they?' O'Neil asked.

'Rebecca Sheffield. She lives in San Diego. And Linda Whitfield is in Portland.'

'Have they kept out of trouble?'

'Think so. No police records I could find. Linda lives with her brother and his wife. She works for a church. Rebecca runs a consulting service for small businesses. My impression is they've put the past behind them.'

'You have their numbers?'

The writer flipped through a notebook of fat pages. His handwriting was sloppy and large, the notes voluminous.

'There was a third woman in the Family,' Dance said, recalling the research she'd done for the interview.

'Samantha McCoy. She disappeared years ago. Rebecca said she changed her name and moved away. Apparently she was sick of being known as one of "Daniel's girls". I've done a little searching but I haven't been able to find her yet.'

'Any leads?'

'West Coast somewhere is all that Rebecca heard.'

Dance said to TJ, 'Find her. Samantha McCoy.'

The curly-haired agent bounded off to the corner of the room. He looked like an elf too, she reflected.

Nagle found the numbers of the two women and Dance wrote them down. She placed a call to Rebecca Sheffield in San Diego.

'Women's Initiatives,' the receptionist said in a voice with a faint Latino accent. 'May I help you?'

A moment later Dance found herself speaking to the head of the company, a no-nonsense woman with a low, raspy voice. The agent explained about Pell's escape. Rebecca Sheffield was shocked.

Angry too. 'I thought he was in some kind of superprison.'

'He didn't escape from there. It was the county courthouse lockup.'

Dance asked if the woman had any thoughts on where Pell might be going, who his accomplice could be, other friends he might contact.

Rebecca couldn't, though. She said that she'd joined the Family just a few months before the Croyton murders. But she added that she'd gotten a call from someone about a month earlier, supposedly a writer. 'I assumed he was legit. But he might've had something to do with the escape. Murray or Morton was the first name. I think I've got his number somewhere.'

'It's all right. He's here with us. We've checked him out.'

Rebecca could offer nothing more about Samantha McCoy's whereabouts or new identity. Then, uneasy, she said, 'Back then, eight years ago, I didn't turn him in, but I did cooperate with the police. Do you think I'm in danger?'

'I couldn't say. But until we reapprehend him, you might want to contact the San Diego police.' Dance gave the woman her numbers at CBI and her mobile, and Rebecca told her she'd try to think of anyone who might help Pell or know where he'd go.

The agent pushed down the button on the phone cradle and let it spring back up again. Then she dialed the second number, which turned out to be the Church of the Holy Brethren in Portland. She was connected to Linda Whitfield, who hadn't heard the news either. Her reaction was completely different: silence, broken by nearly inaudible muttering. All Dance caught was 'dear Jesus'.

Praying, it seemed, not an exclamation. The voice faded, or she was cut off.

'Hello?' Dance asked.

'Yes, I'm here,' Linda said.

Dance asked the same questions she'd put to Rebecca Sheffield.

Linda hadn't heard from Pell in years – though they'd stayed in touch for about eighteen months after the Croyton murders. Finally she'd stopped writing and had heard nothing from him since. Nor did she have any information about Samantha McCoy's whereabouts, though she too told Dance about a call from Morton Nagle last month. The agent reassured her they were aware of him and convinced he wasn't working with Pell.

Linda could offer no leads as to where Pell would go. She had no idea of who his accomplice might be.

'We don't know what he has in mind,' Dance told the woman. 'We have no reason to believe you're in danger, but –'

'Oh, Daniel wouldn't hurt me,' she said quickly.

'Still, you might want to tell your local police.'

'Well, I'll think about it.' Then she added, 'Is there a hotline I can call and find out what's going on?'

'We don't have anything like that set up. But the press's covering it closely. You can get the details on the news as fast as we know them.'

'Oh, my brother doesn't have a television.'

No TV? 'Well, if there are any significant developments, I'll let you know. And if you can think of anything else, please call.' Dance gave her the phone numbers and hung up.

A few moments later CBI chief Charles Overby strode into the room. 'Press conference went well, I think. They asked some prickly questions. They always do. But I fielded them okay, I have to say. Stayed one step ahead. You see it?' He nodded at the TV in the corner. No one had bothered to turn up the volume to hear his performance.

'Missed it, Charles. Been on the phone.'

'Who's he?' Overby asked. He'd been staring at Nagle as if he should know him.

Dance introduced them and instantly the writer disappeared from the agent-in-charge's radar screen instantly. 'Any progress at all?' A glance at the maps.

'No reports anywhere,' Dance told him. Then explained that she'd contacted two of the women who'd been in Pell's Family. 'One's from San Diego, one's from Portland, and we're looking for the other right now. At least we know the first two aren't the accomplice.'

'Because you believe them?' Overby asked. 'You could tell that from the tone of their voices?'

None of the officers in the room said anything. So it was up to Dance to let her boss know he'd missed the obvious. 'I don't think they could've set the gas bombs and gotten back home by now.'

A brief pause. Overby said, 'Oh, you called them where they live. You didn't say that.'

Kathryn Dance, former reporter and jury consultant, had played in the real world for a long time. She avoided TJ's glance and said, 'You're right, Charles, I didn't. Sorry.'

The CBI head turned to O'Neil. 'This's a tough one, Michael. Lots of angles. Sure glad you're available to help us out.'

'Glad to do what I can.'

This was Charles Overby at his best. Using the words 'help us' to make clear who was running the show, while also tacitly explaining that O'Neil and the MCSO were on the line too.

*Stash the blame . . .*

Overby announced he was headed back to the CBI office and left the conference room.

Dance now turned to Morton Nagle. 'Do you have any research about Pell I could look at?'

'Well, I suppose. But why?'

'Maybe help us get some idea of where he's going,' O'Neil said.

'Copies,' the writer said. 'Not the originals.'

'That's fine,' Dance told him. 'One of us'll come by later and pick them up. Where's your office?'

Nagle worked out of a house he was renting in Monterey. He gave Dance the address and phone number, then began packing up his camera bag.

Dance glanced down at it. 'Hold on.'

Nagle noticed her eyes on the contents. He smiled. 'I'd be happy to.'

'I'm sorry?'

He picked up a copy of one of his true-crime books, *Blind Trust*, and with a flourish autographed it for her. 'Thanks.' She set it down and pointed at what she'd actually been looking at. 'Your camera. Did you take any pictures this morning? Before the fire?'

'Oh.' He smiled wryly at the misunderstanding. 'Yes, I did.'

'It's digital?'

'That's right.'

'Can we see them?'

Nagle picked up the Canon and began to push buttons. Dance and O'Neil hunched close over the tiny screen on the back. Dance detected a new aftershave. She felt comfort in his proximity.

The writer scrolled through the pictures. Most of them were of people walking into the courthouse, a few artistic shots of the front of the building in the fog.

Then the detective and the agent simultaneously said, 'Wait.' The image they were looking at depicted the driveway that led to where the fire had occurred. They could make out someone behind a car, just the head and shoulders visible, wearing a blue jacket, a baseball cap and sunglasses.

'Look at the arm.'

Dance nodded. It seemed the person's arm trailed behind, as if wheeling a suitcase.

'Is that time stamped?'

Nagle called up the readout. 'Nine twenty-two.'

'That'd work out just right,' Dance said, recalling the fire marshal's estimate of the time the gas bomb had been planted.

'Can you blow up the image?' she asked.

'Not in the camera.'

TJ said he could on his computer, though, no problem. Nagle gave the memory card to him, and Dance sent TJ back to CBI headquarters, reminding him, 'And Samantha McCoy. Track her down. The aunt too. Bakersfield.'

'You bet, boss.'

Rey Carraneo was still outside, canvassing for witnesses. But Dance believed that the accomplice had fled too; now that Pell had probably eluded the roadblocks, there was no reason for him to stay around. She sent him back to headquarters as well.

Nagle said, 'I'll get started on the copies . . . Oh, don't forget.' He handed her the autographed paperback. 'I know you'll like it.'

When he was gone Dance held it up. 'In all my free time.' And gave it to O'Neil for his collection.

# Chapter
# NINE

At lunch hour a woman in her mid-twenties was sitting on a patio outside the Whole Foods grocery store in Monterey's Del Monte Center.

A pale disk of sun was slowly emerging, as the blanket of fog burned away.

She heard a siren in the distance, a dove cooing, a horn, a child crying, then a child laughing. Jennie Marston thought, Angel songs, angel songs . . .

The scent of pine filled the cool air. No breeze. Dull light. A typical California day on the coast, but everything about it was intensified.

Which is what happens when you're in love and about to meet your boyfriend.

*Anticipation . . .*

Some old pop song, Jennie thought. Her mother sang it from time to time, her smoker's voice harsh and off-key, often slurred.

Blonde, *authentic* California blonde, Jennie sipped her coffee. It was expensive but good. This wasn't her kind of store (the twenty-four-year-old part-time caterer was an Albertsons girl, a Safeway girl), but Whole Foods was a good meeting place.

She was wearing close-fitting jeans, a light pink blouse and, underneath, a red Victoria's Secret bra and panties. Like the coffee, the lingerie was a luxury she couldn't afford. But some things you had to splurge on. (Besides, Jennie reflected, the garments were really a gift, in a way: for her boyfriend.)

Which made her think of other indulgences. Rubbing her nose, *flick, flick,* on the bump.

Stop it, she told herself.

But she didn't. Another two flicks.

*Angel songs . . .*

Why couldn't she have met him a year later? She'd've had the cosmetic work done by then and now she'd be beautiful. At least she could do *something* about the nose and boobs. She only wished she could fix the toothpick shoulders and boyish hips but those were beyond the talents of talented Dr Ginsberg.

*Skinny, skinny, skinny . . . And the way you eat! Twice what I do and look at me. God gave me a daughter like you to test me.*

Watching the unsmiling women wheeling their grocery carts to their mommy vans, Jennie wondered, Do *they* love their husbands? They couldn't possibly be as much in love as she was with her boyfriend. She felt sorry for them.

Jennie finished her coffee and returned to the store, looking at massive pineapples and heads of funny-shaped lettuce and perfectly lined-up steaks and chops. She spent most of her time studying the baked goods and pastry, the way one painter examines another's canvas. Good . . . Not so good. She wasn't hungry and didn't want to buy anything – it was way expensive. She was just too squirrelly to stay in one place.

*That's what I should've named you. Stay Still Jennie. For fuck's sake, girl. Sit down.*

Looking at the produce, looking at the rows of meat.

Looking at the women with boring husbands.

She wondered if the intensity she felt for her boyfriend was simply because it was all so new. Would it fade after a while? But one thing in their favor was that they were older; this wasn't that stupid passion of your teenage years. They were mature people. And most important was their souls' connection, which comes along so rarely. Each knew exactly how the other felt.

'Your favorite color's green,' he'd shared with her the first time they'd spoken. 'I'll bet you sleep under a green comforter. It soothes you at night.'

Oh my God, he was so right. It was a blanket, not a comforter. But it was green as grass. What kind of man had *that* intuition?

Suddenly she paused, aware of a conversation nearby. Two of the bored housewives weren't so bored at the moment.

'Somebody's dead. In Salinas. It just happened.'

Salinas? Jennie thought.

'Oh, the escape from that prison or whatever? Yeah, I just heard about it.'

'David Pell, no, Daniel. That's it.'

'Isn't he, like, Charles Manson's kid or something?'

'I don't know. But I heard some people got killed.'

'He's not Manson's kid. No, he just called himself that.'

'Who's Charles Manson?'

'Are you kidding me? Remember Sharon Tate?'

'Who?'

'Like, when were you born?'

Jennie approached the women. 'Excuse me, what's that you're talking about? An escape or something?'

'Yeah, from this jail in Salinas. Didn't you hear?' one of the short-haired housewives asked, glancing at Jennie's nose.

She didn't care. 'Somebody was killed, you said?'

'Some guards and then somebody was kidnapped and killed, I think.'

They didn't seem to know anything more.

Her palms damp, heart uneasy, Jennie turned and walked away. She checked her phone. Her boyfriend had called a while ago but nothing since then. No messages. She tried the number. He didn't answer.

Jennie returned to the turquoise Thunderbird. She put the radio on the news, then twisted the rearview mirror toward her. She pulled her makeup and brush from her purse.

*Some people got killed . . .*

Don't worry about it, she told herself. Working on her face, concentrating the way her mother had taught her. It was one of the nice things the woman had done for her. 'Put the light here, the dark here – we've got to do something with that nose of yours. Smooth it in, blend it. Good.'

Though with her mother, the nice could be shattered in an instant.

*Well, it looked fine until you messed it up. Honestly, what's wrong with you? Do it again. You look like a whore.*

Daniel Pell was strolling down the sidewalk from the small covered garage connected to an office building in Monterey.

He'd had to abandon Billy's Honda Civic earlier than he'd planned. He'd heard on the news that the police had found the Worldwide Express truck, which meant they would probably assume he was in the Civic. He'd apparently evaded the roadblocks just in time.

How 'bout *that*, Kathryn?

Now he continued along the sidewalk, with his head down. He wasn't concerned about being out in public, not yet. Nobody would expect him here. Besides, he looked different. In addition to the civilian clothes he was smooth-shaven. After dumping Billy's car he'd slipped into the back parking lot of a motel, where he'd gone through the trash. He'd found a discarded razor and a tiny bottle of the motel's giveaway body lotion. Crouching by the Dumpster, he'd used them to shave off the beard.

He now felt the breeze on his face, smelled something in the air: ocean and seaweed. First time in years. He loved the scent. In Capitola prison the air you smelled was the air they decided to send to you through the air conditioner or heating system and it didn't smell like anything.

A squad car went past.

*Hold fast . . .*

Pell was careful to maintain his pace, not looking around, not deviating from his route. Changing your behavior draws attention. And that puts you at a disadvantage, gives people information about you. They can figure out *why* you changed, then use it against you.

That's what had happened at the courthouse.

*Kathryn . . .*

Pell had had the interrogation all planned out: If he could do so without arousing suspicion, he was going to get some information from whoever was interviewing him, learn how many guards were in the courthouse, for instance, and where they were.

But then to his astonishment she'd gotten very close to his plan.

*Now let's think about the wallet. Where could that've come from? . . .*

So he'd been forced to change his plans. And fast. He'd done the best he could but the braying alarm told him she'd anticipated him. If she'd done that just five minutes earlier, he would've been back in the Capitola prison van. The escape plan would've turned to dust.

Kathryn Dance . . .

Another squad car drove past quickly.

Still no glances his way and Pell kept on course. But he knew it was time to get out of Monterey. He slipped into the crowded open-air shopping center. He noted the stores, Macy's, Mervyns and the smaller ones selling Mrs See's Candy, books (Pell loved and devoured them – the more you knew, the more control you had), video games, sports equipment, cheap clothes and cheaper jewelry. The place was packed. It was June; many schools were out of session.

One girl, college age, came out of a store, a bag over her shoulder.

Beneath her jacket was a tight red tank top. One glance at it, and the swelling began inside him. The bubble, expanding. (The last time he'd intimidated a con, and bribed a guard, to swing a conjugal visit with the con's wife in Capitola was a year ago. A long, long year . . .)

He stared at her, following only a few feet behind, enjoying the sight of the hair and her tight jeans, trying to smell her, trying to get close enough to brush against her as he walked past, which is an assault just as surely as being dragged into an alley and stripped at knifepoint.

Rape, Daniel Pell knew, is in the eye of the beholder.

Ah, but then she turned into another store and vanished from his life.

My loss, dear, he thought.

But not yours, of course.

In the parking lot, Pell saw a robin's-egg-blue Ford Thunderbird. Inside he could just make out a woman, brushing her long blonde hair.

Ah . . .

Walking closer. Her nose was bumpy and she was a skinny little thing, not much in the chest department. But that didn't stop the balloon within him growing, ten times, a hundred. It was going to burst soon.

Daniel Pell looked around. Nobody else nearby.

He walked forward through the rows of cars, closing the distance.

Jennie Marston finished with her hair. This particular aspect of her body she loved. It was shiny and thick and when she spun her head it flowed like a shampoo model's in a slo-mo TV commercial. She twisted the Thunderbird's rearview mirror back into position. Shut the radio off. Touched her nose, the bump.

Stop it!

As she was reaching for the door handle she gave a gasp. It was opening on its own.

Jennie froze, staring up at the wiry man who was leaning down.

For three or four seconds neither of them moved. Then he pulled the door open. 'You're the picture of delight, Jennie Marston,' he said. 'Prettier than I imagined.'

'Oh, Daniel.' Overwhelmed with emotion – fear, relief, guilt, a big burning sun of feeling – Jennie Marston could think of nothing else to say. Breathless, she slipped out of the car and flew into her boyfriend's arms, shivering and holding him so tightly that she squeezed a soft, steady hiss from his narrow chest.

# Chapter
# TEN

They got into the T-bird and she pressed her head against his neck as Daniel carefully surveyed the parking lot and the road nearby.

Jennie was thinking how difficult the past month had been, forging a relationship through email, rare phone calls and fantasy, never seeing her lover in person. Still, she knew that it was so much better to build love this way – from a distance. It was like the women on the home front during a war, the way her mother would talk about her father in Vietnam. That was all a lie, of course, she'd later learned, but it didn't take away the larger truth: that love should be first about two souls and only later about sex. What she felt for Daniel Pell was unlike anything she'd ever experienced.

Exhilarating.

Frightening too.

She felt the tears start. No, no, stop it. Don't cry. He won't like it if you cry. Men get mad at that.

But he asked gently, 'What's the matter, lovely?'

'I'm just so happy.'

'Come on, tell me.'

Well, he didn't sound mad. She debated, then said, 'Well, I was wondering. There were some women. At the grocery store. Then I put the news on. I heard . . . somebody got burned real bad. A policeman. And then two people were killed, stabbed.' Daniel had said he just wanted the knife to threaten the guards. He wasn't going to hurt anybody.

'What?' he snapped. His blue eyes grew hard.

No, no, what're you doing? Jennie asked herself. You made him mad!

Why did you ask him that? Now you've fucked everything up! Her heart fluttered.

'They did it again. They always do it! When I left, nobody was hurt. I was so careful! I got out the fire door just like we'd planned and slammed it.' Then he nodded. 'I know . . . sure. There were other prisoners in a cell near mine. They wanted me to let them out too, but I wouldn't. I'll bet they started to riot and when the guards went to stop them, that's when those two got killed. Some of them had shivs, I'll bet. You know what that is?'

'A knife, right?'

'Homemade knife. That's what happened. And if somebody got burned, it was because he was careless. I looked carefully – there was no one else out there when I got through the fire. And how could I attack three people all by myself? Ridiculous. But the police and the news're blaming me for it, like they always do.' His lean face was red. 'I'm the easy target.'

'Just like that family eight years ago,' she said timidly, trying to calm him. Daniel had told her how he and his friend had gone to the Croytons' house to pitch a business idea to the computer genius. But when they got there his friend, it seemed, had a whole different idea – he was going to rob the couple. He knocked Daniel out and started killing the family. Daniel had come to and tried to stop him. Finally he'd had to kill his friend in self-defense.

'They blamed me for that – because you know how we *hate* it when the killer dies. Somebody goes into a school and shoots students and kills himself. We want the bad guy alive. We need somebody to blame. It's human nature.'

He was right, Jennie reflected. She was relieved, but also terrified that she'd upset him. 'I'm sorry, honey. I shouldn't've mentioned anything.'

She expected him to tell her to shut up, maybe even get out of the car and walk away. But to her shock he smiled and stroked her hair. 'You can ask me anything.'

She hugged him again. Felt more tears on her cheek and touched them away. The makeup had clotted. She backed away, staring at her fingers. Oh, no. Look at this! She wanted to be pretty for him.

The fears coming back, digging away.

*Oh, Jennie, you're going to be wearing your hair like that? You sure you want to? . . . You don't want bangs? They'd cover up that high forehead of yours.*

What if she didn't live up to his expectations?

Daniel Pell took her face in his strong hands. 'Lovely, you're the most beautiful woman on the face of the earth. You don't even need makeup.'

Like he could see right into her thoughts.

Crying again. 'I've been worried you wouldn't like me.'

'Wouldn't *like* you. Baby, I love you. What I emailed you, remember?'

Jennie remembered every word he'd written. She looked into his eyes and kneaded his hands. 'Oh, you're such a beautiful person.' She pressed her lips against his. Though they made love in her imagination at least once a day, this was their first kiss. She felt his teeth against her lips, his tongue. They stayed locked together in this fierce embrace for what seemed like forever, though it could have been a mere second. Jennie had no sense of time. She wanted him inside her, pressing hard, his chest pulsing against hers.

Souls are where love should start, but you've got to get the bodies involved pretty damn soon. She slipped her hand along his bare, muscular leg.

He gave a laugh. 'Tell you what, lovely, maybe we'd better get out of here.'

'Sure, whatever you want.'

He asked, 'You have the phone I called you on?' Daniel had told her to buy three prepaid cell phones with cash. She handed him the one she'd answered when he'd called just after he'd escaped. He took it apart and pulled the battery and SIM card out. He threw them into a trash can and returned to the car.

'The others?'

She produced them. He handed her one and put the other in his pocket.

He said, 'We ought to –'

A siren sounded nearby, close. They both froze.

Angel songs, Jennie thought, then recited this good-luck mantra a dozen times.

The sirens faded into the distance.

'Let's go, lovely.'

She nodded. 'They might come back.' Nodding after the sirens.

Daniel smiled. 'I'm not worried about that. I just want to be alone with you.'

Jennie felt a shiver of happiness down her spine. It almost hurt.

The west central regional headquarters of the California Bureau of Investigation, home to dozens of agents, was a two-story modern structure, near Highway 68, indistinguishable from the others around it: functional rectangles of glass and building stone, housing doctors' and lawyers' offices, architectural firms, computer companies and the like. The landscaping was meticulous and boring, the parking lots always half-empty. The countryside rose and fell in gentle hills, which were at the moment bright green, thanks to recent rain. Often the ground was as brown as Colorado during a dry spell.

A United Express jet banked sharply and low, then leveled off, vanishing over the trees for the touchdown at nearby Monterey Peninsula Airport.

Kathryn Dance and Michael O'Neil were in the CBI's ground-floor conference room, directly beneath her office. They stood side-by-side, staring at a large map on which the roadblocks were indicated – this time with pushpins, not entomological Post-it notes. There had still been no sightings of the Worldwide Express driver's Honda, and the net had been pushed farther back, now eighty miles away.

Kathryn Dance glanced at O'Neil's square face and read in it a complicated amalgam of determination and concern. She knew him well. They'd met years ago when she was a jury consultant, studying the demeanor and responses of prospective jurors during voir dire and advising lawyers which to choose and which to reject. She'd been hired by federal prosecutors to help them select jurors in a RICO trial in which O'Neil was a chief witness. (Curiously, she'd met her late husband under parallel circumstances when she was a reporter covering a trial in Salinas and he was a prosecution witness.)

Dance and O'Neil had become friends and stayed close over the years. When she'd decided to go into law enforcement and got a job with the regional office of the CBI she'd found herself working frequently with him. Stan Fishburne, then the agent-in-charge, was one mentor, O'Neil the other. He taught her more about the art of investigation in six months than she'd learned during her entire formal training. They complemented each other well. The quiet, deliberate man preferred traditional police techniques, like forensics, undercover work, surveillance and running confidential informants, while Dance's specialty was canvassing, interrogation and interviewing.

She knew she wouldn't be the agent she was today without O'Neil's help. Or his humor and patience (and other vital talents: like making sure she took her Dramamine *before* she went out on his boat).

Though their approach to their job and their talents differed, their instincts were identical and they were closely attuned to each other. She was amused to see that, while he'd been staring at the map, in fact he'd been sensing signals from her too.

'What is it?' he asked.

'How do you mean?'

'Something's bothering you. More than just finding yourself in the driver's seat here.'

'Yep.' She thought for a minute. That was one thing about O'Neil; he often forced her to put her tangled ideas in order before speaking. She explained, 'Bad feeling about Pell. I got this idea that the guards' deaths meant nothing to him. Juan too. And that Worldwide Express driver? He's dead, you know.'

'I know . . . You think Pell *wants* to kill?'

'No, not wants to. Or doesn't. What he wants is whatever serves his interest, however small. In a way, that seems scarier, and makes it harder to anticipate him. But let's hope I'm wrong.'

'You're never wrong, boss.' TJ appeared, carrying a laptop. He set it up on the battered conference table under a sign, *Most Wanted Statewide*. Below it were the ten winners of that contest, reflecting the demographics of the state: Latino, Anglo, Asian and African American, in that order.

'You find the McCoy woman or Pell's aunt?'

'Not yet. My troops're on the case. But check this out.' He adjusted the computer screen.

They hovered around the screen, on which was a high-resolution image of the photograph from Morton Nagle's camera. Now larger and clearer, it revealed a figure in a denim jacket on the driveway that led to the back of the building, where the fire had started. The shadow had morphed into a large black suitcase.

'Woman?' O'Neil asked.

They could judge the person's height by comparing it to the automobile nearby. About Dance's height, five six. Slimmer, though, she noted. The cap and sunglasses obscured the head and face, but through the vehicle's window you could see hips slightly broader than a man's would be for that height.

'And there's a glint. See that?' TJ tapped the screen. 'Earring.'

Dance glanced at the hole in his lobe, where a diamond or metal stud occasionally resided.

'Statistically speaking,' TJ said in defense of his observation.

'Okay. I agree.'

'A blonde woman, about five six or so,' O'Neil summarized.

Dance said, 'Weight one-ten, give or take.' She had a thought. She called Rey Carraneo in his office upstairs, asked him to join them.

He appeared a moment later. 'Agent Dance.'

'Go back to Salinas. Talk to the manager of the You Mail It store.' The accomplice had most likely recently checked out the Worldwide Express delivery schedule at the franchise. 'See if anyone there remembers a woman fitting her general description. If so, get a picture on EFIS.'

The Electronic Facial Identification System is a computer-based version of the old Identi-Kit, used by investigators to re-create suspects' likenesses from the recollections of witnesses.

'Sure, Agent Dance.'

TJ hit some buttons and the jpeg zipped wirelessly to the color printer in his office. Carraneo would pick it up there.

TJ's phone rang. 'Yo.' He jotted notes during a brief conversation, which ended with, 'I love you, darling.' He hung up. 'Vital statistics clerk in Sacramento. B-R-I-T-N-E-E. Love that name. She's very sweet. Way too sweet for me. Not to say it couldn't work out between us.'

Dance lifted an eyebrow, the kinesic interpretation of which was: 'Get to the point.'

'I put her on the case of the missing Family member, capital F. Five years ago Samantha McCoy changed her name to Sarah Monroe. So she wouldn't have to throw out her monogrammed underwear, I'd guess. Then *three* years ago, somebody of that name marries Ronald Starkey. There goes the monogram ploy. Anyway, they live in San Jose.'

'Sure it's the same McCoy?'

'The real McCoy, you mean. I've been waiting to say that. Yep. Good old Social Security. With a parole board backup.'

Dance called Directory Assistance and got Ronald and Sarah Starkey's address and phone number.

'San Jose,' O'Neil said. 'That's close enough.' Unlike the other two women in the Family to whom Dance had already spoken, Samantha could have planted the gas bomb this morning and been home in an hour and a half.

'Does she work?' Dance asked.

'I didn't check that out. I will, though, you want.'

'We want,' O'Neil said. TJ didn't report to him, and in the well-established hierarchy of law enforcement CBI trumped MCSO. But a request from Chief Deputy Michael O'Neil was the same as a request from Dance. Or even higher.

A few minutes later TJ returned to say that the tax department revealed that Sarah Starkey was employed by a small educational publisher in San Jose.

Dance got the number. 'Let's see if she was in this morning.'

O'Neil asked, 'How're you going to do that? We can't let her know we suspect anything.'

'Oh, I'll lie,' Dance said breezily. She called the publisher from a caller-ID-blocked line. When a woman answered, Dance said, 'Hi. This is the El Camino Boutique. We have an order for Sarah Starkey. But the driver said she wasn't there this morning. Do you know what time she'll be getting in?'

'Sarah? I'm afraid there's some mistake. She's been here since eight thirty.'

'Really? Well, I'll talk to the driver again. Might be better to deliver it to her house. If you could not mention anything to Mrs Starkey, I'd appreciate it. It's a surprise.' Dance hung up. 'She was there all morning.'

TJ applauded. 'And the Oscar for the best performance by a law enforcer deceiving the public goes to . . .'

O'Neil frowned.

'Don't approve of my subversive techniques?' Dance asked.

With his typical wry delivery O'Neil said, 'No, it's just that you're going to have to send her *something* now. The receptionist's going to dime you out. Tell her she's got a secret admirer.'

'I know, boss. Get her one of those balloon bouquets. "Congratulations on not being a suspect."'

Dance's administrative assistant, short, no-nonsense Maryellen Kresbach, walked into the room with coffee for all (Dance never asked; Maryellen always brought). The mother of three wore clattery high heels and favored complicated, coiffed hair and impressive fingernails.

The crew in the conference room thanked. Dance sipped the excellent coffee. Wished Maryellen had brought some of the cookies sitting on her desk. She envied the woman's ability to be both a domestic powerhouse and the best assistant Dance had ever had.

The agent noticed that Maryellen wasn't leaving after delivering the caffeine.

'Didn't know if I should bother you. But Brian called.'

'He did?'

'He said you might not have gotten his message on Friday.'

'You gave it to me.'

'I know I did. I didn't tell him I did. And I didn't tell him I didn't. So.'

Feeling O'Neil's eyes on her, Dance said, 'Okay, thanks.'

'You want his number?'

'I have it.'

'Okay.' Her assistant continued to stand resolutely in front of her boss, nodding slowly.

Well, this is a rather spiny moment.

Dance didn't want to talk about Brian Gunderson.

The trill of the conference-room phone saved her.

She answered, listened for a moment and said, 'Have somebody bring him to my office right away.'

# Chapter
# ELEVEN

The large man, in a California Department of Corrections and Rehabilitation uniform, sat in front of her desk, a workaday slab of government-issue furniture on which lay random pens, a lamp, various commendations and photos: of the two children, of Dance with a handsome silver-haired man, of her mother and father, and of two dogs, each paired with one of the youngsters. A dozen files also rested on the cheap laminate. They were facedown.

'This is terrible,' said Tony Waters, a senior guard from Capitola Correctional Facility. 'I can't tell you.'

Dance detected traces of a southeastern accent in the distraught voice. The Monterey Peninsula drew people from all over the world. Dance and Waters were alone at the moment. Michael O'Neil was checking on the forensics from the scene of the escape.

'You were in charge of the wing where Pell was incarcerated?' Dance asked.

'That's right.' Bulky and with stooped shoulders, Waters sat forward in the chair. He was in his mid-fifties, she estimated.

'Did Pell say anything to you about where he's headed?'

'No, ma'am. I've been racking my brain since it happened. That was the first thing I did when I heard. I sat down and went through everything he'd said in the past week or more. But, no, nothing. For one thing, Daniel didn't talk a lot. Not to us, the hacks.'

'Did he spend time in the library?'

'Huge amount. Read all the time.'

'Can I find out what?'

'It's not logged and the cons can't check anything out.'

'How about visitors?'

'Nobody in the last year.'

'And telephone calls? Are they logged?'

'Yes, ma'am. But not recorded.' He thought back. 'He didn't have many, aside from reporters wanting to interview him. But he never called back. I think maybe he talked to his aunt once or twice. No others I remember.'

'What about computers, email?'

'Not for the prisoners. We have that for ourselves, of course. They're in a special area – a control zone. We're very strict about that. You know, I was thinking about it and if he communicated with anybody on the outside –'

'Which he had to do,' Dance pointed out.

'Right. It had to be through a con being released. You might want to check there.'

'I thought of that. I've talked to your warden. She tells me that there were only two releases in the past month and their parole officers had them accounted for this morning. They could've gotten messages to someone, though. The officers're checking that out.'

Waters, she'd noted, had arrived empty-handed, and Dance now asked, 'Did you get our request for the contents of his cell?'

The guard's mood darkened. He was shaking his head, looking down. 'Yes, ma'am. But it was empty. Nothing inside at all. Had been empty for a couple of days actually.' He looked up, his lips tight, as he seemed to be debating. Then his eyes dipped as he said, 'I didn't catch it.'

'Catch what?'

'The thing is, I've worked the Q, Soledad and Lompoc. Half-dozen others. We learn to look for certain things. See, if something big's going down, the cons' cells change. Things'll disappear – sometimes it's evidence that they're going to make a run, or evidence of shit a con's done that he doesn't want us to know about. Or what he's *going* to do. Because he knows we'll look over the cell with a microscope after.'

'But with Pell you didn't think about him throwing everything out.'

'We never had an escape from Capitola. It can't happen. And they're watched so close, it's almost impossible for one con to move on another – kill him, I mean.' The man's face was flushed. 'I should've thought better. If it'd been Lompoc, I'd've known right away something was going down.' He rubbed his eyes. 'I screwed up.'

'That'd be a tough leap to make,' Dance reassured him. 'From house-keeping to escaping.'

He shrugged and examined his nails. He wore no jewelry but Dance could see the indentation of a wedding band. It occurred to her that, for once, this was no badge of infidelity but a concession to the job. Probably, circulating among dangerous prisoners, it was better not to wear anything they might steal.

'Sounds like you've been in this business for a while.'

'Long time. After the army I got into corrections. Been there ever since.' He brushed his crew-cut, grinning. 'Sometimes seems like forever. Sometimes seems like just yesterday. Two years till I retire. In a funny way, I'll miss it.' He was at ease now, realizing he wouldn't be horse-whipped for not foreseeing the escape.

She asked about where he lived, his family. He was married and held up his left hand, laughing; her deduction about the ring proved correct. He and his wife had two children, both bound for college, he said proudly.

But while they chatted, a silent alarm was pulsing within Dance. She had a situation on her hands.

Tony Waters was lying.

Many falsehoods go undetected simply because the person being deceived doesn't expect to be lied to. Dance had asked Waters here only to get information about Daniel Pell, so she wasn't in interrogation mode. If Waters had been a suspect or a hostile witness, she'd have been looking for stress signs when he gave certain answers, then kept probing those topics until he admitted lying and eventually told the truth.

This process only works, though, if you determine the subject's non-deceptive baseline behavior *before* you start asking the sensitive questions, which Dance, of course, had had no reason to do because she'd assumed he'd be truthful.

Even without a baseline comparison, though, a perceptive kinesic interrogator can sometimes spot deception. Two clues signal lying with some consistency: One is a very slight increase in the pitch of the voice, because lying triggers an emotional response within most people, and emotion causes vocal cords to tighten. The other signal is pausing before and during answering, since lying is mentally challenging. One who's lying has to think constantly about what he and other people have said previously about the topic, then craft a fictitious response that's consistent with those prior statements and what he believes the interrogator knows.

In her conversation with the guard, Dance had become aware that at several points his voice had risen in pitch and he had paused when there was no reason for him to. Once she caught on to this, she looked back to other behaviors and saw that they suggested deception: offering more information than necessary, digressing, engaging in negation movement – touching his head, nose and eyes particularly – and aversion, turning away from her.

As soon as there's evidence of deception, an interview turns into an interrogation, and the officer's approach changes. It was then that she'd broken off the questions about Pell and begun talking about topics he'd have no reason to lie about – his personal life, the Peninsula, and so on. This was to establish his baseline behavior.

As she was doing this, Dance performed her standard four-part analysis of the subject himself, to give her an idea of how to tactically plan the interrogation.

First, she asked, what was his role in the incident? She concluded that Tony Waters was at best an uncooperative witness; at worst, an accomplice of Pell's.

Second, had he a motive to lie? Of course. Waters didn't want to be arrested or lose his job because, intentionally or through negligence, he'd helped Daniel Pell escape. He might also have a personal or financial interest in aiding the killer.

Third, what was his personality type? Interrogators need this information to adjust their own demeanor when questioning the subject – should they be aggressive or conciliatory? Some officers simply determine whether the subject is an introvert or extrovert, which gives a pretty good idea of how assertive to be. Dance, though, preferred a more comprehensive approach, trying to assign code letters from the Myers-Briggs personality type indicator, which includes three other attributes in addition to introvert or extrovert: thinking or feeling, sensing or intuitive, judging or perceiving.

Dance concluded that Waters was a thinking-sensing-judging-extrovert, which meant that she could be more blunt with him than with a more emotional, internalized subject, and could use various reward-punishment techniques to break down the lies.

Finally, she asked, what kind of 'liar's personality' does Waters have? There are several types: for instance, manipulators, or 'High Machiavellians' (after the ruthless Italian prince), lie with impunity, seeing nothing wrong with it, using deceit as a tool to achieve their goals in love, business, politics – or crime. Other types include social liars, who lie to entertain, and adaptors, insecure people who lie to make positive impressions.

She decided that, given his career as a lifelong prison guard and the ease with which he'd tried to take charge of the conversation and lead her away from the truth, Waters was in yet another category. He was an 'actor', someone for whom control was an important issue. They don't lie regularly, only when necessary, and are less skilled than High Machs, but they're good deceivers.

Dance now took off her glasses – with chic dark-red frames – and, on the pretense of cleaning them, set them aside and put on narrower lenses encased in black steel, the 'predator specs' she'd worn when interrogating Pell. She rose, walked around the desk and sat in the chair beside him.

Interrogators refer to the immediate space around a human being as the 'proxemic zone', ranging from 'intimate', six to eighteen inches, to 'public', ten feet away and beyond. Dance's preferred space for interrogation was within the intermediate 'personal' zone, about two feet away.

Waters noted the move with curiosity but he said nothing about it. Nor did she.

'Now, Tony. I'd just like to go over a few things one more time.'

'Sure, whatever.' He lifted his ankle to his knee – a move that seemed relaxed but was, in fact, a glaring defense maneuver.

She returned to a topic that, she now knew, had raised significant stress indicators in Waters. 'Tell me again about the computers at Capitola.'

'Computers?'

Responding with a question was a classic indicator of deception; the subject is trying to buy time to decide where the interrogator is going and how to frame a response.

'Yes, what kind do you have?'

'Oh, I'm not a tech guy. I don't know.' His foot tapped. 'Dells, I think.'

'Laptops or desktops?'

'We have both. Mostly they're desktops. Not that there're, like, hundreds of them, you know.' He offered a conspiratorial smile. 'State budgets and everything.' He told a story about recent financial cuts at the Department of Corrections, which Dance found interesting only because it was such a bald attempt at distracting her.

She steered him back. 'Now, access to computers in Capitola. Tell me about it again.'

'Like I said, cons aren't allowed to use them.'

Technically, this was a true statement. But he hadn't said that cons *don't* use them. Deception includes evasive answers as well as outright lies.

'*Could* they have access to them?'

'Not really.'

Sort of pregnant, kind of dead.

'How do you mean that, Tony?'

'I should've said, no, they can't.'

'But you mentioned office workers and guards have access.'

'Right.'

'Now, why couldn't a con use a computer?'

Waters had originally said that this was because they were in a 'control zone'. She recalled an aversion behavior and a slight change in pitch when he'd used the phrase.

He now paused for just a second as – she supposed – he was trying to recall what he'd said. 'They're in an area of limited access. Only non-violent cons are allowed there. Some of them help out in the office, supervised, of course. Administrative duty. But they can't use the computers.'

'And Pell couldn't get in there?'

'He's classified as One A.'

Dance noticed the non-responsive answer. And the blocking gesture – a scratch of his eyelid – when he gave it.

'And that meant he wasn't allowed in any . . . what were those areas again?'

'LA locations. Limited access.' He now remembered what he'd said earlier. 'Or control zones.'

'Controlled or control?'

A pause. 'Control zone.'

'*Controlled* – with an "ed" on the end – would make more sense. You're sure that's not it?'

He grew flustered. 'Well, I don't know. What difference does it make? We use 'em both.'

'And you use that term for other areas too? Like the warden's office and the guards' locker room – would they be control zones?'

'Sure . . . I mean, some people use that phrase more than others. I picked it up at another facility.'

'Which one would that be?'

A pause. 'Oh, I don't remember. Look, I made it sound like it's an official name or something. It's just a thing we say. Everybody inside uses shorthand. I mean, prisons everywhere. Guards're "hacks"; prisoners are "cons". It's not official or anything. You do the same at CBI, don't you? Everybody does.'

This was a double play: Deceptive subjects often try to establish camaraderie with their interrogators ('you do the same') and use generalizations and abstractions ('everybody', 'everywhere').

Dance asked in a low, steady voice, 'Whether authorized or not, in whatever zone, have Daniel Pell and a computer ever been in the same room at the same time at Capitola?'

'I've never seen him on a computer, I swear. Honestly.'

The stress that people experience when lying pushes them into one of four emotional states: they're angry, they're depressed, they're in denial or they want to bargain their way out of trouble. The words that Waters had just used –' I swear' and 'honestly' – were expressions that along with his agitated body language, very different from his baseline, told Dance that the guard was in the denial stage of deception. He just couldn't accept the truth of whatever he'd done at the prison and was dodging responsibility for it.

It's important to determine which stress state the subject is in because that allows the interrogator to decide on a tactic for questioning. When the subject is in the anger phase, for instance, you encourage him to vent until he exhausts himself.

In the case of denial, you attack on the facts.

Which was what she now did.

'You have access to the office where the computers are kept, right?'

'Yeah, I do, but so what? All the hacks do . . . Hey, what is this? I'm on your side.'

A typical denier's deflection, which Dance ignored. 'And you said it's possible some prisoners would be that office. Has Pell ever been in there?'

'Nonviolent felons are the only ones allowed in –'

'Has Pell ever been in there?'

'I swear to God I never saw him.'

Dance noted adaptors – gestures meant to relieve tension: finger-flexing, foot-tapping, his shoulder aimed toward her (like a football player's defensive posture) and more frequent glances at the door (liars actually glance at routes by which they can escape the stress of the interrogation).

'That's about the fourth time you haven't answered my question, Tony. Now, was Pell ever in any room in Capitola with a computer?'

The guard grimaced. 'I'm sorry. I didn't mean to be, you know, difficult. I just was kind of flustered, I guess. I mean, like, I felt you were accusing *me* of something. Okay, I never saw him on a computer, really. I wasn't lying. I've been pretty upset by this whole thing. You can imagine that.' His shoulders drooped, his head lowered a half inch.

'Sure I can, Tony.'

'Maybe Daniel could've been.'

Her attack had made Waters realize that it was more painful to endure the battering of the interrogation than to own up to what he was lying about. Like turning a light switch, Waters was suddenly in the bargaining phase of deception. This meant the subject was close to dropping the deception but was still holding back the full truth, in an effort to escape punishment. Dance knew that she had to abandon the frontal assault and offer him some way to save face.

In an interrogation the enemy isn't the liar, but the lie.

'So,' she said in a friendly voice, sitting back, out of his personal zone, 'it's possible that at some point, Pell could've gotten access to a computer?'

'I guess it could've happened. But I don't know for sure he was on one.' His head drooped even more. His voice was soft. 'It's just . . . it's hard, doing what we do. People don't understand. Being a hack. What it's like.'

'I'm sure they don't,' Dance agreed.

'We have to be teachers and cops, everything. And –' his voice lowered conspiratorially '– Admin's always looking over our shoulders, telling us to do this, do that, keep the peace, let them know when something's going down.'

'Probably like being a parent. You're always watching your children.'

'Yeah, exactly. It's like having children.' Wide eyes – an affect display, revealing his emotion.

Dance nodded emphatically. 'Obviously, Tony, you care about the cons. And about doing a good job.'

People in the bargaining phase want to be reassured and forgiven.

'It was nothing really. What happened.'

'Go ahead.'

'I made a decision.'

'It's a tough job you have. You must have to make hard decisions every day.'

'Ha. Every *hour*.'

'So what did you have to decide?'

'Okay, see, Daniel was different.'

Dance noted the use of the first name. Pell had gotten Waters to believe they were buddies and exploited the faux friendship. 'How do you mean?'

'He's got this . . . I don't know, power or something over people. The Aryans, the OGs, the Lats . . . He goes where he wants to and nobody touches him. Never seen anybody like him inside before. People do things for him, whatever he wants. People tell him things.'

'And so he gave you information. Is that it?'

'*Good* information. Stuff nobody couldn't've got otherwise. Like, there was a guard selling meth. A con overdosed on it. There's no way we could've found out who was the source. But Pell let me know.'

'Saved lives, I'll bet.'

'Oh, yes, ma'am. And, say somebody was going to move on somebody else? Gut 'em with a shank, whatever, Daniel'd tell me.'

Dance shrugged. 'So you cut him some slack. You let him into the office.'

'Yeah. The TV in the office had cable, and sometimes he wanted to watch games nobody else was interested in. That's all that happened. There was no danger or anything. The office's a maximum-security lock-down area. There's no way he could've gotten out. I went on rounds and he watched games.'

'How often?'

'Three, four times.'

'So he could've been online?'

'Maybe.'

'When most recently?'

'Yesterday.'

'Okay, Tony. Now tell me about the telephones.' Dance recalled seeing a stress reaction when he'd told her Pell had made no calls except to his aunt; Waters had touched his lips, a blocking gesture. If a subject confesses to one crime, it's often easier to get him to confess to another.

Waters said, 'The other thing about Pell, everybody'll tell you, he was into sex, way into sex. He wanted to make some phone-sex calls and I let him.'

But Dance immediately noticed deviation from the baseline and concluded that although he was confessing, it was to a small crime, which usually means that a bigger one is lurking.

'Did he now?' she asked bluntly, leaning close once again. 'And how did he pay for it? Credit card? Nine-hundred number?'

A pause. Waters hadn't thought out the lie; he'd forgotten you had to pay for phone sex. 'I don't mean like you'd call up one of those numbers in the backs of newspapers. I guess it sounded like that's what I meant. Daniel called some woman he knew. I think it was somebody who'd written him. He got a lot of mail.' A weak smile. 'Fans. Imagine that. A man like him.'

Dance leaned a bit closer. 'But when you listened there wasn't any sex, was there?'

'No, I –' He must've realized he hadn't said anything about listening in. But by then it was too late. 'No. They were just talking.'

'You heard both of them?'

'Yeah, I was on the third line.'

'When was it?'

'About a month ago, the first time. Then a couple more times. Yesterday. When he was in the office.'

'Are calls *there* logged?'

'No. Not local ones.'

'If it was long distance it would be.'

Eyes on the floor. Waters was miserable.

'What, Tony?'

'I got him a phone card. You call an eight-hundred number and punch in a code, then the number you want.'

Dance knew them. Untraceable.

'Really, you have to believe me. I wouldn't've done it, except the information he gave me . . . it was good. It saved –'

'What were they talking about?' she asked in a friendly voice. You're never rough with a confessing subject; they're your new best friend.

'Just stuff. You know. Money, I remember.'

'What about it?'

'Pell asked how much she'd put together and she said ninety-two hundred bucks. And he said, "That's all?"'

Pretty expensive phone sex, Dance reflected wryly.

'Then she asked about visiting hours and he said it wouldn't be a good idea.'

So he hadn't wanted her to visit. No record of them together.

'Any idea of where she was?'

'He mentioned Bakersfield. He said specifically, "To Bakersfield."'

Telling her to go to his aunt's place and pick up the hammer to plant in the well.

'And, okay, it's coming back to me now. She was telling him about cardinals.'

'Catholic?'

A laugh, though a desperate one. 'No, birds. Cardinals and humming-birds in the backyard. And then Mexican food. "Mexican is comfort food." That's what she said.'

'Did her voice have an ethnic or regional accent?'

'Not that I could tell.'

'Was it low or high, her voice?'

'Low, I guess. Kind of sexy.'

'Did she sound smart or stupid?'

'Jeez, I couldn't tell.' He sounded exhausted.

'Is there anything else that's helpful, Tony? Come on, we really need to get this guy.'

'Not that I can think of. I'm sorry.'

She looked him over and believed that, no, he didn't know anything more.

'Okay. I think that'll do it for the time being.'

He started out. At the door, he paused and looked back. 'Sorry I was kind of confused. It's been a tough day.'

'Not a good day at all,' she agreed. He remained motionless in the doorway, a dejected pet. When he didn't get the reassurance he sought, he shuffled away.

Dance called Carraneo, currently en route to the You Mail It store, and gave him the information she'd pried from the guard: that his partner didn't seem to have any accent and that she had a low voice. That might help the manager remember the woman more clearly.

She then called the warden of Capitola and told her what had happened. The woman was silent for a moment, then offered a soft 'Oh.'

Dance asked if the prison had a computer specialist. It did, and she'd have him search the computers in the administrative office for online activity and emails yesterday. It should be easy since the staff didn't work on Sunday and Pell presumably had been the only one online – if he had been.

'I'm sorry,' Dance said.

'Yeah. Thanks.'

The agent was referring not so much to Pell's escape but to yet another consequence of it. Dance didn't know the warden but supposed that to run a superprison, she was talented at her job and the work was important to her. It was a shame that her career in corrections, like that of Tony Waters, would soon be over.

# Chapter
## TWELVE

She'd done well, his little lovely.

Followed the instructions perfectly. Getting the hammer from his aunt's garage in Bakersfield (how had Kathryn Dance figured *that* one out?). Embossing the wallet with Robert Herron's initials. Then planting them in the well in Salinas. Making the fuse for the gas bomb (she'd said it was as easy as following a recipe for a cake). Planting the bag containing the fire suit and knife. Hiding clothes under the pine tree.

Pell, though, hadn't been sure of her ability to look people in the eye and lie to them. So he hadn't used her as getaway driver from the courthouse. In fact, he'd made sure that she wasn't anywhere near the place when he escaped. He didn't want her stopped at a roadblock giving everything away because she stammered and flushed with guilt.

Now, shoes off as she drove (he found that kinky), a happy smile on her face, Jennie Marston was chattering away in her sultry voice. Pell had wondered if she'd believe the story about his innocence in the deaths at the courthouse. But one thing that had astonished Daniel Pell in all his years of getting people to do what he wanted was how often they flung logic and self-preservation to the wind and believed what they wanted to – that is, what *he* wanted them to.

Still, that didn't mean Jennie would buy everything he told her, and in light of what he had planned for the next few days, he'd have to monitor her closely, see where she'd support him and where she'd balk.

They drove through a complicated route of surface streets, avoiding the highways with their potential roadblocks.

'I'm glad you're here,' she said, voice tentative as she rested a hand on his knee with ambivalent desperation. He knew what she was feeling: torn between pouring out her love for him and scaring him off. The gushing would win out. Always did with women like her. Oh, Daniel Pell knew all about the Jennie Marstons of the world, the women breathlessly seduced by bad boys. He'd learned about them years ago, being an habitual con. You're in a bar and you drop the news that you've done time, most women'll blink and never come back from their next restroom visit. But there're some who'll get wet when you whispered about the crime you'd done and the time you'd served. They'd smile in a certain way, lean close and want to hear more about your dark side.

That included murder – depending on how you couched it.

And Daniel Pell knew how to couch things.

Yes, Jennie was your classic bad-boy lover. You wouldn't guess it to look at her, the skinny caterer with straight blonde hair, a pretty face marred by a bumpy nose, dressing like a suburban mom at a Mary Chapin Carpenter concert.

Hardly the sort to write to lifers in places like Capitola.

*Dear Daniel Pell:*

*You don't know me but I saw a special about you, it was on A&E, and I don't think it told the whole truth. I have also bought all the books I could find on you and read them and you are a fascinating man. And even if you did what they say I'm sure there were extreme circumstances about it. I could see it in your eyes. You were looking at the camera but it was like you were looking right at me. I have a background that is similar to yours, I mean your childhood (or absense of childhood (!) and I can understand where you are coming from. I mean totally. If you would like to, you can write me.*

*Very sincerely,*
*Jennie Marston*

She wasn't the only one, of course. Daniel Pell got a lot of mail. Some praising him for killing a capitalist, some condemning him for killing a family, some offering advice, some seeking it. Plenty of romantic overtures too. Most of the ladies, and men, would tend to lose steam after a few weeks, as reason set in. But Jennie had persisted, her letters growing more and more passionate.

*My Dearest Daniel:*

*Today I was driving in the desert. Out near Palomar Observatory, where they have the big telescope. The sky was so big, it was dusk and there were stars just coming out. I couldn't stop thinking about you. About how you said no one understands you and blames you for bad things you didn't do, how hard that's got to be. They don't see into you, they don't see the truth. Not like I do. You would never say it because your modest but they don't see what a perfect human being you are.*

*I stopped the car, I couldn't help myself, I was touching myself all over, you know doing what (I'll bet you do, you dirty boy!) We made love there, you and me, watching the stars, I say 'we' because you were there with me in spirit. I'd do anything for you, Daniel . . .*

It was such letters – reflecting her total lack of self-control and extraordinary gullibility – that had made Pell decide on her for the escape.

He now asked, 'You were careful about everything, weren't you? Nobody can trace the T-bird?'

'No. I stole it from a restaurant. There was this guy I went out with a couple years ago. I mean, we didn't sleep together or anything.' She added this too fast, and he supposed they'd spent plenty of time humping like clueless little bunnies. Not that he cared. She continued, 'He worked there and when I'd hang out I saw that nobody paid any attention to the valet-parking key box. So Friday I took the bus over there and waited across the street. When the valets were busy I got the keys. I picked the Thunderbird because this couple had just went inside so they'd be there for a while. I was on the One-oh-one in, like, ten minutes.'

'You drive straight through?'

'No, I spent the night in San Luis Obispo – but I paid cash, like you said.'

'And you burned all the emails, right? Before you left?'

'Uh-huh.'

'Good. You have the maps?'

'Yep, I do.' She patted her purse.

He looked over her body. The small swell of her chest, the thin legs and butt. Her long blonde hair. Women let you know right up front the kind of license you have with them, and Pell knew he could touch her whenever and wherever he wanted. He put his hand on the nape of her neck. How thin, fragile. She made a sound that was actually purring.

The swelling within him continued to grow.

The purring too.

He waited as long as he could.

But the bubble won.

'Pull over there, baby.' He pointed toward a road under a grove of oak trees. It seemed to be a driveway to an abandoned farmhouse in the middle of an overgrown field.

She hit the brakes and turned down the road. Pell looked around. Not a soul he could see.

'Here?'

'This's good.'

His hand slid from her neck down the front of her pink blouse. It looked new. She'd bought it just for him, he understood.

Pell lifted her face and pressed his lips against hers softly, not opening his mouth. He kissed her lightly, then backed away, making her come to him. She grew more and more frantic, the more he teased.

'I want you in me,' she whispered, reaching into the back, where he heard the crinkle of a bag. A Trojan appeared in her hand.

'We don't have much time, baby. They're looking for us.'

She got the message.

However innocent they look, girls who love bad boys know what they're doing (and Jennie Marston didn't look all that innocent). She unbuttoned her blouse and leaned over to the passenger seat, rubbing the padded bra against his crotch. 'Lie back, sweetie. Close your eyes.'

'No.'

She hesitated.

'I want to watch you,' he whispered. Never give them more power than you have to.

More purring.

She unzipped his shorts and bent down.

Only a few minutes later he was finished. She was as talented as he'd expected – Jennie didn't have many resources, so she exploited the ones she had – and the event was fine, though when they got into the privacy of a motel room he'd up the ante considerably. But for now, this would do. And as for her, Pell knew his explosive, voluminous completion was satisfaction enough.

He turned his eyes to hers. 'You're wonderful, lovely. That was so special.'

She was so drunk on emotion that even the most trite porn-movie dialogue would have sounded to her like a declaration of love out of an old-time novel.

'Oh, Daniel.'

He sat back and adjusted his clothes.

Jennie buttoned the blouse. Pell looked at the pink cloth, the embroidery, the metal tips on the collar.

She noticed him. 'You like?'

'It's nice.' He glanced out the window and studied the fields around them. Not worried about police, more intent on her. Aware she was studying the blouse.

Hesitantly Jennie said, 'It's awfully pink. Maybe too much. I just saw it and thought I'd get it.'

'No, it's fine. It's interesting.'

As she fastened the buttons she glanced at the pearl dots, then the embroidery, the cuffs. She'd probably had to work a whole week to afford it.

'I'll change later if you want.'

'No, if you like it, that's fine,' he said, getting his tone just right, like a singer hitting a difficult note. He glanced at the garment once more, then he leaned forward and kissed her – the forehead, not the mouth, of course. He scanned the field again. 'We should get back on the road.'

'Sure.' She wanted him to tell her more about the blouse. What was wrong with it? Did he hate pink? Did an ex-girlfriend have a shirt like it? Did it make her boobs look small?

But, of course, he said nothing.

Jennie smiled when he touched her leg and she put the car in gear. She returned to the road, glancing down one last time at the blouse, which, Pell knew, she would never wear again. His goal had been for her to throw it out; he had a pretty good idea that she would.

And the irony was that the blouse looked really good on her, and he liked it quite a bit.

But offering his subtle disapproval and watching her reaction gave him a nice picture of exactly where she was. How controllable, how loyal.

A good teacher always knows the exact state of his student's progress.

Michael O'Neil sat in a chair in Dance's office, rocking back and forth on its rear legs, his shoes on her battered coffee table. It was his favorite way to sit. (Kinesically Dance put the habit down to nervous energy –

and a few other issues, which, because she was so close to him, she chose not to analyze in more depth.)

He, TJ Scanlon and Dance were gazing at her phone, from whose speaker a computer tech from Capitola prison was explaining, 'Pell *did* get online yesterday, but apparently he didn't send any emails – at least not then. I couldn't tell about earlier. Yesterday he only browsed the Web. Now he erased the sites he visited but he forgot about erasing search requests. I found what he was looking up.'

'Go ahead.'

'He did a Google search for "Alison" and "Nimue". He searched those together, as limiting terms.'

Dance asked for spellings.

'Then he did another. "Helter Skelter".'

O'Neil and Dance shared a troubled glance. The phrase was the title of a Beatles song, which Charles Manson was obsessed with. He had used the term to refer to an impending race war in America. It was also the title of the award-winning book about the cult leader by the man who'd prosecuted him.

'Then he went to Visual-Earth dot com. Like Google Earth. You can see satellite pictures of practically everywhere on the planet.'

Great, Dance thought. Though it turned out not to be. There was no way to narrow down what he'd looked for.

'It could've been highways in California, it could've been Paris or Key West or Moscow.'

'And what's "Nimue"?'

'No idea.'

'Does it mean anything in Capitola?'

'No.'

'Any employees there named Alison?'

The disembodied voice of the techie said, 'Nope. But, I was going to say, I might be able to find out what sites he logged on to. It depends on whether he just erased or shredded them. If they're shredded, forget it. But if they're just dumped I might be able to find them floating around in the free space somewhere on the hard drive.'

'Anything you can do would be appreciated,' Dance said.

'I'll get right on it.'

She thanked him and they disconnected.

'TJ, check out "Nimue".'

His fingers flew over the keyboard. The results came up and he scrolled through them. After a few minutes he said, 'Hundreds of thousands of hits. Looks like a lot of people use it as a screen name.'

O'Neil said, 'Somebody he knew online. Or a nickname. Or somebody's real last name.'

Staring at the screen, TJ continued, 'Trademarks too: cosmetics, electronic equipment – hm, sex products . . . Never seen one of *those* before.'

'TJ,' Dance snapped.

'Sorry.' He scrolled again. 'Interesting. Most references are to King Arthur.'

'As in *Camelot*?'

'I guess.' He continued to read. 'Nimue was the Lady of the Lake. This wizard, Merlin, fell in love with her – he was like a hundred or something and she was sixteen. Now *that*'ll guarantee you twenty minutes on *Dr. Phil*.' He read some more. 'Merlin taught her how to be a sorceress. Oh, and she gave King Arthur this magic sword.'

'Excalibur,' O'Neil said.

'What?' TJ asked.

'The sword. Excalibur. Haven't you heard any of this before?' the detective asked.

'Naw, I didn't take Boring Made-up Stuff in college.'

'I like the idea that it's somebody he was trying to find. Cross-check "Nimue" with "Pell, Alison, California, Carmel, Croyton." Anything else?'

O'Neil suggested, 'The women: Rebecca Sheffield, Samantha McCoy and Linda Whitfield.'

'Good.'

After several minutes of frantic typing the agent looked over at Dance. 'Sorry, boss. Zip.'

'Check the search terms out with VICAP, NCIC and the other main criminal databases.'

'Will do.'

Dance stared at the words she'd written. What did they mean? Why had he risked going online to check them out?

*Helter Skelter, Nimue, Alison* . . .

And what had he been looking at on Visual-Earth? A place he intended to flee to, a place he intended to burglarize?

She asked O'Neil, 'What about the crime scene forensics at the courthouse?'

The detective consulted his notes. 'No red flags. Almost everything was burned or melted. The gas was in plastic milk jugs inside a cheap roller suitcase. Sold in a dozen places – Wal-Mart, Target, stores like that. The fireproof bag and fire suit were made by Protection Equipment, Inc., New Jersey. Available all over the world but most are sold in Southern California.'

'Brushfires?'

'Movies. For stuntmen. A dozen outlets. Not much to follow up on, though. There're no serial numbers. They couldn't lift any prints off the bag or the suit. Now, the additives in the gas mean it was BP but we can't narrow it down to a particular station. The fuse was homemade. Rope soaked in slow-burning chemicals. None of them're traceable either.'

'TJ, what's the word on the aunt?'

'Zip so far. I'm expecting a breakthrough any moment.'

Her phone rang. It was another call from Capitola. The warden was with the prisoner who claimed he had some information about Daniel Pell. Did Dance want to talk to him now?

'Sure.' She hit the speakerphone button. 'This is Agent Dance. I'm here with Detective O'Neil.'

'Hey. I'm Eddie Chang.'

'Eddie,' the warden added, 'is doing a five-to-eight for bank robbery. He's in Capitola because he can be a bit . . . slippery.'

'How well did you know Daniel Pell?' Dance asked.

'Not really good. Nobody did. But I was somebody who, you know, wasn't no threat to him, so he kind of opened up to me.'

'And you've got some information on him?'

'Yes, ma'am.'

'Why're you helping us?' O'Neil asked.

'Up for parole in six months. I help you, it'll go good for me. Provided you catch him, of course. If you don't, I think I'll stay in the Big C here until you do, now that I'm rolling over on him.'

O'Neil asked, 'Did Pell talk about girlfriends or anyone on the outside? Particularly a woman?'

'He bragged about the women he'd had. He'd give us these great stories. It was like watching a porn film. Oh, man, we loved those stories.'

'You remember any names? Someone named Alison?'

'He never mentioned anybody.'

After what Tony Waters had told her, Dance suspected that Pell was making up the sex stories – using them as incentives to get the cons to do things for him. She asked, 'So, what do you want to tell us?'

'I have this idea where he might be headed.' Dance and O'Neil shared a glance. 'Outside of Acapulco. There's a town there, Santa Rosario, in the mountains.'

'Why there?'

'Okay, what it was, maybe a week ago we were sitting around bullshitting and there was a new con, Felipe Rivera, doing a back-to-back 'cause he got trigger happy during a GTA. We were talking and Pell finds out he was from Mexico. So Pell's asking him about this Santa Rosario. Rivera'd never heard of it, but Pell's pretty anxious to find out more, so he describes it, like trying to jog his memory. It's got a hot spring, and it's not near any big highways, and there's this steep mountain nearby . . . But Rivera couldn't remember anything. Then Pell shut up about it and changed the subject. So I was figuring that's what he might've had in mind.'

Dance asked, 'Before that, had he ever mentioned Mexico?'

'Maybe. Can't say as I recall.'

'Think back, Eddie. Say, six months, a year. Did Pell ever talk about someplace *else* he'd like to go?'

Another pause. 'No. Sorry. I mean, no place he thought was, man, I've gotta go there because it's kick-ass, or whatever.'

'How about somewhere he was just interested in? Or curious about?'

'Oh, hey, a couple times he mentioned that Mormon place.'

'Salt Lake City.'

'No. The state. Utah. What he liked was that you could have a lot of wives.'

*The Family* . . .

'He said in Utah the police don't give you any shit because it's the Mormons who run the state and they don't like the FBI or the state police snooping around. You can do whatever you want in Utah.'

'When did he tell you that?'

'I don't know. A while ago. Last year. Then maybe a month ago.'

Dance glanced at O'Neil and he nodded.

'Let me call you back. Can you wait there for a minute?'

A laugh from Chang. 'And where would I go?'

She disconnected, then called Linda Whitfield and, after her, Rebecca Sheffield. Neither woman knew of any interest Pell had ever had in either Mexico or Utah. As for the attraction of Mormon polygamy, Linda said he'd never mentioned it. Rebecca laughed. 'Pell liked *sleeping* with several women. That's different from being *married* to several women. Real different.'

Dance and O'Neil walked upstairs to Charles Overby's office and briefed him about the possible destinations, as well as the three references they'd found in the Google search, and the crime-scene results.

'Acapulco?'

'No. It was a plant, I'm sure. He asked about it just last week and in front of other cons. It's too obvious. Utah's more likely. But I've got to find out more before I can give an opinion about that one.'

'Well, front burner it, Kathryn,' Overby said. 'I just got a call from *The New York Times*.' His phone rang.

'It's Sacramento on two, Charles,' his assistant said. He sighed and grabbed the handset.

Dance and O'Neil left and just as they got into the hallway, his phone rang too.

As they walked, she glanced at him several times. Michael O'Neil's affect displays – signals of emotion – were virtually invisible most of the time, but they were obvious to her. She deduced the call was about Juan Millar. She could see clearly how upset he was about his fellow officer's injury. She couldn't recall the last time he'd been so troubled.

O'Neil hung up and gave her a summary of the detective's condition: It was the same as earlier but he'd been awake once or twice.

'Go see him,' Dance said.

'You sure?'

'I'll follow up here.'

Dance returned to her office, pausing to pour up more coffee from the pot near Maryellen Kresbach, who said nothing more about phone messages, though Dance sensed she wanted to.

*Brian called . . .*

This time she helped herself to the chocolate chip cookie she'd been fantasizing about. Sitting at her desk, she called Chang and the warden back.

'Eddie, I want to keep going. I want you to tell me more about Pell. Anything about him you can remember. Things he said, things he did. What made him laugh, what made him mad.'

A pause. 'I don't know what to tell you, really.' He sounded confused.

'Hey, how's this for an idea? Pretend somebody was going to set me up on a date with Pell. What would you tell me about him before we went out?'

'A date with Daniel Pell? Whoa, that's one fucking scary thought.'

'Do your best, Cupid.'

# Chapter
# THIRTEEN

Back in her office, Dance heard the frog croak again and she picked up her cell phone.

The caller was Rey Carraneo, reporting that the manager of the You Mail It franchise on San Benito Way in Salinas *did* remember a woman in the store about a week ago. 'Only, she didn't mail anything, Agent Dance. She just asked about when the different delivery services stopped there. Worldwide Express was the most regular, he told her. Like clockwork. He wouldn't've thought anything about it, except that he saw her outside a few days later, sitting on a park bench across the street. I'd guess she was checking the times herself.'

Unfortunately, Carraneo couldn't do an EFIS image because she'd worn the baseball cap and dark sunglasses then too. Nor had the manager seen her car.

They disconnected, and she wondered again when the Worldwide Express driver's body would be found.

More violence, more death, another family altered.

*The ripples of consequence can spread almost forever.*

It was just as that recollection of Morton Nagle's words was passing through her mind that Michael O'Neil called. Coincidentally, his message was about the fate of that very driver.

Dance was in the front seat of her Taurus.

'From the CD player a song by the original Fairfield Four gospel singers did its best to distract her from the carnage of the morning.

*'I'm standing in the safety zone . . .'*

Music was Kathryn Dance's salvation. Policework for her wasn't test tubes and computer screens. It was people. Her job required her to blend her mind and heart and emotions with theirs and stay close to them so that she could discern the truths they knew but hesitated to share. The interrogations were usually difficult and sometimes wrenching and the memories of what the subjects had said and done, often horrendous crimes, never left her completely.

If Alan Stivell's Celtic harp melodies, or Natty Bo and Beny Billy's irrepressible ska-Cubano tunes or Lightnin' Hopkins's raw, zinging chords were churning in her ears and thoughts, she tended not to hear the shocking replays of her interviews with rapists and murderers and terrorists.

Dance now lost herself in the scratchy tones of the music from a half-century ago.

'Roll, Jordan, roll . . .'

Five minutes later she pulled into an office park on the north side of Monterey, just off Munras Avenue, and climbed out. She walked into the ground-floor garage, where the Worldwide Express driver's red Honda Civic sat, trunk open, blood smeared on the sheet metal. O'Neil and a town cop were standing beside it.

Someone else was with them.

Billy Gilmore, the driver Dance had been sure was Pell's next victim. To her shock, he'd been found very much alive.

The heavyset man had some bruises and a large bandage on his forehead – covering the cut that was apparently the source of the blood – but, it turned out, the injuries weren't from being beaten by Pell; he'd cut himself shifting around in the trunk to get comfortable. 'I wasn't trying to get out. I was afraid to. But somebody heard me, I guess, and called the police. I was supposed to stay in there for three hours, Pell told me. If I didn't he said he'd kill my wife and kids.'

'They're okay,' O'Neil explained to Dance. 'We've got them in protection.' He related Billy's story about Pell's hijacking the truck, then the car. The driver had confirmed that Pell was armed.

'What was he wearing?'

'Shorts, a dark windbreaker, baseball cap, I think. I don't know. I was really freaked-out.'

O'Neil had called in the new description to the roadblocks and search parties.

Pell had given Billy no idea where he was ultimately going, but was very clear about directions to this garage. 'He knew just where it was and that it'd be deserted.'

The woman accomplice had checked this out too, of course. She'd met him here and they'd headed for Utah, presumably.

'Do you remember anything else?' she asked.

Just after he'd slammed the trunk lid, Billy said, he'd heard the man's voice again.

'Somebody was with him?'

'No, it was just him. I think he was making a call. He had my phone.'

'Your phone?' Dance asked, surprised. A glance at O'Neil, who immediately called the Sheriff's Office technical-support people and had the techs get in touch with the driver's cell phone service provider to set up a trace.

Dance asked if Billy had heard anything that Pell said. 'No. It was just mumbling to me.'

O'Neil's mobile rang and he listened for a few minutes and said to Dance, 'Nope. It's either destroyed or the battery's out. They can't find a signal.'

Dance looked around the garage. 'He's dumped it somewhere. Let's hope nearby. We should have somebody check the trashcans – and the drains in the street.'

'Bushes too,' O'Neil said and sent two of his deputies off on the task.

TJ joined them. 'He *did* come this way. Call me crazy, boss, but this isn't on the route I *myself* would take to Utah.'

Whether or not Pell was headed for Utah, his coming to downtown Monterey was surprising. It was a small town and he'd easily be spotted, and there were far fewer escape routes than if he'd gone east, north or south. A risky place to meet his accomplice, but a brilliant move. This was the last place they'd expect him.

One other question nagged.

'Billy, I need to ask you something. Why are you still alive?'

'I . . . Well, I begged him not to hurt me. Practically got on my hands and knees. It was embarrassing.'

It was also a lie. Dance didn't even need a baseline to see the stress flood through the man's body. He looked away and his face flushed. 'I need to know the truth. It could be important,' she said.

'Really. I was crying like a baby. I think he felt sorry for me.'

'Daniel Pell has never felt sorry for a human being in his life,' O'Neil said.

'Go on,' Dance said softly.

'Well, okay . . .' He swallowed and his face turned bright red. 'We made a deal. He was going to kill me. I'm sure he was. I said if he'd let me live . . .' Tears filled his eyes. It was hard to watch the misery but Dance needed to understand Pell, and why this man was still alive, when two others had been killed under similar circumstances.

'Go on,' she said softly.

'I said if he let me live I'd do anything for him. I meant give him money or something. But he said he wanted me to . . . well, he saw my wife's picture and he liked how she looked. So he . . . he asked me to tell him about the things we did together. You know, intimate things.' He stared at the concrete floor of the garage. 'Like, he wanted all the details. I mean, everything.'

'What else?' Dance prompted.

'Naw, that was it. It was so embarrassing.'

'Billy, please tell me.'

His eyes filled with tears. His jaw was trembling.

'What?'

A deep breath. 'He got my home phone number. And he said he'd call me at night sometime. Maybe next month, maybe six months. I'd never know. And when he called, my wife and me were supposed to go in the bedroom. And, you know . . .' The words caught in his throat. 'I was supposed to leave the phone off the hook so he could listen to us. Pam had to say some things he told me.'

Dance glanced at O'Neil, who exhaled softly. 'We'll catch him before anything like that happens.'

The man wiped his face. 'I almost told him, "No, you fucker. Go ahead and kill me." But I couldn't.'

'Go see your family. And get out of town for a while.'

'I almost told him that. I really did.'

A medical tech led him back to the ambulance.

O'Neil whispered, 'What the hell're we up against here?'

Echoing Dance's exact thought.

'Detective, I've got a phone,' an MCSO deputy called as he joined them. 'Was up the street in a trashcan. The battery was in another can, across the street.'

'Good catch,' O'Neil told the man.

Dance took a pair of latex gloves from TJ, pulled them on, then took the phone and replaced the battery. She turned it on and scrolled through recent calls. None had been received but five had been made since the escape. She called them out to O'Neil, who was on the phone with his tech people again. They did a reverse lookup.

The first wasn't a working number; it wasn't even a real exchange prefix – which meant that the call to the accomplice about Billy's family had never occurred. It was simply to frighten him into cooperating.

The second and third calls were to another number, which turned out to be a prepaid mobile phone. It was presently off, probably destroyed; there was no signal to triangulate on.

The last two numbers were more helpful. The first was a 555-1212 call, directory assistance. The area code was Utah. The last number – the one Pell had was presumably gotten from the operator – was an RV campsite outside Salt Lake City.

'Bingo,' TJ said.

Dance called the number and identified herself. She asked if they'd received a call forty minutes ago. The clerk said that she had, a man from Missouri, driving west, who was curious how much it cost to park a small Winnebago there by the week.

'Any other calls around that time?'

'My mother and two of the guests here, complaining about something or other. That was all.'

'Did the man say when he'd be arriving?'

'No.'

Dance thanked the woman and told her to call them immediately if he contacted them again. She explained to O'Neil and TJ what the RV camp manager had said and then phoned the Utah State Police – she was friends with a captain in Salt Lake City – and told him the situation. The USP would immediately send a surveillance team to the campsite.

Dance's eyes slipped to the miserable driver, staring at the ground again. She felt sorry for him; the man would live for the rest of his life with the horror he'd experienced today – perhaps less the kidnapping itself than the degradation of Pell's deal.

She thought again of Morton Nagle; Billy had escaped with his life, but was yet another victim of Daniel Pell.

'Should I tell Overby about Utah?' TJ asked. 'He'll want to get word out.'

She was interrupted, though, by a phone call. 'Hold on,' she told the young agent. She answered. It was the computer specialist from Capitola prison. Excited, the young man said that he'd managed to find one site that Pell had visited. It had to do with the Helter Skelter search.

'It was pretty smart,' the man said. 'I don't think he had any interest in the term itself. He used it to find a bulletin board where people post messages about crime and murder. It's called "Manslaughter". There're different categories, depending on the type of crime. One's "The Bundy Effect", about serial killers. Ted Bundy, you know? "Helter Skelter" is devoted to cult murders. I found a message that had been posted on Saturday, and I think it was meant for him.'

Dance said, 'And he didn't type in the URL to Manslaughter dot com directly, in case we checked the computer and we'd find the website.'

'Right. He used the search engine instead.'

'Clever. Can you find out who posted it?'

'It was anonymous. No way to trace it.'

'And what did it say?'

He read her the short message, only a few lines long. There was no doubt it was intended for Pell; it gave the last-minute details of the escape. The poster of the message added something else at the end, but, as Dance listened, she shook her head. It made no sense.

'I'm sorry, could you repeat that?'

He did.

'Okay,' Dance said. 'Appreciate it. Forward me a copy of that.' She gave her email address.

'Anything else I can do, let me know.'

Dance disconnected and stood silently for a moment, trying to fathom the message. O'Neil noticed her troubled face but didn't disturb her with questions.

She debated and then came to a decision. She called Charles Overby and told him about the camper park in Utah. Her boss was delighted at the news; he now had something concrete for the media.

Then, thinking about the conversation with Eddie Chang about her imaginary date with Pell, she called Rey Carraneo back and sent him on another assignment. As the young agent digested her request he said uncertainly, 'Well, sure, Agent Dance. I guess.'

She didn't blame him; the task was unorthodox, to say the least. Still, she said, 'Pull out all the stops.'

'Uhm.'

She deduced he hadn't heard the expression.

'Move fast.'

# Chapter
# FOURTEEN

'We're getting sand dabs.'

'Okay,' Jennie agreed. 'What's that?'

'These little fish. Like anchovies, but they're not salty. We'll get sandwiches. I'm having two. You want two?'

'Just one, honey.'

'Put vinegar on them. They have that at the tables.'

Jennie and Pell were in Moss Landing, north of Monterey. On the land side the massive Duke Power plant's twin stacks soared into the air. Across the highway was a small spit of land, an island really, accessible only by bridge. On this strip of sandy soil were marine service companies, docks and the rambling, massive structure where Pell and Jennie now sat: Jack's Seafood. It had been in business for three-quarters of a century. John Steinbeck, Joseph Campbell and Henry Miller – as well as Monterey's most famous madam, Flora Woods – would sit around the stained, scarred tables, arguing, laughing and drinking till the place closed, and sometimes until much later.

Now Jack's was a commercial fishery, seafood market and cavernous restaurant, all rolled into one. The atmosphere was much less bohemian and volatile than in the '40s and '50s, but in compensation the place had been featured on the Food Channel.

Pell remembered it from the days when they'd lived not far away, in Seaside. The Family didn't go out to eat much, but he'd send Jimmy or Linda to buy sand dab sandwiches, fries and coleslaw. He just loved the food and he was real happy the restaurant hadn't closed up.

He had some business to take care of in the area, but there'd be a little delay before he could proceed with that, some preparations to make, information to find. Besides, he was starving and figured he could take a chance being out in public. The police wouldn't be looking for a happy tourist couple – especially here, since they believed he was halfway to Utah by now, according to the news story he'd heard on the radio, some pompous ass named Charles Overby making the announcement.

Jack's had an outdoor patio with a view of the fishing boats and the bay, but Pell wanted to stay inside and keep an eye on the door. Carefully avoiding the urge to adjust the uncomfortable automatic pistol in his back waistband, Pell sat down at the table, Jennie beside him. She pressed her knee against his.

Pell now sipped his iced tea. He glanced at her and saw her watching a revolving carousel with tall cakes in it.

'You want dessert after the sand dabs?'

'No, honey. They don't look very good.'

'They don't?' They didn't to *him*; Pell didn't have a sweet tooth. But they were some pretty damn big hunks of cake. Inside, in Capitola, you could bargain a piece for a whole carton of cigarettes.

'They're just sugar and white flour and flavorings. Corn syrup and cheap chocolate. They look good and they're sweet but they don't taste like anything.'

'For your catering jobs, you wouldn't make those?'

'No, no, I'd never do that.' Her voice was lively as she nodded toward the merry-go-round of pastry. 'People eat a lot of that stuff because it's not satisfying, and they want more. I make a chocolate cake without any flour at all. It's chocolate, sugar, ground nuts, vanilla and egg yolks. Then I pour a little raspberry glaze on the top. You just need a few bites of that and you're happy.'

'Sounds pretty good.' He thought it was repulsive. But she was telling him about herself, and you always encouraged people to do that. Get 'em drunk, let 'em ramble. Knowledge was a better weapon than a knife. 'Is that what you do mostly? Work for bakeries?'

'Well, I like baking best, 'cause I have more control. I make everything myself. On the other food lines you have people prepping part of the dishes.'

Control, he reflected. Interesting. He filed that fact away.

'Then sometimes I serve. You get tips when you serve.'

'I'll bet you get good ones.'

'I can, yeah. Depends.'

'And you like it? . . . What're you laughing at?'

'Just . . . I don't know the last time anybody – I mean a boyfriend – asked me if I like my job . . . Anyway, sure, serving's fun. And sometimes I pretend I'm not just serving. I pretend it's *my* party, with my friends and family.'

Outside the window a hungry seagull hovered over a piling, then landed clumsily, looking for scraps. Pell had forgotten how big they were.

Jennie continued, 'It's like when I bake a cake, say, a wedding cake. Sometimes I just think it's the little happinesses that're all we can count on. You bake the best cake you can and people enjoy it. Oh, not forever. But what on earth makes you happy forever?'

Good point. 'I'll never eat anybody's cake but yours.'

She gave a laugh. 'Oh, sure you will, sweetie. But I'm happy you said that. Thank you.'

These few words had made her sound mature. Which meant, in control. Pell felt defensive. He didn't like it. He changed the subject. 'Well, I hope you like your sand dabs. I love them. You want another iced tea?'

'No, I'm fine for now. Just sit close to me. That's what I want.'

'Let's look over the maps.'

She opened her bag and took them out. She unfolded one and Pell examined it, noticing how the layout of the Peninsula had changed in the past eight years. Then he paused, aware of a curious feeling within him. He couldn't quite figure out the sensation. Except that it was real nice.

Then he realized: He was free.

His confinement, eight years of being under someone else's control, was over, and he could now start his life over again. After finishing up his missions here, he'd leave for good and start another Family. Pell glanced around him, at the other patrons in the restaurant, noting several of them in particular: the teenage girl, two tables away, her silent parents hunched over their food, as if actually having a conversation would be torture. The girl, a bit plump, could be easily seduced away from home when she was alone in an arcade or Starbucks. It would take him two days, tops, to convince her it was safe to get into the van with him.

And, at the counter, the young man about twenty (he'd been denied a beer when he'd 'forgotten' his ID). He was inked – silly tattoos, which he probably regretted – and wore shabby clothes, which, along with his meal of soup, suggested money problems. His eyes zipped around the restaurant, settling on every female older than 16 or so. Pell knew exactly what it would take to sign the boy up in a matter of hours.

Pell noted too the young mother, single, if the naked ring finger told the truth. She sat slouching in a funk – man problems, of course. She was hardly aware of her baby in a stroller by her side. She never once looked down at the child, and good luck if it started crying; she'd lose patience fast. There was a story behind her defeated posture and resentful eyes, though Pell didn't care what it might be. The only message of interest to him was that her connection to the child was fragile. Pell knew that if he could lure the woman to join them, it wouldn't take much work to separate mother and child, and Pell would become an instant father.

He thought of the story his aunt Barbara had read him when he'd stayed with her in Bakersfield: the Pied Piper of Hamelin, the man who spirited away the children of a medieval German town, dancing as they followed, when the citizens refused to pay him for eliminating a rat infestation. The story had made a huge impression on Pell and stayed with him. As an adult he read more about the incident. The real facts were different from the Brothers Grimm and popular versions. There were probably no rats involved, no unpaid bills; a number of children simply disappeared from Hamelin and were never found again. The disappearance – and the parents' reportedly apathetic response – remained a mystery.

One explanation was that the children, infected with plague or a disease that induced dancelike spasms, were led out of town to die because the adults feared contagion. Another was that the Pied Piper organized a religious pilgrimage for children, who died on the road in some natural disaster or when they were caught in a military conflict.

There was another theory, though, which Pell preferred. That the children left their parents willingly and followed the Pied Piper to Eastern Europe, then being colonized, where they created settlements of their own, with him as their absolute leader. Pell loved the idea that someone had the talent to lure away dozens – some said more than 100 – youngsters from their families and become their substitute parent. What sorts of skills had the Piper been born with, or perfected?

He was lulled from his daydreams by the waitress, who brought their food. His eyes strayed to her breasts, then down to the food.

'Looks scrumptious, sweetie,' Jennie said, staring at her plate.

Pell handed her a bottle. 'Here's the malt vinegar. You put that on them. Just sprinkle it on.'

'Okay.'

He took one more look around the restaurant: the sullen girl, the edgy boy, the distant mother . . . He wouldn't pursue any of them now, of course. He was simply ecstatic to see that so many opportunities beckoned. After life was settled, in a month or so, he'd begin hunting again – the arcades, the Starbucks, the parks, the schoolyards and campuses, McDonald's.

*The Pied Piper of California . . .*

Daniel Pell's attention turned to his lunch and he began to eat.

The cars sped north on Highway 1.

Michael O'Neil was behind the wheel of his unmarked MCSO Ford, Dance beside him. TJ was in a CBI pool Taurus right behind them, and two Monterey Police cruisers were tailing them. The CHP was sending several cars to the party too, and the nearest town, Watsonville, was sending a squad car south.

O'Neil was doing close to eighty. They could've gone faster but traffic was heavy. Portions of the road were only two lanes. And they used only lights, no sirens.

They were presently en route to where they believed Daniel Pell and his blonde accomplice were, against all odds, eating a leisurely lunch.

Kathryn Dance had her doubts about Pell's destination of Utah. Her intuition told her that, like Mexico, Utah too was probably a false lead, especially after learning that Rebecca and Linda had never heard Pell talk about the state, and after the mobile phone had been found conveniently discarded near the Worldwide Express driver's car. And, most important, he'd left the driver alive to report to the police about the phone and that he'd heard Pell making a call. The sexual game he'd played with Billy was one excuse for keeping him alive, but it struck Dance that, however kinky, no escapee would waste time on a porn encounter like that.

But then she'd heard from the computer tech at Capitola, who'd read to her the message that the accomplice had posted on the 'Manslaughter' bulletin board in the 'Helter Skelter' category.

**Package will be there about 9:20. WWE delivery truck at San Benito at 9:50. Orange ribbon on pine tree. Will meet in front of grocery store we mentioned.**

This was the first part of the message, a final confirmation of the escape plan. What had been so surprising to Dance, though, was the final sentence.

**Room all set and checking on those locations around Monterey you wanted.**
**- Your lovely.**

Which suggested, to everyone's astonishment, that Pell might be staying nearby.

Dance and O'Neil could deduce no reason for this. It was madness. But if he *was* staying, Dance decided to make him feel confident enough to show himself. And so she'd done what she never would have otherwise. She'd used Charles Overby. She knew that once she told him about Utah, he'd run to the press immediately and announce that the search was now focused on the routes east. This would, she hoped, give Pell a false sense of security and make him more likely to appear in public.

But where might that be?

She hoped the answer to that question might be found in her conversation with Eddie Chang, getting a sense of what Daniel Pell had hinted appealed to him, his interests and urges. Sex figured prominently, Chang told her, which meant he might head for massage parlors, brothels or escort agencies, but there were few on the Peninsula. Besides, he had his female partner, who presumably would be satisfying him in that department.

'What else?' she'd asked Chang.

'Oh, I remember something. Food.'

Daniel Pell, it seemed, had a particular love of seafood, especially a tiny fish known as the sand dab. He had mentioned on several occasions that there were only four or five restaurants in the Central Coast area that knew how to cook them right. And he was opinionated about how they should be prepared. Dance got the names of the restaurants Chang could remember. Three had closed in the years since Pell had gone into prison, but one at Fisherman's Wharf in Monterey and one in Moss Landing were still open.

That was the unorthodox assignment Dance had given Rey Carraneo: calling those two restaurants – and any others up and down the Central Coast with similar menus – and telling them about the escaped prisoner, who might be in the company of a slight woman with blonde hair.

It was a long shot, and Dance didn't have much hope that the idea would pay off. But Carraneo had just heard back from the manager of Jack's, the landmark restaurant at Moss Landing. A couple was in there at the moment, and he thought they were acting suspicious – sitting inside where they could see the front door, which the boyfriend kept looking at, when most patrons were outside. The man was clean-shaven and wearing sunglasses and a cap so they couldn't really tell if he was Pell. The woman appeared to be blonde, though she too had a cap and shades on. But the ages of the couple were right.

Dance had called the manager of the restaurant directly and asked if someone there could find out which car the couple had arrived in. The manager didn't have any idea. But the lot wasn't crowded and one of the busboys had gone outside and, in Spanish, given Dance the tag numbers of all the cars parked in the small lot.

A fast DMV check revealed that one, a turquoise Thunderbird, had been stolen just last Friday – though, curiously, not in the area but in Los Angeles.

Maybe it was a false alarm. But Dance decided to move on the place; if nothing else, they'd collar a car thief. She'd alerted O'Neil, and then told the manager, 'We'll be there as soon as we can. Don't do anything. Just ignore him and act normally.'

'Act normal,' the man said with a shaking voice. 'Yeah, right.'

Kathryn Dance was now anticipating her next interrogation session with Pell, when he was back in custody. The number one question she was eager to learn the answer to: Why was he staying in the area?

Cruising through Sand City, a commercial strip along Highway 1, the traffic grew lighter, and O'Neil punched the accelerator hard. They'd be at the restaurant in ten minutes.

# Chapter
# FIFTEEN

'Are those the best thing you ever tasted?'

'Oh, honey, they're good. Sandy dabs.'

'Sand dabs,' Pell corrected. He was thinking of having a third sandwich.

'So, that was my ex,' she continued. 'I never see him or hear from him. Thank God.'

She'd just given him the details of the husband – an accountant and businessman and a wimpy little guy, believe it or not – who'd put her in the hospital twice with internal injuries, once with a broken arm. He'd screamed at her when she forgot to iron the sheets, screamed at her when she didn't get pregnant after only one month of trying, screamed at her when the Lakers lost. He'd told her that her tits were like a boy's, which was why he couldn't get it up. He'd told her in front of his friends that she'd 'look okay' if she got her nose fixed.

A petty man, Pell thought, controlled by everything except himself.

Then he heard the further installments of the soap opera: the boyfriends after the divorce. They seemed like him, bad boys. But Pell Lite, he thought. One was a petty thief who lived in Laguna, between L.A. and San Diego. He worked low-stakes scams. One sold drugs. One was a biker. One was just a shit.

Pell had been through his share of therapy. Most of it was pointless but sometimes a shrink came up with some good insights, which Pell filed away (not for his own mental health, of course, but because they were such helpful weapons to use against people).

So why did Jennie go for bad boys? Obvious to Pell. They were like her mother; subconsciously she kept flinging herself at them in hopes they'd change their ways and love, not ignore or use, her.

This was helpful for Pell to know but he could have told her: By the way, lovely, don't bother. We don't change. We never, ever change. Write that down and keep it close to your heart.

Of course, though, he kept these wise words to himself.

She stopped eating. 'Honey?'

'Uhm?'

'Can I ask you a question?'

'Sure, lovely.'

'You never said anything about those, you know, girls you were living with. When they arrested you. The Family.'

'Guess I didn't.'

'Did you stay in touch with them or anything? What were their names?'

He recited, 'Samantha, Rebecca and Linda. Jimmy too – the one who tried to kill me.'

Her eyes flicked toward him. 'Would you rather I didn't ask about them?'

'No, it's okay. You can ask me anything.'

Never tell someone not to talk about a subject. Keep a smile on your face and suck out every bit of information you can. Even if it hurts.

'Did they turn you in, the women?'

'Not exactly. They didn't even know we were going to the Croytons', Jimmy and me. But they didn't back me up after I got arrested. Linda, she burnt some evidence and lied to the police. But even her, she finally caved and helped them.' A sour laugh. 'And look at what I did for them. I gave them a home. Their own parents didn't give a shit about them. I gave them a family.'

'Are you upset? I don't want to upset you.'

'No.' Pell smiled. 'It's okay, lovely.'

'Do you think about them much?'

Ah, so that's it. Pell had worked hard all his life to spot the subtext beneath people's comments. He now realized that Jennie was jealous. It was a petty emotion, one that was easy to put down, but it was also a central force in the universe.

'Nope. I haven't heard from them for years. I wrote for a while. Linda was the only one who answered. But then she said her lawyer told her it'd look bad for her parole and she stopped. Felt bad about that, I have to say.'

'I'm sorry, honey.'

'For all I know, they're dead, or maybe married and happy. I was mad at first but then I understood that I'd made a mistake with them. I picked wrong. Not like you. You're good for me; they weren't.'

She lifted his hand to her mouth and kissed his knuckles one at a time.

Pell was studying the map again. He loved maps. When you were lost, you were helpless, out of control. He remembered how maps – well, the *lack* of a map – played a role in the history of this area of California, where they sat right now, in fact, Monterey Bay. In the Family, years ago, Linda had read aloud after dinner, all of them sitting in a circle. Pell had often picked works by local authors and books that were set here, and he remembered one, a history of Monterey. The bay had been discovered by the Spanish in the early 1600s. The *Bahia de Monte Rey*, named after a rich patron of the expedition, was considered a real plum – fertile land, a perfect port, strategic location – and the governor wanted to build a major colony there. Unfortunately after the explorers sailed away, they managed to lose the bay entirely.

A number of expeditions tried unsuccessfully to locate it again. With every passing year Monterey Bay took on mythical proportions. One of the largest contingents of explorers departed from San Diego and headed north on land, determined to find the bahia. Constantly at risk from the elements and the grizzly bears, the conquistadors covered every inch of the state up to San Francisco – and still managed to miss the huge bay altogether.

Simply because they had no accurate map.

When he'd managed to get online in Capitola, he'd been thrilled with a website called Visual-Earth, where you could click on a map and an actual satellite photo of the place you wanted to see came up on screen. He was astonished at this. There were some important things to look at, so he hadn't had a chance to browse. Pell looked forward to the time when his life was more settled and he could spend hours on the site.

Now, Jennie was pointing out some locations on the map open in front of them and Pell was taking in the information. But, as always, he was also listening to everything around him.

'He's a good puppy. Just needs more training.'

'It's a long drive, but if we take our time, it'll be a blast. You know?'

'I ordered ten minutes ago. Could you see what's taking so long?'

At this last comment, Pell glanced at the counter.

'Sorry,' explained a middle-aged man at the cash register to a customer.

'Just a little short staffed today.' The man, the owner or manager, was uneasy and looked everywhere except at Pell and Jennie.

*Smart people can figure out why you changed, then use it against you.*

When Pell had ordered their food, there were three or four waitresses shuttling back and forth between the kitchen and the tables. Now this man was the only one working. He'd sent all his employees into hiding.

Pell leapt up, knocking over the table. Jennie dropped her fork and jumped to her feet.

The manager stared at them in alarm.

'You son of a bitch,' Pell muttered and pulled the pistol from his waistband.

Jennie screamed.

'No, no . . . I –' The manager debated for a second and fled into the kitchen, abandoning his customers, who screamed and spilled onto the floor for cover.

'What is it, honey?' Jennie's voice was panicked.

'Let's go. The car.' He grabbed the map and they fled.

Outside, in the distance, south, he could see tiny flashing lights.

Jennie froze, panicked, whispering, 'Angel songs, angel songs . . .'

'Come on!'

They leapt in. He slammed the car into reverse, then shifted gears and gunned the engine, heading for Highway 1, over the narrow bridge. Jennie nearly slipped out of her seat as they hit the uneven pavement on the other side of the structure. On the highway Pell turned north, got about a hundred yards then skidded to a stop. Coming the other way was another police car.

Pell glanced to his right and floored the accelerator, heading directly for the front gate of the power plant, a massive, ugly structure, something that belonged not here on this picture-postcard seashore but in the refineries of Gary, Indiana.

Dance and O'Neil were no more than five minutes from Moss Landing.

Her fingers tapped the grip of the Glock, resting high on her right hip. She'd never fired her gun in the line of duty and wasn't much of a shot – weaponry didn't come naturally to her. Also, with children in the house she was uneasy carrying the weapon (at home she kept it in a solid lockbox beside her bed, and only she knew the combination).

Michael O'Neil, on the other hand, was a fine marksman, as was TJ. She was glad she was with them.

But would it come to a fight? she wondered. Dance couldn't say, of course. But she knew she'd do whatever was necessary to stop the killer.

The Ford now squealed around the corner and then up a hill.

As they crested it O'Neil muttered. 'Oh, hell . . .'

He jammed the brake pedal. 'Hold on!'

Dance gasped and grabbed the dashboard as they went into a fierce skid. The car came to a stop halfway on the shoulder, only five feet from a semi stopped in the middle of the road. The highway was completely blocked all the way to Moss Landing. The opposite lanes were moving, but slowly. Several miles ahead Dance could see flashing lights and realized officers were turning back the traffic.

A roadblock?

O'Neil called Monterey County central dispatch on his Motorola. 'It's O'Neil.'

'Go ahead, sir. Over.'

'We're on One, northbound, just short of Moss Landing. Traffic's stopped. What's the story?'

'Right. Be advised. There's . . . they're evacuating Duke Power. Fire or something. It's pretty bad. They've got multiple injuries. Two fatalities.'

Oh, no, Dance thought, exhaling a sigh. Not more deaths.

'Fire?' O'Neil asked.

'Just what Pell did at the courthouse.' Dance squinted. She could see a column of black smoke. Emergency planners took seriously any risk of a conflagration around here. Several years ago a huge fire had raged through an abandoned oil tank at the power facility. The plant was now gas operated – not oil – and the odds of a serious fire were much less. Still, security would have frozen Highway 1 in both directions and started to evacuate anyone nearby.

O'Neil snapped, 'Tell CHP or Monterey Fire or whoever's running the scene to clear a path. We've got to get through. We're in pursuit of that escapee. Over.'

'Roger, Detective . . . Hold on . . .' Silence for a minute. Then: 'Be advised. Just heard from Watsonville Fire. I don't know . . . Okay, the plant's *not* burning. The fire's just a car in front of the main gate. I don't know who called in the eleven-forty-one. No injuries that anybody can tell. That was a false report . . . And we've got some calls from Jack's. The suspect pulled a gun and fled.'

'Hell, he made us,' O'Neil muttered.

Dance took the microphone. 'Roger. Are *any* police on the scene?'

'Stand by . . . Affirmative. One Watsonville officer. The rest are fire and rescue.'

'*One* officer,' Dance said, scowling, shaking her head.

'Tell him that Daniel Pell's there somewhere. And he *will* target innocents and officers.'

'Roger. I'll relay that.'

Dance wondered how the sole officer would fare; Moss Landing's worst crimes were DUIs and auto and boat thefts.

'You get all that, TJ?'

'Fuck,' was the reply from the speaker. TJ didn't bother much with radio codes.

O'Neil slammed the microphone into the cradle in frustration.

Their plea to move the traffic along wasn't having any effect.

Dance told him, 'Let's try to get up there anyway. I don't care if we need bodywork.'

O'Neil nodded. He hit the siren and started along the shoulder, which was sandy in parts, rocky in others, and in several places barely passable.

But slowly the motorcade made its way forward.

# Chapter
# SIXTEEN

When they arrived at Moss Landing, Pell and his girlfriend were nowhere to be seen.

Dance and O'Neil parked. A moment later TJ too pulled up, beside the burned Thunderbird, which was still smoldering.

'Pell's car,' she pointed out. 'The one stolen from L.A. on Friday.' She told TJ to find the manager of Jack's.

The Watsonville cop, O'Neil and other officers spread out to search for witnesses. Many of them had left, probably scared off by the flames from the T-bird and the piercing siren from the power plant – maybe even thinking it was a nuclear reactor that was melting down.

Dance interviewed several people near the power plant. They reported that a wiry man and a blonde, driving the Thunderbird – it had been turquoise before the fire – had sped over the bridge from Jack's Seafood, then stopped abruptly in front of the power plant. They'd gotten out and a moment later the car had erupted in flames.

The couple had run across the road to the shore side, one person reported, but nobody saw what became of them after that. Apparently Pell had called 911 himself to report that the plant was burning and there were injuries and two deaths.

Dance looked around her. They'd need another car; you couldn't escape from here on foot. But then her eyes focused on the bay. With the traffic jam, it would make more sense to steal a boat. She corralled several local officers, trotted across the highway, and they spent fifteen frantic minutes talking to the people on the shoreline, to find out if Pell had taken a vessel. Nobody reported seeing the couple, nor were any boats missing.

A waste of time.

Returning to the highway, Dance noticed a store across from the power plant, a shack selling souvenirs and candy. There was a **CLOSED** sign on the door but inside Dance believed she could see a woman's face, looking out.

Was Pell inside with her?

Dance gestured to a deputy, told him of her concern, and together they stepped to the door. She rapped on it. No response.

Another knock, and slowly the door opened. A round woman with short curly hair glanced in alarm at their hands, resting on their guns, and asked breathlessly, 'Yes?'

Eyes on the dim interior behind her, Dance asked, 'Could you please step outside?'

'Uhm, sure.'

'Is anyone else in there?'

'No. What –?'

The deputy pushed past her and flicked the lights on. Dance joined him. A fast search revealed that the tiny place was unoccupied.

Dance returned to the woman. 'Sorry for the disturbance.'

'No, that's okay. This's scary. Where did they go?'

'We're still searching. Did you see what happened?'

'No. I was inside. When I looked out there was the car burning. I kept thinking about the oil tank fire a few years ago. That was a bad one. Were you here for that?'

'I was. I could see it from Carmel.'

'We knew it was empty, the tank. Or pretty much empty. But we were all freaked out. And those wires. Electricity can be pretty spooky.'

'So you're closed?'

'Yeah. I was going to leave early anyway. Didn't know how long the highway would be closed. Not many tourists'd be interested in saltwater taffy with a power plant on fire across the highway.'

'Imagine not. I'd like to ask why you wondered where they went.'

'Oh, a dangerous man like that? I'd hope he'd get arrested as fast as possible.'

'But you said "they". How did you know there were several people?'

A pause. 'I –'

Dance gazed at her with a smile but with unwavering eyes. 'You said you didn't see anything. You looked out only after you heard the siren.'

'I think I talked to somebody about it. Outside.'

*I think . . .*

A denial flag expression. Subconsciously the woman would feel she was giving an opinion, not a deceptive statement.

'Who told you?' Dance persisted.

'I didn't know them.'

'A man or a woman?'

Another hesitation. 'A girl, a woman. From out of state.' Her head was turned away and she was rubbing her nose – an aversion/negation cluster.

'Where's your car?' Dance asked.

'My –?'

Eyes play an ambiguous role in kinesic analysis. There's the belief among some officers that if a suspect looks to his left under your gaze, it's a sign of lying. Dance knew that was just an old cops' tale; averting eyes – unlike turning the body or face away from the interrogator – has no correlation to deception; direction of eye gaze is too easily controlled.

But eyes are still very revealing.

As Dance was talking to the woman, she'd noticed her looking at a particular place in the parking lot. Every time she did, she displayed general stress indicators: shifting her weight, pressing her fingers together. Dance understood: Pell had stolen her car and said that he as with the infamous partner would kill her family if she said anything. Just as with the Worldwide Express driver.

Dance sighed, upset. If the woman had come forward when they'd first arrived, they might have Pell by now.

Or if I hadn't blindly believed the CLOSED sign and knocked on the door sooner, she added to herself bitterly.

'I –' The woman started to cry.

'I understand. We'll make sure you're safe. What kind of car?'

'It's a dark blue Ford Focus. Three years old. There's a bumper sticker about global warming on it. And a dent in the –'

'Where did they go?'

'North.'

Dance got the tag number and called O'Neil, who would in turn relay a message to MCSO dispatch for an announcement to all units about the car.

As the clerk made arrangements to stay with a friend until Pell's recapture, Dance stared at the lingering cloud of smoke around the Thunderbird. Angry. She'd made a sharp deduction from Eddie Chang's information and they'd come up with a solid plan for the apprehension. But it had been a waste.

TJ joined her, with the manager of Jack's Seafood. He gave his story of the events, clearly omitting a few facts, probably that he'd inadvertently tipped off Pell about the police. Dance couldn't blame him. She remembered Pell from the interview – how sharp and wary he was.

The manager described the woman, who was skinny and pretty in a 'mousy way' and had looked at the man adoringly throughout most of the meal. At first he'd thought they were honeymooners. She couldn't keep her hands off him. He put her age at mid-twenties. The manager added that they'd pored over a map during much of the meal. 'What was it of?'

'Here, Monterey County.'

Michael O'Neil joined her, flipping closed his phone. 'No reports of the Focus,' he said. 'But with the evacuation it must've gotten lost in the traffic. Hell, he could've turned south and driven right past us.'

Dance called Carraneo over. The young man looked tired. He'd had a busy day but it wasn't over yet. 'Find out everything you can about the T-bird. And start calling motels and boardinghouses from Watsonville down to Big Sur. See if any blonde women checked in by themselves and listed a Thunderbird as their car on the registration form. Or if anybody saw a T-bird. If the car was stolen on Friday, she'd've checked in Friday, Saturday or Sunday.'

'Sure, Agent Dance.'

She and O'Neil both stared west, over the water, which was calm. The sun was a wide, flat disk, low over the Pacific, the fierce beams muted; the fog hadn't arrived yet but the late-afternoon sky was hazy, grainy. Monterey Bay looked like a flat, blue desert. He said, 'Pell's taking a huge risk staying around here. He's got something important to do.'

It was just then that she got a call from someone who, she realized, might have some thoughts about what the killer might have in mind.

# Chapter
## SEVENTEEN

There are probably ten thousand streets named Mission in California, and James Reynolds, the retired prosecutor who eight years earlier had won the conviction of Daniel Pell, lived on one of the nicer ones.

He had a Carmel ZIP code, though this street wasn't in the cute part of town – that storybook area flooded on the weekends with tourists (whom the locals simultaneously love and hate). Reynolds was in working Carmel, but it was not exactly the wrong side of the tracks. He had a precious three-quarters acre of secluded property not far from the Barnyard, the landscaped multilevel shopping center where you could buy jewelry and art and complicated kitchen gadgets, gifts and souvenirs.

Dance now pulled into the long driveway, reflecting that people with so much property were either the elite of recent money – neurosurgeons or geeks who survived the Silicon Valley shakeout – or long-time residents. Reynolds, who'd made his living as a prosecutor, had to be the latter.

The tanned, balding man in his mid-sixties met her at the door, ushered her inside.

'My wife's at work. Well, at *volunteer*. I'm cooking dinner. Come on into the kitchen.'

As she followed him along the corridor of the brightly lit house Dance could read the man's history in the many frames on the wall. The East Coast schools, Stanford Law, his wedding, the raising of two sons and a daughter, their graduations.

The most recent photos had yet to be framed. She nodded at a stack of pictures, on the top of which was one of a young woman, blonde and beautiful in her elaborate white dress, surrounded by her maids of honor. 'Your daughter? Congratulations.'

'The last to fly the nest.' He gave her a thumbs-up and grinned. 'How 'bout you?'

'Oh, the weddings're a while off. I've got middle school next on the agenda.'

She also noticed a number of framed newspaper pages: big convictions he'd won. And, she was amused to see, trials he'd lost. He noticed her looking at one and chuckled. 'The wins are for ego. The losses're for humility. I'd take the high ground and say that I learned something from the not-guilties. But the fact is, sometimes juries're just out to lunch.'

She knew this very well from her previous job as jury consultant.

'Like with our boy Pell. The jury should've recommended the death penalty. But they didn't.'

'Why not? Extenuating circumstances?'

'Yep, if that's what you call fear. They were scared the Family would come after them for revenge.'

'But they didn't have a problem convicting him.'

'Oh, no. The case was solid. And I ran the prosecution hard. I picked up on the Son-of-Manson theme – I was the one who called him that in the first place. I pointed out all the parallels: Manson claimed he had the power to control people. A history of petty crimes and a cult of subservient women. He was behind the deaths of a rich family. And in Pell's house, crime scene found dozens of books about Manson, underlined and annotated.

'Pell actually helped get himself convicted,' Reynolds added with a smile. 'He played the part. He'd sit in court and stare at the jurors, trying to intimidate, scare them. He tried it with me too. I laughed at him and said I didn't think psychic powers had any effect on lawyers. The jury laughed too. It broke the spell.' He shook his head. 'Not enough to get him the needle, but I was happy with consecutive life sentences.'

'You also prosecuted the three women in the Family?'

'I pled them out. It was pretty much minor stuff. They didn't have anything to do with the Croyton thing. I'm positive of that. Before they ran into Pell, none of them'd ever been picked up for anything worse than drinking in public or a little pot, I think. Pell brainwashed them . . . Jimmy Newberg was different. He had a history of violence – some aggravateds and felony drug charges.'

In the spacious kitchen, decorated entirely in yellow and beige,

Reynolds put an apron on. He'd apparently slipped it off to answer the door. 'I took up cooking after I retired. Interesting contrast. Nobody likes a prosecutor. But –' He nodded at a large orange skillet filled with cooking seafood '– my cioppino? *Everybody* loves that.'

'So,' Dance said, looking around with an exaggerated frown. 'This is what a kitchen looks like.'

'Ah, a take-out queen. Like me when I was a working bachelor.'

'My poor kids. The good news is that they're learning defensive cooking. For last Mother's Day? They made me strawberry crepes.'

'And all you had to do was clean up. Here, try a bowl.'

She couldn't resist. 'Okay, just a sample.'

He dished up a portion. 'It needs red wine to accompany.'

'That I'll pass on.' She tried the stew. 'Excellent!'

Reynolds had been in touch with Sandoval and the Monterey County sheriff and learned the latest details of the manhunt, including the information that Pell was staying in the area. (Dance noted that, regarding the CBI, he'd called *her* and not Charles Overby.)

'I'll do whatever I can to help you nail this bastard.' The former prosecutor meticulously sliced a tomato. 'Just name it. I've already called the county storage company. They're bringing me all my notes from the case. Probably ninety-nine percent of them won't be helpful, but there could be a nugget or two. And I'll go through every damn page, if I have to.' Dance glanced at his eyes, which were dark coals of determination, very different from, say, Morton Nagle's sparkle. She had never worked any cases with Reynolds, but knew he'd be a fierce and uncompromising prosecutor.

'That'd be very helpful, James. Appreciate it.' Dance finished the stew and, rinsing the bowl, placed it in the sink. 'I didn't even know you were in the area. I'd heard you retired to Santa Barbara.'

'We have a little place there. But we're here most of the year.'

'Well, when you called, I got in touch with MCSO. I'd like to have a deputy stationed outside.'

Reynolds dismissed the idea. 'I've got a good alarm system. I'm virtually untraceable. When I became lead prosecutor I started getting threats – those Salinas gang prosecutions. I had my phone unlisted and transferred title to the house to a trust. There's no way he could find me. And I've got a carry permit for my six-gun.'

Dance wasn't going to take no for an answer. 'He's already killed several times today.'

A shrug. 'Sure, what the hell. I'll take a babysitter. Can't hurt – my younger son's here visiting. Why take chances?'

Dance scooted onto a stool. She rested her maroon wedge Aldos on the supports. The straps on the shoes were inlaid with bright daisies. Even ten-year-old Maggie had more conservative taste than she did when it came to shoes, which were one of Dance's passions.

'For now, could you tell me something about the murders eight years ago? It might give me an idea of what he's up to.'

Reynolds sat on an adjoining stool, sipping wine. He ran through the facts of the case: How Pell and Jimmy Newberg had broken into the house of William Croyton in Carmel, killed the businessman, his wife and two of their three children. They'd all been stabbed to death. Newberg too. 'My theory was that he balked about murdering the kids and got into a fight with Pell, who killed *him*.'

'Any history between Pell and Croyton?'

'Not that we could establish. But Silicon Valley was at its peak then, and Croyton was one of the big boys. He was in the press all the time – he not only designed most of the programs himself, he was the chief of sales too. Larger-than-life kind of guy. Big, sunburned, loud . . . Work hard, play hard. Not the most sympathetic victim in the world. Pretty ruthless businessman, rumors of affairs, disgruntled employees. But if murder was a crime only against saints, we prosecutors'd be out of a job.

'His company had been burglarized a couple of times in the year before the killing. The perps got away with computers and software, but Santa Clara County could never come up with a suspect. No indication that Pell had anything to do with it. But I always wondered if it could've been him.'

'What happened to the company after he died?'

'It was acquired by somebody else, Microsoft or Apple or one of the game companies, I don't know.'

'And his estate?'

'Most of it went in trust to his daughter, and I think some to his wife's sister, the aunt who took custody of the girl. Croyton'd been in computers ever since he was a kid. He had probably ten, twenty million dollars' of old hardware and programs that he left to Cal State-Monterey Bay. The computer museum there's really impressive, and techies come from all over the world to do research in the archives.'

'Still?'

'Apparently so. Croyton was way ahead of his time, it seems.'

'And rich.'

'Way rich.'

'That was the actual motive for the killings?'

'Well, we never knew for sure. On the facts, it was a plain-vanilla burglary. I think Pell read about Croyton and thought it'd be a cakewalk to pick up some big bucks.'

'But his take was pretty skimpy, I read.'

'Few thousand. Would've been a small case. Except for five dead bodies, of course. Almost six – good thing that little girl was upstairs.'

'What's her story?'

'Poor kid. You know what they called her?'

'"The Sleeping Doll".'

'Right. She didn't testify. Even if she'd seen something, I wouldn't've subjected her to the stand, not with that prick in the courtroom. I had enough evidence anyway.'

'She didn't remember anything?'

'Nothing helpful. She went to bed early that night.'

'Where is she now?'

'No idea. She was adopted by the aunt and uncle and they moved away.'

'What was Pell's defense?'

'They'd gone there with some business idea. Newberg snapped and killed everybody. Pell tried to stop him, they fought and Pell, quote, "had" to kill him. But there was no evidence Croyton had a meeting planned – the family was in the middle of dinner when they showed up. Besides, the forensics were clear: time of death, fingerprints, trace, blood spatter, everything. Pell was the doer.'

'In prison Pell got access to a computer. Unsupervised.'

'That's not good.'

She nodded. 'We found some things he searched for. Do they mean anything to you? One was "Alison".'

'It wasn't one of the girls in the Family. I don't know anybody else connected to him with that name.'

'Another word he searched was "Nimue". A character out of mythology. King Arthur legend. But I'm thinking it's a name or screen name of somebody Pell wanted to get in touch with.'

'Sorry, nothing.'

'Any other ideas about what he might have in mind?'

Reynolds shook his head. 'Sorry. It was a big case – for me. And for the county. But, the fact is, it wasn't remarkable. He was caught red-handed, the forensics were waterproof and he was a recidivist with a history of criminal activity going back to his early teens. I mean, this guy and the Family were on watch lists in beach communities from Big Sur to Marin. I'd've had to screw up pretty bad to lose.'

'All right, James. I'd better get going,' she said. 'Appreciate the help. If you find something in the files let me know.'

He gave her a solemn nod, no longer a dabbling retiree or kindly father-of-the-bride. She could see in Reynolds's eyes the fierce determination that had undoubtedly characterized his approach in court. 'I'll do anything I can to help get that son of a bitch back where he belongs. Or into a body bag.'

They'd separated, and now, several hundred yards apart, they made their way on foot to a motel in quaint Pacific Grove, right in the heart of the Peninsula.

Pell walked leisurely and wide-eyed, like a dumbfounded tourist who'd never seen surf outside *Baywatch*.

They were in a change of clothing, which they'd bought at a Goodwill store in a poor part of Seaside (where he'd enjoyed watching Jennie hesitate, then discard her beloved pink blouse). Pell was now in a light-gray windbreaker, cords, and cheap running shoes, a baseball cap on backward. He also carried a disposable camera. He would occasionally pause to take pictures of the sunset, on the theory that one thing escaped killers rarely do is stop to record panoramic seascapes, however impressive.

He and Jennie had driven east from Moss Landing in the stolen Ford Focus, taking none of the major roads and even cutting through a Brussels sprout field, aromatic with the scent of human gas. Eventually they'd headed back toward Pacific Grove. But when the area became more populous, Pell knew it was time to ditch the wheels. The police would learn about the Focus soon. He hid it in tall grass in the middle of a large field off Highway 68, marked with a 'For Sale – Commercial Zoned' sign.

He decided they should separate on the hike to the motel. Jennie didn't like it, not being with him, but they stayed in touch via their prepaid mobiles. She called every five minutes until he told her it was probably better not to, because the police might be listening in.

Which they weren't, of course, but he was tired of the honey-bunny chatter and wanted to think.

Daniel Pell was worried.

How had the police tracked them to Jack's?

He ran through the possibilities. Maybe the cap, sunglasses and shaved face hadn't fooled the manager at the restaurant, though who'd believe that a murderous escapee would sit down like a day-tripper from San Francisco to devour a plate of tasty sand dabs fifteen miles from the detention center he'd just redecorated with fire and blood?

Finding that the T-bird was stolen was another possibility. But why would somebody run the tag of a car stolen four hundred miles away? And even if it was boosted, why call out the 101st Airborne just for a set of stolen wheels – unless they knew it had some connection to Pell?

And the cops were supposed to believe he was headed to that camper park outside of Salt Lake City he'd called.

*Kathryn?*

He had a feeling she hadn't bought into the Utah idea, even after the trick with Billy's phone and leaving the driver alive on purpose. Pell wondered if she'd put out the announcement about Utah to the press intentionally, to flush him into the open.

Which had, in fact, worked, he reflected angrily.

Wherever he went, he had a feeling, she'd be supervising the manhunt for him.

Pell wondered where she lived. He thought again about his assessment of her in the interview – her children, her husband – recalled when she'd given her subtle reactions, when she didn't.

Kids? Yes. Husband, probably not. A divorce didn't seem likely. He sensed good judgement and loyalty within her.

Pell paused and took a snap of the sun easing into the Pacific Ocean. It was really quite a sight.

Kathryn as a widow. Interesting idea. He felt the swelling within him again.

Somehow he managed to tuck it away.

For the time being.

He bought a few things at a store, a little bodega, which he picked because he knew his picture wouldn't be looping on the news every five minutes; he was right, the tiny set showed only a Spanish-language soap opera.

Pell met up with Jennie in Asilomar, the beautiful park, which featured a crescent of beach for die-hard surfers and, closer to Monterey, an increasingly rugged shoreline of rocks and crashing spray.

'Everything all right?' she asked cautiously.

'Fine, lovely. We're doing fine.'

She led him through the quiet streets of Pacific Grove, a former Methodist retreat, filled with colorful Victorian and Tudor bungalows. In five minutes she announced, 'Here we are.' She nodded at the Sea View Motel. The building was brown, with small lead windows, a wood shingle roof and plaques of butterflies above the doors. The village's claim to fame, other than being the last dry town in California, was the monarchs – tens of thousands of the insects would cluster here from fall to spring.

'It's cute, isn't it?'

Pell guessed. Cute didn't mean anything to him. What mattered was that the room faced away from the road and there were driveways off the back parking lot that would be perfect escape routes. She'd gotten exactly the kind of place she was supposed to.

'It's perfect, lovely. Just like you.'

Another smile on her smooth face, but a half-hearted one; she was still shaken by the incident at Jack's restaurant. Pell didn't care. The bubble within him had started expanding once more. He wasn't sure whether Kathryn was driving it, or Jennie.

'Which one's ours?'

She pointed. 'Come on, honey. I have a surprise for you.'

Hm. Pell didn't like surprises.

She unlocked the door.

He nodded toward it. 'After you, lovely.' And reached into his waistband, gripping the pistol. He tensed, ready to push her forward as a sacrificial shield and start shooting at the sound of a cop's voice.

But it wasn't a setup. The place was empty. He looked around. It was even nicer than the outside suggested. Ritzy. Expensive furniture, drapes, towels, even bathrobes. Some nice paintings too. Seashores, the Lonesome Pine, and more goddamn butterflies.

And candles. Lots of them. Everywhere you could put a candle there was a candle.

Oh, that was the surprise. They weren't, thank God, lit. That's all he'd need – come back from an escape to find his hideaway on fire.

'You have the keys?'

She handed them to him.

Keys. Pell loved them. Whether for a car, a motel room, a safe deposit box or a house, whoever possesses the keys is in control.

'What's in there?' she asked, glancing at the bag. She'd been curious earlier, when they met on the beach not long ago, he knew. Purposely he had'nt told her.

'Just some things we needed. And some food.'

Jennie blinked in surprise. 'You bought food?'

What, was this the first time her man had bought her groceries?

'I could've done that,' she said quickly. Then nodding at the kitchen-ette, she added a perfunctory, 'So. I'll cook you a meal.'

Odd phrase. She's been taught to think that. By her ex, or one of the abusive boyfriends. Tim the biker.

*Shut up and go cook me a meal . . .*

'That's okay, lovely. I'll do it.'

'You?'

'Sure.' Pell knew men who insisted that 'the wife' feed them. They thought they were kings of the household, to be waited on. It gave them some sense of power. But they didn't understand that when you depended on someone for anything, you were weakened. (Also, how stupid can you be? You know how easy it is to mix rat poison into soup?) Pell was no chef but, even years ago, when Linda was the Family's cook, he liked to hang out in the kitchen, help her, keep an eye on things.

'Oh, and you got Mexican!' She laughed as she pulled out the ground beef, tortillas, tomatoes, canned peppers and sauces.

'You said you liked it. Comfort food . . . Hey, lovely.' He kissed her head. 'You were real steady today at the restaurant.'

Turning away from the groceries, she looked down. 'I got kind of freaked, you know. I was scared. I didn't mean to scream.'

'No, no, you held fast. You know what that means?'

'Not really.'

'It's an old expression sailors used to say. They'd tattoo it on their fingers, so when you made fists, you'd see it spelled out. "Hold fast." It means not running away.'

She laughed. 'I wouldn't run away from you.'

He touched his lips to her head, smelled sweat and discount perfume. She rubbed her nose.

'We're a team, lovely.' Which got her to stop rubbing. Pell noted that.

He went into the bathroom, peed long and then washed up. When he stepped outside he found a second surprise.

Jennie'd stripped down. She was wearing only a bra and panties, holding a cigarette lighter, working on the candles.

She glanced up. 'You said you liked red.'

Pell grinned, walked to her. Ran his hand down her bony spine.

'Or would you rather eat?'

He kissed her. 'We'll eat later.'

'Oh, I want you, baby,' she whispered. It was clearly a line she'd used often in the past. But that didn't mean it wasn't true now.

He took the lighter. 'We'll do atmosphere later.' He kissed her, pulled her hips to him.

She smiled – an unqualified one now – and pressed harder against his crotch. 'I think you want me too.' A purr.

'I do want you, lovely.'

'I like it when you call me that.'

'You have any stockings?' he asked.

She nodded. 'Black ones. I'll go put them on.'

'No. That's not what I want them for,' he whispered.

# Chapter
# EIGHTEEN

One more errand before this hard day was over.

Kathryn Dance pulled up to a modest house in the netherworld between Carmel and Monterey.

When the huge military base, Fort Ord, was *the* industry in the area, medium-rank officers would live and, often, retire here. Before that, in the fishing and cannery days, foremen and managers lived here. Dance parked in front of a modest bungalow and walked through the picket-fence gate and along the stony path to the front door. A minute later a freckled, cheerful woman in her late thirties greeted her. Dance identified herself. 'I'm here to see Morton.'

'Come on in,' Joan Nagle said, smiling, the lack of surprise – and concern – in her face telling Dance that her husband had given her some of the details of his role in the events of today, though perhaps not all.

The agent stepped into a small living room. The half-full boxes of clothes and books – mostly the latter – suggested that they'd just moved in. The walls were covered with the cheap prints of a seasonal rental. Again the smells of cooking assaulted her – but this time the scent was of hamburger and onions, not Italian herbs.

A cute, round girl in pigtails, wearing wire-rimmed glasses, was holding a drawing pad. She looked up and smiled. Dance waved to her. She was about Wes's age. On the couch, a boy in his mid-teens was lost in the chaos of a video game, pushing buttons as if civilization depended on him.

Morton Nagle appeared in the doorway, tugging at his waistband. 'Hello, hello, hello, Agent Dance.'

'Kathryn, please.'

'Kathryn. You've met my wife, Joan.' A smile. 'And . . . hey, Eric, put that . . . Eric!' he called in a loud, laughing voice. 'Put that away.'

The boy saved the game – Dance knew how vital *that* was – and set the controller down. He bounded to his feet.

'This's Eric. Say hello to Agent Dance.'

'Agent? Like FBI?'

'Like that.'

'Sweet!'

Dance shook the hand of the teenager, as he stared at her hip, looking at the gun.

The girl, still clutching her sketchbook, came up shyly.

'Well, introduce yourself,' her mother urged.

'Hi.'

'What's your name?' Dance asked.

'Sonja.'

Sonja's weight's a problem, Dance noted. Her parents better address it pretty soon, though given their physiques she doubted they understood the problems their daughter was already facing. The agent's kinesics expertise gave her many insights into people's psychological and emotional difficulties, but she continually had to remind herself that her job was law enforcer, not therapist.

Nagle said, 'I've been following the news. You almost caught him?'

'Minutes away,' she said, grimacing.

'Can I get you anything?' his wife asked.

'No, thanks,' Dance said. 'I can only stay a minute.'

'Come on into my office,' Nagle said.

They walked into a small bedroom, which smelled of cat pee. A desk and two chairs were the only pieces of furniture. A laptop, the letters worn off the A, H and N keys, sat beside a desk lamp that had been taped together. There were stacks of paper everywhere and probably two or three hundred books, in boxes and littering the shelves, covering the radiator and piled on the floor.

'I like my books around me.' A nod toward the living room. 'They do too. Even Mr Wizard on the video game there. We pick a book and then every night I read from it out loud.'

'That's nice.' Dance and her children did something similar, though it usually involved music. Wes and Mags devoured books, but they preferred to read on their own.

'Of course, we still find time for true culture . . . *Survivor* and *24*.'
Nagle's eyes just wouldn't stop sparkling. He gave another of his chuckles
when he saw her note the volume of material he had for her. 'Don't
worry. *That* one's yours, the small one.' He gestured toward a box of
videotapes and photocopied sheets.

'Sure I can't get you anything?' Joan asked from the doorway.

'Nothing, thanks.'

'You can stay for dinner if you like.'

'Sorry, no.'

She smiled and left. Nagle nodded after her. 'She's a physicist.' And
added nothing more.

Dance told Nagle the latest details in the case and explained that she
was pretty sure Pell was staying in the area.

'That'd be crazy. Everybody on the Peninsula's looking for him.'

'You'd think.' She explained about his search at Capitola, but Nagle
could contribute no insights about Alison or Nimue. Nor did he have
any clue why the killer had been browsing a satellite-photo site.

She glanced at the box he'd prepared for her. 'Is there a bio in there?
Something brief?'

'Brief? No, not really. But if you want a synopsis I could do it, sure.
Three, four pages?'

'That'd be great. It'll take me forever to pull it together from all of
that.'

'*All* of that?' Chuckling. 'That's nothing. By the time I'm ready to write
the book, I'll have fifty times more notes and sources. But, sure, I'll gin
up something.'

'Hi,' a youthful voice said.

Dance smiled at Sonja in the doorway.

An envious glance at the agent's figure, then hair. 'I saw you looking
at my drawings. When you came in?'

'Honey, Agent Dance is busy.'

'No, it's okay.'

'Do you want to see them?'

Dance sank to her knees to look at the sketchpad. They were pictures
of butterflies, surprisingly well done.

'Sonja, these are beautiful. They could be in a gallery on Ocean in
Carmel.'

'You think?'

'Definitely.'

She flipped back a page. 'This one's my favorite. It's a swallowtail.'

The picture was of a dark blue butterfly. The color was iridescent.

'It's sitting on a Mexican sunflower. They get nectar from that. When I'm at home we go out into the desert and I draw lizards and cactuses.'

Dance remembered that the writer's full-time residence was Scottsdale.

Sonja continued, 'Here, my mommy and I go out in the woods and we take pictures. Then I draw them.'

Nagle said, 'She's the James Audubon of butterflies.'

Joan appeared in the doorway and ushered the child out.

'Think that'll do any good?' Nagle asked, gesturing at the box.

'I don't know. But I sure hope so. We need some help.'

Dance said good night, turned down another dinner invitation and returned to the car.

She set the box on the seat next to her. The photocopies beckoned her and she was tempted to turn on the dome light and have a look now. But the material would have to wait. Kathryn Dance was a good investigator, just as she'd been a good reporter and a good jury consultant. But she was also a mother and a widow. And the unique confluence of *those* roles required her to know when to pull back from her other job. It was now time to be home.

# Chapter
# NINETEEN

This was known as the Deck.

An expanse of gray, pressure-treated wood, twenty by thirty feet, extending from the kitchen of Dance's house into the backyard and filled with mismatched lawn chairs, loungers and tables. Tiny electric Christmas lights, some amber globes, a sink and a large refrigerator were the main decorations, along with a few anemic plants in terra-cotta bowls. A narrow stairway led down to the backyard, hardly landscaped, though it *was* filled with plenty of natural flora: scrub oak and maple trees, monkey flowers, asters, lupine, potato vines, clover and renegade grass.

A stockade fence provided separation from the neighbors. Two birdbaths and a feeder for hummingbirds hung from a branch near the stairs. Two wind chimes lay on the ground where Dance, in her pajamas, had dumped them at 3:00 a.m. one particularly stormy night a month ago.

The classic Victorian house – dark green with gray, weathered banisters, shutters and trim – was in the northwestern part of Pacific Grove; if you were willing to risk a precarious lean, you could catch a glimpse of ocean, about a half-mile away.

Dance spent plenty of time on the Deck. It was often too cold or misty for an early breakfast but on lazy weekends, after the sun had melted the fog, she and the children might come here after a walk on the beach with the dogs and have bagels and cream cheese, coffee and hot chocolate. Hundreds of dinner parties, large and small, had been hosted on the uneven planks.

The Deck was where her husband, Bill, had told his parents firmly that he was marrying Kathryn Dance and, by corollary, not the Napa socialite his mother had championed for several years – an act braver for him than much of what he'd done with the FBI.

The Deck was where they'd had his memorial service.

It was also a gathering-place for friends both within and outside the law enforcement community on the Peninsula. Kathryn Dance enjoyed her friendships but after Bill's death she'd chosen to spend her free time with her children, not wanting to take them to bars or restaurants with other adults. So she brought the friends into their world.

There was beer and soda in the outdoor fridge, and usually a bottle or two of basic Central Coast chardonnay or pinot grigio and cabernet. A stained, rusty but functional barbecue grill sat here as well, and there was a bathroom downstairs, accessible from the backyard. It wasn't unusual for Dance to come home and find her mother or father, friends or colleagues from the CBI or MCSO, enjoying a beer or coffee.

All were welcome to stop by whether she was home or away, whether the visitors announced their intentions or not, though even if she was home she might not join them. A tacit but well-understood rule held that, while people were always welcome anytime outside, the house itself was off limits, except for planned parties; privacy, sleep and homework were sacred.

Dance now climbed the steep stairs from her side yard and walked onto the Deck, carrying the box of photocopies and tapes, on top of which was perched a prepared chicken dinner she'd bought at Albertsons. The dogs greeted her, a black flat-coated retriever and a black-and-tan German shepherd. She rubbed ears and flung a few mangy stuffed toys, then continued on to two men sitting in plastic chairs.

'Hi, honey.' Stuart Dance looked younger than his seventy years. He was tall, with broad shoulders and a full head of unruly white hair. His hours at sea and on the shore had taken a toll on his skin; a few scars from the dermatologist's scalpel and laser were evident too. Technically retired, he still worked at the aquarium several days a week, and nothing in the universe could keep him from the rocky shoals of the coast.

He and his daughter brushed cheeks.

'Hnnn.' From Albert Stemple, another Major Crimes agent with the CBI. The massive, shaved-headed man wore boots, jeans, a black T-shirt. There were scars on his face too, and others he'd alluded to – in places that didn't see much sunlight, though a dermatologist hadn't been the source. He was drinking a beer, feet sticking out in front of him. The CBI was not known for its cowboys, but Albert Stemple was your basic, make-my-own-rules Wild Bill Hickock. He had more collars than any other agent, as well as more official complaints (he was most proud of the latter).

'Thanks for keeping an eye on things, Al. Sorry it's later than I'd planned.' Thinking of Pell's threats during the interrogation – and at his remaining in the area, Dance had asked Stemple to babysit until she returned home. (O'Neil too had arranged for local officers to keep an eye on her house as long as the escapee was at large.)

Stemple grunted. 'Not a problem. Overby'll buy me dinner.'

'Charles said that?'

'Naw. But he'll buy me dinner. Quiet here. I walked around a couple times. Nothin' strange.'

'You want a soda for the road?'

'Sure.' The big man helped himself to two Anchor Steams from the fridge. 'Don't worry. I'll finish 'em 'fore I get in the car. So long, Stu.' He clomped along the Deck, which creaked under his weight.

He disappeared and she heard the Crown Victoria start up fifteen seconds later and peel away, the open beers undoubtedly resting between his massive thighs.

Dance glanced through the streaked windows into the living room. Her eyes settled on a book sitting on the coffee table in the living room. It jogged her memory. 'Hey, did Brian call?'

'Oh, your friend? The one who came to dinner?'

'Right.'

'What was his last name?'

'Gunderson.'

'The investment banker.'

'That's the one. Did he call?'

'Not that I know. You want to ask the kids?'

'No, that's okay. Thanks again, Dad.'

'No worries.' An expression from his days in New Zealand. He turned away, rapping on the window. 'Bye!'

'Grandpa, wait!' Maggie ran outside, her chestnut braid flapping behind her. She was clutching a book. 'Hi, Mom,' she said enthusiastically. 'When'd you get home?'

'Just now.'

'You didn't *say* anything!' exclaimed the ten-year-old, poking her glasses up on her nose.

'Where's your brother?'

'I don't know. His room. When's dinner?'

'Five minutes.'

'What're we having?'

'You'll see.'

Maggie held the book up to her grandfather and pointed out a small gray-purple, nautilus-like sea shell. 'Look. You were right.' Maggie didn't try to pronounce the words.

'A Columbian Amphissa,' he said and pulled out the pen and notebook he was never without. Jotted. Three decades older than his daughter and he needed no glasses. Most of her genetic proclivities derived from her mother, Dance had learned.

'A tide-drift shell,' he said to Dance. 'Very rare here. But Maggie found one.'

'It was just *there*,' the girl said.

'Okay, I'm headed home to the staff sergeant. She's fixing dinner and my presence is required. 'Night, all.'

''Bye, Grandpa.'

Her father climbed down the stairs, and Dance thanked fate or God or whatever might be, as she often did, for a good, dependable male figure in the life of a widow with children.

On her way to the kitchen her phone rang. Rey Carraneo reported that the Thunderbird at Moss Landing had been stolen from the valet parking lot of an upscale restaurant on Sunset Boulevard in Los Angeles the previous Friday. There were no suspects. They were expecting the report from LAPD but, like most car thefts, there were no forensics. Also he'd had no luck finding the hotel, motel or boardingroom the woman might've checked into. 'There're a lot of them,' he confessed.

Welcome to the Monterey Peninsula. 'We've got to stash the tourists somewhere, Rey. Keep at it. And say hi to your wife.'

Dance began unpacking dinner.

A lean boy with sandy hair wandered into the sunroom beside the kitchen. He was on the phone. Though only twelve, Wes was nearly as tall as his mother. She wiggled a finger at him and he wandered over to her. She kissed him on the forehead and he didn't cringe. Which was the same as 'I love you very much, mother dear.'

'Off the phone,' she said. 'Dinnertime.'

'Like, gotta go.'

'Don't say "like".'

'What're we having?' The boy hung up.

'Chicken,' Maggie said dubiously.

'You like Albertsons.'

'What about bird flu?'

Wes snickered. 'Don't you know anything? You get it from *live* chickens.'

'It *was* alive once,' the girl countered.

From the corner where his sister had backed him, Wes said, 'Well, it's not an Asian chicken.'

'Hell-*o*. They migrate. And how you die is you throw up to death.'

'Mags, not at dinnertime!' Dance said.

'Well, you do.'

'Oh, like chickens migrate? Yeah, right. And they don't have bird flu here. Or we would've heard.'

Sibling banter. But there was a little more to it, Dance believed. Her son remained deeply affected by his father's death. This made him more sensitive to mortality and violence than most boys his age. Dance steered him away from those topics – a tough job for a woman who tracked down felons for a living. She now announced, 'As long as the chicken's cooked, it's fine.' Though she wasn't sure this was right and wondered if Maggie would dispute it.

But her daughter was lost in her seashell book.

The boy said, 'Oh, mashed potatoes too. You rock, Mom.'

Maggie and Wes set the table and laid out the food, while Dance washed up.

When she returned from the bathroom, Wes asked, 'Mom, aren't you going to change?' He was looking at her black suit.

'I'm starving. I can't wait.' Not sharing that the real reason she'd kept the outfit on was to wear her weapon. Usually the first thing she did upon coming home was to put on jeans and a T-shirt and slip the gun into the lockbox beside her bed.

*Yeah, it's a tough life being a cop. The little ones spend a lot of time alone, don't they? They'd probably love some friends to play with . . .*

Wes glanced once more at her suit as if he knew exactly what she'd been thinking.

But then they turned to the food, eating and talking about their day – the children's at least. Dance, of course, said nothing about hers. Wes was in a sports camp in Monterey, Maggie at a music camp in Carmel. Each seemed to be enjoying the experience. Thank goodness neither of them asked about Daniel Pell.

When dinner was over, the trio cleaned the table and did the dishes – her children always had a share of the housework. When they were through, Wes and Maggie headed into the living room to read or play video games.

Dance logged onto her computer and checked email. Nothing about the case, though she had several about her other 'job'. She and her friend Martine Christiansen, ran a website called 'American Tunes'. after the famous Paul Simon song from the 1970s.

Kathryn Dance was not a bad musician, but a brief attempt at a full-time career as a singer and guitarist had left her dissatisfied (which, she was afraid, was how *she*'d left her audiences). She decided that her real talent was for *listening* to music and encouraging other people to, as well.

On her infrequent vacations or on long weekends, she'd head off in search of homemade music, often with the children and dogs in tow. A 'folklorist' was the name of the avocation or, more popularly, 'song catcher'. Alan Lomax was perhaps the most famous, collecting music from Louisiana to the Appalachians for the Library of Congress throughout the mid-twentieth century. While his taste had run to black blues and mountain music, Dance's scavenger hunt took her farther afield, to places reflecting the changing sociology of North America: music grounded in Latino, Caribbean, Nova Scotian, Canadian, urban African American and Native American cultures.

She and her best friend, Martine Christensen, helped the musicians copyright their original material, posted the taped songs and distributed to them the money that listeners paid for downloads.

When the day came when Dance was no longer willing or able to track down criminals, she knew music would be a good way to spend retirement.

Her phone rang. She looked at the caller ID number.

'Well, hello.'

'Hey there,' Michael O'Neil said. 'How'd it go with Reynolds?'

'Nothing particularly helpful. But he's checking his old files from the Croyton case.' She added that she'd picked up Morton Nagle's material too, but hadn't had a chance to look through it yet.

O'Neil told her that the Focus stolen from Moss Landing hadn't been located, and they'd discovered nothing else helpful at Jack's Seafood. The techs had lifted fingerprints from the T-bird and the utensils: Pell's and others that were common to both locations, presumably the woman's.

A search through state and federal databases revealed she had no record.

'We did find one thing we're a little troubled about. Peter Bennington –'

'Your crime lab guy.'

'Right. He said there was acid on the floorboard of the T-bird, driver's seat side, the part that didn't burn. It was recent. Peter said it was a corrosive acid – pretty diluted but Watsonville Fire soaked the car to cool it so it could've been pretty strong when Pell left it there.'

'You know me and evidence, Michael.'

'Okay, the bottom line is that it was mixed with the same substance found in apples, grapes and candy.'

'You think Pell was . . . what? Poisoning something?'

Food was the raison d'etre of Central California. There were thousands of acres of fields and orchards, a dozen big wineries and other food processors all within a half hour drive.

'It's a possibility. Or maybe he's hiding out in an orchard or vineyard. We scared him at Moss Landing and he gave up on staying in a motel or boardinghouse. Think about the Pastures . . . We ought to get some people searching.'

'Have you got anybody available?' she asked.

'I can shift some troops. Get CHP too. Hate to pull them off the search downtown and along One, but I don't think we have any choice.'

Dance agreed. She relayed to him Carraneo's information about the T-bird.

'Not racing forward at the speed of light, are we?'

'Nup,' she agreed.

'What're you up to?'

'Schoolwork.'

'I thought the kids were out for the summer.'

'*My* schoolwork. On the manhunt.'

'I'm headed your way right now. Want some help sharpening your pencils and cleaning the blackboard?'

'Bring an apple for the teacher, and you're on.'

# Chapter
# TWENTY

'Hi, Michael,' Wes said, slapping a high five.

'Hey there.'

They talked about the boy's tennis camp – O'Neil played too – and about restringing rackets. Her lean, muscular son was skillful at most sports he tried, though he was now concentrating on tennis and soccer. He wanted to try karate or aikido, but Dance deflected him from martial arts. Sometimes the boy boiled over with anger – its source his father's death – and she didn't like encouraging fighting as a sport.

O'Neil had undertaken a mission to keep the boy's mind occupied with healthy diversions. He'd introduced him to two activities that were polar opposites: collecting books and spending time on O'Neil's favorite spot on earth: Monterey Bay. (Dance sometimes thought the detective had been born in the wrong era and could easily picture him as the captain of an old-time sailing ship, or a fishing vessel in the 1930s.) Sometimes, while Dance had a mother–daughter outing with Maggie, Wes would spend the afternoon on O'Neil's boat fishing or whale watching. Dance was violently seasick unless she popped Dramamine, but Wes had been born with sea legs.

They talked now about a fishing trip in a few weeks, then Wes said good night and wandered off to his room.

Dance poured some wine. O'Neil was a red-wine drinker and preferred cabernet. She had a pinot grigio. They walked into the living room, sat on the couch. O'Neil happened to be on the cushion that was directly beneath Dance's wedding picture. The detective and Bill Swenson had been good friends and had worked together a number of times. There had been a brief window before his death during which Dance, her husband and O'Neil were all active law enforcers; they'd even worked on a case together. Bill, federal. Dance, state. O'Neil, county.

With a loud snap, the detective opened the plastic box of take-out sushi he'd brought. The crackle was a modern-day Pavlovian bell, and the two dogs leapt up and bounded toward him: Dylan, the German shepherd, named for the singer-songwriter, of course, and Patsy, the flat-coated retriever, dubbed in honor of Ms Cline, Dance's favorite C&W singer.

'Can I give them . . . ?' He held up a piece of maguro tuna with the chopsticks.

'Not unless you want to brush their teeth.'

'Sorry, guys,' O'Neil said to the dogs.

She too declined an offer for sushi and he started to eat, not bothering to open the soy sauce or wasabi. He looked very tired. Maybe it was just too much trouble to wrestle with the packets.

'One thing I wanted to ask,' Dance said. 'Is the sheriff okay with CBI running the manhunt?'

O'Neil set down the chopsticks and ran his hand through his salt-and-pepper hair. 'Well, I'll tell you. When my father was in 'Nam his platoon sometimes had to take out Vietcong tunnels. Sometimes they'd find booby traps. Sometimes they'd find armed VC. It was the most dangerous job in the war. Dad developed this fear that stayed with him all his life.'

'Claustrophobia?'

'No. Volunteer-phobia. He cleared one tunnel, then never raised his hand again. Nobody can quite figure out why exactly you stepped forward on this one.'

She laughed. 'You're assuming I did.' She told him about Overby's gambit to seize control of the manhunt, ahead of CHP and O'Neil's own office.

'Wondered about that. Just for the record, we miss the Fish as much as you do.'

Stanley Fishburne, the former head of CBI.

'No, *not* as much as we do,' Dance said definitively.

'Okay, probably not. But in answer to your question, everybody's de-*lighted* you're on point here. God bless and more power to you.'

Dance moved aside piles of magazines and books, then spread Morton Nagle's material out in front of them. Maybe the sheets represented only a small percentage of the books, clippings and notes filling Nagle's study, but there was still a daunting quantity.

She found an inventory of the evidence and other items removed from Pell's house in Seaside after the Croyton murders. There were a dozen books about Charles Manson, several large files, and a note from the crime-scene officer:

*Item No. 23. Found in the box where the Manson books were kept: Trilby, novel by George du Maurier. Book had been read numerous times. Many notes in margins. Nothing relevant to case.*

'You ever heard of it?' she asked.

O'Neil read a huge amount and his large collection, filling his den, contained just about every genre of book that existed. But this was one he hadn't heard of.

Dance got her laptop, went online and looked it up. 'This is interesting. George du Maurier was Daphne du Maurier's grandfather.' She read several synopses and reviews of the book. 'Seems like *Trilby* was a huge bestseller, a *Da Vinci Code* of the time. Svengali?'

'Know the name – it means a mesmerizer. But nothing else.'

'Interesting. The story's about a failed musician, Svengali, who meets a young beautiful singer – her first name's Trilby. But she wasn't very successful. Svengali falls in love with her but she won't have anything to do with him. So he hypnotizes her. Her career's successful, but she becomes his mental slave. In the end, Svengali dies and – because du Maurier believed a robot can't survive without its master – she dies too.'

'Guess there was no sequel.' O'Neil flipped through a stack of notes. 'Nagle have any thoughts about what he's up to?'

'Not really. He's writing us a bio. Maybe there'll be something in it.'

For the next hour they sifted through the photocopies, looking for references to any place or person in the area that Pell might've had an interest in, some reason for him to stay on the Peninsula. Nor was there any reference to Alison or Nimue from the killer's Google search.

Nothing.

Most of the video tapes were feature TV magazine reports about Pell, the Croyton murders or about Croyton himself, the flamboyant, larger-than-life Silicon Valley entrepreneur.

'Sensationalist crap,' O'Neil announced.

'*Superficial* sensationalist crap.' Exactly what Morton Nagle objected to in the coverage of crime and war.

But there were two others, police interview tapes that Dance found more illuminating. One was for a burglary bust, thirteen years ago.

*'Who are your next of kin, Daniel?'*

*'I don't have any. No family.'*

*'Your parents?'*

*'Gone. Long gone. I'm an orphan, you could say.'*

*'When did they die?'*

*'When I was seventeen. But my dad'd left before that.'*

*'You and your father get along?'*

*'My father? That's a hard story.'*

Pell gave the officer an account of his abusive father, who had forced young Daniel to pay rent from the age of thirteen. He'd beat the boy if he didn't come up with the money – and beat the mother as well if she defended her son. This, he explained, was why he'd taken to stealing. Finally the father had abandoned them. Coincidentally his separated parents had died the same year – his mother of cancer, his father in a drunk-driving accident. At seventeen Pell was on his own.

*'And no siblings, hm?'*

*'No, sir . . . I always thought that if I had somebody to share that burden with, I would've turned out differently . . . And I don't have any children myself, either. That's a regret, I must say . . . But I'm a young man. I've got time, right?'*

*'Oh, if you get your act together, Daniel, there's no reason in the world you couldn't have a family of your own.'*

*'Thank you for saying that, Officer. I mean that. Thank you. And what about you, Officer? You a family man? I see you're wearing a wedding ring.'*

The second police tape was from a small town in the Central Valley twelve years ago, where he'd been arrested for petty larceny.

*'Daniel, listen here, I'm gonna be askin' you a few questions. Don't go and lie to us now, okay? That'll go bad for you.'*

*'No, sir, Sheriff. I'm here to be honest. Tell God's truth.'*

*'You do that and you and me'll get along just fine. Now, how come was it you was found with Jake Peabody's TV set and VCR in the back of your car?'*

*'I bought 'em, Sheriff. I swear to you. On the street. This Mexican fellow?*

*We was talking, and he said he needed some money. Him and his wife had a sick kid, he told me.'*

'See what he's doing?' Dance asked.

O'Neil shook his head.

'The first interviewer's intelligent. He speaks well, uses proper grammar, syntax. Pell responded exactly the same way. The second officer? Not as well educated as the first, makes grammatical mistakes. Pell picks up on that and echoes him. "We was talking." Or "Him and his wife." It's a trick High Machiavellians use.' A nod at the set. 'Pell is in total control of both interrogations.'

'I don't know, I'd give him a B-minus for the sob stories,' O'Neil judged. 'Didn't buy any sympathy from me.'

'Let's see.' Dance found the disposition reports that Nagle had included with the copies of the tapes. 'Sorry, Professor. *They* gave him As. Reduced the first charge from burglary one to a receiving stolen, suspended. The second? He was released.'

'I stand corrected.'

They looked through the material for another half-hour. Nothing else was useful.

O'Neil looked at his watch. 'Got to go.' Wearily he rose and she walked him outside. He scratched the dogs' heads.

'Hope you can make it to Dad's party tomorrow.'

'Let's hope it'll all be over with by then.' He climbed into his Volvo and headed down the misty street.

Her phone croaked.

'Lo?'

'Hey, boss.'

She could hardly hear; loud music crashed in the background. 'Could you turn that down?'

'I'd have to ask the band. Anything new about Juan?'

'No change.'

'I'll go see him tomorrow . . . Listen —'

'I'm trying.'

'Ha. First, Pell's aunt? Her name's Barbara Pell. But she's brain-fried. Bakersfield P.D. say she's got Alzheimer's or something. Doesn't know the time of day but there's a work shed or garage behind the house with some tools in it and some other things of Pell's. Anybody could've just strolled in and walked out with the hammer. Neighbors didn't see anything. Surprise, surprise, surprise.'

'Was that Andy Griffith?'

'Same show. Gomer Pyle.'

'Bakersfield's going to keep an eye on the woman's house?'

'That's affirmative . . . Now, boss, I got the skinny for you. On Winston.'

'Who?'

'Winston Kellogg, the FBI guy. The one Overby's bringing in to babysit you.'

*Babysit . . .*

'Could you pick a different word?'

'To oversee you. To ride herd. Subjugate.'

'TJ.'

'Okay, here's the scoop. He's forty-four. Lives in Washington now but comes from the West Coast. Former military, army.'

Just like my late husband, she thought. The military part, as well as the age.

'Detective with Seattle PD, then joined the bureau. He's with a division that investigates cults and related crimes. They track down the leaders, handle hostage negotiations and hook up cult members with deprogrammers. It was formed after Waco.'

That was the standoff in Texas between law officers and the cult run by David Koresh. The assault to rescue the members had ended tragically. The compound burned and most of the people inside died, including a number of children.

'He's got a good rep in the bureau. He's a bit of a straight arrow but he's not afraid to get his hands dirty. That's a direct quote from my buddy and I have no clue what it means. Oh, one other thing, boss. The Nimue search. No VICAP or other law enforcement reports. And I've only checked out a few hundred screen names online. Half of them're expired and the ones that are still active seem to belong to sixteen-year-old geeks. The real surnames are mostly European and I can't find anyone who's got a connection out here. But I did find a variation that's interesting.'

'Really? What?'

'It's an online role-playing game. You know those?'

'For a computer, right? One of those big boxes with wires in it?'

'Touché, boss. It's set in the Middle Ages and what you do is kill trolls and dragons and rescue damsels. Kind of what we do for a living, when you think about it. Anyway, the reason it didn't show up at first is that it's spelled differently N-i-X-m-u-e. The logo is the word "Nimue" with a big red X in the middle. It's one of the hottest games online nowadays. Hundreds of millions in sales. Ah, whatever happened to Ms-Pac-Man, my personal favorite?'

'I don't think Pell's the sort who's into computer games.'

'But he is definitely the sort who *killed* a man who wrote software.'

'Good point. Look into that. But I'm still leaning toward the idea it's somebody's name or screen name.'

'Don't worry, boss. I can check 'em both out, thanks to all the leisure time you give me.'

'Enjoying the band?'

'Double touché.'

Dance let Dylan and Patsy out for their bedtime business, then made a fast search of the property. No unrecognized cars were parked nearby. She got the animals back inside. Normally they'd sleep in the kitchen but tonight she let them have the run of the house; they made a huge racket when strangers came around. She also armed the window and door alarms.

Dance went into Maggie's room and listened to her play a brief Mozart piece on the keyboard. Then kissed her good night and shut the light out.

She sat for a few minutes with Wes while he told her about a new kid at the camp who'd moved to town with his parents a few months ago. They'd enjoyed playing some practice matches today.

'You want to ask him and his folks over tomorrow? To Grandpa's birthday?'

'Naw. I don't think so.'

After his father's death Wes had also become shier and more reclusive.

'You sure?'

'Maybe later. I don't know . . . Mom?'

'Yes, dearest son.'

An exasperated sigh.

'Yes?'

'How come you've still got your gun?'

Children . . . nothing whatsoever gets by them.

'Forgot all about it. It's going in the safe right now.'

'Can I read for a while?'

'Sure. Ten minutes. What's the book?'

'*Lord of the Rings.*' He opened, then closed it. 'Mom?'

'Yes?'

But nothing more was forthcoming. Dance thought she knew what was on his mind. She'd talk if he wanted to. But she hoped he didn't; it'd been a really long day.

Then he said, 'Nothing,' in a tone she understood to mean: There *is* something but I don't want to talk about it yet. He returned to Middle Earth.

She asked, 'Where are the hobbits?' A nod at the book.

'In the Shire. The horsemen are looking for them.'

'Fifteen minutes.'

''Night, Mom.'

Dance slipped the Glock into the safe. She reset the lock to a simple three-digit code, which she could open in the dark. She tried it now, with her eyes closed. It took no more than two seconds.

She showered, donned sweats and slipped under the thick comforter, the sorrows of the day wafting around her like the scent of lavender from the potpourri dish nearby.

Where are you? she thought to Daniel Pell. Who's your partner?

What are you doing at this moment? Sleeping? Driving through neighborhoods, looking for someone or something? Are you planning to kill again?

How can I figure out what you have in mind, staying close?

Drifting off to sleep, she heard in her mind lines from the tape she and Michael O'Neil had just listened to.

'And I don't have any children myself, either. That's a regret, I must say ... But I'm a young man. I've got time, right?'

'Oh, if you get your act together, Daniel, there's no reason in the world you couldn't have a family of your own.'

Dance's eyes opened. She lay in bed for a few minutes, staring at a configuration of shadows on the ceiling. Then, pulling on slippers, she made her way into the living room. 'Go back to sleep,' she said to the two dogs, who nonetheless continued to watch her attentively for the next hour or so as she prowled once again through the box that Morton Nagle had prepared for her.

# Chapter
# TWENTY-ONE

Kathryn Dance, TJ beside her, was in Charles Overby's corner office, early-morning rain pelting the windows. Tourists thought the climate in Monterey Bay tended toward frequent overcasts threatening showers. In fact, the area was usually desperate for rain, the gray overhead nothing more than standard-issue West Coast fog. Today, however, the precipitation was the real thing.

'I need something, Charles.'

'What's that?'

'An okay for some expenses.'

'For what?'

'We're not making any headway. There're no leads from Capitola, the forensics aren't giving us any answers, no sightings of him. And most important I don't know why he's staying in the area.'

'What do you mean, expenses?' Charles Overby was a man of focus.

'I want the three women who were in the Family.'

'Arrest them? I thought they were in the clear.'

'No, I want to interview them. They lived with him; they've got to know him pretty well.'

*Oh, if you get your act together, Daniel, there's no reason in the world you couldn't have a family of your own . . .*

It was this line from the police interview tape that had inspired the idea.

*A to B to X . . .*

'We want to hold a Family reunion,' said cheerful TJ. She knew he'd been partying late but his round face, under the curly red hair, was as fresh as if he'd walked out of a spa.

Overby ignored him. 'But why would they want to help us? They'd be sympathetic to him, wouldn't they?'

'No. I've talked to two of them, and they have no sympathy for Pell. The third changed her identity to put that whole life behind her. That's not sympathetic either.'

'Why bring them here? Why not interview them where they live?'

'I want them together. It's a gestalt interviewing approach. Their memories would trigger one another's. I was up till two reading about them. Rebecca wasn't with the Family very long – just a few months – but Linda lived with Pell for over a year, and Samantha for two.'

'Have you already talked to them?' The question was coy, as if he suspected her of pulling an end run.

'No,' Dance said. 'I wanted to ask you first.'

He seemed satisfied that he wasn't being outmaneuvered. Still, he shook his head. 'Airfare, guards, transportation . . . Red tape. I really doubt I could get it through Sacramento. It's too out of the box.' He noticed a frayed thread on his cuff and plucked it out. 'I'm afraid I have to say no. Utah. I'm sure that's where he's headed now. After the scare at Moss Landing. It'd be crazy for him to stay around. Is the USP surveillance team up and running?'

'Yep,' TJ told him.

'Utah'd be good. Real good.'

Meaning, Dance understood: *They* nail him and CBI gets the credit, with no more loss of life in California. USP misses him, it's *their* flub.

'Charles, I'm sure Utah's a false lead. He's not going to point us there and –'

'Unless,' her boss said triumphantly, 'it's a double twist. Think about it.'

'I did, and it's not Pell's profile. I really want to go forward with my idea.'

'I'm not sure . . .'

A voice from behind her. 'Can I ask what that idea is?'

Dance turned to see a man in a dark suit, powder blue shirt and striped blue-and-black tie. Not classically handsome – he had a bit of a belly, prominent ears and, if he were to look down, a double chin would blossom. But he had unwavering, amused brown eyes and a flop of hair, identical brown, that hung over his forehead. His posture and appearance hinted at an easy-going nature. He had a faint smile on narrow lips.

Overby asked, 'Can I help you?'

Stepping closer, the man offered an FBI identification card. Special Agent Winston Kellogg.

'The babysitter is in the building,' TJ said, *sotto voce*, his hand over his mouth. She ignored him.

'Charles Overby. Thanks for coming, Agent Kellogg.'

'Please, call me Win. I'm with the bureau's MVCC.'

'That's –'

'Multiple Victims Coercive Crimes Division.'

'That's the new term for cults?' Dance asked.

'We used to call it Cult Unit actually. But that wasn't PCP.'

TJ frowned. 'Drugs?'

'Not a "politically correct phrase".'

She liked that and laughed. 'I'm Kathryn Dance.'

'TJ Scanlon.'

'Thomas Jefferson?'

TJ gave a cryptic smile. Even Dance didn't know his full name. It might even have been just TJ.

Addressing all of the CBI agents, Kellogg offered, 'I want to say something up front. Yeah, I'm the Fed. But I don't want to ruffle feathers. I'm here as a consultant – to give you whatever insights I can about how Pell thinks and acts . . . I'm happy to take the backseat.'

Even if he didn't mean it 100 percent, Dance gave him credit for the reassurance. It was unusual in the world of law enforcement egos to hear one of the Washington folk say something like this.

'Appreciate that,' Overby said.

Kellogg turned to the CBI chief. 'Have to say that was a good call of yours yesterday, checking out the restaurants. I never would've thought of that one.'

Overby hesitated, then said, 'Actually, I think I told Amy Grabe that *Kathryn* here came up with that idea.'

TJ cleared his throat softly and Dance didn't dare look his way.

'Well, whoever, it was a good idea.' He turned to Dance. 'And what were you suggesting just now?'

Dance reiterated it.

The FBI agent nodded. 'Getting the Family back together. Good. Very good. They've gone through a process of deprogramming by now. Even if they haven't seen therapists, the passage of time alone would take care of any remnants of Stockholm syndrome. I really doubt they'd have any loyalty to him. I think we should pursue it.'

There was silence for a moment. Dance wasn't going to bail out Overby, who finally said, 'It *is* a good idea. Absolutely. The only problem is our budget. See, recently we –'

'We'll pay,' Kellogg said. Then he shut up and simply stared at Overby.

Dance wanted to laugh.

'You?'

'I'll get a bureau jet to fly them here, if we need one. Sound okay to you?'

Robbed of the only argument he could think of on such short notice, the CBI chief said, 'How can we refuse a Christmas present from Uncle Sam? Thanks, amigo.'

Dance, Kellogg and TJ were in Dance's office, when Michael O'Neil stepped inside. The men introduced each other and shook hands.

'No more hits on the forensics from Moss Landing,' he said, 'but we're hopeful about the Pastures of Heaven and vineyards. We've got health department people sampling products too. In case he's adulterated them with acid.' He explained to Kellogg about the trace found in the Thunderbird during Pell's escape.

'Any reason why he'd do that?'

'Diversion. Or maybe he just wants to hurt people.'

'Physical evidence isn't my expertise, but sounds like a good lead.' Dance noted that the FBI agent had been looking aside as O'Neil gave him the details, concentrating hard as he memorized them.

Then Kellogg said, 'It might be helpful to give you some insights into the cult mentality. At MVCC we've put together a general profile, and I'm sure some or all of it applies to Pell. I hope it'll help you formulate a strategy.'

'Good,' O'Neil said. 'I don't think we've ever seen anybody quite like this guy.'

Dance's initial skepticism about a cult expert's usefulness had faded now that it was clear Pell had an agenda they couldn't identify. She wasn't sure that the killer was, in fact, like any other perp she'd come across.

Kellogg leaned against her desk. 'First, like the name of my unit suggests, we consider the members of a cult "victims", which they certainly are. But we have to remember that they can be just as dangerous as the leader. Charles Manson wasn't even present at the Tate–LaBianca killings. It was the members who committed the murders.

'Now, in speaking of the leader, I'll tend to say "he", but women can be just as effective and as ruthless as men. And often they're more devious.

'So here's the basic profile. A cult leader isn't accountable to any authority except his own. He's always in charge one hundred percent. He dictates how the subjects spend every minute of their time. He'll assign work and keep them occupied, even if it's just busywork. They should never have any free time to think independently.

'A cult leader creates his own morality – which is defined solely as what's good for him and what will perpetuate the cult. External laws are irrelevant. He'll make the subjects believe it's morally right to do what he tells them – or what he suggests. Cult leaders are masters at getting their message across in very subtle ways, so that even if they're caught on a wiretap their comments won't incriminate them specifically. But the subjects understand the shorthand.

'He'll polarize issues and create conflicts based on them versus us, black and white. The cult is right and anyone who's not in the cult is wrong and wants to destroy them.

'He won't allow any dissent. He'll take extreme views, outrageous views, and wait for a subject to question him – to test loyalty. Subjects are expected to give everything to him – their time, their money.'

Dance told him about the ninety-two hundred dollars. 'Sounds like the woman is financing Pell's escape.'

Kellogg nodded. 'They're also expected to make their bodies available. And hand over their children sometimes.

'He'll exercise absolute control over the subjects. They have to give up their pasts. He'll give them new names, often something fanciful or reflective of how he sees them. He'll tend to pick vulnerable people and play on their insecurities. He looks for loners and makes them abandon their friends and family. They come to see him as a source of support and nurture. He'll threaten to withhold himself from them – that's probably his most powerful weapon.

'I could go on for hours but that gives you a rough idea of Daniel Pell's thought processes.' Kellogg lifted his hands. He seemed like a professor. 'What does all this mean for us? For one thing, it says something about his vulnerabilities. It's tiring to be a cult leader. You have to monitor your members constantly, look for dissension, eradicate it as soon as you find it. So when external influences exist – like out on the street, in public places – they're particularly wary. In their own environments, though, they're more relaxed. And therefore more careless and vulnerable.

'Look at what happened at that restaurant. He was constantly monitoring, because he was in public. If he'd been in his own house, you probably would've gotten him.

'The other implication is this: The accomplice, that woman, will believe Pell is morally right and that he's justified in killing. That means two things: We won't get any help from her, and she's as dangerous as he is. Yes, she's a victim, but that doesn't mean she won't kill you if she has a chance . . . Well, those are some general thoughts.'

Dance glanced at O'Neil. She knew he had the same reaction as hers: impressed with Kellogg's knowledge of his specialty. Maybe, for once, Charles Overby had made a good decision, even if his motive was to cover his ass.

Still, though, thinking of what he'd told them about Pell, she was dismayed at what they were up against. She had firsthand knowledge of the killer's intelligence, but if Kellogg's profile was even partially correct the man seemed a particularly dangerous threat.

Dance thanked Kellogg, and the meeting broke up – O'Neil headed for the hospital to check on Juan Millar, TJ to find a temporary office for the FBI agent.

Dance pulled out her mobile and found Linda Whitfield's phone number in the recent-calls log. She hit redial.

'Oh, Agent Dance. Have you heard anything new?'

'No, I'm afraid not.'

'We've been listening to the radio . . . I heard you almost caught him yesterday.'

'That's right.'

More muttering. Prayer again, Dance assumed. 'Ms Whitfield?'

'I'm here.'

'I'm going to ask you something and I'd like you to think about it before you answer.'

'Go on.'

'We'd like you to come here and help us.'

'*What?*' she whispered.

'Daniel Pell is a mystery to us. We're pretty sure he's staying on the Peninsula. But we can't figure out why. Nobody knows him better than you, Samantha and Rebecca. We're hoping you can help us figure it out.'

'Are they coming?'

'You're the first one I've called.'

A pause. 'But what could I possibly do?'

'I want to talk to you about him, see if you can think of anything that suggests what his plans might be, where he might be going.'

'But I haven't heard from him in seven or eight years.'

'There could be something he said or did back then that'll give us a clue. He's taking a big risk staying here. I'm sure he has a reason.'

'Well . . .'

Dance was familiar with how mental defense processes work. She could imagine the woman's brain frantically looking for – and rejecting or holding onto – reasons why she couldn't do what the agent asked. She wasn't surprised when she heard, 'The problem is I'm helping my brother and sister-in-law with their foster children. I can't just up and leave.'

Dance remembered that she lived with the couple. She asked if they could handle the children for a day or two. 'It won't be any longer than that.'

'I don't think they could, no.'

The verb 'think' has great significance to interrogators. It's a denial flag expression – like 'I don't remember' or 'probably not'. Its meaning: I'm hedging but not flatly saying no. The message to Dance was that the couple could easily handle the children.

'I know it's a lot to ask. But we need your help.'

After a pause the woman offered excuse two: 'And even if I could get away I don't have any money to travel.'

'We'll fly you in a private jet.'

'Private?'

'An FBI jet.'

'Oh, my.'

Dance dealt with excuse three before it was raised: 'And you'll be under very tight security. No one will know you're here, and you'll be guarded twenty-four hours a day. Please. Will you help us?'

More silence.

'I'll have to ask.'

'Your brother, your supervisor at work? I can give them a call and –'

'No, no, not them. I mean Jesus.'

Oh . . . 'Well, okay.' After a pause Dance asked, 'Could you check with Him pretty soon?'

'I'll call you back, Agent Dance.'

They hung up. Dance called Winston Kellogg and let him know they were awaiting divine intervention regarding Whitfield. He seemed amused. 'That's one long-distance call.'

Dance decided she definitely wouldn't let Charles Overby know whose permission was required. Was this whole thing such a great idea, after all?

She then called Women's Initiatives in San Diego. When Rebecca Sheffield answered, she said, 'Hi. It's Kathryn Dance again, in Monterey. I was –'

Rebecca interrupted. 'I've been watching the news for the past twenty-four hours. What happened? You almost had him and he got away?'

'I'm afraid so.'

Rebecca gave a harsh sigh. 'Well, are you catching on now?'

'Catching on?'

'The fire at the courthouse. The fire at the power plant. Twice, arson. See the pattern? He found something that worked. And he did it again.'

Exactly what Dance had thought. She didn't defend herself, though, but merely said, 'He's not quite like any escapee we've ever seen.'

'Well, yeah.'

'Ms Sheffield, there's something –'

'Hold on. First, there's one thing I want to say.'

'Go ahead,' Dance said uneasily.

'Forgive me, but you people don't have a clue what you're up against. You need to do what I tell people in my seminars. They're about empowerment in business. A lot of women think they can get together with their friends for drinks and dump on their idiotic bosses or their exes or their abusive boyfriends, and, presto, they're cured. Well, it doesn't work like that. You can't stumble around, you can't wing it.'

'Well, I appreciate –'

'First, you identify the problem. An example. You're not comfortable dating. Second, identify the *facts* that are the source of the problem. You were date-raped once. Three, structure a solution. You don't dive into dating and ignore your fears. You don't curl up in a ball and forget men. You make a plan: start out slowly, see men at lunchtime, meet them in public places, only go out with men who aren't physically imposing and who don't invade your personal space, who don't drink, et cetera. You get the picture. Then, slowly, you expand who you see. After three months or six or a year you've solved the problem. Structure a plan and stick to it. See what I'm saying?'

'I do, yes.'

Dance thought two things: First, the woman's seminars probably drew sell-out crowds. Second, she wouldn't want to hang out with Rebecca Sheffield socially. She wondered if the woman was finished.

She wasn't.

'Okay, now I have a seminar today I can't cancel. But if you haven't caught him by tomorrow morning I want to come up there. Maybe there are some things I can remember from eight years ago that'll help. Or is that against some policy or something?'

'No, not at all. It's a good idea.'

'All right. Look, I have to go. What were you going to ask me?'

'Nothing important. Let's hope everything works out before then, but if not I'll call and make arrangements to get you here.'

'Sounds like a plan,' the woman said briskly and hung up.

# Chapter
# TWENTY-TWO

In the Sea View Motel, Daniel Pell looked up from Jennie's computer, where he'd been online, and saw the woman easing toward him seductively.

Jennie offered a purr and whispered, 'Come on back to bed, baby. Fuck me.'

Pell switched screens so she wouldn't see what he was searching for and slipped his arm around her narrow waist.

Men and women exercise power over each other every day. Men have a harder time at first. They have to work their way inside a woman's defenses, build subtle connections, find her likes and dislikes and fears, all of which she tries to keep hidden. It could take weeks or months to get the leash on. But once you had her, you were in charge for as long as you wanted.

*Oh, we're like, you know, soul mates . . .*

A woman, on the other hand, had tits and a pussy and all she had to do was get them close to a man – sometimes not even that – and she could get him to do virtually anything. The woman's problem came later. When the sex was over, her control dropped off the radar screen.

Jennie Marston had been in charge a few times since the escape, no question about it: in the front seat of the T-bird, then in bed with her trussed up tight with the stockings, and another – more leisurely and much better – on the floor with some accessories that greatly appealed to Daniel Pell. (Jennie, of course, didn't care for that particular brand of sex but her reluctant acquiescence was a lot more exciting than if she'd really been turned on.)

The spell she'd woven was now subdued, though. But a teacher never lets his student know he's not attentive. Pell grinned and looked at her body as if he were sorely tempted. He sighed. 'I wish I could, lovely. But you tired me out. Anyway, I need you to run an errand for me.'

'Me?'

'Yep. Now that they know I'm here, I need you to do it by yourself.' The news stories were now reporting that he was probably still in the vicinity. He had to be much more careful.

'Oh, all right. But I'd rather fuck you.' A little pout. She was probably one of those women who thought the expression worked with men. It didn't, and he'd teach her so at some point. But there were more important lessons to be learned at the moment.

He said, 'Now, go cut your hair.'

'My hair.'

'Yeah. And dye it. The people at the restaurant saw you. I bought some brown dye for you. At the Mexican store.' He pulled a box out of the bag.

'Oh. I thought that was for you.'

She smiled awkwardly, gripping a dozen strands, fingers twining them.

Daniel Pell had no agenda with the haircut other than making it more difficult to recognize her. He understood, though, that there was something more, another issue. Jennie's hair was like the precious pink blouse, and he was instantly intrigued. He remembered her sitting in the T-bird when he'd first seen her in the Whole Foods parking lot, proudly brushing away.

*Ah, the information we give away . . .*

She didn't want to cut it. In fact, she *really* didn't want to. Long hair meant something to her. He supposed she'd let it grow at some point as protection from her vicious self-image. Some emblem of pathetic triumph over her flat chest and bumpy nose.

Jennie remained on the bed. After a moment she said, 'Sweetheart, I mean, I'll cut it, sure. Whatever you want.' Another pause. 'Of course, I was thinking: Wouldn't it be better if we left now? After what happened at the restaurant? I couldn't stand it if anything happened to you . . . Let's just get another car and go to Anaheim! We'll have a nice life. I promise, baby! I'll make you happy. I'll support us. You can stay home until they forget about you.'

'That sounds wonderful, lovely. But we can't leave yet.'

'Oh.'

She wanted an explanation. Pell said only, 'Now go cut it.' He added in a whisper, 'Cut it short. Real short.'

He handed her scissors. Her hands trembled as she took them.

'Okay.' Jennie walked into the small bathroom, clicked on all the lights. From her training at the Hair Cuttery, where she used to work, or because she was stalling, she spent some moments pinning up the strands before cutting them. She stared into the mirror, fondling the scissors uneasily. She closed the door partway.

Pell moved to a spot on the bed where he could see her clearly. Despite his protests earlier, he found his face growing flushed, and the bubble starting to build inside him.

Go ahead, lovely, do it!

Tears streaking down her cheeks, she lifted a clump of hair and began to cut. Breathing deeply, then cutting. She wiped her face, then cut again.

Pell was leaning forward, staring.

He tugged his pants down, then his underwear. He gripped himself, hard. Every time a handful of blonde hair cascaded to the floor, he stroked.

Jennie wasn't proceeding very quickly. She was trying to get it right. And she had to pause often to catch her breath from the crying and wipe the tears.

Pell was wholly focused on her.

His breathing came faster and faster. Cut it, lovely. Cut it!

Once or twice he came close to finishing but he managed to slow down just in time.

He was, after all, the king of control.

Monterey Bay Hospital is a beautiful place, located off a winding stretch of Highway 68 – a multiple-personality route that piggybacks on express-ways and commercial roads and even village streets, from Pacific Grove through Monterey and on to Salinas. Sixty-eight is the jugular vein of John Steinbeck country.

Kathryn Dance knew the hospital well. She'd delivered her son and daughter here. She'd held her father's hand after the bypass surgery in the cardiac ward and she'd sat beside a fellow CBI agent as he strug-gled to survive three gunshot wounds in the chest.

She'd identified her husband's body in the MBH morgue.

The facility was in the piney hills approaching Pacific Grove. The low, rambling buildings were landscaped with gardens and a forest surrounded the grounds; patients might awaken from surgery to find, outside their windows, hummingbirds hovering or deer gazing at them in wary, narrow-eyed curiosity.

The portion of the Critical Care Unit where Juan Millar was presently being tended, however, had no view. Nor was there any patient-pleasing décor, just matter-of-fact posters of phone numbers and procedures incomprehensible to lay people, and stacks of functional medical equipment. He was in a small glass-walled room, sealed off to minimize the risk of infection.

Dance now joined Michael O'Neil outside the room. Her shoulder brushed his. She felt an urge to take his arm. Didn't.

She stared at the injured detective, recalling his shy smile in Sandy Sandoval's office.

*Crime Scene boys love their toys . . . I heard that somewhere.*

'He say anything since you've been here?' she asked.

'No. Been out the whole time.'

Looking at the injuries, the bandages, Dance decided out was better. Much better.

They returned to the CCU waiting area, where some of Millar's family sat – his parents and an aunt and two uncles, if she'd gotten the introductions right. She doled out her heartfelt sympathy to the grim-faced family.

'Katie.'

Dance turned to see a solid woman with short gray hair and large glasses. She wore a colorful overblouse, from which dangled one badge identifying her as E. Dance, RN, and another indicating that she was attached to the cardiac care unit.

'Hey, Mom.'

O'Neil and Edie Dance smiled at each other.

'No change?' Dance asked.

'Not really.'

'Has he said anything?'

'Nothing intelligible. Did you see our burn specialist, Dr Olson?'

'No,' her daughter replied. 'Just got here. What's the word?'

'He's been awake a few more times. He moved a little, which surprised us. But he's on a morphine drip, so doped up he didn't make any sense when the nurse asked him some questions.' Her eyes strayed to the patient in the glass-enclosed room. 'I haven't seen an official prognosis, but there's hardly any skin under those bandages. I've never seen a burn case like that.'

'It's that bad?'

'I'm afraid so. What's the situation with Pell?'

'Not many leads. He's in the area. We don't know why.'

You still want to have Stu's party tonight?' Edie asked.

'Sure. The kids're looking forward to it. I might have to do a hit-and-run, depending. But I still want to have it.'

'You'll be there, Michael?'

'Plan to. Depending.'

'I understand. Hope it works out, though.'

Edie Dance's pager beeped. She glanced at it. 'I've got to get to Cardiac. If I see Dr Olson I'll ask him to stop by and brief you.'

Her mother left. Dance glanced at O'Neil, who nodded. He showed a badge to the Critical Care nurse and she helped them both into gowns and masks. The two officers stepped inside. O'Neil stood while Dance pulled up a chair and scooted forward. 'Juan, it's Kathryn. Can you hear me? Michael's here too.'

'Hey, partner.'

'Juan?'

Though the right eye, the uncovered one, didn't open, it seemed to Dance that the lid fluttered slightly.

'Can you hear me?'

Another flutter.

O'Neil said in a low and comforting voice, 'Juan, I know you're hurting. We're going to make sure you have the best treatment in the country.'

Dance said, 'We want this guy. We want him bad. He's in the area. He's still here.'

The man's head moved.

'We need to know if you saw or heard anything that'll help us. We don't know what he's up to.'

Another gesture of the head. It was subtle but Dance saw the young man's swaddled chin move slightly. 'Did you see something? Nod if you saw or heard something.'

Now, no motion.

'Juan,' she began, 'did –'

'Hey!' a male voice shouted from the doorway. 'What the fuck do you think you're doing?'

Her first thought was that the man was a doctor and that her mother would be in trouble for letting Dance into the room unsupervised. But the speaker was a young, sturdy Latino in a business suit. Juan's brother.

'Julio,' O'Neil said.

The nurse ran up. 'No, no, please close the door! You can't be inside without a mask –'

He waved a stiff arm at her and continued speaking to Dance. 'He's in that condition and you're *questioning* him?'

'I'm Kathryn Dance with the CBI. Your brother might know something helpful about the man who caused this.'

'Well, he's not going to be very fucking helpful if you kill him.'

'I'll call security if you don't close the door this minute,' the nurse snapped.

Julio held his ground. Dance and O'Neil stepped out of the room and into the hallway, closing the door behind them. They took off the gowns and masks.

In the corridor the brother got right into her face. 'I can't believe it. You have no respect –'

'Julio,' Millar's father said, stepping toward his son. His stocky wife, her jet-black hair disheveled, joined him.

Julio ignored everyone but Dance. 'That's all you care about, right? He tells you what you want to know and then he can die?'

She remained calm, recognizing a young man out of control. She didn't take his anger personally. 'We're very anxious to catch the man who did this to him.'

'Son, please! You're embarrassing us.' His mother touched his arm.

'Embarrassing you?' he mocked. Then turned to Dance again. 'I asked around. I talked to some people. Oh, I know what happened. You sent him down into the fire.'

'I'm sorry?'

'You sent him downstairs at the courthouse to the fire.'

She felt O'Neil stiffening but he restrained himself. He knew Dance wouldn't let other people fight her battles. She leaned closer to Julio. 'You're upset, we're all upset. Why don't we –'

'You picked *him*. Not Mikey here. Not one of your CBI people. The one Chicano cop – and you sent him.'

'Julio,' his father said sternly. 'Don't say that.'

'You want to know something about my brother? Hm? Do you know he wanted to get into CBI? But they didn't let him in. Because of who he was.'

This was absurd. There was a high percentage of Latinos in all California law-enforcement agencies, including the CBI. Her best friend in the bureau, Major Crimes Agent Connie Ramirez, had more decorations than any agent in the history of the west central office.

But his anger wasn't about ethnic representation in state government, of course. It was about fear for his brother's life. Dance had a lot of experience with anger; like denial and depression, it was one of the stress response states exhibited by deceitful subjects. When somebody's throwing a tantrum, the best approach is simply to let him tire himself out. Intense rage can be sustained only for a short period.

'He wasn't good enough to get a job with you, but he was good enough to send to get burned up.'

'Julio, please,' his mother implored.

'Don't *do* that, Mama! You let them get away with shit every time you say things like that.'

Tears slipped down the woman's powdered cheeks, leaving fleshy trails.

The young man turned back to Dance, 'It was Latino Boy you sent, it was the *chulo.*'

'That's enough,' his father barked, taking his son's arm.

The young man pulled away. 'I'm calling the papers. I'm going to call KHSP. They'll get a reporter here and they'll find out what you did. It'll be on all the news.'

'Julio –' O'Neil began.

'No, you be quiet, you Judas. You two worked together. And you let her sacrifice him.' He pulled out his mobile phone. 'I'm calling them. Now. You're going to be so fucked.'

Dance said, 'Can I talk to you for a moment, just us?'

'Oh, now you're scared.'

The agent stepped aside.

Ready for battle, Julio faced her, holding the phone like a knife, and leaned into Dance's personal proxemic zone.

Fine with her. She didn't move an inch, looked into his eyes. 'I'm very sorry for your brother, and I know how upsetting this is to you. But I won't be threatened.'

The man gave a bitter laugh. 'You're just like –'

'Listen to me,' she said calmly. 'We don't know for sure what happened but we *do* know that a prisoner disarmed your brother. He had the suspect at gunpoint, then he lost control of his weapon and of the situation.'

'You're saying it was his fault?' Julio asked, eyes wide.

'Yes. That's exactly what I'm saying. Not my fault, not Michael's fault.

Your brother's. It didn't make him a bad cop. But he *was* at fault. And if you turn this into a public issue, that fact is going to come out in the press.'

'You threatening me?'

'I'm telling you that I won't have this investigation jeopardized.'

'Oh, you don't know what you're doing, lady.' He turned and stormed down the corridor.

Dance watched him, trying to calm down. She breathed deeply. Then joined the others.

'I'm so sorry about that,' Mr Millar said, his arm around his wife's shoulders.

'He's upset,' Dance said.

'Please, don't listen to him. He says things first and regrets them later.'

Dance didn't think that the young man would be regretting a single word. But she also knew he wasn't going to be calling reporters anytime soon.

The mother said to O'Neil, 'And Juan's always saying such nice things about you. He doesn't blame you or anybody. I know he doesn't.'

'Julio loves his brother,' O'Neil reassured them. 'He's just concerned about him.'

Dr Olson arrived. The slightly built, calm man, briefed the officers and the Millars. The news was pretty much the same. They were still trying to stabilize the patient. As soon as the dangers from shock and sepsis were under control he'd be sent to a major burn and rehab center. It was very serious, the doctor admitted. He couldn't say one way or the other if he'd survive but they were doing everything they could.

'Has he said anything about the attack?' O'Neil asked.

The doctor looked over the monitor with still eyes. 'He's said a few words but nothing coherent.'

The parents continued their effusive apologies for their younger son's behavior. Dance spent a few minutes reassuring them, then she and O'Neil said good-bye and headed outside.

The detective was jiggling his car keys.

A kinesics expert knows that it's impossible to keep strong feelings hidden. Charles Darwin wrote, 'Repressed emotion almost always comes to the surface in some form of body motion.' Usually it's revealed as hand or finger gestures or tapping feet – we may easily control our words, glances and facial expressions but we exercise far less conscious mastery over our extremities.

Michael O'Neil was wholly unaware that he was playing with his keys.

She said, 'He's got the best doctors in the area here. And Mom'll keep an eye on him. You know her. She'll manhandle the chief of the department into his room if she thinks he needs special attention.'

A stoic smile. Michael O'Neil was good at that.

'They can do pretty miraculous things,' she said. Not having any idea what doctors could or couldn't do. She and O'Neil had had a number of occasions on which to reassure each other over the past few years, mostly professionally, sometimes personally, like her husband's death or O'Neil's father's deteriorating mental state. Neither of them did a very good job expressing sympathy or comfort; platitudes seemed to diminish the relationship. Usually the other's simple presence worked much better.

'Let's hope.'

As they approached the exit she took a call from FBI agent Winston Kellogg, in his temporary quarters at CBI. Dance paused and O'Neil continued on into the lot.

She told Kellogg about Millar. And she learned from him that a canvass by the FBI in Bakersfield had located no witnesses who'd seen anybody break into Pell's aunt's tool shed or garage to steal the hammer. As for the wallet bearing the initials *R.H.*, found in the well with the hammer, the federal forensic experts were unable to trace it to a recent buyer.

'And, Kathryn, I've got the jet tanked up in Oakland, if Linda Whitfield gets the okay from on high. One other thing? That third woman?'

'Samantha McCoy?'

'Right. Have you called her?'

At that moment Dance happened to look across the parking lot. She saw Michael O'Neil pausing as a tall, attractive blonde approached him. The woman smiled at O'Neil, slipped her arms around him and kissed him. He kissed her back.

'Kathryn,' Kellogg asked, 'you there?'

'What?'

'Samantha McCoy?'

'Sorry.' Dance looked away from O'Neil and the blonde. 'No. I'm driving up to San Jose now. If she's gone to this much trouble to keep her identity quiet I want to see her in person. I think it'll take more than a phone call to convince her to help us out.'

She disconnected and walked up to O'Neil and the woman he was embracing.

'Kathryn.'

'Anne, how are you?' Dance asked Michael O'Neil's wife.

'Fine, thanks.'

'The kids?'

'Last day of school was Friday, so they're in heaven. Maggie and Wes?'

'Already in their camps.'

Anne O'Neil nodded toward the hospital. 'I came to see Juan. Mike said he's not doing very well.'

'No. It's pretty bad. He's unconscious now. But his parents are there. They'd be glad for some company, I'm sure.'

Anne had a small Leica camera slung over her shoulder. Thanks to the landscape photographer Ansel Adams and the f64 Club, Northern and Central California made up one of the great photography meccas in the world. Anne ran a gallery in Carmel that sold collectible photographs, 'collectible' generally defined as those taken by photographers no longer among the living: Adams, Alfred Stieglitz, Edward Weston, Imogen Cunningham, Henri Cartier-Bresson. Anne was also a stringer for several newspapers, including big dailies in San Jose and San Francisco.

Dance said, 'Michael told you about the party tonight? My father's birthday.'

'He did. I think we can make it.' Anne kissed her husband again and headed into the hospital. 'See you later, honey.'

"Bye, dear.'

Dance nodded good-bye and climbed into her car, tossing the Coach purse onto the passenger seat. She stopped at Shell for gas, coffee and a cake donut and headed onto Highway 1 north, getting a beautiful view of Monterey Bay. She noted that she was driving past the campus of Cal State at Monterey Bay, on the site of the former Fort Ord (probably the only college in the country overlooking a restricted area filled with unexploded ordnance). A large banner announced what seemed to be a major computer conference this weekend. The school, she recalled, was the recipient of much of the hardware and software in William Croyton's estate. She reflected that if computer experts were still doing research based on the man's contributions from eight years ago, he must've been a true genius. The programs that Wes and Maggie used seemed to be outdated in a year or two tops. How many brilliant innovations had Daniel Pell denied the world by killing William Croyton?

Dance flipped through her notebook and found the number of Samantha McCoy's employer, called and asked to be connected, ready to hang up if she answered. But the receptionist said she was working at home that day. Dance disconnected and had TJ text-message her Mapquest directions to the woman's house.

A few minutes later the phone rang, just as she hit play on the CD. She glanced at the screen. Coincidentally the Fairfield Four resumed their gospel singing as Dance said hello to Linda Whitfield, who was calling from her church office.

*'Amazing grace, how sweet the sound . . .'*

'Agent Dance –'

'Call me Kathryn. Please.'

*'. . . that saved a wretch like me . . .'*

'I just wanted you to know. I'll be there in the morning to help you, if you still want me.'

'Yes, I'd love for you to come. Somebody from my office will call about the arrangements. Thank you so much.'

*'. . . I once was lost, but now I am found . . .'*

A hesitation. Then she said in a formal voice, 'You're welcome.'

Two out of three. Dance wondered if the reunion might work after all.

# Chapter
# TWENTY-THREE

Sitting in front of the open window of the Sea View Motel, Daniel Pell typed awkwardly on the computer keyboard. He'd managed some access to computers at the Q and at Capitola, but he hadn't had time to sit down and really get to know how they worked. He'd been pounding away on Jennie's portable all morning. Ads, news, porn . . . it was astonishing.

But even more seductive than the sex was his ability to get information, to find things about people. Pell had ignored the smut and been hard at work. First he'd read everything he could about Jennie – recipes (a ton of them), emails, her bookmarked pages, making sure she was essentially who she claimed to be (she was). Then he searched for some people from his past – important to find them – but he didn't have much luck. He then tried tax records, deeds offices, vital statistics. But you needed a credit card for almost everything, he learned. And credit cards, like cell phones, left obvious trails.

Then he had a brainstorm and searched through the archives of the local newspapers and TV stations. That proved much more helpful. He jotted information, a lot of it.

Among the names on his list was 'Kathryn Dance'.

He enjoyed doodling a funereal frame around it.

The search didn't give him all the information he needed, but it was a start.

Always aware of his surroundings, he noticed a black Toyota Camry pull into the lot and pause outside the window. He gripped the gun. Then he smiled as the car parked exactly seven spaces away.

She climbed out.

That's my girl.

*Holding fast . . .*

She walked inside.

'You did it, lovely.' Pell glanced at the Camry. 'Looks nice.'

She kissed him fast. Her hands were shaking. And she couldn't control her excitement. 'It went great! It really did, sweetie. At first he was kind of freaked and I didn't think he was going to do it. He didn't like the thing about the license plates but I did everything you told me and he agreed.'

'Good for you, lovely.'

Jennie had used some of her cash – she'd withdrawn $9,200 to pay for the escape and tide them over for the time being – to buy a car from a man who lived in Marina. It would be too risky to have it registered in her real name so she'd persuaded him to leave his own plates on it. She'd told him that her car had broken down in Modesto and she'd have the plates in a day or two. She'd swap them and mail his back. This was illegal and really stupid. No man would ever do that for some other guy, even one paying cash. But Pell had sent Jennie to handle it – a woman in tight jeans, a half-buttoned blouse and red bra on fine display. (Had it been a woman selling the car, Pell would have dressed her down, lost the makeup, given her four kids, a dead soldier for a husband and a pink breast cancer ribbon. You can never be *too* obvious, he'd learned.)

'Nice. Oh, can I have the car keys?'

She handed them over. 'Here's what else you wanted.' Jennie set two shopping bags on the bed. Pell looked through them and nodded approvingly.

She got a soda from the minifridge. 'Honey, can I ask you something?'

His natural reluctance to answer questions – at least truthfully – surfaced again. But he smiled. 'You can, anything.'

'Last night, when you were sleeping you said something. You were talking about God.'

'God. What'd I say?'

'I couldn't tell. But it was definitely "God".'

Pell's head turned slowly toward her. He noticed his heart rate increase. He found his foot tapping, which he stopped.

'You were really freaking out. I was going to wake you up but that's not good. I read that somewhere. *Reader's Digest*. Or *Health*. I don't know. When somebody's having a bad dream, you should never wake them up. And you said, like, "Fuck no".'

'I said that?'

Jennie nodded. 'Which was weird. 'Cause you never swear.'

That was true. People who used obscenities had much less power than people who didn't.

'What was your dream about?' she asked.

'I don't remember.'

'Wonder why you were dreaming about God.'

For a moment he felt a curious urge to tell her about his father. Then: What the hell're you thinking of?

'No clue.'

'I'm *kinda* into religion,' she said uncertainly. 'A little. More spiritual stuff than Jesus, you know?'

'Well, about Jesus, I don't think he was the son of God or anything, but I'll tell you, I respect Him. He could get anybody to do whatever He wanted. I mean, even now, you just mention the name and, bang, people'll hop to in a big way. That's power. But all those religions, the organized ones, you give up too much to belong to them. You can't think the way you want to. They control you.'

Pell glanced at her blouse, the bra. The swelling began again, the high-pressure center growing in his belly.

He tried to ignore it and he looked back at the notes he'd taken from his online searches and the map. Jennie clearly wanted to ask what he had in mind but couldn't bring herself to. She'd be hoping he was looking for routes out of town, roads that would lead ultimately to Orange County.

'I've got a few things to take care of, baby. I'll need you to give me a ride.'

'Sure, just say when.'

He was studying the map carefully, and he looked up to see that she'd stepped away.

Jennie returned a moment later, carrying a few things, which she'd gotten from a bag in the closet. She set these on the bed in front of him, then knelt on the floor. It was like a dog bringing her master a ball, ready to play.

Pell hesitated. But then he reminded himself that it's okay to give up a little control from time to time, depending on the circumstances.

He reached for her but she lay down and rolled over on her belly all by herself.

\* \* \*

There are two routes to San Jose from Monterey. You can take Highway 1, which winds along the coast through Santa Cruz, then cut over on vertigo-inducing 17, through artsy Los Gatos, where you can buy crafts and crystals and incense and tie-dyed Janis Joplin dresses (and, okay, Roberto Cavalli and D&G).

Or you can just take the Highway 156 cut-off to the 101 and, if you've got government tags, burn however much gas you want to get up to the city in an hour.

Kathryn Dance chose the second.

Gospel was gone and she was listening to Latin music – the Mexican singer Julieta Venegas. Her soulful 'Verdad' was pounding from the speakers.

The Taurus was doing ninety as she zipped through Gilroy, the garlic capital of the world. Not far away was Castroville (ditto, artichokes) and Watsonville, with its sweeping pelt of berry fields and mushroom farms. She liked these towns and had no patience for the detractors who laughed at the idea of crowning an artichoke queen or standing in line for the petting tanks at Monterey's own Squid Festival. After all, these chicer-than-thou urbanites were the ones who paid obscene prices for imported olive oil and balsamic vinegar to whip up those very artichokes and cala-mari rings.

These burgs were homey and honest and filled with history. And they were also her turf, falling within the west central region of the CBI.

She saw a sign luring tourists to a vineyard in Morgan Hill, and had a thought.

Dance called Michael O'Neil.

'Hey,' he said.

'I was thinking about the acid they found in the Thunderbird at Moss Landing. Any word?'

'Peter's techs've been working on it but they still don't have any specific leads.'

'How many bodies we have searching the orchards and vineyards?'

'About fifteen CHP, five of our people, some Salinas uniforms. They haven't found anything.'

'I've got an idea. What is the acid exactly?'

'Hold on.'

Eyes slipping between the road and the pad of paper resting on her knee, she jotted the incomprehensible terms as he spelled them.

'So kinesics isn't enough? You have to master forensics too?'

'A wise woman knows her limitations. I'll call you in a bit.'

Dance then hit speed dial and listened to a phone ring two thousand miles away.

A click as it answered. 'Amelia Sachs.'

'Hi, it's Kathryn.'

'How're you doing?'

'Well, been better.'

'Can imagine. We've been following the case. How's that officer? The one who was burned?'

Dance was surprised that Lincoln Rhyme, the well-known forensic scientist in New York City, and Amelia Sachs, his partner and a detective with the NYPD, had been following the story of Pell's escape. 'Not too good, I'm afraid.'

'We were talking about Pell. Lincoln remembers the original case. In ninety-nine. When he killed that family. Are you making headway?'

'Not much. He's smart. Too smart.'

'That's what we're gathering from the news. How're the kids?'

'Fine. We're still waiting for that visit. My parents too. They want to meet you both.'

Sachs gave a laugh. 'I'll get him out there soon. It's a challenge.'

Lincoln Rhyme didn't like to travel. This wasn't owing to the problems associated with his disability (he was a quadriplegic). He simply didn't like to travel.

Dance had met Rhyme and Sachs last year when she'd been teaching a course in the New York area and had been tapped to help them on a case. They'd stayed in touch. She and Sachs in particular had grown close. Women in the tough business of policing tend to do that.

'Any word on our other friend?' Sachs asked.

This reference was to the perp they'd been after in New York last year. The man had eluded them and vanished, possibly to California. Dance had opened a CBI file but then the trail grew cold and it was possible that the perp was now out of the country.

'I'm afraid not. Our office in L.A.'s still following up on the leads. I'm calling about something else. Is Lincoln available?'

'Hold on a minute. He's right here.'

There was a click and Rhyme's voice popped into her phone. 'Kathryn.'

Rhyme was not the sort for chitchat, but he spent a few minutes conversing with her – nothing about her personal life or the children, of course. His interest was the cases she was working. Rhyme was a scientist, with very little patience for the 'people' side of policing, as he put it. Yet, on their recent case together, he'd grown to understand and value kinesics (though being quick to point out that it was based on scientific methodology and not, he said contemptuously, gut feeling).

He now said, 'Wish you were here. I've got a witness we'd love for you to grill on a multiple homicide case. You can use a rubber hose if you want.'

She could picture him in his red motorized wheelchair, staring at a large flat screen hooked up to a microscope or computer. He loved evidence the same way she loved interrogation.

'Wish I could. But I've got my hands full.'

'So I hear. Who's doing the lab work?'

'Peter Bennington.'

'Oh, sure. I know him. Cut his teeth in L.A. Took a seminar of mine. Good man.'

'Got a question about the Pell situation.'

'Sure. Go ahead.'

'We've got some evidence that might lead to what he's up to – maybe tainting food – or where he's hiding. But either one's taking a lot of manpower to check out. I have to know if it makes sense to keep them committed. We could really use them elsewhere.'

'What's the evidence?'

'I'll do the best I can with the pronunciation.' Eyes shifting between the road and her notebook. 'Carboxylic acid, ethanol and malic acid, amino acid and glucose.'

'Give me a minute.'

She heard his conversation with Amelia Sachs, who apparently went online into one of Rhyme's own databases. She could hear the words clearly; unlike most callers, the criminalist was unable to hold his hand over the phone when speaking to someone else in the room.

'Okay, hold on, I'm scrolling through some things now . . .'

'You can call me back,' Dance said. She hadn't expected an answer immediately.

'No . . . just hold on . . . Where was the substance found?'

'On the floor of Pell's car.'

'Hm. Car.' Silence for a moment. Then Rhyme was muttering to himself. Finally he asked, 'Any chance that Pell had just eaten in a restaurant? A seafood restaurant or a British pub?'

She laughed out loud. 'Seafood, yes. How on earth did you know?'

'The acid's vinegar – malt vinegar specifically, because the amino acids and glucose indicate caramel coloring. My database tells me it's common in British cooking, pub food and seafood. Thom? You remember him? He helped me with that entry.'

'Of course. Say hi for me.' Rhyme's caregiver was also quite a cook. Last December he'd served her a boeuf bourguignon that was the best she'd ever had.

'Sorry it doesn't lead to his front door,' the criminalist said.

'No, no, that's fine, Lincoln. I can pull the troops off the areas we had them searching. Send them to where they'll be better used.'

'Call anytime. That's one perp I wouldn't mind a piece of.'

They said good-bye.

Dance disconnected, called O'Neil and told them it was likely that the acid had come from Jack's restaurant and wouldn't lead them to Pell or his mission here. It was probably better for the officers to search for the killer.

She hung up and continued her drive north on the familiar highway, which would take her to San Francisco where the eight-lane Highway 101 eventually funneled into just another city street, Van Ness. Now, eighty miles north of Monterey, Dance turned west and made her way into the sprawl of San Jose, a city that stood as the antithesis of Los Angeles narcissism in the old Burt Bacharach/Hal David tune 'Do You Know the Way to San Jose?' Nowadays, of course, thanks to Silicon Valley, San Jose flexed an ego of its own.

Mapquest led her through a maze of large developments until she came to one filled with nearly identical houses; if the symmetrically planted trees had been saplings when they'd gone in, Dance estimated the neighborhood was about twenty-five years old. Modest, nondescript, small – still, each house would sell for well over a million dollars.

She found the house she sought and passed it by, parking across the street a block away. She walked back to the address, where a red Jeep and a dark blue Acura sat in the driveway and a big plastic tricycle rested on the lawn. Dance could see lights inside the house. She walked to the front porch. Rang the bell. Her cover story was prepared in case Samantha McCoy's husband or children answered the door. It seemed unlikely that the woman had kept her past a secret from her spouse, but it would be better to start out on the assumption that she had. Dance needed the woman's cooperation and didn't want to alienate her.

The door opened and she found herself looking at a slim woman with a narrow, pretty face, resembling the actress Cate Blanchett. She wore chic, blue-framed glasses and had curly brown hair. She stood in the doorway, head thrust forward, bony hand gripping the jamb.

'Yes?'

'Mrs Starkey?'

'That's right.' The face was very different from that in the pictures of Samantha McCoy eight years ago; she'd had extensive cosmetic surgery. But her eyes told Dance instantly that there was no doubt of her identity. Not their appearance, but the flash of horror, then dismay.

The agent said quietly, 'I'm Kathryn Dance. California Bureau of Investigation.' The woman's glance at the ID, discreetly held low, was so fast that she couldn't possibly have read a word on it.

From inside, a man's voice called, 'Who is it, honey?'

Samantha's eyes firmly fixed on Dance's, she replied, 'That woman from up the street. The one I met at Safeway I told you about.'

Which answered the question about how secret her past was. She also thought: Smooth. Good liars are always prepared with credible answers, and they know the person they're lying to. Samantha's response told Dance that her husband had a bad memory of casual conversation and that Samantha had thought out every likely situation in which she'd need to lie.

The woman stepped outside, closed the door behind her and they walked halfway to the street. Without the softening filter of the screen door, Dance could see how haggard the woman looked. Her eyes were red and the crescents beneath were dark, her facial skin dry, her lips cracked. A fingernail was torn. It seemed she'd gotten no sleep. Dance understood why she was 'working at home' today.

A glance back at the house. Then she turned to Dance and, with imploring eyes, whispered, 'I had *nothing* to do with it, I swear. I heard he had somebody helping him, a woman. I saw that on the news, but –'

'No, no, that's not what I'm here about. I checked you out. You work for that publisher on Figueroa. You were there all day yesterday.'

Alarm. 'Did you –'

'Nobody knows. I called about delivering a package.'

'That . . . Toni said somebody tried to deliver something, they were asking about me. That was you.' The woman rubbed her face, then crossed her arms. Gestures of negation. She was steeped in stress.

'That was your husband?' Dance asked.

She nodded.

'He doesn't know?'

'He doesn't even suspect.'

Amazing, Dance reflected. 'Does *anyone* know?'

'A few of the clerks at the courthouse where I changed my name. My parole officer.'

'What about friends and family?'

'My mother's dead. My father couldn't care less about me. They didn't have anything to do with me before I met Pell. After the Croyton murders, they stopped returning my phone calls. And my old friends? Some stayed in touch for a while but being associated with somebody like Daniel Pell? Let's just say they found excuses to disappear from my life as fast as they could. Everybody I know now I met after I became Sarah.' A glance back at the house, then she turned her uneasy eyes to Dance. 'What do you want?' A whisper.

'I'm sure you're watching the news. We haven't found Pell yet. But he's staying in the Monterey area. And we don't know why. Rebecca and Linda are coming to help us.'

'They are?' She seemed astonished.

'And I'd like you to come down there too.'

'*Me?*' Her jaw trembled. 'No, no, I couldn't. Oh, please . . .' Her voice started to break.

Dance could see the fringes of hysteria. She said quickly, 'Don't worry. I'm not going to ruin your life. I'm not going to say anything about you. I'm just asking for help. We can't figure him out. You might know some things —'

'I don't know anything. Really. Daniel Pell's not like a husband or brother or friend. He's a monster. He used us. That's all. I lived with him for two years and I still couldn't begin to tell you what was going on in his mind. You have to believe me. I swear.'

Classic denial flags, signaling not deception but the stress from a past she couldn't confront.

'You'll be completely protected, if that's what —'

'No. I'm sorry. I wish I could. You have to understand, I've created a new life for myself. But it's taken so much work, and it's so fragile.'

One look at the face, the horrified eyes, the quivering jaw, told Dance that there was no chance of her agreeing. 'I understand.'

'I'm sorry. I just can't do it.'

Samantha turned and walked to the house. At the door, she looked back and gave a big smile.

Has she changed her mind? Dance was momentarily hopeful.

Then the woman waved. "Bye!' she called. 'Good seeing you again.'

Samantha McCoy and her lie walked back into the house. The door closed.

# Chapter
# TWENTY-FOUR

'Did you hear about that?' Susan Pemberton asked César Gutierrez, sitting across from her in the hotel bar, as she poured sugar into her latte. She gestured toward a TV from which an anchorman was reading news above a local phone number.

**Escapee Hotline.**

'Wouldn't it be Escap*er*?' Gutierrez asked.

Susan blinked. 'I don't know.'

The businessman continued, 'I didn't mean to be light about it. It's terrible. He killed two people, I heard.' The handsome Latino sprinkled cinnamon into his cappuccino, then sipped, spilling a bit of spice on his slacks. 'Oh, look at that. I'm such a klutz.' He laughed. 'You can't take me anywhere.'

He wiped at the stain, which only made it worse. 'Oh, well.'

This was a business meeting – Susan, who worked for an event-planning company, was going to put together an anniversary party for his parents – but, being currently single, the thirty-nine-year-old woman automatically sized him up from a personal perspective, noting he was only a few years older than she and wore no wedding ring.

They'd disposed of the details of the party – cash bar, chicken and fish, open wine, fifteen minutes to exchange new vows and then dancing to a DJ.

And now they were chatting over coffee before she went back to the office to work up an estimate.

'You'd think they would've got him by now.' Then Gutierrez glanced outside, frowning.

'Something wrong?' Susan asked.

'It sounds funny, I know. But just as I was getting here I saw this car pull up. And somebody who looked a little like him, Pell, got out.' He nodded at the TV.

'Who? The killer?'

He nodded. 'And there was a woman driving.'

The TV announcer had just repeated that his accomplice was a young woman.

'Where did he go?'

'I wasn't paying attention. I think toward the parking garage, by the bank.'

She looked toward the place.

Then the businessman gave a smile. 'But that's crazy. He's not going to be here.' He nodded past where they were looking. 'What's that banner? I saw it before.'

'Oh, the concert on Friday. Part of a John Steinbeck celebration. You read him?'

The businessman said, 'Oh, sure. *East of Eden. The Long Valley.* You ever been to King City? I love it there. Steinbeck's grandfather had a ranch.'

She touched her palm reverently to her chest. '*Grapes of Wrath* . . . the best book ever written.'

'And there's a concert on Friday, you were saying? What kind of music?'

'Jazz. You know, because of the Monterey Jazz Festival. It's my favorite.'

'I love it too,' Gutierrez said. 'I go to the festival whenever I can.'

'Really?' Susan resisted an urge to touch his arm.

'Maybe we'll run into each other at the next one.'

Susan said, 'I worry . . . Well, I just wish more people would listen to music like that. Real music. I don't think kids are interested.'

'Here's to that.' Gutierrez tapped his cup to hers. 'My ex . . . she lets our son listen to rap. Some of those lyrics? Disgusting. And he's only twelve years old.'

'It's not music,' Susan announced. Thinking: So. He has an ex. Good. She'd vowed never to date anyone over forty who hadn't been married.

He hesitated and asked, 'You think you might be there? At the concert?'

'Yeah, I will.'

'Well, I don't know your situation, but if you were going to go, you want to hook up there?'

'Oh, César, that'd be fun.'

*Hooking up* . . .

Nowadays that was as good as a formal invitation.

Gutierrez stretched. He said he wanted to get on the road. Then he added he'd enjoyed meeting her and, without hesitating, gave her the holy trinity of phone numbers: work, home and mobile. He picked up his briefcase and they started for the door together. She noticed, though, that he was pausing, his eyes, through dark-framed glasses, examining the lobby. He frowned again, brushing uneasily at his moustache.

'Something wrong?'

'I think it's that guy,' he whispered. 'The one I saw before. There, you see him? He was here, in the hotel. Looking our way.'

The lobby was filled with tropical plants. She had a vague image of someone turning and walking out of the door.

'Daniel *Pell*?'

'It couldn't be. It's stupid . . . Just, you know, the power of suggestion or something.'

They walked to the door, stopped. Gutierrez looked out. 'He's gone.'

'Think we should tell somebody at the desk?'

'I'll give the police a call. I'm probably wrong but what can it hurt?' He pulled out his cell phone and dialed 911. He spoke for a few minutes, then disconnected. 'They said they'd send somebody to check it out. Didn't sound real enthusiastic. Of course, they're probably getting a hundred calls an hour. I can walk you to your car, if you want.'

'Wouldn't mind that.' She wasn't so much worried about the escapee; she just liked the idea of spending more time with Gutierrez.

They walked along the main street in downtown, Alvarado. Now it was the home of restaurants, tourist shops and coffeehouses – a lot different from the wild west avenue it was a hundred years ago, when soldiers and Cannery Row workers drank, hung out in the brothels and occasionally shot it out in the middle of the street.

As Gutierrez and Susan walked along, their conversation was subdued and they both looked around them. She realized the streets were unusually deserted. Was that because of the escape? She began to feel uneasy.

Her office was next to a construction site a block from Alvarado. There were piles of building materials here; if Pell had come this way, she reflected, he could easily be hiding behind them, waiting. She slowed.

'That's your car?' Gutierrez asked.

She nodded.

'Something wrong?'

Susan gave a grimace and an embarrassed laugh. She told him she was worried about Pell hiding in the building supplies.

He smiled. 'Even if he *was* here he wouldn't attack two of us together. Come on.'

'César, wait,' she said, reaching into her purse. She handed him a small, red cylinder. 'Here.'

'What's this?'

'Pepper spray. Just in case.'

'I think we'll be okay. But how does it work?' Then he laughed. 'Don't want to spray myself.'

'All you have to do is point it and push there. It's ready to go.'

They continued to the car and by the time they got there, Susan was feeling foolish. No crazed killers were lurking behind the piles of bricks. She wondered if her skittishness had lost her points in the potential date department. She didn't think so. Gutierrez seemed to enjoy the role of gallant gentleman.

She unlocked the doors.

'I better give this back to you,' he said, holding out the spray.

Susan reached for it.

But Gutierrez lunged fast, grabbed her hair and jerked her head back fiercely. He shoved the nozzle of the canister into her mouth, open in a stifled scream.

He pushed the button.

Agony, reflected Daniel Pell, is perhaps the fastest way to control somebody.

Still in his apparently effective disguise as a Latino businessman, he was driving Susan Pemberton's car to a deserted location near the ocean, south of Carmel.

Agony . . . Hurt them bad, give them a little time to recover, then threaten to hurt them again. Experts say torture isn't efficient. That's wrong. It isn't *elegant*. It isn't *tidy*. But it works real well.

The spray up Susan Pemberton's mouth and nose had been only a second in duration but from her muffled scream and thrashing limbs he knew the pain was nearly unbearable. He let her recover. Brandished the spray in front of her panicked, watering eyes. And immediately got from her exactly what he wanted.

He hadn't planned on the spray, of course; he had duct tape and a knife in the briefcase. But he'd decided to change his plans when the woman, to his amusement, handed the canister to him – well, to his alter ego César Gutierrez.

Daniel Pell had things to do in public and, with his picture running every half-hour on local television, he had to become someone else. After she'd wheedled the Toyota out of a gullible seller with an interest in a woman's cleavage, Jennie Marston had bought cloth dye and instant-tan cream, which he'd mixed into a recipe for a bath that would darken his skin. He dyed his hair and eyebrows black and used Skin–Bond and hair clippings to make a realistic moustache. Nothing he could do about the eyes. If there were contact lenses that made blue brown, he didn't know where to find them. But the glasses – cheap tinted reading glasses with dark frames – would distract from the colour.

Earlier in the day Pell had called the Brock Company and gotten Susan Pemberton, who'd agreed to meet about planning an anniversary party. He dressed in a cheap suit Jennie'd bought at Mervyns and met the events planner at the Doubletree where he got to work, doing what Daniel Pell did best.

Oh, it had been nice! Playing Susan like a fish was a luxurious high, even better than watching Jennie cut her hair or discard blouses or wince when he used the coat hanger on her narrow butt.

He now replayed the techniques: finding a common fear (the escaped killer) and common passions (John Steinbeck and jazz, which he knew little about, but he was a good bluffer); playing the sex game (her glance at his bare ring finger and stoic smile when he'd mentioned children told him all about Susan Pemberton's romantic life); doing something silly and laughing about it (the spilled cinnamon); arousing her sympathy (his bitch of an ex-wife ruining his son); being a decent person (the party for his beloved parents, his chivalry in walking her to the car); belying suspicion (the fake call to 911).

Little by little gaining trust – and therefore gaining control.

What a total high it was to practice his art once again in the real world.

Pell found the turn-off. It led through a dense grove of trees toward the ocean. Jennie had spent the Saturday before the escape doing some reconnaissance for him and had discovered this deserted place. He continued along the sand-swept road, passing a sign that declared the property private. He beached Susan's car in sand at the end of the road, well out of sight of the highway. Climbing out, he heard the surf crash over an old pier not far away. The sun was low and spectacular.

He didn't have to wait long. Jennie was early. He was happy to see that; people who arrive early are in your control. Always be wary of those who make you wait. She parked, climbed out and walked to him. 'Honey, I hope you didn't have to wait long.' She hungrily closed her mouth around his, gripping his face in both her hands. Desperate.

Pell came up for air.

She laughed. 'It's hard to get used to you like this. I mean, I knew it was you but, still, I did a double-take, you know. But it's like me and my short hair – it'll grow back and you'll be white again.'

'Come here.' He took her hand and sat on a low sand dune, pulled her down next to him.

'Aren't we leaving?' she asked.

'Not quite yet.'

A nod at the Lexus. 'Whose car is that? I thought your friend was going to drop you off.'

He said nothing. They looked west at the Pacific Ocean. The sun was a pale disk just approaching the horizon, growing more fiery by the minute.

She'd be thinking: Does he want to talk, does he want to fuck me? What's going on?

Uncertainty . . . Pell let it run up. She'd be noticing that he wasn't smiling.

Concern flowed in like high tide. He felt the tension in her hand and arm.

Finally he asked, 'How much do you love me?'

She didn't hesitate, though Pell noted something cautious in her response. 'As big as that sun.'

'Looks small from here.'

'I mean as big as the sun really is. No, as big as the *universe*,' she added quickly, as if trying to correct a wrong answer in class.

Pell was quiet.

'What's the matter, Daniel?'

'I have a problem. And I don't know what to do about it.'

She tensed. 'A problem, sweetheart?'

So it's 'sweetie' when she's happy, 'sweetheart' when she's troubled. Good to know. He filed that away.

'That meeting I had?' He'd told her only that he was going to meet someone about a 'business thing'.

'Uh-huh.'

'Something went wrong. I had all the plans made. This woman was going to pay me back a lot of money I'd loaned her. But she lied to me.'

'What happened?'

Pell was looking Jennie right in the eye. He reflected quickly that the only person who'd ever caught him lying was Kathryn Dance. But thinking of her was a distraction so he put her out of his mind. 'She had her own plans, it turned out. She was going to use me. And you too.'

'Me? She knows me?'

'Not your name. But from the news she knows we're together. She wanted me to leave you.'

'Why?'

'So she and I could be together. She wanted to go away with me.'

'This was somebody you used to know?'

'That's right.'

'Oh.' Jennie fell silent.

*Jealousy . . .*

'I told her no, of course. There's no way I'd even think about that.'

An attempted purr. It didn't work.

*Sweetheart . . .*

'And Susan got mad. She said she was going to the police. She'd turn us both in.' Pell's face contorted with pain. 'I tried to talk her out of it. But she wouldn't listen.'

'What happened?'

He glanced at the car. 'I brought her here. I didn't have any choice. She was trying to call the police.'

Alarmed, Jennie looked up and didn't see anybody in the car.

'In the trunk.'

'Oh, God. Is she –'

'No,' Pell answered slowly, 'she's okay. She's tied up. That's the problem. I don't know what to do now.'

'She still wants to turn you in?'

'Can you believe it?' he asked breathlessly. 'I begged her. But she's not right in the head. Like your husband, remember? He kept hurting you even though he knew he'd get arrested. Susan's the same. She can't control herself.' He sighed angrily. 'I was fair to her. And she cheated me. She spent all the money. I was going to pay you back with it. For the car. For everything you've done.'

'You don't have to worry about the money, sweetheart. I want to spend it on us.'

'No, I'm going to pay you back.' Never, ever let a woman know you want her for her money.

He kissed her in a preoccupied way. 'But what're we going to do now?'

Jennie avoided his gaze and stared into the sun. 'I . . . I don't know, sweetheart. I'm not . . .' Her voice ran out of steam, just like her thoughts.

He squeezed her leg. 'I can't let anything hurt us. I love you so much.'

Faintly: 'And I love you, Daniel.'

He took the knife from his pocket. Stared at it. 'I don't want to. I really don't. People've been hurt yesterday because of us.'

Us. Not *me*.

She caught the distinction. He could sense it in the stiffening of her shoulders.

He continued, 'But I didn't do that intentionally. It was accidental. But this . . . I don't know.' He turned the knife over and over in his hand.

She pressed against him, staring at the blade, flashing in the sunset. She was shivering hard.

'Will you help me, lovely? I can't do it by myself.'

Jennie started to cry. 'I don't know, sweetheart. I don't think I can.' Her eyes were fixed on the rump of the car.

Pell kissed her head. 'We can't let anything hurt us. I couldn't live without you.'

'Me too.' She sucked in breath. Her jaw was quivering as much as her fingers.

'Help me, please.' A whisper. He rose, helped her to her feet and they continued to the Lexus. He gave her the knife, closed his hand around hers. 'I'm not strong enough alone,' he confessed. 'But together . . . we can do it together.' He looked at her, eyes bright. 'It'll be like a pact. You know, like a lovers' pact. It means we're bonded as close as two people can be. Like blood brothers. We'd be blood *lovers*.'

He reached into the car and hit the trunk-release button. Jennie barked a faint scream at the sound.

'Help me, lovely. Please.' He led her toward the trunk.

Then she stopped.

She handed him the knife, sobbing. 'Please . . . I'm sorry. I'm so sorry, sweetheart. Don't be mad. I can't do it. I just can't.'

Pell said nothing, just nodded. Her miserable eyes, her tears reflecting red from the melting sun.

It was an intoxicating sight.

'Don't be mad at me, Daniel. I couldn't stand it if you were mad.'

Pell hesitated for three heartbeats, the perfect length of time to hatch uncertainty. 'It's okay. I'm not mad.'

'Am I still your lovely?'

Another pause. 'Of course you are.' He told her to go wait in the car. 'I –'

'Go wait for me. It's okay.' He said more and Jennie walked back to the Toyota. He continued to the trunk of the Lexus and looked down.

At Susan Pemberton's lifeless body.

He'd killed her an hour before, in the parking lot of her building. Suffocated her with duct tape.

Pell had never intended that Jennie help him kill the woman. He'd known she'd balk. This whole incident was merely another lesson in the education of his pupil.

She'd moved a step closer to where he wanted her. Death and violence were on the table now. For at least five or ten seconds she'd considered slipping the knife into a human body, prepared to watch the blood flow, prepared to watch a human life vanish. Last week she'd never have been able to conceive of the thought; next week she'd consider it for a longer period.

Then she might actually agree to help him kill someone. And later still? Maybe he could get her to the point where she'd commit murder by herself. He'd gotten the girls in the Family to do things they hadn't wanted to – but only petty crimes. Nothing violent.

Daniel Pell, though, believed he had the talent to turn Jennie Marston into a robot who would do whatever he ordered, even kill.

He slammed the trunk. Then he snagged a pine branch and used it to obscure the footprints in the sand. He returned to the car, sweeping behind him. He told Jennie to drive up the road until the car was on gravel, then obliterated the tire prints as well. He joined her. 'I'll drive,' he said.

'I'm sorry, Daniel,' she said, wiping her face. 'I'll make it up to you.'

Begging for reassurance.

But the lesson plan dictated that he give no response whatsoever.

# Chapter
# TWENTY-FIVE

He was a curious man, Kathryn Dance was thinking.

Morton Nagle tugged at his sagging pants and sat down at the coffee table in her office, opening a battered briefcase.

He was a bit of a slob, his thinning hair disheveled, goatee unevenly trimmed, gray shirt cuffs frayed, body spongy. But he seemed comfortable with his physique, Dance the kinesics analyst assessed. His mannerisms, precise and economical, were stress-free. His eyes, with their elfin twinkle, performed triage, deciding instantly what was important and what wasn't. When he'd entered her office, he'd ignored the décor, noted what Dance's face revealed (probably exhaustion), gave young Rey Carraneo a friendly but meaningless glance and fixed immediately on Winston Kellogg.

And after he learned Kellogg's employer, the writer's eyes narrowed a bit further, wondering what an FBI agent was doing here.

Compared with earlier, Kellogg was dressed unfederal today – in a beige checkered sports coat, dark slacks and blue dress shirt. He wore no tie. Still, his behavior was right out of the bureau, as noncommittal as their agents always are. He told Nagle only that he was here as an observer, 'helping out'.

The writer offered one of his chuckles, which seemed to mean: I'll get you to talk.

'Rebecca and Linda have agreed to help us,' Dance told him.

He lifted an eyebrow. 'Really? And the other one, Samantha?'

'No, not her.'

Nagle extracted three sheets of paper from his briefcase. He set them on the table. 'My mini opus, if that's not an oxymoron. A brief history of Daniel Pell.'

Kellogg scooted his chair next to Dance's. Unlike with O'Neil, she could detect no aftershave.

The writer repeated what he'd said to Dance the day before: His book wasn't about Pell himself, but about his victims. 'I'm looking into everybody affected by the Croytons' deaths. Even employees. Croyton's company was eventually bought by a big software developer and hundreds of people were laid off. Maybe that wouldn't have happened if he hadn't died. And what about his profession? *That's* a victim too. He was one of the most innovative computer designers in Silicon Valley at the time. He had dozens of copyrights on programs and hardware that were way ahead of their time. A lot of them didn't even have patents on any application back then, they were so advanced. Now they're gone. Maybe some were revolutionary programs for medicine or science or communications.'

Dance remembered thinking the same as she'd driven past the Cal State campus that was the recipient of much of Croyton's estate.

Nagle continued, with a nod toward what he'd written. 'It's interesting – Pell changes his autobiography depending on whom he's talking to. Say, he needs to form a connection with somebody whose parents died at a young age. Well, to them Pell says he was orphaned at ten. Or he has to exploit somebody whose father was in the military, then he was the army brat of a soldier killed in combat. To hear him tell it, there are about twenty different Pells. Well, here's the truth:

'He was born in Bakersfield, October of nineteen sixty-three. The seventh. But he tells everyone that his birthday is November twenty-second. That was the day Lee Harvey Oswald shot Kennedy.'

'He admired a presidential assassin?' Kellogg asked.

'No, apparently he considered Oswald a loser. He thought he was too pliable and simpleminded. But what he admired was the fact that one man, with one act, could affect so much. Could make so many people cry, change the entire course of a country – well, the world.

'Now, Joseph Pell, his father, was a salesman, mother a receptionist, when she could keep a job. Middle-class family. Mom – Elizabeth – drank a lot, have to assume she was distant, but no abuse, no incarceration. Died of cirrhosis when Daniel was in his mid-teens. With his wife gone, the father did what he could to raise the boy but Daniel couldn't take anyone else being in charge. Didn't do well with authority figures – teachers, bosses and especially his old man.'

Dance mentioned the tape she and Michael O'Neil had watched, the comments about his father charging rent, beating him, abandoning the family, his parents dying.

Nagle said, 'All a lie. But his father was undoubtedly a hard character for Pell to deal with. He was religious – *very* religious, very strict. He was an ordained minister – some conservative Presbyterian sect in Bakersfield – but he never got a church of his own. He was an assistant minister but finally was released. A lot of complaints that he was too intolerant, too judgmental about the parishioners. He tried to start his own church, but the Presbyterian synod wouldn't even talk to him so he ended up selling religious books and icons, things like that. But we can assume that he'd made his son's life miserable.

Religion was not central to Dance's own life. She, Wes and Maggie celebrated Easter and Christmas, though the chief icons of the faith were a rabbit and a jolly fellow in a red suit, and she doled out to the children her own brand of ethics – solid, incontrovertible rules common to most of the major sects. Still, she'd been in law enforcement long enough to know that religion often played a role in crime. Not only premeditated acts of terrorism but more mundane incidents. She and Michael O'Neil had spent nearly ten hours together in a cramped garage in the nearby town of Marina, negotiating with a fundamentalist minister intent on killing his wife and daughter in the name of Jesus because the teenage girl was pregnant. (They saved the family but Dance came away with an uneasy awareness of what a dangerous thing spiritual rectitude can be.)

Nagle continued, 'Pell's father retired, moved to Phoenix and remarried. His second wife died two years ago and Joseph died last year, heart attack. Pell apparently hadn't stayed in touch. No uncles on either side and one aunt, in Bakersfield.'

'The one with Alzheimer's?'

'Yes. Now, he does have a brother.'

Not an only child, as he'd claimed.

'He's older. Moved to London years ago. He runs the sales operation of a U.S. importer/exporter. Doesn't give interviews. All I have is a name. Richard Pell.'

Dance said to Kellogg, 'I'll have somebody track him down.'

'Cousins?' the FBI agent asked.

'The aunt never married.' Tapping the bio he'd written. 'Now, Pell's later teens, he was constantly in and out of juvenile detention – mostly for larceny, shoplifting, car theft. But he has no long history of violence.

His early record was surprisingly peaceful. There's no evidence of street brawling, no violent assaults, no signs he ever lost his temper. One officer suggested that it seemed Pell would only hurt somebody if it was tactically useful, and that he didn't enjoy – or hate – violence. It was a tool.'

Dance thought of her earlier assessment, killing emotionlessly whenever it was expedient.

'Now, no history of drugs. Pell apparently's never been a user. And he doesn't – or didn't – drink any alcohol.'

'What about education?'

'Now that's interesting. He's brilliant. When he was in high school he tested off the charts. He got As in independent study classes, but never showed up when attendance was required. In prison he taught himself law and handled his own appeal in the Croyton case.'

She thought of his comment during the interview, about Hastings Law School.

'And he took it all the way to the California Supreme Court – just last year they ruled against him. Apparently it was a big blow. He thought for sure he'd get off.'

'Well, he may be smart but not smart enough to stay out of jail.' Kellogg tapped a paragraph of the bio that described maybe seventy-five arrests. '*That's* a rap sheet.'

'And it's the tip of the iceberg; Pell usually got *other* people to commit the crimes. There're probably hundreds of other offenses he was behind that somebody else got nailed for. Robbery, burglary, shoplifting, pickpocketing. That was how he lived. Getting people around him to do the dirty work.'

'Oliver,' Kellogg said.

'What?'

'Charles Dickens. *Oliver Twist* . . . You ever read it?'

Dance said, 'Saw the movie.'

'Good comparison. Fagin, the guy who ran the gang of pickpockets. That was Pell.'

'"Please, sir, I want some more,"' Kellogg said in a Cockney accent. It was lousy. Dance laughed and he shrugged.

'Pell left Bakersfield and moved to L.A., then San Francisco. Hung out with some people there, was arrested for a few things, nothing serious. No word on him for a while – until he's picked up in Northern California in a homicide investigation.'

'Homicide?'

'Yep. The murder of Charles Pickering in Redding. Pickering was a county worker. He was found stabbed to death in the hills outside of town about an hour after he was seen talking to somebody who looked like Pell. Vicious killing. He was slashed dozens of times. Bloodbath. But Pell had an alibi – a girlfriend he was with. And there was no physical evidence. The local police held him for a week on vagrancy, but finally gave him a pass. The case was never solved.

'Then he gets the Family together in Seaside. A few more years of theft, shoplifting. Some assaults. An arson or two. Pell was suspected in the beating of a biker who lived nearby, but the man wouldn't press charges. A month or so after that came the Croyton murders. From then on – well, until yesterday – he was in prison.'

Dance asked, 'What does the girl have to say?'

'Girl?'

'The Sleeping Doll. Theresa Croyton.'

'What could she tell you? She was asleep at the time of the murders. That was established.'

'Was it?' Kellogg asked. 'By who?'

'The investigators at the time, I assume.' Nagle's voice was uncertain. He'd apparently never thought about it.

'She'd be, let's see, seventeen now,' Dance calculated. 'I'd like to talk to her. She might know some things that'd be helpful. She's living with her aunt and uncle, right?'

'Yes, they adopted her.'

'Could I have their number?'

Nagle hesitated. His eyes swept the desktop; they'd lost their sparkle. 'Is there a problem?'

'Well, I promised the aunt I wouldn't say anything to anybody about the girl. She's very protective of her niece. Even *I* haven't met her yet. At first the woman was deadset against my talking to her. I think she might agree eventually but if I gave you her number, I doubt very much she'd talk to you, and I suspect I'd never hear from her again.'

'Just tell us where she lives. We'll get the name from Directory Assistance. I won't mention you.'

He shook his head. 'They changed their last name, moved out of the area. They were afraid somebody in the Family would come after them.'

'You gave Kathryn the names of the women,' Kellogg pointed out.

'They were in the phone book and in public records. You could've gotten them yourself. Theresa and her aunt and uncle are very unpublic.'

'*You* found them,' Dance said.

'Through some confidential sources. Who, I guarantee, want to stay even more confidential now that Pell's escaped. But I know this's important . . . I'll tell you what I'll do. I'll go see the aunt in person. Tell her you want to talk to Theresa about Pell. I'm not going to try to persuade them. If they say no, that's it.'

Kellogg nodded. 'That's all we're asking. Thanks.'

Looking over the bio, Dance said, 'The more I learn about him, the less I know.'

The writer laughed, the sparkle returning to his face. 'Oh, you want to know the why of Daniel Pell?' He dug through his briefcase, found a stack of papers and flipped to a yellow tab. 'Here's a quote from one of his prison psych interviews. For once he was being candid.' Nagle read:

> *Pell: You want to analyze me, don't you? You want to know what makes me tick? You surely know the answer to that one, Doctor. It's the same for everybody: family, of course. Daddy whipped me, Daddy ignored me, Mommy didn't breastfeed me, Uncle Joe did who knows what. Nature or nurture, you can lay everything at your family's feet. But if you think too much about 'em, next thing you know, every single relative and ancestor you ever had is in the room with you and you're paralyzed. No, no, the only way to survive is to let 'em all go and remember that you're who you are and that's never going to change.*
>
> *Interviewer: Then who are you, Daniel?*
>
> *Pell (laughing): Oh, me? I'm the one tugging the strings of your soul and making you do things you never though you were capable of. I'm the one playing my flute and leading you to places you're afraid to go. And let me tell you, Doctor, you'd be astonished at how many people want their puppeteers and their Pied Pipers. Absolutely astonished*

'I have to get home,' Dance said after Nagle had left. Her mother and the children would be anxiously awaiting her for Dad's party.

Kellogg tossed the comma of hair off his forehead. It fell back. He tried again. She glanced at the gesture and noticed something she hadn't seen before – a bandage protruding above the collar of his shirt.

'You hurt?'

A shrug. 'Got winged. A takedown in Chicago the other day.'

His body language told her he didn't want to talk about it and she didn't push. But then he said, 'The perp didn't make it.' In a certain tone and with a certain glance. It was how she told people that she was a widow.

'I'm sorry. You handling it okay?'

'Fine.' Then he added, 'Okay, not fine. But I'm handling it. Sometimes that's the best you can do.'

On impulse she asked, 'Hey, you have plans tonight?'

'Brief the SAC., then a bath at the hotel, a scotch, a burger and sleep. Well, okay, two scotches.'

'Have a question.'

He lifted an eyebrow.

'You like birthday cake?'

After only a brief pause he said, 'It's one of my favorite food groups.'

# Chapter
# TWENTY-SIX

'Mom, look. We deck-orated it! D-E-C-K.'

Dance kissed her daughter. 'Mags, that's funny.'

She knew the girl had been bursting, waiting to share the pun.

The Deck did look nice. The kids had been busy all afternoon, getting ready for the party. Banners, Chinese lanterns, candles everywhere. (They'd learned from their mom; when it came to entertaining, Kathryn Dance's guests might not get gourmet food, but they were treated to great atmosphere.)

'When can Grandpa open his presents?' Both Wes and Maggie had saved up allowance money and bought Stuart Dance outdoor gear – waders and a net. Dance knew her father'd be happy with anything his grandchildren got him but those particular items he would definitely use.

'Presents after the cake,' Edie Dance announced. 'And that's after dinner.'

'Hi, Mom.' Dance and her mother didn't always hug but tonight Edie clasped her close as an excuse to whisper that she wanted to talk to her about Juan Millar.

The women walked into the living room. Dance saw immediately that her mother was troubled.

'What is it?'

'He's still hanging in there. He's come to a couple of times.' A glance around to make sure, presumably, that the children were nowhere nearby. 'Only for a few seconds each time. He couldn't possibly give you a statement. But . . .'

'What, Mom?'

She lowered her voice even further. 'I was standing near him. Nobody else was in earshot. I looked down and his eyes were open. I mean the one that's not bandaged. His lips were moving. I bent down. He said . . .' Edie glanced around again. 'He said, "Kill me." He said it twice. Then he closed his eyes.'

'Is he in that much pain?'

'No, he's so medicated he can't feel a thing. But he could look at the bandages. He could see the equipment. He's not a stupid man.'

'His family's there?'

'Most of the time. Well, that brother of his round the clock. He watches us like a hawk. He's convinced we're not giving Juan good treatment because he's Latino. And he's made a few more comments about you.'

Dance grimaced.

'Sorry, but I thought you should know.'

'I'm glad you told me.'

She was very troubled – not about Julio Millar, of course. She could handle him. No, it was the young detective's hopelessness.

*Kill me . . .*

Dance asked, 'Did Betsey call?'

'Ah, your sister can't be here,' Edie said in a breezy tone, whose subtext was irritation that their younger daughter wouldn't make the four-hour drive from Santa Barbara for her father's birthday party. Of course, with the Pell manhunt ongoing, Dance probably wouldn't've driven *there*, had the situation been reversed. According to an important rule of families, though, hypothetical transgressions aren't offenses, and that Dance was present, even by default, meant that, this time, Betsey earned the black mark.

They returned to the Deck and Maggie asked, 'Mom, can we let Dylan and Patsy out?'

'We'll see.' The dogs could be a little boisterous at parties. And tended to get too much human food for their own good.

'Where's your brother?'

'In his room.'

'What's he doing?'

'Stuff.'

Dance locked the weapon away for the party – an MCSO deputy was on security detail was parked outside. She showered fast and changed.

She found Wes in the hallway. 'No T-shirt. It's your grandfather's birthday.'

'Mom. It's clean.'

'Polo. Or your blue-and-white button-down.' She knew the contents of his closet better than he did.

'Oh, okay.'

She looked closely at his downcast eyes. His demeanor had nothing to do with a change of shirt. 'What's the matter?'

'Nothing.'

'Come on, spill.'

'Spill?'

'It's from my era. Tell me what's on your mind.'

'Nothing.'

'Go change.'

Ten minutes later she was setting out mounds of luscious appetizers, offering a silent prayer of thanks to Trader Joe's.

In a dress shirt, cuffs buttoned and tails tucked, Wes strafed past and grabbed a handful of nuts. A whiff of aftershave followed. He looked good. Being a parent was a challenge, but there was plenty to be proud of too.

'Mom?' He tossed a cashew into the air. Caught it in his mouth.

'Don't do that. You could choke.'

'Mom?'

'What?'

'Who's coming tonight?'

Now the eyes fished away and his shoulder was turned toward her. That meant another agenda lay behind the question. She knew what was bothering him – the same as last night. And now it was time to talk.

'Just us and a few people.' Sunday evening there'd be a bigger event, with many of Stuart's friends, at the Marine Club near the aquarium in Monterey. Today, her father's actual birthday, she'd invited only eight or so people for dinner. She continued, 'Michael and his wife, Steve and Martine, the Barbers . . . That's about it. Oh, and somebody who's working with us on a case. He's from Washington.'

He nodded. 'That's all? Nobody else?'

'That's all.' She pitched him a bag of pretzels, which he caught with one hand. 'Set those out. And make sure there're some left for the guests.'

A much-relieved Wes headed off to start filling bowls.

What the boy had been worried about was the possibility that Dance had invited Brian Gunderson. The Brian who was the source of the book sitting prominently nearby, the Brian whose phone call to Dance at CBI headquarters Maryellen Kresbach had so diligently reported.

*Brian called . . .*

The forty-year-old investment banker had been a blind date, courtesy of Maryellen, who was as compulsive about, and talented at, match-making as with baking, brewing coffee and running the professional life of CBI agents.

Brian was smart and easy-going and funny too; on their first date he'd listened to her description of kinesics and promptly sat on his hands. 'So you can't figure out my intentions.' That dinner had turned out to be quite enjoyable. Divorced, no children (though he wanted them). Brian's investment-banking business was hectic, and with his and Dance's busy schedules the relationship had by necessity moved slowly. Which was fine with her. Long married, recently widowed, she was in no hurry.

After a month of dinners, coffee and movies, she and Brian had taken a long hike and found themselves on the beach at Asilomar. A golden sunset, a slew of sea otters playing near shore . . . How could you resist a kiss or two? They hadn't. She remembered liking that. Then feeling guilty for liking. But liking it more than feeling guilty.

*That* part of your life you can do without for a while, but not forever.

Dance had had no particular plans for the future with Brian and was happy to take it easy, see what developed.

But Wes had intervened. He was never rude or embarrassing, but he made clear in a dozen ways a mother could clearly read that he didn't like anything about Brian. Dance had graduated from grief-counseling but she still saw a therapist occasionally. The woman told her how to introduce a possible romantic interest to the children, and she'd done everything right. But Wes had outmaneuvered her. He grew sullen and passive-aggressive whenever the subject of Brian came up or when she returned from seeing him.

That's what he'd been wanting to ask about last night when he was reading *Lord of the Rings*.

Tonight, in his casual question about attendance at the party, the boy really meant, Is Brian coming?

And the corollary: Have you two really broken up?

Yes, we have. (Though Dance wondered if Brian felt differently. After all, he'd called several times since the breakup.)

The therapist had said Wes's behavior was normal, and Dance could work it out if she remained patient and determined. Most important, though, she couldn't let her son control her. But in the end she decided she wasn't patient or determined enough. And so, two weeks ago, she'd broken it off. She'd been tactful, explaining that it was just a little too soon after her husband's death; she wasn't ready. Brian had been upset but had taken the news well. No parting shots. And they'd left the matter open.

*Let's just give it some time . . .*

In truth the breakup was a relief; parents have to pick their battles, and, she decided, skirmishing over romance wasn't worth the effort just now. Still, she was pleased about his calls and had found herself missing him.

Carting wine outside onto the Deck, she found her father with Maggie. He was holding a book and pointing to a picture of a deep-sea fish that glowed.

'Hey, Mags, that looks tasty,' Dance said.

'Mom, gross.'

'Happy birthday, Dad.' She hugged him.

'Thank you, dear.'

Dance arranged platters, dumped beer into the cooler, then walked into the kitchen and pulled out her mobile. She checked in with TJ and Carraneo. They'd had no luck with the physical search for Pell, nor come across any leads to the missing Ford Focus, anyone with the names or screen names Nimue or Alison, or hotels, motels or boardinghouses Pell and his accomplice might be staying.

She was tempted to call Winston Kellogg, thinking he might be shying, but she decided not to. He had all the vital statistics; he'd either show or not.

Dance helped her mother with more food and, returning to the Deck, greeted the neighbors, Tom and Sarah Barber, who brought with them wine, a birthday present and their gangly mixed-breed dog, Fawlty.

'Mom, please!' Maggie called, her meaning clear.

'Okay, okay, let 'em out of doggy jail.'

Maggie freed Patsy and Dylan from the bedroom and the three canines galloped into the backyard, knocking one another other down and checking out new scents.

A few minutes later another couple appeared on the Deck. Fortyish Steven Cahill could've been a Birkenstock model, complete with corduroy slacks and salt-and-pepper ponytail. His wife, Martine Christensen, belied her surname; she was sultry, dark and voluptuous. You'd have thought think the blood in her veins was Spanish or Mexican but her ancestors predated all the Californian settlers. She was part Ohlone Indian – the loose affiliation of tribelets hunting and gathering from Big Sur to San Francisco Bay. For hundreds, possibly thousands of years, the Ohlone had been the sole inhabitants of this region of the state.

Some years ago Dance had met Martine at a concert at a community college in Monterey, a descendant of the famed Monterey Folk Festival, where Bob Dylan had made his West Coast debut in '65, and that a few years later had morphed into the even more famous Monterey Pop Festival, which brought Jimi Hendrix and Janis Joplin to the world's attention.

The concert where Dance and Martine had met was less culture-breaking than its predecessors, but more significant on a personal level. The women had hit it off instantly and had stayed long after the last act finished, talking music. They'd soon become best friends. It was Martine who'd practically broken down Dance's door on several occasions following Bill's death. She'd waged a persistent campaign to keep her friend from sinking into the seductive world of reclusive widowhood. While some people avoided her and others (her mother, for instance) plied her with exhausting sympathy, Martine embarked on a campaign that could be called ignoring sorrow. She cajoled, joked, argued and plotted. Despite Dance's reticence, she realized that, damn it, the tactic had worked. Martine was perhaps the biggest influence in getting her life back on track.

Steve's and Martine's children, twin boys a year younger than Maggie, followed them up the stairs, one toting his mother's guitar case, the other a present for Stuart. After greetings, Maggie herded the boys into the backyard.

The adults gravitated to a rickety candlelit table.

Dance saw that Wes was happier than he'd been in a long time. He was a natural social director and was now organizing a game for the children.

She thought again about Brian, then let it go.

'The escape. Are you . . . ?' Martine's melodious voice faded once she saw that Dance knew what she was talking about.

'Yep. I'm running it.'

'So the bugs hit you first,' her friend observed.

'Right in the teeth. If I have to run off before the cake and candles, that's why.'

'It's funny,' said Tom Barber, a local journalist and freelance writer, 'we spend all our time lately thinking about terrorists. They're the new "in" villains. And suddenly somebody like Pell sneaks up behind you. You tend to forget that it's people like him who might be the worst threat to most of us.'

Barber's wife added, 'People're staying home. All over the Peninsula. They're afraid.'

'Only reason I'm here,' Steven Cahill said, 'is because I knew there'd be folks packing heat.'

Dance laughed.

Michael and Anne O'Neil arrived with their two children, Amanda and Tyler, nine and ten. Once again Maggie clambered up the stairs. She escorted the new youngsters to the backyard, after stocking up on sodas and chips.

Dance pointed out wine and beer, then headed into the kitchen to help. But her mother said, 'You've got another guest.' She indicated the front door, where Dance found Winston Kellogg.

'I'm empty-handed,' he confessed.

'I've got more than we'll ever eat. You can take a doggy bag home, if you want. By the way, you allergic?'

'To pollen, yes. Dogs? No.'

Kellogg had changed again. The sports coat was the same but he wore a Polo shirt and jeans, Topsiders and yellow socks.

He noted her glance. 'I know. For a Fed I look surprisingly like a soccer dad.'

She directed him through the kitchen and introduced him to Edie. Then they continued on to the Deck, where he was inundated with more introductions. She remained circumspect about his role here, and Kellogg said merely that he was in town from Washington and was 'working with Kathryn on a few projects.'

Then she took him to the stairs leading down to the backyard and introduced him to the children. Dance caught Wes and Tyler looking at him closely, undoubtedly for armament, and whispering to each other.

O'Neil joined the two agents.

Wes waved enthusiastically to the deputy and, with another glance at Kellogg, returned to their game, which he was apparently making up on the run. He was laying out the rules. It seemed to involve outer space and invisible dragons. The dogs were aliens. The twins were royalty of some kind and a pine cone was either a magic orb or a hand grenade, perhaps both.

'Did you tell Michael about Nagle?' Kellogg asked.

She gave a brief synopsis of what they'd learned about Pell's history and added that the writer was going to see if Theresa Croyton would talk to them.

'So, you think Pell's here because of the murders back then?' O'Neil asked.

'I don't know,' she said. 'But I need all the information I can get.'

The placid detective gave a smile and said to Kellogg, 'No stone left unturned. That's how I describe her policing style.'

'Which I learned from him,' Dance said, laughing, and nodding at O'Neil.

Then the detective said, 'Oh, I was thinking about something. Remember one of Pell's phone conversations from Capitola was about money?'

'Ninety-two hundred dollars,' Kellogg said. She was impressed at his memory.

'Well, here's what I thought: We know the Thunderbird was stolen in Los Angeles. It's logical to assume that's where Pell's girlfriend's from. How 'bout we contact banks in L.A. County and see if any women customers've withdrawn that amount in the past, say, month or two?'

Dance liked the idea, though it would mean a lot of work.

O'Neil said to Kellogg, 'That'd have to come from you folks: FBI Treasury, IRS or Homeland Security, I'd guess.'

'It's a good idea. Just thinking out loud, though, I'd say we'd have a manpower problem.' He echoed Dance's concern. 'We're talking millions of customers. I know the L.A. bureau couldn't handle it, and Homeland'd laugh. And if she was smart she'd make small withdrawals over a period of time. Or cash third-party checks and stash the money.'

'Oh, sure. Possibly. But it'd be great to ID his girlfriend. You know, "A second suspect—"'

'"—logarithmically increases the chances for detection and arrest,"' Kellogg finished the quotation from an old textbook on law enforcement. Dance and O'Neil quoted it often.

Smiling, Kellogg held O'Neil's eye. 'We Feds don't have quite the resources people think we do. I'm sure we couldn't come up with the bodies to man the phones. Be a huge job.'

'I wonder. You'd think it'd be pretty easy to check databases, at least with the big chain banks.' Michael O'Neil could be quite tenacious.

Dance asked, 'Would you need a warrant?'

O'Neil said, 'Probably to release the name you would. But if a bank wanted to cooperate they could run the numbers and tell us if there was a match. We could get a warrant for the name and address in a half-hour.'

Kellogg sipped his wine. 'The fact is, there's another problem. I'm worried if we go to the SAC. or Homeland with something like that – too tenuous – we might lose support we'd need later for something more solid.'

'Crying wolf, hm?' O'Neil nodded. 'Guess you have to play more politics at that level than we do here.'

'But let's think about it. I'll make some calls.'

O'Neil looked past Dance's shoulder. 'Hey, happy birthday, young man.'

Stuart Dance, wearing a badge that said 'Birthday Boy', handmade by Maggie and Wes, shook hands, refilled O'Neil's and Dance's wineglasses and said to Kellogg, 'You're talking shop. Not allowed. I'm stealing you away from these children, come play with the adults.'

Kellogg gave a shy laugh and followed the man to the candlelit table, where Martine had her battered Gibson guitar out of the case and was organizing a sing-along. Dance and O'Neil stood alone. She saw Wes looking up. He'd apparently been studying the adults. He turned away, back to the *Star Wars* improvisation.

'He seems good,' O'Neil said, tilting his head toward Kellogg.

'Winston? Yes.'

Typically, O'Neil carried no grudge about the rejection of his suggestions. He was the antithesis of pettiness.

'He take a hit recently?' O'Neil tapped his neck.

'How'd you know?' The bandage wasn't visible tonight.

'He was touching it the way you touch a wound.'

She laughed. 'Good kinesic analysis. Yeah, just happened. He was in Chicago. The perp got a round off first, I guess, and Win took him out. He didn't go into detail.'

They fell silent, looking over the backyard, the children, the dogs, the lights glowing brighter in the encroaching dusk. 'We'll get him.'

'Will we?' she asked.

'Yep. He'll make a mistake. They always do.'

'I don't know. He's something different. Don't you feel that?'

'No. He's not different. He's just *more*.' Michael O'Neil – the most widely read person she knew – had surprisingly simple philosophies of life. He didn't believe in evil or good, much less God or Satan. Those were all abstractions that deflected you from your job, which was to catch people who broke rules that humans had created for their own health and safety.

No good, no bad. Just destructive forces that had to be stopped. To Michael O'Neil, Daniel Pell was a tsunami, an earthquake, a tornado. He watched the children playing, then said, 'I gather that guy you've been seeing . . . It's over with?'

*Brian called . . .*

'You caught that, hm? Busted by my own assistant.'

'I'm sorry. Really.'

'You know how it goes,' Dance said, noting she'd spoken one of those sentences that were meaningless flotsam in a conversation.

'Sure.'

Dance turned to see how her mother was coming with dinner. She saw O'Neil's wife looking at the two of them. Anne smiled.

Dance smiled back. She said to O'Neil, 'So, let's go join the sing-along.'

'Do I have to sing?'

'Absolutely not,' she said quickly. He had a wonderful speaking voice, low with a natural vibrato. He couldn't stay on key under threat of torture.

After a half-hour of music, gossip and laughter, Edie Dance, her daughter and granddaughter set out Worcestershire-marinated flank steak, salad, asparagus and potatoes au gratin. Dance sat beside Winston Kellogg, who was holding his own very well among strangers. He even told a few jokes, with a deadpan delivery that reminded her of her late husband, who had shared not only Kellogg's career but his easy-going nature – at least once the federal ID card was tucked away.

The conversation ambled from music to Anne O'Neil's critique of San Francisco arts, to politics in the Middle East, Washington and Sacramento, to the far more important story of a sea otter pup born in captivity at the aquarium two days ago.

It was a comfortable gathering: friends, laughter, food, wine, music.

Though, of course, complete comfort eluded Kathryn Dance. Pervading the otherwise fine evening, like the moving bass line of Martine's old guitar, was the thought that Daniel Pell was still at large.

# WEDNESDAY

## Chapter
# TWENTY-SEVEN

Kathryn Dance was sitting in a cabin at the Point Lobos Inn – the first time she'd ever been in the expensive place. It was an upscale lodge of private cabins on a quiet road off Highway 1, south of Carmel, abutting the rugged and beautiful state park after which the inn had been named. The Tudor-style place was secluded – a long driveway separated it from the road – and the deputy in the Monterey Sheriff's Office car stationed in front had a perfect view of all approaches, which was why she'd picked it.

Dance checked in with O'Neil. At the moment he was following up on a missing person report in Monterey. Calls to TJ and Carraneo too. TJ had nothing to tell her, and the Latino agent said he was still having no luck finding a cheap motel or boardinghouse where Pell might be. 'I've tried all the way up to Gilroy and –'

'*Cheap* hotels?'

A pause. 'That's right, Agent Dance. I didn't bother with the expensive ones. Didn't think an escapee'd have much money to spend on them.'

Dance recalled Pell's secret phone conversation in Capitola, the reference to $9200. 'Pell's probably thinking that's exactly what *you're* thinking. Which means . . .' She let Carraneo pick up her thought.

'That it'd be smarter for him to stay in an expensive one. Hm. Okay. I'll get on it. Wait. Where are you right now, Agent Dance? Do you think he –?'

'I've already checked out everybody here,' she assured him. She hung up, looked at her watch again and wondered: Is this hare-brained scheme really going to do any good?

Five minutes later, a knock on the door. Dance opened it to see massive CBI Agent Albert Stemple towering over a woman in her late twenties. Stocky Linda Whitfield had a pretty face, untouched by makeup, and short, red hair. Her clothes were a bit shabby: black stretch pants with shiny knees and a red sweater dangling threads; its V-neck framed a pewter cross. Dance detected no trace of perfume, and Linda's nails were unpolished and cut short.

The women shook hands. Linda's grip was firm.

Stemple's brow lifted. Meaning, Is there anything else?

Dance thanked him and the big agent set down Linda's suitcase and ambled off. Dance locked the door and the woman walked into the living room of the two-bedroom cabin. She looked at the elegant place as if she'd never stayed anywhere nicer than a Days Inn. 'My.'

'I've got coffee going.' A gesture toward the small kitchen.

'Tea, if there's any.'

Dance made a cup. 'I'm hoping you won't have to stay long. Maybe not even overnight.'

'Any more on Daniel?'

'Nothing new.'

Linda looked at the bedrooms as if choosing one would commit her to staying longer than she wanted to. Her serenity wavered, then returned. She picked a room and took her suitcase inside, returned a moment later and accepted the cup of tea, poured milk in and sat. 'I haven't been on an airplane in years,' she said. 'And that jet . . . it was amazing. So small, but it pushed you right back in your seat when we took off. There was an FBI agent on board. She was very nice.'

They sat on comfortable couches, a large coffee table between them. She looked around the cabin again. 'My, this is nice.'

It sure was. Dance wondered what the FBI accountants would say when they saw the bill. The cabin was nearly six hundred a night.

'Rebecca's on her way. But maybe you and I could just get started.'

'And Samantha?'

'She wouldn't come.'

'You talked to her then?'

'I went to see her.'

'Where is she? . . . No, wait, you can't tell me that.'

Dance smiled.

'I heard she had plastic surgery and changed her name and everything.'

'That's true, yes.'

'At the airport I bought a newspaper to see what was going on?'

Dance wondered about the absence of a TV in her brother's house, where she lived; was it an ethical or cultural decision? Or an economic one? You could get a cable ready set for a few hundred bucks nowadays. Still, Dance noted that the heels of Linda's shoes were virtually worn away.

'It said there was no doubt he killed those guards.' She set down the tea. 'I was surprised by that. Daniel wasn't violent. He'd only hurt someone in self-defense.'

Though, looked at from Pell's point of view, that was exactly why he'd slaughtered the guards. 'But,' Linda continued, 'he *did* let somebody go. That driver.'

Only because it served his interest.

Dance asked about the killing of the government worker in Redding.

'Charles Pickering?' The woman's eyes scanned the appliances in the kitchen as she thought back. 'Never heard Daniel mention him. But if the police let him go, I guess that means he didn't do it.'

Interesting logic. 'How did you meet Pell?'

'It was about ten years ago. In Golden Gate Park. San Francisco. I'd run away from home and was sleeping there. Daniel, Samantha and Jimmy were living in Seaside, along with a few other people. They'd travel up and down the coast, like gypsies. They'd sell things they'd bought or made. Sam and Jimmy were pretty talented; they'd make picture frames, CD holders, tie racks. Things like that.

'Anyway, I'd run away that weekend – no big deal, I did it all the time – and Daniel saw me near the Japanese Garden. He sat down and we started talking. Daniel has this gift. He listens to you. It's like you're the center of the universe. It's really, you know, seductive.'

'And you never went back home?'

'No, I did. I always wanted to run away and just keep going. My brother did. He left home at eighteen and never looked back. But I wasn't brave enough to. My parents – we lived in San Mateo – they were real strict. Like drill instructors. My father was head of Santa Clara Bank and Trust, and he –'

'Wait, *that* Whitfield?'

'Yep. The multimillionaire Whitfield. The one who financed a good portion of Silicon Valley and survived the crash. The one who was going into politics – until a certain daughter of his made the press in a big way.' A wry smile. 'Ever met anybody who's been disowned by her parents? You have now . . .

'When I was growing up they were very authoritarian. I had to do everything the way they insisted. How I made my room, what I wore, what I was taking in school, what my grades were going to be. I got spanked until I was fourteen and I think he only stopped because my mother told my father it wasn't a good idea with a girl that age . . . They claimed it was because they loved me, they wanted me to be successful and happy. But, no, they were just control freaks. They were trying to turn me into a little doll for them to dress up and play with.

'So I go back home but all the time I was there I couldn't get Daniel out of my head. We'd only talked for, I don't know, a few hours. But it was wonderful. He treated me like I was a real person. He told me to trust my judgment. That I was smart, I was pretty.' A grimace. 'Oh, I wasn't really – not either of those things. But when he said it I believed him.

'One morning my mother came to my room and told me to get up and get dressed. We were going to visit my aunt or somebody. And I was supposed to wear a skirt. I wanted to wear jeans. It wasn't a formal thing – we were just going to lunch. But she made a big deal out of it. She screamed at me. "No daughter of mine . . ." You get the idea. Well, I grabbed my backpack and just left. I was afraid I'd never find Daniel but I remembered he'd told me he'd be in Santa Cruz that week, at a flea market on the boardwalk.'

The boardwalk was a famous amusement park on the beach. A lot of young people hung out there, at all hours of the day. Dance reflected that it'd make a good hunting ground if Daniel Pell was on the prowl for victims.

'He'd hang out there a lot. That's where he met Jimmy, and later Rebecca. So I hitched a ride down Highway One, and there he was. He looked happy to see me. Which I don't think my parents ever did.' She laughed. 'I asked if he knew a place I could stay. I was nervous about that, hinting. But he said, "You bet I do. With us."'

'In Seaside?'

'Uh-huh. We had a little bungalow there. It was nice.'

'You, Samantha, Jimmy and Pell?'

'Right.'

Her body language told Dance that she was enjoying the memory: the easy position of the shoulders, the crinkles beside the eyes and the illustrator hand gestures, which emphasize the content of the words and suggest the intensity of the speaker's reaction to what he or she is saying.

Linda picked up her tea again and sipped it. 'Whatever the papers said – cult, drug orgies – that was wrong. It was really homey and comfortable. I mean, no drugs at all, or liquor. Some wine at dinner sometimes. Oh, it was nice. I loved being around people who saw you for who you were, didn't try to change you, respected you. I ran the house. I was sort of the mother, I guess you could say. It was so nice to be in charge, for a change. Not getting yelled at for having my own opinion.'

'What about the crimes?'

Linda grew tense. 'There was *that*. Some. Not as much as people say. A little shoplifting, things like that. And I never liked it. Never.'

A few negation gestures here, but Dance sensed she wasn't being deceptive; the kinesic stress was due to her minimizing the severity of the crimes. The Family had done much worse than just shoplifting, Dance knew. There were burglary counts, and grand larceny, as well as purse snatching and pickpocketing – both crimes against persons and under the penal code, more serious than those against property.

'But we didn't have any choice. To be in the Family you had to participate.'

'What was it like living with Daniel?'

'It wasn't as bad as you'd think. You just had to do what he wanted.'

'And if you didn't?'

'He never hurt us. Not physically. Mostly, he'd . . . withdraw.'

Dance recalled Kellogg's profile of a cult leader.

*He'll threaten to withhold himself from them, and that's a very powerful weapon.*

'He'd turn away from you. And you'd get scared. You never knew if that was the end for you and you'd get thrown out. Somebody in the church office was telling me about these reality shows? *Big Brother, Survivor?*'

Dance nodded.

'She was saying how popular they were. I think that's why people're obsessed with them. There's something terrifying about the idea of being kicked out of your family.' She shrugged and fondled the cross on her chest.

'You got a longer sentence than the others. For destroying evidence. What was that story?'

The woman's lips grew tight. 'It was stupid. I panicked. All I knew was that Daniel called and said Jimmy was dead and something had gone wrong at this house where they'd had a meeting. We were supposed to pack up and get ready to leave, the police might be after him soon. Daniel kept all these books about Charles Manson in the bedroom and clippings and things. I burned some before the police got there. I thought it'd look bad if they knew he had this thing for Manson.'

It had, Dance reflected, recalling how the prosecutor had used the Charles Manson theme to help him win a conviction.

Responding to Dance's questions, Linda said more about her recent life. In jail she'd become devoutly religious and, after her release, moved to Portland, where she'd gotten a job working for a local Protestant church. She'd joined it because her brother was a deacon there.

She was seeing a 'nice Christian' man in Portland and was the nanny, in effect, for her brother and sister-in-law's foster children. She wanted to become a foster parent herself – she'd had medical problems and could have no children of her own – but that was hard with the prison conviction. She added, in a tone of conclusion, 'I don't have many material things, but I like my life. It's a *rich* life, in the good sense of the word.'

A knock on the door intruded. Dance's hand strayed toward her heavy pistol.

'It's TJ, boss. I forgot the secret password.'

Dance opened the door and the young agent entered with another woman. Slim and tall, in her mid-thirties, she carried a leather backpack slung over her shoulder.

Kathryn Dance rose to greet the second member of the Family.

# Chapter
# TWENTY-EIGHT

Rebecca Sheffield was a few years older than her fellow Family member. She was athletic-looking and gorgeous, though Dance thought that the short crop of prematurely gray hair, the brash jewelry and the absence of makeup made her look austere. She wore jeans and a white silk T-shirt under a brown suede jacket.

Rebecca shook Dance's hand firmly but she immediately turned her attention to Linda, who was rising and gazing at her with a steady smile.

'Well, look who it is.' Rebecca stepped forward and hugged Linda.

'After all these years.' Linda's voice choked. 'My, I think I'm going to cry.' And she did.

They dropped the embrace but Rebecca continued to hold the other woman's hands tightly. 'It's good to see you, Linda.'

'Oh, Rebecca . . . I've prayed for you a lot.'

'You're into that now? You didn't use to know a cross from a Star of David. Well, thanks for the prayers. Not sure they took.'

'No, no, you're doing such good things. Really! The church office has a computer. I saw your website. Women starting their own businesses. It's wonderful. I'm sure it does a lot of good.'

Rebecca seemed surprised that Linda had kept up with her.

Dance pointed out the available bedroom and Rebecca carried her backpack into it, and used the restroom.

'You need me, boss, just holler.' TJ left and Dance locked the door behind him.

Linda picked up her teacup, fiddled with it, not taking a sip. How people love their props in stressful situations, Dance reflected. She'd interrogated suspects who clutched pens, ashtrays, food wrappers and even their shoes to dull the stress.

Rebecca returned and Dance offered her some coffee.

'You bet.'

Dance poured and set out milk and sugar. 'There's no public restaurant here, but they have room service. Order whatever you'd like.'

Sipping the coffee, Rebecca said, 'I've got to say, Linda, you're looking good.'

A blush. 'Oh, I don't know. I'm not in the shape I'd like. You're glamorous. And thin. I *love* your hair.'

Rebecca laughed. 'Hey, nothing like a couple years in prison to turn you gray, hm? Hey, no ring. You're not married?'

'Nope.'

'Me either.'

'You're kidding. You were going to marry some hunky Italian sculptor. I thought for sure you'd be hooked up now.'

'Not easy to find Mr Right when they hear your boyfriend was Daniel Pell. I read about your father in *BusinessWeek*. Something about his bank expanding.'

'Really? I wouldn't know.'

'You're still not talking?'

Linda shook her head. 'My brother doesn't talk to them either. We're two poor church mice. But it's for the best, believe me. You still paint?'

'Some. Not professionally.'

'No? Really?' Linda turned to Dance, her eyes shining. 'Oh, Rebecca was so good! You should see her work. I mean, she's the best.'

'Just sketch for fun now.'

They spent a few minutes catching up. Dance was surprised that though they both lived on the West Coast they hadn't communicated since the trial.

Rebecca glanced at Dance. 'Samantha joining our coffee klatch? Or whatever her name is now?'

'No, just the two of you.'

'Sam was always the timid one.'

'"Mouse", remember?' Linda said.

'That's right. That's what Pell called her. His Mouse.'

They refilled their cups and Dance got down to work, asking Rebecca the same basic questions she'd asked Linda.

'I was the last one to get suckered in by Mr Pell,' the thin woman said sourly. 'It was only . . . when?' A glance at Linda, who said, 'January. Just four months before the Croyton situation.'

*Situation*. Not *murders*.

'How did you meet Pell?' Dance asked.

'Back then I was bumming around the West Coast, making money doing sketches of people at street fairs and on the beach, you know. I had my easel set up and Pell stopped by. He wanted his portrait done.'

Linda gave a coy smile. 'I seem to remember you didn't do much sketching. You two ended up in the back of the van. And were there for a long, long time.'

Rebecca's smile was of embarrassment. 'Well, Daniel had *that* side to him, sure . . . In any case, we *did* spend time talking too. And he asked me if I wanted to hang out with them in Seaside. I wasn't sure at first – I mean, we all knew about Pell's reputation, and the shoplifting and things like that. But I just said to myself, hell, I'm a bohemian, I'm a rebel and artist. Screw my lily-white suburban upbringing . . . go for it. And I did. It worked out well. There were good people around me, like Linda and Sam. I didn't have to work nine to five and could paint as much as I wanted. Who could ask for anything more in life? Of course, it turned out I'd also joined up with Bonnie and Clyde, a band of thieves. That *wasn't* so good.'

Dance noticed Linda's placid face darken at the comment.

After release from jail, Rebecca explained, she became involved in the women's movement. 'I figured me kowtowing to Pell – treating him like the king of the roost – set the feminist cause back a few years and I wanted to make it up to them.'

Finally, after a lot of counseling, she'd started a consulting service to help women open and finance small businesses. She'd been at it ever since. She must do well for herself, Dance thought, to judge from the jewelry, clothes and Italian shoes, which if the agent's estimate was right (Dance could be an expert footwear witness) cost the same as her best two pairs put together.

Another knock on the door. Winston Kellogg arrived. Dance was happy to see him – professionally and personally. She'd enjoyed getting to know him on the Deck last night. He'd been surprisingly social, for a hard-traveling Fed. Dance had attended a number of functions with her husband's federal coworkers and found most of them quiet and focused, reluctant to talk. But Win Kellogg, along with her parents, had been the last to leave the party.

He now greeted the two women and, in keeping with protocol, showed them his ID. He poured himself some coffee. Up until now Dance had been asking background information but with Kellogg here it was time to get to the crux of the interview.

'All right, here's the situation. Pell is probably still in the area. We can't figure out where or why. It doesn't make any sense; most escapees get as far away as they can from the site of the jail break.'

She told them in detail of how the plan at the courthouse had unfolded and the developments to date. The women listened with interest – and shock or revulsion – to the specifics.

'First, let me ask you about his accomplice.'

'That woman I read about?' Linda asked. 'Who is she?'

'We don't know. Apparently blonde and young. Age is roughly mid-twenties.'

'So he's got a new girlfriend,' Rebecca said. 'That's our Daniel. Never without one.'

Kellogg said, 'We don't exactly know the relationship. She was probably a fan of his. Apparently prisoners, even the worst, get plenty of women throwing themselves at their feet.'

Rebecca laughed and glanced at Linda. '*You* get any love letters when you were inside? I didn't.'

Linda gave a polite smile.

'There's a chance,' Dance said, 'that she isn't a stranger. She'd've been very young at the time the Family was together but I was wondering if she could be somebody you know.'

Linda frowned. 'Mid-twenties now . . . she'd've been a teenager then. I don't remember anyone like that.'

Rebecca added, 'When I was in the Family, it was only the five of us.'

Dance jotted a note. 'Now, I want to talk about what your life was like then. What Pell said and did, what interested him, what his plans were. I'm hoping something you remember will give us a clue as to what he's up to.'

'Step one, define the problem. Step two, get the facts.' Rebecca's eyes were on Dance.

Both Linda and Kellogg looked blank. Dance, of course, knew what she was talking about. (And was thankful that the woman wasn't in the mood to deliver another lecture, like yesterday.) 'Jump in with whatever you want. If you have an idea that sounds bizarre, go ahead and tell us. We'll take whatever we can get.'

'I'm game,' Linda said.

Rebecca offered, 'Shoot.'

Dance asked about the structure of life in the Family.

'It was sort of a commune,' Rebecca said, 'which was weird for me, growing up in capitalistic, sitcom suburbia, you know.'

As they described it, the arrangement was a little different, though, from what a communist cadre might expect. The rule seemed to be: From each according to what Daniel Pell demanded of them; to each according to what Daniel Pell decided.

Still, the Family worked pretty well, at least on a practical level. Linda had made sure the household ran smoothly and the others contributed. They ate well and kept the bungalow clean and in good repair. Both Samantha and Jimmy Newberg were talented with tools and home improvement. For obvious reasons – stolen property stored in a bedroom – Pell didn't want the owner to paint or fix broken appliances, so they had to be completely self-sufficient.

Linda said, 'That was one of Daniel's philosophies of life. "Self-Reliance" – the essay by Ralph Waldo Emerson. I read it out loud a dozen times. He loved to hear it.'

Rebecca was smiling. 'Remember reading at night?'

Linda explained that Pell believed in books. 'He loved them. He made a ceremony out of throwing out the TV. Almost every night I'd read something aloud, with everyone else gathered in a circle on the floor. Those were nice nights.'

'Were there any neighbors or other friends in Seaside he had a particular connection with?'

'We didn't have friends,' Rebecca said. 'Pell wasn't like that.'

'But some people he'd met would come by, stay for a while, then leave. He was always picking up people.'

'Losers like us.'

Linda stiffened slightly. Then said, 'Well, I'd say people down on their luck. Daniel was generous. Gave them food, money sometimes.'

You give a hungry man food, he'll do what you want, Dance reflected, recalling Kellogg's profile of a cult leader and his subjects.

They continued reminiscing but the conversation didn't trigger any recollections of who the houseguests might've been. Dance moved on. 'There are some things he searched for online recently. I was wondering if they mean anything to you. One was "Nimue". I was thinking it might be a name. A nickname or computer screen name maybe.'

'No. I've never heard of it. What does it mean?'

'It's a character out of the King Arthur legend.'

Rebecca looked at the younger woman. 'Hey, did you read us any of those stories?'

But Linda never had. Nor had they heard of an Alison.

Dance then said, 'Tell me about a typical day in the Family.'

Rebecca seemed at a loss for words. 'We'd get up, have breakfast . . . I don't know.'

Shrugging, Linda said, 'We were just a *family*. We talked about what families talk about. The weather, plans, trips we were going to take. Money problems. Who was going to be working where. Sometimes I'd stand in the kitchen after breakfast, doing dishes and just cry – because I was so happy. I had a real family at last.'

Rebecca agreed that their life hadn't been very different from anyone else's, though she clearly wasn't as sentimental as her sister-in-crime.

The discussion meandered and they revealed nothing helpful. In interviewing and interrogation, it's a well-known rule that abstractions obscure memories, while specifics trigger them. Dance now said, 'Do this for me: Pick a particular day. Tell me about it. A day you'd both remember.'

Neither could think of one that stood out, though.

Then Dance suggested, 'Think of a holiday: Thanksgiving, Christmas.'

Linda offered, 'How about that Easter?'

'My first holiday there. My *only* holiday. Sure. That was fun.'

Linda described making an elaborate dinner with food that Sam, Jimmy and Rebecca had 'come up with'. Dance spotted the euphemism instantly; it meant the trio had stolen the groceries.

'I cooked a turkey,' Linda said. 'I smoked it all day in the backyard. My, that was fun.'

Prodding, Dance asked, 'So there you are, you two and Samantha – she was the quiet one, you said.'

'The Mouse.'

'And the young man who was with Pell at the Croytons,' Kellogg said. 'Jimmy Newberg. Tell us about him.'

Rebecca said, 'Right. He was a funny little puppy. He was a runaway too. From up north, I think.'

'Good-looking. But he wasn't all there.' Linda tapped her forehead.

A laugh from her comrade. 'He'd been a stoner.'

'But he was a genius with his hands. Carpentry, electronics, everything.

He was totally into computers, even wrote his own programs. He'd tell us about them and none of us could understand what he was talking about. He wanted to get some website going – remember, this was *before* everybody had one. I think he was actually pretty creative. I felt bad for him. Daniel didn't like him that much. He'd lose patience with him. He wanted to kick him out, I think.'

'Besides, Daniel was a ladies' man. He didn't do well with other men around.'

Dance steered them back to the holiday.

'It was a pretty day,' Linda continued. 'The sun was out. It was warm. We had music going. Jimmy'd put together a real good sound system.'

'Did you say grace?'

'No.'

'Even though it was Easter?'

Rebecca said, 'I suggested it. But Pell said no.'

Linda said, 'That's right. He got upset.'

His father, Dance supposed.

'We played some games in the yard. Frisbee, badminton. Then I put dinner out.'

Rebecca said, 'I'd boosted some good cabernet and we girls and Jimmy had wine – Pell didn't drink. Oh, I got pretty wasted. Sam did too.'

'And we ate a lot.' Linda gripped her belly.

Dance continued to probe. She was aware that Winston Kellogg had dropped out of the conversation. He might be the cult expert but he was deferring to her expertise now. She appreciated that.

Linda said, 'After dinner we just hung out and talked. Sam and I sang. Jimmy was tinkering with his computer. Daniel was reading something.'

The recollections came more frequently now, a chain reaction.

'Drinking, talking, a family holiday.'

'Yeah.'

'You remember what you talked about?'

'Oh, just stuff, you know . . .' Linda fell silent. Then she said, 'Wait. That reminds me of one thing you might want to know about.' She tilted her head slightly. It was a recognition response, though from the focus of her eyes – on a nearby vase filled with artificial amaryllis – the thought was not fully formed. Dance said nothing; you can often erase an elusive memory by asking someone about it directly.

The woman continued, 'It wasn't Easter. It was another dinner. But thinking about Easter reminded me. Daniel and I were in the kitchen. He was watching me cook. And there was a big crash from next door. The neighbors were fighting. He said he couldn't wait to get out of Seaside. To his mountaintop.'

'Mountaintop?'

'Yeah.'

Kellogg asked, '*His?*'

'That's what he said.'

'Did he own some property?'

'He never mentioned anything specific. Maybe he meant "his" in the sense that it was something he *wanted* to have someday.'

Rebecca knew nothing about it.

Linda said, 'I remember clearly. He wanted to get away from everybody. Just us, just the Family. Nobody else around. I don't think he said anything about it before or after that.'

'But not Utah? You both said he never mentioned that.'

'No.' Rebecca agreed. 'But, wait. You know, thinking of that . . . I don't know if it's helpful but I remember something too. Along those same lines. We were in bed one night and he said, 'I need to make a big score. Come up with enough money just to get away from everybody.' I remember that. He said, "A big score".'

'What did he mean? A robbery to buy some property?'

'Could be.'

'Linda?'

She had to plead ignorance and seemed troubled that he hadn't shared everything with her.

Dance asked the obvious question: 'Could the big score have been the Croyton break-in?'

'I don't know,' Rebecca said. 'He never told us that's where he and Jimmy were going that night.'

Dance speculated: Maybe he *did* steal something valuable from Croyton's house, after all. When the police were closing in, he hid it. She thought of the car he'd driven to the break-in. Had it been searched thoroughly? Where was it now? Maybe destroyed, maybe owned by someone else. She made a note to try to find the vehicle. Also, to check deed registries to see if Pell owned any property.

Mountaintop . . . Could that have been what he'd been looking for online in Capitola on the Visual-Earth website? Dozens of sizeable peaks were within an hour's drive of the Peninsula.

There were still questions, but Dance was pleased at their progress. Finally, she felt she had some insights into the mind of Daniel Pell. She was about to ask more questions when her phone rang. 'Excuse me.'

She answered it.

'Kathryn. It's me.'

She pressed the phone closer to her head. 'TJ, what's up?' And steeled herself. The fact that he hadn't called her 'boss' meant he was about to deliver bad news.

# Chapter
# TWENTY-NINE

Kathryn Dance and Winston Kellogg walked along a road covered with a thin coat of damp sand toward TJ and Michael O'Neil, who stood at the open trunk of a late-model Lexus. Another man was there too, one of the officers from the Coroner's Division, which in Monterey County is part of the MCSO. The balding, round deputy greeted her. 'Kathryn.'

Dance introduced him to Kellogg, then peered into the trunk. The victim, a woman, lay on her side. Her legs were bent and her hands and mouth were duct-taped. Her nose and face were bright red. Blood vessels had broken.

O'Neil said, 'Susan Pemberton. Lived in Monterey. Single, thirty-nine.'

'Probable COD is suffocation?'

The coroner officer added, 'And we've got capillary dilation and membrane inflammation and distension. That residue there? I'm sure it's capsicum oleoresin.'

'He hit her with pepper spray and then duct-taped her.'

The coroner officer nodded.

'Terrible,' O'Neil muttered.

Dying alone, in pain, an ignominious trunk her coffin. A burst of raw anger at Daniel Pell swept through Dance.

It turned out, O'Neil explained, that Susan's was the disappearance that he'd been looking into.

'We're sure it's Pell?'

'It's him,' the Coroner's Division officer said. 'Prints match.'

O'Neil added, 'I've ordered field prints tests done for every homicide in the area.'

'Any idea of the motive?'

'Maybe. She worked for an event-planning company. He apparently used her to get in and tell him where all the files were. He stole everything. Crime scene's been through the office. Nothing conclusive so far, except his prints.'

'Any clue why?' Kellogg asked.

'Nope.'

'How'd he find her?'

'Her boss said she left the office about five last night to meet a prospective client for drinks.'

'Pell, you think?'

O'Neil shrugged. 'No idea. Her boss didn't know who. Maybe Pell saw them and followed.'

'Next of kin?'

'Nobody here, doesn't look like,' the Coroner's Division officer said. 'Her parents're in Denver. I'll make that call when I get back to the office.'

'TOD?'

'Last night, maybe seven to nine. I'll know more after the autopsy.'

Pell had left little evidence, except a few faint footsteps in the sand that seemed to lead toward the beach then were lost in the pale grass littering the dunes. No other prints or treadmarks were visible.

What was in the files he'd stolen? What didn't he want them to know?

Kellogg was walking around the area, getting a feel for the crime scene, maybe considering it in light of his specialty, cult mentality.

Dance told O'Neil about Rebecca's idea that Pell was after a big score, presumably so that he could buy an enclave somewhere.

'"Mountaintop" was what Linda said. And the big score might've been the Croyton break-in.' She added her idea that maybe Pell had hidden something of Croyton's in the getaway car.

'I think it was why he was searching Visual-Earth. To check the place out.'

'Interesting theory,' O'Neil said. He and Dance would often brainstorm when they were working cases together. Occasionally they'd come up with some truly bizarre theories about the crimes they were investigating. Sometimes those theories actually turned out to be right.

Dance told TJ to check out the status of the vehicle Pell had been driving on the night of the Croyton murders and if there'd been an inventory of the car's contents. 'And see if Pell owns property anywhere in the state.'

'Will do, boss.'

Dance looked around. 'Why'd he abandon the car here? He could've gone east into the woods, and nobody would've found it for days. It's a lot more visible here.'

Michael O'Neil pointed at a narrow pier extending into the ocean. 'The T-bird's out of commission. He's ditched the stolen Ford Focus by now. Maybe he got away by boat.'

'Boat?' Dance asked.

'His footsteps go that way. None head back to the road.'

Kellogg was nodding but it was a slow gesture and it said, I don't think so. 'It's a little rough, don't you think, to dock a boat there?'

'Not for somebody who knows what they're doing.'

'Could you?'

'Me? Sure. Depending on the wind.'

A pause as Winston Kellogg looked over the scene. The rain started coming down steadily. He didn't seem to notice. 'My thinking is that he started that way for some reason, maybe to lead us off. But then he turned and headed back over the dunes to the road, met his accomplice somewhere along here.'

Phrases like 'my thinking' and 'I'm of the opinion that' are what Dance called verbal anesthetic. Their purpose is to take the sting out of a speaker's critical or contrary statement. The new kid on the block was reluctant to disagree with O'Neil but evidently felt that he was wrong about the boat.

'Why do you think that?' Dance asked.

'That old windmill.'

At the turnoff where the beach road left the main highway was an abandoned gas station, under a decorative two-story windmill.

'How long's it been there?'

'Forty, fifty years, I'd guess. The pumps only have two windows for the price – like no one ever believed gas would ever cost more than 99 cents.'

Kellogg continued, 'Pell knows the area. His accomplice's probably from out of town. He picked this place because it's deserted but also because there's a landmark you can't miss. "Turn right at the windmill."'

O'Neil's face revealed he wasn't swayed. 'Could be. Of course, if that was the only reason, you'd wonder why he didn't pick someplace closer to town. Be easier to direct his accomplice to a place like that, and there are plenty of deserted areas that'd work. And think about it, the Lexus was stolen and had a body in the trunk. He'd definitely want to dump it as soon as possible.'

'Maybe, makes sense,' Kellogg conceded. He looked around, squinting in the mist. 'But I'm leaning toward something else. I think he was drawn here not because of the pier but because it's deserted and it's a beach. He's not a ritualistic killer but most cult leaders have a mystical bent, and water often figures in that. Something happened here, almost ceremonial, I'd say. It might've involved the woman with him. Maybe sex after the kill. Or maybe something else?'

'What?'

'I can't say. My guess is she met him here. For whatever he had in mind.'

'But,' O'Neil pointed out, 'there's no evidence of another car, no evidence that he turned around and walked back to the road. You'd think there'd be some prints.'

Kellogg said, 'He could've covered his tracks.' Pointing to a portion of the sand-covered road. 'Those marks don't look natural. He could've swept over them with brush or leaves. Maybe even a broom. I'd excavate that whole area.'

O'Neil: 'I'm thinking it can't hurt to check on stolen vessels. And I'd rather crime scene ran the pier now.'

The tennis volley continued, the FBI agent offering, 'With this wind and rain . . . I really think the road should be first.'

'You know, Win, I think we'll go with the pier.'

Kellogg tipped his head, meaning: It's your crime scene team; I'm backing down. 'Fine with me. I'll search it myself if you don't mind.'

'Sure. Go right ahead.'

Without a look at Dance – he had no desire to test loyalties – the FBI agent returned to the area with the dubious markings.

Dance turned and walked along a clean zone back to her car, glad to leave the crime scene behind. Forensic evidence wasn't her expertise.

Neither were strong-willed rams butting horns.

The visage of grief.

Kathryn Dance knew it well. From her days as a journalist, interviewing survivors of crimes and accidents. From her days as a jury consultant, watching the faces of the witnesses and victims recounting injustices and personal injury.

From her own life too. As a widow: looking in the mirror, staring eye

to eye with a very different Kathryn Dance, the lipstick hovering before
easing away from the mask of a face.

Why bother, why bother?

Now, she was seeing the same look as she sat in Susan Pemberton's
office, across from the dead woman's boss, Eve Brock.

'It's not real to me.'

No, it never is.

The crying was over but only temporarily, Dance sensed. The stocky
middle-aged woman held herself in tight rein. Sitting forward, legs tucked
under the chair, shoulders rigid, jaw set. The kinesics of grief matched
the face.

'I don't understand the computer and the files. Why?'

'I assume there was something he wanted to keep secret. Maybe he
was at an event years ago and he didn't want anybody to know about
it.' Dance's first question to the woman had been: Was the company in
business before Pell went to prison? Yes, it was.

The crying began again. 'One thing I want to know. Did he . . . ?'

Dance recognized a certain tone and answered the incomplete question: 'There was no sexual assault.' She asked the woman about the client
Susan was going to meet, but she knew no details.

'Would you excuse me for a moment?' Eve Brock was about to
surrender to her tears.

'Of course.'

Eve headed for the ladies' room.

Dance looked at Susan Pemberton's walls, filled with photos of past
jobs: weddings; bar and bat mitzvahs; anniversary parties; outings and
events for local corporations, banks and fraternal groups; political fund
raisers and high school and college events. The company also worked
with funeral homes to cater receptions after an interment.

She saw, to her surprise, the name of the mortician who had handled
her husband's funeral.

Eve Brock returned, her face red, eyes puffy. 'I'm sorry.'

'Not a problem at all. So she met that client after work?'

'Yes.'

'Would they go for drinks or coffee somewhere?'

'Probably.'

'Nearby?'

'Usually. Alvarado.' The main street in downtown Monterey. 'Or maybe
Del Monte Center, Fisherman's Wharf.'

'Any favorite watering hole?'

'No. Wherever the client wanted to go.'

'Excuse me.' Dance found her phone and called Rey Carraneo.

'Agent Dance,' he said.

'Where are you?'

'Near Marina. Still checking on stolen boats for Detective O'Neil. Nothing yet. And no luck on the motels, either.'

'Okay. Keep at it.' She disconnected and called TJ. 'Where are *you*?'

'The emphasis tells me I'm the second choice.'

'But the answer is?'

'Near downtown. Monterey.'

'Good.' She gave him the address of Eve Brock's company and told him to meet her on the street in ten minutes. She'd give him a picture of Susan Pemberton and have him canvass all the bars and restaurants within walking distance, as well as the shopping center and Fisherman's Wharf. Cannery Row too.

'You love me best, boss. Bars and restaurants. My kind of assignment.'

She also asked him to check with the phone company and find out about incoming calls to Susan's phones. She didn't think the client was Pell; he was ballsy, but he wouldn't come to downtown Monterey in broad daylight. But the prospective client might have valuable information about, say, where Susan was going after their meeting.

Dance got the numbers from Eve and recited them to TJ.

After they disconnected, she asked, 'What would be in the files that were stolen?'

'Oh, everything about our business. Clients, hotels, suppliers, churches, bakeries, caterers, restaurants, liquor stores, florists, photographers, corporate PR departments who'd hired us . . . just everything . . .' The recitation seemed to exhaust her.

What had worried Pell so much he'd destroyed the files?

'Did you ever work for William Croyton or his company?'

'For . . . oh, the man he killed, the family. No, we never did.'

'Maybe a subsidiary of his company, or one of his suppliers?'

'I suppose we could have. We do a lot of corporate functions.'

'Do you have backups of the material?'

'Some are in the archives. Tax records, cancelled checks. Things like that. Probably copies of the invoices. But a lot of things I don't bother with. It never occurred to me that somebody would steal them. The copies would be at my accountant's. He's in San Jose.'

'Could you get as many of them as possible?'

'There's so much . . .' Her mind was stalled.

'Limit it to eight years ago, up to May of Ninety-nine.'

It was then that Dance's mind did another of its clicks. Could Pell be interested in something that the woman was planning in the *future?* 'All your upcoming jobs too.'

'I'll do what I can, sure.'

The woman seemed crushed by the tragedy, paralyzed.

Thinking of Morton Nagle's book *The Sleeping Doll,* Dance realized that she was looking at yet one more victim of Daniel Pell.

*I see violent crime like dropping a stone into a pond. The ripples of consequence can spread almost forever.*

Dance got a picture of Susan to give to TJ and walked downstairs to the street to meet him. Her phone rang.

O'Neil's mobile on caller ID.

'Hi,' she said, glad to see the number.

'I have to tell you something.'

'Go ahead.'

He spoke softly and Dance took the news without a single affect display, no revealed emotion.

'I'll be there as soon as I can.'


'It's a blessing, really,' Juan Millar's mother told Dance through her tears.

She was standing next to a grim-faced Michael O'Neil in the corridor of Monterey Bay Hospital, watching the woman do her best to reassure *them* and deflect their own words of sympathy.

Winston Kellogg arrived and walked up to the family, offered condolences and then shook O'Neil's hand, fingers on the detective's biceps, a gesture conveying sincerity among businessmen, politicians and mourners. 'I'm so sorry.'

They were outside the burn unit of the ICU. Through the window they could see the complicated bed and its surrounding spacecraft accoutrements: wires, valves, gauges, instrumentation. In the center was a still mound, covered by a green sheet.

The same color sheet had covered her husband's corpse. Dance recalled seeing it and thinking, frantically, But where did the life go, where did it *go?* At that moment she'd come to loathe this particular shade of green.

Dance stared at the body, hearing in her memory Edie Dance's whispered words.

*He said, 'Kill me.' He said it twice. Then he closed his eyes . . .*

Millar's father was inside the room itself, asking the doctor questions whose answers he probably wasn't digesting. Still, the role of parent who'd survived his son required this – and would require much more in the days ahead.

Kellogg too offered his sympathy to the mother, who chatted away and told him again that her son's death was for the best, there was no doubt, the years of treatment, the years of grafts . . .

'For the best, absolutely,' he said, offering Charles Overby's favorite adverbial crutch.

Edie Dance, working an unplanned late shift, now came down the hall, looking distraught but determined, a visage that her daughter recognized clearly. Sometimes feigned, sometimes genuine, the expression had served her well in the past. Today it would, of course, be a reflection of her true heart.

Now Edie moved straight to Millar's mother. She took the woman by the arm and, recognizing approaching hysteria, bestowed words on her – a few questions about her own state of mind but mostly about her husband's and other children's, all aimed at diverting the woman's focus from this impossible tragedy. Edie Dance was a genius in the art of compassion. It was why she was such a popular nurse.

Rosa Millar began to calm and then to cry, and Dance could see the staggering horror melting into manageable grief. Her husband joined them, and Edie handed his wife over to him like a trapeze artist transferring one acrobat to another in midair.

'Mrs Millar,' Dance said, 'I'd just like to –'

Then found herself flying sideways, barking a scream, hands not dropping to her weapon but rising to keep her head from slamming into one of the carts parked here.

Her first thought: How had Daniel Pell gotten into the hospital?

'No!' O'Neil shouted. Or Kellogg. Probably both. Dance caught herself as she went down on one knee, knocking coils of yellow tubing and plastic cups to the floor.

The doctor too leapt forward, but it was Winston Kellogg who got the enraged Julio Millar in a restraint hold, arm bent backward, and held him down easily with a twisted wrist. The maneuver was fast and seemed effortless.

'No, son!' the father shouted, and the mother cried harder.

O'Neil helped Dance up. No injuries other than what would be bruises come morning, she guessed.

Julio tried to break away but Kellogg, apparently much stronger than he appeared, tugged the arm up slightly. 'Take it easy, don't hurt yourself. Just take it easy.'

'Bitch, you fucking bitch! You killed him! You killed my brother!'

O'Neil said, 'Julio, listen. Your parents are upset enough. Don't make it worse.'

'Worse? How could it be worse?' He tried to kick out.

Kellogg simply sidestepped him and lifted the wrist higher. The young man grimaced and groaned. 'Relax. It won't hurt if you relax.' The FBI agent looked at the parents, their hopeless eyes. 'I'm sorry.'

'Julio,' his father said, 'you hurt her. She's a policewoman. They'll put you in jail.'

'They should put *her* in jail! She's the killer.'

Millar senior shouted, 'No, stop it! Your mother, think about your mother. Stop it!'

Smoothly, O'Neil had his cuffs out. He was hesitating. He glanced at Kellogg. The men were debating. Julio seemed to be relaxing.

'Okay, okay, get off me.'

O'Neil said, 'We'll have to cuff you if you can't control yourself. Understand?'

'Yeah, yeah, I understand.'

Kellogg let go and helped him up.

Everyone's eyes were on Dance. But she wasn't going to take the matter to the magistrate. 'It's all right. There's no problem.'

Julio stared into Dance's eyes. 'Oh, there's a problem. There's a big problem.' He stormed off.

'I'm so sorry,' Rosa Millar said through her tears.

Dance reassured her. 'Does he live at home?'

'No, an apartment nearby.'

'Have him stay with you tonight. Tell him you need his help. For the funeral, to take care of Juan's affairs, whatever you can think of. He's in as much pain as everybody here. He just doesn't know what to do with it.'

The mother had stepped to the gurney where her son lay. She muttered something. Edie Dance walked up to her again and whispered into her ear, touching her arm. An intimate gesture between women who'd been complete strangers until a couple of days ago.

After a moment Edie returned to her daughter. 'You want the kids to spend the night?'

'Thanks. It's probably best.'

Dance said good-bye to the Millar's. 'Is there anything we can do? Anything at all?'

The father answered in a voice that seemed perplexed by the question. 'No, no.' Then he added, 'What else is there to be done?'

# Chapter
# THIRTY

The town of Vallejo Springs in Napa, California, has several claims to fame.

It's the site of a museum featuring many works of Eadweard Muybridge, the nineteenth-century photographer credited with inventing moving pictures (and – a lot more interesting than his art – he was a man who murdered his wife's lover, admitted it in court and got off scot-free).

Another draw is the local vineyards, which produce a particularly fine strain of the merlot grape – one of the three most famous used to make red wine. Contrary to a bad rap generated by a movie of a few years ago, merlot isn't your Yugo of grapes. Just look at Pétrus, a wine from the Pomerol section of Bordeaux, made almost entirely from merlot and perhaps the most consistently expensive wine in the world.

Morton Nagle, though, was now crossing the town limits because of Vallejo Springs's third attraction, albeit one that was known to very few people.

Theresa Croyton, the Sleeping Doll, and her aunt and uncle lived here.

Nagle had done his homework. A month of tracking down twisty leads had turned up a reporter in Sonoma, who'd given him the name of a lawyer who'd done some legal work for the girl's aunt. He'd been reluctant to give Nagle any information but did offer the opinion that the woman was overbearing and obnoxious – and cheap. She'd dunned him on a bill. Once he was convinced that Nagle was a legitimate writer he gave up the town the family lived in and their new name, on a guarantee of anonymity.

'Confidential source' is really just a synonym for spineless.

Nagle had been to Vallejo Springs several times, meeting with the Sleeping Doll's aunt in an attempt to get an interview with the girl (the uncle didn't figure in the equation, he'd learned). She was reluctant but Nagle believed that she would eventually agree.

Now back in this picturesque town, he parked near the spacious house, waiting for the opportunity to talk to the woman alone. He could call, of course. But Nagle felt that phone calls – like email – were an ineffective way of communicating. On a telephone the person you're speaking to is your equal. You have much less control and power of persuasion than if you're there in person.

They can also just hang up.

He had to be careful. He'd noticed the police cruising past the house at frequent intervals. This in itself meant nothing – Vallejo Springs was a rich town and had a large, well-endowed constabulary – but Nagle noticed that the squad cars seemed to slow when they drove past the house of Tod and Mary Bolling, the surname the family had adopted.

He noticed too that there were far more police cars out and about now than last week, which suggested to him what he already suspected: that Theresa was a town sweetheart. The cops would be on high alert to make sure nothing happened to her. If Nagle overstepped, they'd escort him to the town limits and dump him in the dust, like an unwelcome gunslinger in some bad western.

He sat back, eyes on the front door, and thought about opening lines for his book.

*Carmel by the Sea is a village of contradictions, a mecca for tourists, the jewel in the crown of the Central Coast, yet beneath the pristine and the cute you'll find the secretive world of the rich and ruthless from San Francisco, Silicon Valley and Hollywood.*

Hm. Work on that.

Nagle chuckled.

And then he saw the SUV, a white Escalade, pulling out of the Bollings' driveway. The girl's aunt, Mary, was behind the wheel, alone in the car. Good. He'd never get close if Theresa was with her.

Nagle started his car, a Buick worth the price of the SUV's transmission alone, and followed. Theresa's aunt made a stop at a gas station, filled the tank with premium. She chatted with a woman at a nearby pump. The aunt seemed harried. Her gray hair wasn't brushed and she looked tired. Even from the edge of the parking lot, Nagle could make out dark circles under her eyes.

Pulling out of Shell, she drove through the quaint, unmistakably Californian downtown: a street adorned with plants and flowers and quirky sculptures and lined with coffee shops, understated restaurants, a garden center, an independent bookstore, a yoga and pilates place and small retail operations selling wine, crystals, gifts and L.L. Bean-style clothing.

A few hundred yards along the road was the strip mall where the locals shopped, anchored by an Albertsons grocery and a RiteAid drugstore. Mary Bolling parked in the lot and walked inside the grocery store. Nagle parked near her SUV. He stretched, longing for a cigarette, though he hadn't smoked in twenty years.

He continued the endless debate with himself.

So far he hadn't transgressed. Hadn't broken any rules.

He could still head home, no moral harm done.

But should he?

He wasn't sure.

Morton Nagle believed he had a purpose in life, which was to expose evil. It was an important mission, one he felt passionate about. A noble mission.

But the goal was to *reveal* evil, and let people make their own judgments, not to fight it himself. Because once you crossed the line and your purpose became seeking justice, not illuminating it, there were risks. Unlike the police, he didn't have the Constitution telling him what he could and couldn't do, which meant there was the potential for abuse. By asking Theresa Croyton to help find a killer, he was exposing her and her family – himself and his too – to very real dangers. Daniel Pell obviously had no problem killing youngsters.

It was so much better to *write* about human beings and the conflicts in their lives than to make judgments about those conflicts. Let his readers decide what was good or bad, and act accordingly. On the other hand, was it right for him to sit back and let Pell continue his slaughter, when he could do more?

The time for his slippery debate ended, though. Mary Bolling was walking out of Albertsons, wheeling a cart filled with groceries.

Yes or no?

Morton Nagle hesitated only a few seconds, then pulled open the door, stepped out and hitched up his pants. He strode forward.

'Excuse me. Hi, Mrs Bolling. It's me.'

She paused, blinked and stared at him. 'What are you doing here?'

'I –'

'I haven't agreed to let you talk to Theresa.'

'I know, I know . . . That's not –'

'How dare you show up here like this? You're stalking us!'

Her cell phone was in her hand.

'Please,' Nagle said, feeling a sudden desperation to sway her. 'This is something different. I'm here doing a favor for someone. We can talk about the book later.'

'A favor?'

'I drove up from Monterey to ask you something. I wanted to see you in person.'

'What are you talking about?'

'You know about Daniel Pell.'

'Of *course* I know.' She said this as if he were the village idiot.

'There's a policewoman who'd like to talk to your niece. She thinks maybe Theresa can help her find Pell.'

'*What?*'

'Don't worry. There's no risk. She –'

'No risk? Are you mad? You could've led him here!'

'No. He's somewhere in Monterey.'

'Did you tell them where we are?'

'No! This policewoman'll meet her wherever you like. Here. Anywhere. She just wants to ask Theresa –'

'No one is going to talk to her. No one is going to see her.' The woman leaned forward. 'There will be very serious consequences if you don't leave immediately.'

'Mrs Bolling, Daniel Pell has killed –'

'I watch the fucking news. Tell that policewoman, whoever she is, that there's not a single thing Theresa can tell her. And *you* can forget about ever talking to her for your goddamn book.'

'No, wait, please –'

Mary Bolling turned and ran back to the Escalade, as her abandoned shopping cart ambled in the opposite direction down the shallow incline. By the time a breathless Nagle had grabbed the cart just before it slammed into a Mini Cooper, the SUV was spinning tires as it vanished from the lot.

\* \* \*

Not long ago a CBI agent, now *former*, had once called this the 'Gals' Wing'.

He was referring to that part of the Monterey headquarters that happened to be the home of two female investigative agents – Dance and Connie Ramirez – as well as Maryellen Kresbach and the no-nonsense office manager, Grace Yuan.

The unfortunate utterer was a fiftyish agent, one of those fixtures in offices all over the world who wake up counting the days to retirement, and who've done so since their twenties. He'd had his share of collars at the Highway Patrol some years back, but his move to the CBI had been a mistake. He wasn't up to the challenges of the job.

He also apparently lacked any sense of survival.

'And this is the Gals' Wing,' he'd said, loud enough for everyone to hear, during a lunch-hour tour of HQ with a young woman he was wooing.

Dance and Connie Ramirez made eye contact.

That night they went on a pantyhose-buying mission and when the poor agent came to work the next day he found his entire office spider-webbed in mesh, fishnet and glittery synthetic legwear. Some personal hygiene products also figured in the décor. He ran whining to the then CBI head Stan Fishburne, who, bless him, could hardly keep a straight face during the inquisition. 'What do you mean you *only* said, "Gals' Wing", Barton? You actually *said* that? Are you nuts?'

He threatened a complaint to Sacramento, but he didn't last long enough in the CBI to see the matter through. Ironically, after the offender's departure, the population of that portion of the office adopted the moniker instantly and the hallway was now known to everyone in the CBI as 'GW'.

Whose undecorated hallway Kathryn Dance was walking down at the moment.

'Maryellen, hi.'

'Oh, Kathryn, I'm sorry to hear about Juan. We're all going to make a donation. You know where his parents would like it to go?'

'Michael's talking to them now.'

'Your mother called. She's going to stop by with the kids later, if that's okay.'

Dance made sure to see her children whenever she could, even during business hours if a case was taking up a lot of time and she'd be working late. 'Good. How's the Davey situation?'

'It's taken care of,' said the woman firmly. The person in question was Maryellen's son, Wes's age, who'd been having trouble in school because of some issues with what amounted to a preteen gang. Maryellen now relayed the news of the resolution with a look of happy malice, which told Dance that extreme measures had been used to get the offenders transferred or otherwise neutralized.

Dance believed that Maryellen Kresbach would make a great cop.

In her office she dropped her jacket onto a chair, hitched the awkward Glock to the side and sat. She looked through her email. Only one was relevant to the Pell case. His brother, Richard Pell, was replying from London.

*Officer Dance:*

> *I received your forwarded email from the U.S. embassy here. Yes, I heard of the escape, it has made the news here. I have not had any contact with my brother for 12 years, when he came to visit my wife and me in Bakersfield at the same time my wife's twenty-three-year old sister was visiting us from New York. One Saturday we got a call from the police that she'd been detained at a jewelry store downtown for shoplifting.*
>
> *The girl had been an honors student in college and quite involved in her church. She'd never been in any trouble in her life before that.*
>
> *It seemed that she'd been 'hanging out' with my brother and he'd talked her into stealing a 'few things'. I searched his room and found close to $10,000 worth of merchandise. My niece was given probation and my wife nearly left me as a result.*
>
> *I never had anything to do with him again. After the murders in Carmel in '99, I decided to move my family to Europe.*
>
> *If I hear from him, I will certainly let you know, though that is unlikely. The best way to describe my relationship now is this: I've contacted the London Metropolitan Police and they have an officer guarding my house.*

So much for that lead.

Her mobile rang. The caller was Morton Nagle. In an alarmed voice he asked, 'He killed someone else? I just saw the news.'

'I'm afraid so.' She gave him the details. 'And Juan Millar died, the officer who was burned.'

'I'm so sorry. Are there other developments?'

'Not really.' Dance told him that she'd spoken with Rebecca and Linda. They'd shared some information that might prove to be helpful, but nothing was leading directly to Pell's doorstep. Nagle had come across nothing in his research about a 'big score' or a mountaintop.

He had news of his own efforts, though they weren't successful. He'd talked to Theresa Croyton's aunt, but she was refusing to let him, or the police, see the girl.

'She threatened me.' His voice was troubled and Dance was sure that there would be no sparkle in his eyes just now.

'Where are you?'

He didn't say anything.

Dance filled in, 'You're not going to tell me, are you?'

'I'm afraid I can't.'

She glanced at the caller ID, but he was on his mobile, not a hotel or pay phone.

'Is she going to change her mind?'

'I really doubt it. You should've seen her. She abandoned a hundred dollars' worth of groceries and just ran.'

Dance was disappointed. Daniel Pell was a mystery and she was now obsessed with learning everything she could about him. Last year when she'd assisted on that case in New York with Lincoln Rhyme, she'd noted the criminalist's obsessive fascination with every detail of the physical evidence; she was exactly the same – though with the human side of crime.

But there're compulsions like double-checking every detail of a subject's story, and there are compulsions like avoiding sidewalk cracks when you're walking home. You have to know which are vital and which aren't.

She decided they'd have to let the Sleeping Doll lead go.

'I appreciate your help.'

'I did try. Really.'

After hanging up, Dance talked to Rey Carraneo again. Still no luck on the motels and no reports of boats stolen from local marinas.

Just as she hung up, TJ called. He'd heard back from the DMV. The car that Pell had been driving during the Croyton murders hadn't been registered for years, which meant it'd probably been sold for scrap. If he had stolen something valuable from the Croytons' on the night of the murders it was, most likely, lost or melted into oblivion. TJ had also checked the inventory from when the car was impounded. The list was short and nothing suggested that any of the items had come from the businessman's house.

She gave him the news about Juan Millar too, and the young agent responded with utter silence, a sign that he was truly shaken.

A few moments later her phone rang again. It was Michael O'Neil with his ubiquitous, 'Hey. It's me.' His voice was laden with exhaustion; sorrow too. Millar's death was weighing on him heavily.

'Whatever'd been on the pier where we found the Pemberton woman was gone – if there was anything. I just talked to Rey. He tells me there're no reports of any stolen craft so far. Maybe I was off base. Your friend find anything the other way – toward the road?'

She noted the loaded term, 'friend', and replied, 'He hasn't called. I assume he didn't stumble across Pell's address book or a hotel key.'

'And negative on sources for the duct tape, and the pepper spray's sold in ten thousand stores and mail order outlets.'

She told O'Neil that Nagle's attempt to contact Theresa had failed.

'She won't cooperate?'

'Her aunt won't. And she's first base. I don't know how helpful it'd be anyway.'

O'Neil said, 'I liked the idea. She's the only nexus to Pell and that night.'

'We'll have to try harder without her,' Dance said.

'How're you doing?'

'Fine,' he answered.

*Stoic . . .*

A few minutes after they disconnected, Winston Kellogg arrived and Dance asked, 'Any luck at the Pemberton crime scene, the road?'

'Nope. The scene itself – we searched for an hour. No treadmarks, no discarded evidence. Maybe Michael was right. Pell *did* get away by boat from that pier.'

Dance laughed to herself. The chest-bumping males had each just conceded the other might've been right – though she doubted they'd ever admit it to each other.

She updated him on the missing files from Susan Pemberton's office and Nagle's failure to arrange an interview with Theresa Croyton. TJ, she explained, was looking for the client Susan had met with just before Pell had killed her.

Dance glanced at her watch. 'Got an important meeting. Want to come?'

'Is it about Pell?'

'Nope. It's about snack time.'

# Chapter
## THIRTY-ONE

As they walked down the halls of CBI's headquarters Dance asked Kellogg where he lived.

'The District – that's Washington, D.C. to you all. Or that place known as "Inside the Beltway", if you watch the pundits on Sunday-morning talk TV. Grew up in the Northwest – Seattle – but didn't really mind the move east. I'm not a rainy-day kind of guy.'

The talk meandered to personal lives and he volunteered that he and his ex had no children, though he himself had come from a big family. His parents were still alive and lived on the East Coast.

'I've got four brothers. I was the youngest. I think my parents ran out of names and started on consumer products. So, I'm Winston, like cigarettes. Which is a really bad idea when your last name is corn flakes. If my parents had been any more sadistic my middle name'd be Oldsmobile.'

Dance laughed. 'I'm convinced I didn't get invited to the junior prom because nobody wanted to take a Dance to the dance.'

Kellogg had received a degree in psych from the University of Washington then gone into the army.

'CID?' She was thinking about her late husband's stint in the army, where he'd been a Criminal Investigations Division officer.

'No. Tactical planning. Which meant paper, paper, paper. Well, computer, computer, computer. I was fidgety. I wanted to get into the field so I left and joined the Seattle Police Department. Made detective and did profiling and negotiations. But I found the cult mentality interesting. So I thought I'd specialize in it. I know it sounds lame but I just didn't like the idea of bullies preying on vulnerable people.'

She didn't think it was lame at all.

Down more corridors.

'How'd *you* get into this line?' he asked.

Dance gave him a brief version of the story. She'd been a crime reporter for a few years – she'd met her husband while covering a criminal trial (he gave her an exclusive interview in exchange for a date). After she grew tired of reporting, she went back to school and got degrees in psychology and communications, improving her natural gift of observation and an ability to intuit what people were thinking and feeling. She became a jury consultant. But nagging dissatisfaction with that job and a sense that her talents would be more worthwhile in law enforcement, had led her to the CBI.

'And your husband was like me, a feebie?'

'Been doing your homework?' Her late husband, William Swenson, had been a dependable career special agent for the FBI, but he was just like tens of thousands of others. There was no reason for a specialist like Kellogg to have heard of him, unless he'd gone to some trouble to check.

A bashful grin. 'I like to know where I'm going on assignments. And who I'm going to meet when I get there. Hope you're not offended.'

'Not at all. When I interview a subject I learn everything I can about his "terrarium".' Not sharing with Kellogg that she'd had TJ scope out the agent through his friend in the Chico resident agency.

A moment passed and he asked, 'Can I ask what happened to your husband? Line of duty?'

The thud in her belly generated by that question had become less pronounced over the years. 'It was a traffic accident.'

'I'm sorry.'

'Thank you . . . Now, welcome to *Chez* CBI.' Dance waved him into the lunchroom.

They poured coffee and sat at one of the cheap tables.

Her cell chirped. It was TJ. 'Bad news. My bar-hopping days are over. Just as I got started. I found out where the Pemberton woman was before she was killed.'

'And?'

'With some Latino guy in the bar at the Doubletree. A business meeting, some event he wanted her to handle, the waiter thinks. They left about six thirty.'

'You get a credit-card receipt?'

'Yep, but she paid. Business expense. Hey, boss, I think *we* should start doing that.'

'Anything else about him?'

'Zip. Her picture'll be on the news so he might see it and come forward.'

'Susan's phone logs?'

'About forty calls yesterday. I'll check them out when I'm back in the office. Oh, and statewide real estate tax records? Nope, Pell don't own no mountaintops or anything else. I checked Utah too. Nothing there either.'

'Good. I forgot about that.'

'Or Oregon, Nevada, Arizona. I wasn't being diligent. I was just trying to prolong my bar time as much as I could.'

After they hung up she relayed the information to Kellogg, who grimaced. 'A witness, hm? Who'll see her picture on the tube and decide this is a real nice time to take that vacation to Alaska.'

'And I can hardly blame him.'

Then the FBI agent smiled as he looked over Dance's shoulder. She glanced back. Her mother and children were walking into the lunch room.

'Hi, honey,' she said to Maggie, then hugged her son. There'd be a day, pretty soon, when public hugs would be verboten and she was storing up for the drought. He tolerated the gesture well enough today.

Edie Dance and her daughter cast glances each other's way, acknowledging Millar's death but not specifically referring to the tragedy. Edie and Kellogg greeted each other, and exchanged a similar look.

'Mom, Carly moved Mr Bledsoe's wastebasket!' Maggie told her breathlessly. 'And every time he threw something out it went on the floor.'

'Did you keep from giggling?'

'For a while. But then Brendon did and we couldn't stop.'

'Say hello to Agent Kellogg.'

Maggie did. But Wes only nodded. His eyes shifted away. Dance saw the aversion immediately.

'You guys want hot chocolate?' she asked.

'Yay!' Maggie cried. Wes said he would too.

Dance patted her jacket pockets. Coffee was gratis but anything fancier took cash, and she'd left all of hers in the Coach purse in her office. Edie had no change.

'I'll treat,' Kellogg said, digging into his pocket.

Wes said quickly, 'Mom, I want coffee instead.' The boy had sipped coffee once or twice in his life and hated it.

Maggie said, 'I want coffee too.'

'No coffee. It's hot chocolate or soda.' Dance supposed that Wes didn't want something that the FBI man paid for. What was going on here? Then she remembered how his eyes had scanned Kellogg on the Deck the previous night. She thought he'd been looking for his weapon; now she understood he'd been sizing up the man whom Mom had brought to his grandfather's party. Was Winston Kellogg the new Brian, in his eyes?

'Okay,' her daughter said, 'chocolate.'

Wes muttered, 'That's okay. I don't want anything.'

'Come on, I'll loan it to your mom,' Kellogg said, dispensing the coins. The children took them, Wes reluctantly and only after his sister did.

'Thanks,' Wes said.

'Thank you very much,' Maggie offered.

Edie poured coffee. They sat at the unsteady table. Kellogg thanked Dance's mother again for the dinner the other night and asked about Stuart. Then he turned to the children and wondered aloud if they liked to fish.

Maggie said sort of. She didn't.

Wes loved to but responded, 'Not really. You know, it's boring.'

Dance knew the agent had no motive but breaking the ice, his question probably inspired by his conversation with her father at the party about fishing in Monterey Bay. She noted some stress reactions – he was trying too hard to make a good impression, she guessed.

Wes fell silent and sipped his chocolate while Maggie inundated the adults with the morning's events at music camp, including a rerun, in detail, of the trashcan caper.

The agent found herself irritated that the problem with Wes had reared its head yet again . . . and for no good reason. She wasn't even dating Kellogg.

But Dance knew the tricks of parenting and in a few minutes had Wes talking enthusiastically about his tennis match that morning. Kellogg's posture changed once or twice and the body language told Dance that he too was a tennis player and wanted to contribute. But he'd caught on that Wes was ambivalent about him and he smiled as he listened, but didn't add anything.

Finally Dance told them she needed to get back to work, she'd walk them out. Kellogg told her he was going to check in with the San Francisco field office. 'Good seeing you all.' He waved.

Edie and Maggie said good-bye to him. After a moment Wes did too – only so he wouldn't be outdone by his sister, though, Dance sensed.

The agent wandered off up the hallway toward his temporary office.

'Are you coming to Grandma's for dinner?' Maggie asked.

'I'm going to try, Mags.' Never promise if there's a chance you can't deliver.

'But if she can't,' Edie said, 'what're you in the mood for?'

'Pizza,' Maggie said fast. 'With garlic bread. And mint chocolate chip for dessert.'

'And I want a pair of Ferragamos,' Dance said.

'What're those?'

'Shoes. But what we want and what we get are sometimes two different things.'

Her mother put another offer on the table. 'How's a big salad? With blackened shrimp?'

'Sure.'

Wes said, 'That'll be great.' The children were infinitely polite with their grandparents.

'But I think garlic bread can be arranged,' Edie added, which finally pried a smile from him.

Outside the CBI office, one of the administrative clerks was on his way to deliver documents to the Monterey County Sheriff's Office in Salinas.

He noticed a dark car pulling into the lot. The driver, a young woman wearing sunglasses despite the fog, scanned the parking lot. She's uneasy about something, the clerk thought. But, of course, you got that a lot here: people who'd come in voluntarily as suspects or reluctant complaining witnesses. The woman looked at herself in the mirror, pulled on a cap and climbed out. She didn't go to the front door. Instead she approached him. 'Excuse me?'

'Yes, ma'am?'

'This is the California Bureau of Investigation?'

If she'd looked at the building she would've seen the large sign that repeated four of the words in her question. But, being a good public servant, he said, 'That's right. Can I help you?'

'Is this the office where Agent Dance works?'

'Kathryn Dance. Yes.'

'Is she in now?'

'I don't –' The clerk looked across the lot and barked a laugh. 'Well, guess what, miss? That's her, right over there, the younger woman.' He saw Dance with her mother and the two kids, whom the clerk had met on a couple of occasions.

'Okay. Thank you, Officer.'

The clerk didn't correct her. He liked being misidentified as a real law enforcer. He got into his car and pulled out of the driveway. He happened to glance in the rearview mirror and saw the woman standing just where he'd left her. She seemed troubled.

He could've told her she didn't need to be. Kathryn Dance, in his opinion, was one of the nicest people in the whole of the CBI.


Dance closed the door of her mother's Prius hybrid. It hummed out of the lot and the agent waved good-bye. She watched the silver car negotiate the winding road toward Highway 68. She was troubled. She kept imagining Juan Millar's voice in her head.

*Kill me . . .*

The poor man.

Although his brother's lashing out had nothing to do with it, Kathryn Dance *did* feel guilty that she'd picked him to go check on what was happening in the lockup. He was the most logical one, but she wondered if, being younger, he'd been more careless than a more experienced officer might've been. It was impossible to think that Michael O'Neil, or big Albert Stemple, or Dance herself would have let Pell disarm them.

Turning back toward the building, she was thinking of the first few moments of the fire and the escape. They'd had to move so quickly. But should she have waited, thought out her strategy better?

Second-guessing. It went with the territory of being a cop.

Walking toward the main entrance, she hummed Julieta Venegas's song. The notes were swirling through her thoughts, intoxicating – and taking her away from Juan Millar's terrible wounds and terrible words and Susan Pemberton's death . . . and her own son's eyes, flipping from cheerful to stony the moment the boy had seen Dance with Winston Kellogg.

What to do about *that*?

Dance continued through the deserted parking lot toward the front door of CBI, glad that the rain had stopped.

She was nearing the stairs when she heard the scrape of footsteps on the asphalt and turned quickly to see that a woman had come up behind her, silently until now. She was a mere six or so feet away, walking directly toward her.

Dance stopped fast.

The woman did too. She shifted her weight. 'Agent Dance . . . I . . .'

Neither spoke for a moment.

Then Samantha McCoy said, 'I've changed my mind. I want to help.'

# Chapter
# THIRTY-TWO

'I couldn't sleep after you came to see me. And when I heard he'd killed someone else, that woman, I knew I *had* to come.'

Samantha, Dance and Kellogg were in her office. The woman sat upright, gripping the arms of the chair hard, looking from one to the other. Never more than a second's gaze at either. 'You're sure it was Daniel who killed her?'

'That's right,' Kellogg said.

'Why?'

'We don't know. We're looking into it now. Her name was Susan Pemberton. She worked for Eve Brock. Do the names mean anything to you?'

'No.'

'It's an event-planning company. Pell took all their files and presumably destroyed them. There was something in them that he wanted to hide. Or maybe there's an event coming up that he's interested in. Do you have any thoughts about what that might be?'

'I'm sorry, no.'

Dance told her, 'I want to get you together with Linda and Rebecca as soon as possible.'

'They're both here?'

'That's right.'

Samantha nodded slowly.

Kellogg said, 'I need to follow up on a few things here. I'll join you later.'

Dance told Maryellen Kresbach where she'd be and the women left the CBI building. The agent had Samantha park her car in the secure garage under the building, so no one would see it. They then both got into Dance's Ford.

Samantha clicked on her seat belt and then stared straight ahead. Suddenly she blurted, 'One thing, my husband, his family . . . my friends. They still don't know.'

'What did you tell him about being away?'

'A publishing conference . . . And Linda and Rebecca? I'd just as soon they didn't know my new name, about my family.'

'That's fine with me. I haven't given them any details they didn't already know. Now, you ready?'

A shaky smile. 'No. I'm not the least ready. But, okay, let's go.'

When they arrived at the inn Dance checked with the MCSO deputy outside and learned there'd been no unusual activity in or around the cabin. She gestured Samantha out of the car. The woman hesitated and climbed from the vehicle, squinting, taking in everything around her. She'd be vigilant, of course, under the circumstances, but Dance sensed something else lay behind this attentiveness.

Samantha gave a faint smile. 'The smells, the sound of the ocean . . . I haven't been back to the Peninsula since the trial. My husband keeps asking me to drive down for the weekend. I've come up with some doozy excuses. Allergies, car sickness, pressing manuscripts to edit.' Her smile faded. She glanced at the cabin. 'Pretty.'

'It's only got two bedrooms. I wasn't expecting you.'

'If there's a couch, I can sleep on that. I don't want to bother anybody.'

Samantha the unassuming one, the shy one, Dance recalled.

*The Mouse.*

'I hope it'll just be for one night.' Kathryn Dance stepped forward and knocked on the door to the past.

The Toyota smelled of cigarette smoke, which Daniel Pell hated.

He himself never smoked, though he'd bartered cigarettes like a floor broker on a stock exchange when he was inside the Q or Capitola. He would've let the kids in the Family smoke – dependency in someone else is exploitable, of course – but he loathed the smell. Reminded him of growing up, his father sitting in his big armchair, reading the Bible, jotting notes for sermons nobody would ever hear and chain-smoking. His mother nearby too, but smoking *and* drinking and doing nothing else. And his brother, not smoking or doing anything else but hauling young Daniel out from where he was hiding, his closet, the tree house, the basement bathroom. 'I'm not doing all the fucking work myself.'

Though his brother ended up not doing *any* of the work; he just handed Daniel a scrub bucket or toilet brush or dishrag and went to hang with his friends. He'd return to the house occasionally to pound on Daniel if the house wasn't spick and span.

*Cleanliness, son, is next to godliness. There's truth in that. Now, polish the ashtrays. I want them to sparkle.*

So he and Jennie were now driving with the windows down, the scent of pine and cold salty air swirling into the car.

Jennie did that rubby-nose thing, like she was trying to massage the bump out, and was quiet. She was content now, not purring but back on track. His distance last night, after she'd balked at helping him 'kill' Susan Pemberton on the beach, had worked just fine. They'd returned to the Sea View and she'd done the only thing she could to try to win back his love – and spent two strenuous hours proving it. He'd withheld at first, been sullen, and she tried even harder. She was even starting to enjoy the pain. It reminded him of the time the Family had stopped at Carmel Mission years ago. He'd learned about the monks who'd beat themselves bloody, getting a high in the name of God.

But that reminded Daniel Pell of his chunky father looking at him blankly over the Bible, through a cloud of Camel cigarette smoke, so he pushed the memory away.

Last night, after the sex, he'd grown warmer to her. But later he'd stepped outside and pretended to make a phone call.

Just to keep her on edge.

When he'd returned she hadn't asked about the call and he'd just kept flipping through the material he'd gotten from Susan Pemberton's office, and went online once more.

This morning he'd told her he had to go see someone. Let that sit, watched her insecurities roll up – taps on the lumpy nose, a half-dozen 'sweethearts' – and then finally he'd said, 'I'd like it if you came along.'

'Really?' A thirsty dog lapping up water.

'Yep. But, I don't know . . . It might be too hard for you.'

'No, I want to. Please.'

'We'll see.'

She'd pulled him back to bed and they'd continued their balance-of-power game. He let himself be tugged temporarily back into her camp.

Now, though, as they drove, he had no interest in her body whatsoever; he was firmly back in control.

'You understand about yesterday, at the beach? I was in a funny mood. I get that way when something precious to me is endangered.' This was a bit of an apology – who can resist that? – along with the reminder that it might happen again.

'That's one thing I love about you, sweetie.'

Not 'sweetheart' now. Good.

When Pell had had the Family, tucked away all cozy in the town of Seaside, he'd used a lot of techniques for controlling the girls and Jimmy. He'd give them common goals, he'd dispense rewards evenly, he'd dole out tasks but withhold the reason for doing them, he'd keep them in suspense until they were nearly eaten alive by uncertainty.

And – the best way to cement loyalty and avoid dissension – he'd create a common enemy.

He now said to her, 'We have another problem, lovely.'

'Oh. That's where we're going now?' Rub-a-dub on the nose. It was a wonderful barometer.

'That's right.'

'I told you, honey, I don't care about the money. You don't have to pay me back.'

'This doesn't have anything to do with that. It's more important. Much more. I'm not asking you to do what I did last night. I'm not asking you to hurt anybody. But I need some help. And I hope *you* will.'

Carefully playing with the emphasis.

She'd be thinking of the fake phone call last night. Who'd he been talking to? Somebody else he could call on to step in?

'Whatever I can do, sure.'

They passed a pretty brunette, late teens, on the sidewalk. Pell noted immediately her posture and visage – the determined walk, the angry, downcast face, the unbrushed hair – which suggested she'd fled after an argument. Perhaps from her parents, perhaps her boyfriend. So wonderfully vulnerable. A day's work, and Daniel Pell could have her on the road with him.

*The Pied Piper* . . .

But, of course, now wasn't the time and he left her behind, feeling the frustration of a hunter unable to stop by the roadside and take a perfect buck in a field nearby. Still, he wasn't upset; there'd be plenty of other young people like her in his future.

Besides, feeling the gun and knife in his waistband, Pell knew that in just a short period of time his hunt lust would be satisfied.

# Chapter
# THIRTY-THREE

Standing in the open doorway of the cabin at Point Lobos Inn, Rebecca Sheffield said to Dance, 'Welcome back. We've been gossiping and spending your money on room service.' She nodded toward a bottle of Jordan cabernet, which only she was drinking.

Rebecca glanced at Samantha and, not recognizing her, said, 'Hello.' Probably thinking she was another police officer involved in the case.

The women walked inside. Dance shut and double-locked the door.

Samantha looked from one woman to the other. It seemed as if she'd lost her voice, and for a moment Dance believed she'd turn and flee.

Rebecca did a double take and blinked. 'Wait. Oh my God.'

Linda didn't get it, her brows furrowed.

Rebecca said, 'Don't you recognize her?'

'What do you – ? Wait. It's you, Sam?'

'Hello.' The slim woman was racked with uneasiness. She couldn't hold a gaze for more than a few seconds.

'Your face,' Linda said. 'You're so different. My.'

Samantha shrugged, blushing.

'Uh-huh, prettier. And you've got some meat on your bones. Finally. You were a scrawny little thing.' Rebecca walked forward and firmly hugged Samantha. Then, hands on her shoulders, she leaned back. 'Great job . . . What'd they do?'

'Implants, jaw and cheek. Lips and eyes mostly. Nose, of course. And then . . .' She glanced at her round chest. A faint smile. 'But I'd wanted to do that for years.'

Linda, crying, 'I can't believe it.' Another hug.

'What's your new name?'

Not looking at either of them, she said, 'I'd rather not say. And listen, both of you. Please. You can't tell anybody about me. If they catch Daniel and you want to talk to reporters, please don't mention me.'

'No problem with that.'

'Your husband doesn't know?' Linda asked, glancing at Samantha's engagement and wedding rings.

A shake of the head.

'How'd you pull *that* one off?' Rebecca asked.

Samantha swallowed. 'I lie. That's how.'

Dance knew that married couples lie to each other with some frequency, though less often than romantic partners who aren't married. But most lies are trivial; very few involve something as fundamental as Samantha's.

'That's gotta be a pain,' Rebecca said. 'Need a good memory.'

'I don't have any choice,' Samantha added. Dance recognized the kinesic attributes of defensiveness, body parts folding, stature shrinking, crossings, aversions. She was a volcano of stress.

Rebecca said, 'But he has to know you did time?'

'Yes.'

'Then how –?'

'I told him it was a white-collar thing. I helped my boss embezzle some stocks because his wife needed an operation.'

'He believed *that*?'

Samantha gave a timid look to Rebecca. 'He's a good man. But he'd walk out the door if he knew the truth. That I was in a cult –'

'It wasn't a cult,' Linda said quickly.

'Whatever it was, Daniel Pell was behind it. That's reason enough to leave me. And I wouldn't blame him.'

Rebecca asked, 'What about your parents? Do they know anything?'

'My mother's dead, and my father's as involved in my life as he always was. Which is not at all. But I'm sorry, I'd rather not talk about all this.'

'Sure, Sam,' Rebecca said.

The agent now returned to the specifics of the case. First, she gave them the details of the Pemberton killing, the theft of the company's files.

'Are you sure he did it?' Linda asked.

'Yes. The prints are his.'

She closed her eyes and muttered a prayer. Rebecca's face tightened angrily.

Neither of them had ever heard the name Pemberton, nor of the

Brock Company. They couldn't recall any events Pell might've gone to that had been catered.

'Wasn't a black-tie kind of life back then,' Rebecca said.

Dance now asked Samantha about Pell's accomplice, but, like the others, she had no idea who the woman might be. Nor did she recall any references to Charles Pickering in Redding. Dance told them about the email from Richard Pell and asked if they'd ever had any contact with him.

'Who?' Rebecca asked.

Dance explained.

'An *older* brother?' Linda interrupted. 'No, Scotty was younger. And he died a year before I met Daniel.'

'He had a *brother*?' Rebecca asked. 'He said he was an only child.'

Dance told them the story about the crimes Pell had committed with his brother's sister-in-law.

Linda shook her head. 'No, no. You're wrong. His brother's name was Scott and he was mentally disabled. That's one of the reasons we connected so well. My cousin's got cerebral palsy.'

Rebecca said, 'And he told me he was an only child, like me.' A laugh. 'He was lying to get our sympathy. What'd he tell *you*, Sam?'

She was reluctant to answer. Then she said, 'Richard was older. He and Daniel didn't get along at all. Richard was a bully. Their mother was drunk all the time and she never cleaned up so but his father insisted the boys do it. But Richard would force Daniel to do all the work. He beat him up if he didn't.'

'He told *you* the truth?' Linda asked stiffly.

'Well, he just mentioned it.'

'The Mouse scores.' Rebecca laughed.

Linda said, 'He told me he didn't want anybody else in the Family to know about his brother. He only trusted me.'

'I wasn't supposed to mention he was an only child,' Rebecca said.

Linda's face was troubled. 'We all tell fibs sometimes. I'll bet the incident with the niece – what his brother emailed you about? I'll bet that didn't happen at all, or it wasn't so bad, and his brother used it as an excuse to cut things off.'

Rebecca was clearly not convinced of this.

Dance supposed that Pell had identified both Linda and Rebecca as more of a threat to him than Samantha. Linda was the mother of the Family and would have some authority. Rebecca was clearly brash and outspoken. But Samantha . . . he could control her much better and knew she could be trusted with the truth – well, *some* truth.

Dance was glad she'd decided to come help them. She noticed that Samantha was looking at the coffee pot.

'Like some?'

'I'm a little tired. Haven't had much sleep lately.'

'Welcome to the club,' Rebecca said.

Samantha half rose but Dance waved her down. 'Milk, sugar?'

'Oh, don't go to any trouble. Really.'

The agent noticed that Linda and Rebecca shared a faint smile at Samantha's habitual timidity.

*Mouse . . .*

'Thanks. Milk.'

Dance continued, 'Linda mentioned Pell might have wanted to move to the country somewhere, a "mountaintop". Do you have any idea what he was talking about?'

'Well, Daniel told me a bunch of times he wanted to get out to the country. Move the Family there. It was real important to him to get away from everybody. He didn't like neighbors, didn't like the government. He wanted space for more people. He wanted the Family to grow.'

'He did?' Rebecca asked.

Linda said nothing about this.

'Did he ever mention Utah?'

'No.'

'Where could he have had in mind?'

'He didn't say. But it sounded like he'd been doing some serious thinking about it.'

Recalling that he'd possibly used a boat to escape from the Pemberton crime scene, Dance had an idea. She asked, 'Did he ever mention an island?'

Samantha laughed. 'An island? No way.'

'Why not?'

'He's terrified of the water. He's not getting into anything that floats.'

Linda blinked. 'I didn't know that.'

Rebecca didn't either. A wry smile. 'Of course not. He'd only share his fears with his Mouse.'

'Daniel said the ocean's somebody else's world. People have no business being there. You shouldn't be in a place that you can't be master of. Same thing with flying. He didn't trust pilots or airplanes.'

'We were thinking he escaped from the murder scene by boat.'

'Impossible.'

'You're sure?'

'Positive.'

Dance excused herself for a moment, called Rey Carraneo and had him call off the search for stolen boats. She hung up, reflecting that O'Neil's theory was wrong and Kellogg's was right.

'Now, I'd like to think about his motives for staying here. What about money?' She mentioned Rebecca's comment about a big score – a robbery or break-in, a big heist. 'I was thinking he might be here because he hid money or something valuable somewhere. Or has unfinished business. Something to do with the Croyton murders?'

'Money?' Samantha shook her head. 'No, I don't really think that's it.'

Rebecca said firmly, 'I know he said it.'

'Oh, no, I'm not saying he didn't,' the Mouse added quickly. 'Just, he might not have meant "big" in the sense we'd use. He didn't like to commit crimes that'd be too visible. We broke into houses –'

'Well, hardly any,' Linda corrected.

Rebecca sighed. 'Well . . . We pretty much *did*, Linda. And you folks'd been busy before I joined you.'

'It was exaggerated.'

Samantha said nothing to support either woman, and seemed uneasy, as if afraid they'd call on her again to be the tiebreaker. She continued, 'He said if somebody did anything *too* illegal, the press would cover the story and then the police got after you in a big way. We stayed away from banks and check-cashing offices. Too much security, too risky.' She shrugged. 'Anyway, all the stealing – it was never about the money.'

'It wasn't?' Dance asked.

'No. We could've made as much doing legitimate jobs. But that's not what turned Daniel on. What he liked was getting people to do things they didn't want to. That was his high.'

Linda said, 'You make it sound like that's all we did.'

'I didn't mean it like that –'

'We weren't a gang of thugs.'

Rebecca ignored Linda. 'I think he was definitely into making money.'

Samantha smiled uncertainly. 'Well, I just had this sense it was more about manipulating people. He didn't need a lot of money. He didn't want it.'

'He'd have to pay for his mountaintop somehow,' Rebecca pointed out.

'That's true, I guess. I could be wrong.'

Dance sensed this was an important key to understanding Pell, so she asked them about their criminal activities, hoping it might spark some specific memories.

Samantha said, 'He was good, Daniel was. Even knowing what we were doing was wrong, I couldn't help but admire him. He'd know the best places to go for pickpocketing or breaking into houses. How security worked in department stores, what designer labels had security tags and which didn't, what kind of clerk would take returns without receipts.'

Linda said, 'Everybody makes him out to be this terrible criminal. But it was really just a *game* to him. Like, we'd have disguises. Remember? Wigs, different clothes, fake glasses. It was all harmless fun.'

Dance was inclined to believe Samantha's theory that sending the Family out on their missions was more about power than money.

'But what about the Charles Manson connection?'

'Oh,' Samantha said. 'There *was* no Manson connection.'

Dance was surprised. 'But all the press said so.'

'Well, you know the press.'

Samantha was typically reluctant to disagree, but she was clearly certain about this. 'He thought Manson was an example of what *not* to do.'

But Linda shook her head. 'No, no, he had all those books and articles about him.'

Dance recalled that she'd gotten a longer prison sentence because she'd destroyed some of the incriminating material about Manson the night of the Croyton murders. She seemed troubled now that her heroic act might have been pointless.

'The only parallels were that he lived with several women and had us doing crimes for him. Manson wasn't in control of *himself*, Daniel said. He claimed he was Jesus, he tattooed a swastika on his forehead, he thought he had psychic powers, he ranted about politics and race.

'That was another example of emotions controlling you. Just like tattoos and body piercings or weird haircuts. They give people information about you. And information is control. No, he thought Manson did everything wrong. Daniel's heroes were Hitler –'

'Hitler?' Dance asked Samantha.

'Yep. Except he faulted him because of that "Jewish thing". It was a weakness. Pell said that if Hitler could suck it up and live with Jews, even include them in the government, he'd have been the most powerful man in history. But he couldn't control himself, so he deserved to lose the war. He admired Rasputin too.'

'The Russian monk?'

'Right. He worked his way into Nicholas and Alexandra's household. Pell liked Rasputin's use of sex to control people.' Drawing a laugh from Rebecca and a blush from Linda. 'Svengali too.'

'The *Trilby* book?' Dance asked.

'Oh,' she replied. 'You know about that? He loved that story. Linda read it a dozen times.'

'And frankly,' Rebecca said, 'it was pretty bad. All that old-style writing. Melodrama, you know.'

Glancing at her notebook, the agent asked the newcomer about the keywords Pell had searched in prison.

'"Nimue"?' Samantha repeated. 'No. But he had a girlfriend named Alison once.'

'Who?' Linda asked.

'When he was in San Francisco he met her. Before us. She was in this group, sort of like the Family.'

'What're you talking about?' Linda asked.

Samantha nodded. She looked uneasily at Linda. 'But it wasn't his group. He just was bumming around and met Alison and got to know some of the people in that cult, or whatever it was. Daniel wasn't a member – he didn't take orders from *anybody* – but he was fascinated with it, and hung out with them. He learned a lot about how to control people. But they got suspicious of him – he wouldn't join. So he and Alison left. They hitchhiked around the state. Then he got arrested or picked up by the police for something, and she went back to San Francisco. Even when we were together he tried to find her. That's why he'd go up to the Bay area sometimes. I don't know why he'd want to try now.'

'What was her last name?'

'I don't know.'

Dance wondered aloud if Pell was looking for this Alison – or someone named Nimue – for revenge. 'After all, he'd need a pretty good reason to risk going online in Capitola to find somebody.'

'Oh,' Samantha said, 'Daniel didn't believe in revenge.'

Rebecca said, 'I don't know, Sam. What about that biker? That punk up the street? Daniel almost killed him.'

Dance remembered Nagle telling them about a neighbor in Seaside whom Pell had assaulted.

'First of all,' Linda said, 'Daniel didn't do it. That was somebody else.'

'Well, no, he beat the crap out of him. Nearly killed him.'

'But the police let him go.'

Curious proof of innocence, Dance reflected.

'Only because the guy didn't have the balls to press charges.' Rebecca looked at Samantha. 'Was it our boy?'

Samantha shrugged, avoiding their gaze. 'I think so. I mean, yeah, Daniel beat him up.'

Linda looked unconvinced.

'But that wasn't about revenge . . . See, the biker thought he was some kind of neighborhood godfather. He tried to blackmail Daniel, threatened to go to the police about something that never even happened. Daniel went to see him and started playing these mind games with him. But the biker just laughed at him and told Daniel he had one day to come up with the money.

'Next thing there's an ambulance in front of the biker's house. His wrists and ankles were broken. But that wasn't revenge. It was because he was immune to Daniel. If you're immune, then Daniel can't control you, and that makes you a threat. And he said all the time, "Threats have to be eliminated."'

'Control,' Dance said. 'That pretty much sums up Daniel Pell, doesn't it?'

This, it seemed, was one premise from their past that all three members of the Family could agree on.

# Chapter
# THIRTY-FOUR

From the patrol car, the MCSO deputy kept his vigilant eye on his territory: the grounds, the trees, the gardens, the road.

Guard duty – it had to be the most boring part of being a police officer, hands down. Stakeouts came in a close second, but at least then you had a pretty good idea that the surveillee was a bad guy. And *that* meant you might get a chance to draw your weapon and go knock heads.

You'd get to *do* something.

But babysitting witnesses and good guys – especially when the bad guys don't even know where the good ones are – was borrrrring.

All that happened was you got a sore back and sore feet and had to balance the issue of coffee with bathroom breaks and –

Oh, hell, the deputy muttered to himself. Wished he hadn't thought that. Now he realized he had to pee.

Could he risk the bushes? Not a good idea, considering how nice this place was. He'd ask to use one inside. First he'd make a fast circuit just to be sure everything was secure, then go knock on the door.

He climbed out of the car and walked down the main road, looking around at the trees, the bushes. Still nothing odd. Typical of what you'd see around here: a limo driving past slowly, the driver actually wearing one of those caps like they did in the movies. A housewife across the street was having her gardener arrange flowers beneath her mailbox before he planted them, the poor guy frustrated at her indecision.

The woman looked up and saw the deputy, nodded his way.

He nodded back, flashing on a wispy fantasy of her coming over and saying how much she liked a man in a uniform. The deputy had heard stories of cops making a traffic stop and the women 'paying the fine' behind a row of trees near the highway or in the back of a squad car (the seat of a Harley Davidson figured in some versions, as well). But those were always I-know-somebody-who-knows-somebody stories. It'd never happened to any of his friends. He suspected too that if anybody – even this desperate housewife – proposed a romp, he couldn't even get it up.

Which put him in mind of the geography below the belt again and how much he needed to relieve himself.

Then he noticed the housewife was waving to him and approaching. He stopped.

'Is everything okay around here, Officer?'

'Yes, ma'am.' Ever noncommittal.

'Are you here about that car?' she asked.

'Car?'

She gestured. 'Up there. About ten minutes ago I saw it park, but the driver, he sort of pulled up in between some trees. I thought it was a little funny, parking that way. You know, we've had a few break-ins around here lately.'

Alarmed now, the deputy stepped closer to where she was indicating. Through the bushes he saw a glint of chrome or glass. The only reason to drive a car that far off the road was to hide it.

Pell, he thought.

Reaching for his gun, he took a step up the street.

*Wssssh.*

He glanced back at the odd sound just as the shovel, swung by the housewife's gardener, slammed into his shoulder and neck, connecting with a dull ring.

A grunt. The deputy dropped to his knees, his vision filled with a dull yellow light, black explosions going off in front of him. 'Please, no!' he begged.

But the response was simply another blow of the shovel, this one better aimed.

Dressed in his dirt-stained gardener outfit, Daniel Pell dragged the cop into the bushes where he couldn't be seen. The man wasn't dead, just groggy and hurting.

Quickly he stripped off the deputy's uniform and put it on, rolled up the cuffs of the too-long slacks. He duct-taped the officer's mouth and cuffed him with his own bracelets. He slipped the cop's gun and extra clips into his pocket, placed the Glock he'd brought with him in the holster; he was familiar with that weapon and had dry fired it often enough to be comfortable with the trigger pull.

Glancing behind him, he saw Jennie retrieving the flowers from the patch of dirt around the neighbor's mailbox and dumping them into a shopping bag. She'd done a good job in her role as housewife. She'd distracted the cop perfectly and she'd hardly flinched when Pell had smacked the poor bastard with the shovel.

The lesson of 'murdering' Susan Pemberton had paid off; she'd moved closer to the core darkness within her. But he'd still have to be careful now. Killing the deputy would be over the top. Still, she was coming along nicely; Pell was ecstatic. Nothing made him happier than transforming someone into a creature of his own making.

'Get the car, lovely.' He handed her the gardener outfit.

A smile blossoming, full. 'I'll have it ready.' She turned and hurried up the street with the clothes, shopping bag and shovel. She glanced back, mouthing, 'I love you.'

Pell watched her, enjoying the confident stride.

Then he turned away and walked slowly up the driveway that led to the house of the man who'd committed an unforgivable sin against him, a sin that would spell the man's death: former prosecutor James Reynolds.

Daniel Pell peered through a crack in the curtain of a front window. He saw Reynolds on a cordless phone, holding a bottle of wine, walking from one room to another. A woman – his wife, Pell guessed – walked into what seemed to be the kitchen. She was laughing.

Pell had thought it'd be easy to find almost anybody nowadays, computers, the Internet, Google. He'd discovered some information about Kathryn Dance, which would be useful. But James Reynolds was invisible. No phone listing, no tax records, no addresses in any of the old state and county directories or bar association lists.

He would eventually have found the prosecutor through public records, Pell supposed, but could hardly browse through the very county government building he'd just escaped from. Besides, he had very little time. He needed to finish his business in Monterey and leave.

But then he'd had his brainstorm and turned to the archives of local newspapers on the Internet. He'd found a listing in the *Peninsula Times* about the prosecutor's daughter's wedding. He'd called the venue where the event was held, the Del Monte Spa and Resort, and found the name of the wedding planner, the Brock Company. A bit of coffee – and pepper spray – with Susan Pemberton had earned Pell the files that contained the name and address of the man who'd paid for the fete, James Reynolds.

And now here he was.

More motion inside.

A man in his late twenties, it seemed, was also in the house. Maybe a son – the brother of the bride. He'd have to kill them all, of course, and anyone else inside. He didn't care one way or the other about hurting the family but he couldn't leave anyone alive. Their deaths were simply a practical matter, to give Pell and Jennie more time to get away. At gunpoint he'd force them into a closed space – a bathroom or den – then use the knife, so no one would hear shots. With some luck, the bodies wouldn't be found until after he'd finished his other mission here on the Peninsula and be long gone.

Pell now saw the prosecutor hang up his phone and start to turn. Pell ducked back, checked his pistol and pressed the doorbell. There was the rustle of noise from inside. A shadow filled the peephole. Pell stood where he could be seen in his uniform, though he was looking down casually.

'Yes? Who is it?'

'Mr Reynolds, it's Officer Ramos.'

'Who?'

'I'm the relief deputy. I'd like to talk to you.'

'Just a second. I've got something on the stove.'

Pell gripped his pistol, feeling that a huge irritation was about to be relieved. He suddenly felt aroused. He couldn't wait to get Jennie back to the Sea View. Maybe they wouldn't make it all the way to the motel. He'd take her in the backseat. Pell now stepped into the shadows of a large, tangled tree beside the door, enjoying the feel of the heavy gun in his hand. A minute passed. Then another. He knocked again. 'Mr Reynolds?'

'Pell, don't move!' a voice shouted. It was coming from outside, behind him. 'Drop the weapon.' The voice was Reynolds's. 'I'm armed.'

No! What had happened? Pell shivered with anger. He nearly vomited he was so shaken and upset.

'Listen to me, Pell. If you move one inch I will shoot you. Take the weapon in your left hand by the barrel and set it down. Now!'

'What? Sir, what are you talking about?'

No, no! He'd planned this so perfectly! He was breathless with rage.

He gave a brief glance behind him. There was Reynolds, holding a large revolver in both hands. He knew what he was doing and didn't seem the least bit nervous.

'Wait, wait, Prosecutor Reynolds. My name's Hector Ramos. I'm the relief –'

He heard the click as the hammer on Reynolds's gun cocked.

'Okay! I don't know what this is about. But okay. Jesus.' Pell took the barrel in his left hand and crouched, lowering it to the deck.

When, with a screech, the black Toyota skidded into the driveway and braked to a stop, the horn blaring.

Pell dropped flat to his belly, swept up the gun and began firing in Reynolds's direction. The prosecutor crouched and fired several shots himself but, panicked, missed. Pell then heard the distant keening of sirens. Torn between self-preservation and his raw lust to kill the man, he hesitated a second. But survival won out. He sprinted down the driveway, toward Jennie, who had opened the passenger door for him.

He tumbled inside and they sped away, Pell finding some bleak satisfaction in emptying his weapon toward the house, hoping for at least one mortal hit.

# Chapter
# THIRTY-FIVE

Dance, Kellogg and James Reynolds stood in his dewy front lawn, amid pristine landscaping, lit by the pulse of colored lights.

The prosecutor's first concern, he explained, was that no one had been hit by his, or Pell's, slugs. He'd fired in defensive panic – he was still shaken – and even before the car had skidded away he was troubled that a bullet might have injured a neighbor. He'd run to the street to look at the car's tags, but the vehicle was gone by then so he jogged to the houses nearby. No one had been injured by a stray shot, though. The deputy in the bushes outside the house would have some bad bruises, a concussion and very sore muscles, but nothing more serious than that, the medics reported.

When the doorbell rang and 'Officer Ramos' announced his presence at the front door, Reynolds had actually been on the phone with Kathryn Dance, who was telling him urgently that Pell, possibly disguised as a Latino, knew where he lived and was planning to kill him. The prosecutor had drawn his weapon and sent his wife and son into the basement to call 911. Reynolds had slipped out a side door and come up behind the man. He'd been seconds away from shooting to kill; only the girlfriend's intervention had saved Pell.

The prosecutor now stepped away to see how his wife was doing, then returned a moment later. 'Pell took all this risk just for revenge? I sure called that one wrong.'

'No, James, it wasn't revenge.' Without mentioning her name – reporters were already starting to show up – Dance explained about Samantha McCoy's insights into Pell's psychology and told him about the incident in Seaside, where the biker had laughed at him. 'You did the same thing in court. When he tried to control you, remember? That meant you were immune to him. And, even worse, you controlled him – you turned him into Manson, into somebody else somebody he had no respect for. He was your puppet. Pell couldn't allow that. You were too much of a danger to him.'

'That's not revenge?'

'No, it was about his future plans,' Dance said. 'He knew you wouldn't be intimidated, and that you had some insights and information about him – maybe even something in the case notes. And he knew that you were the sort who wouldn't rest until he was recaptured. Even if you were retired.'

She remembered the prosecutor's determined visage in his house. *Whatever I can do . . .*

'You wouldn't be afraid to help us track him down. That made you a threat. And, like he said, threats have to be eliminated.'

'What do you mean by the "future"? What's he got in mind?'

'That's the big question. We just don't know.'

'But how the hell did you manage to call two minutes before he showed up?'

Dance shrugged. 'Susan Pemberton.'

'The woman killed yesterday?'

'She worked for Eve Brock.'

His eyes flashed in recognition. 'The caterer, I mean, the event-planner who handled Julia's wedding. He found me through her? Brilliant.'

'At first I thought Pell used Susan to get into the office and *destroy* some evidence. Or to get information about an upcoming event. I kept picturing her office, all the photos on the walls. Some were of local politicians, some were of weddings. Then I remembered seeing the pictures of your daughter's wedding in your living room. The connection clicked. I called Eve Brock and she told me that, yes, you'd been a client.'

'How'd you know about the Latino disguise?'

She explained that Susan had been seen in the company of a slim Latino man not long before she'd been killed. Linda had told them about Pell's use of disguises. 'Becoming Latino seemed a bit far-fetched. But apparently it wasn't.' She nodded at a cluster of bullet holes in the prosecutor's front wall.

Finished with their canvassing, TJ and Rey Carraneo arrived to report that there'd been no sightings of the killer's new wheels.

Michael O'Neil too joined them. He'd been with the crime scene officers as they'd worked the street and the front yard.

O'Neil nodded politely toward Kellogg, as if the recent disagreements were long forgotten. Crime scene, he reported, hadn't discovered much at all. They'd found shell casings from a 9mm pistol, some useless tire prints (they were so worn the technicians couldn't ID the brand) and 'about a million samples of trace that'll lead us nowhere.' The latter information was delivered with the sour hyperbole O'Neil slung out when frustrated.

And, he added, the guard gave only a groggy and inarticulate description of his attacker and the girl with him, but he couldn't add anything to what they already knew.

Reynolds called his daughter, since Pell now knew her and her husband's names, and told her to leave town until the killer was recaptured. Reynolds's wife and other son would join them, but the prosecutor refused to leave. He was going to stay in the area – though at a separate hotel, under police guard – until he'd had a chance to review the Croyton murder files, which should arrive from the county court archives soon. He was more determined than ever to help them get Pell.

Most of the officers left – two stayed to guard Reynolds and his family, and two were keeping the reporters back – and soon Kellogg, O'Neil and Dance were alone, standing on the fragrant grass.

'I'm going back to Point Lobos,' Dance said to both of the men. Then to Kellogg: 'You want me to drop you off at HQ, for your car?'

'I'll go with you to the inn,' Kellogg said. 'If that's okay.'

'Sure.' 'What about you, Michael? Want to come with us?' She could see that Millar's death was still weighing heavily on him.

The deputy glanced at Kellogg and Dance, standing side by side, like a couple in front of their suburban house saying good-night to guests after a dinner party. He said, 'Think I'll pass. I'll make a statement to the press then stop by to see Juan's family.' He exhaled, sending a stream of breath into the cool night. 'Been a long day.'

He was exhausted.

And his round belly contained pretty much an entire bottle of Vallejo Springs's smooth merlot wine. There was no way Morton Nagle was going to drive home tonight through a tangle of combat traffic that involved the sprawl of Contra Costa County, then the equally daunting roads around San Jose. He'd found a motel not far from the vineyards he'd moped around in all day and checked in. He washed his face and hands, ordered a club sandwich from room service and uncorked the wine.

Waiting for the food to arrive, he called his wife and spoke to her and the children, then got through to Kathryn Dance.

She told him that Pell had tried to kill the prosecutor in the Croyton trial.

'Reynolds? No!'

'Everybody's all right,' Dance said. 'But he got away.'

'You think maybe that was his goal? Why he was staying in the area?'

The agent explained she didn't think so. She believed he'd intended to kill Reynolds as a prelude to his real plan, because he was frightened of the prosecutor. But what that real plan might be continued to elude them. Dance sounded tired, discouraged.

Apparently he did too.

'Morton,' Dance asked, 'are you all right?'

'I'm just wondering how bad my headache'll be tomorrow morning.'

Room service knocked on the door. He said good-bye and hung up the phone.

Nagle ate the meal without much appetite and channel surfed, seeing virtually nothing that flickered by on the screen.

The large man lay back in bed, kicking off his shoes. As he sipped from a plastic glass of wine he was thinking of a color photo of Daniel Pell in *Time* magazine years ago. The killer's head was turned partially away but the unearthly blue eyes stared straight into the camera. They seemed to follow you wherever you were, and you couldn't shake the thought that even if you closed the magazine he'd continue to stare into your soul.

Nagle was angry that he'd failed in his attempt to get the aunt's agreement, that the trip here had been a waste of time.

But then he told himself that, at least, he'd stayed true to his journalist's ethics and protected his sources and protected the girl. He'd been as persuasive as he could with the aunt but hadn't stepped over any moral boundaries and told Kathryn Dance the girl's new name and location.

No, Nagle realized, he'd done everything right in a difficult situation.

Growing drowsy, he found he was feeling better. He'd go home tomorrow, back to his wife and children. He'd do the best he could with the book. He'd heard from Patricia Sheffield and she was game to go ahead – she'd been making a lot of notes on life in the Family – and wanted to sit down with him when he returned. She was sure she could convince Linda Whitfield to be interviewed, as well. And there were certainly no lack of victims of Daniel Pell to write about.

Finally, drunk and more or less content, Morton Nagle drifted off to sleep.

# Chapter
# THIRTY-SIX

They sat around the TV, leaning forward, watching the news like three reunited sisters.Which in a way they were, thought Samantha McCoy.

'Can you believe that?' Rebecca asked in a low, angry voice.

Linda, who with Sam was cleaning up the remnants of a room-service dinner, shook her head in dismay.

James Reynolds, the prosecutor, had been the target of Daniel Pell.

Sam was very disturbed by the assault. She remembered Reynolds well. A stern but reasonable man, he'd negotiated what her lawyer had said were fair plea bargains. Sam, in fact, had thought he was quite lenient. There was no evidence that they'd had any involvement in the Croyton deaths – Sam, like the others, was stunned and horrified at the news. Still, the Family's record of petty crimes was extensive and if he'd wanted to, James Reynolds could have gone to trial and probably gotten much longer sentences from a jury.

But he was sympathetic to what they'd been through; he realized they'd fallen under the spell of Daniel Pell. He called it the Stockholm syndrome, which Sam had looked up. It was an emotional connection that victims develop with their hostage takers or kidnappers. Sam was happy to accept Reynolds's leniency, but she wasn't going to let herself off the hook by blaming her actions on some psychological excuse. Every single day she felt bad about the thefts and letting Pell run her life. She hadn't been kidnapped; she'd lived with the Family voluntarily.

A picture came on the TV: an artist's rendering of Pell with darker skin, moustache and black hair, glasses and a vague Latino look. His disguise.

'That's way bizarre,' Rebecca offered.

The knock on the door startled them. Kathryn Dance's voice announced her arrival. Linda rose to let her in.

Samantha liked her – a cop with a great smile, who wore an iPod like her gun and had shoes with bold daisies embossed on the straps. She'd like a pair of shoes like that. Sam rarely bought fun or frivolous things for herself. Sometimes she'd window-shop and think, Neat, I'd like one of those. But then her conscience rumbled, and she decided, no, I don't deserve it.

Winston Kellogg too was smiling, but his was different from Dance's. It seemed like his badge, something to be flashed, saying: I'm really not what you think. I'm a federal agent, but I'm human too. He was appealing. Kellogg wasn't really handsome, certainly not in a classic way. He had a bit of double chin, was a little round in the middle. But his manner and voice and eyes made him sexy.

Glancing at the TV screen, Dance asked, 'You heard?'

Linda said, 'I'm so happy he's all right. His family was there too?'

'They're all fine.'

'On the news, they mentioned a deputy was hurt?' Rebecca asked.

Kellogg said, 'He'll be all right.' He went on to explain how Pell and his partner had planned the man's murder, killing the other woman, Susan Pemberton, yesterday, solely to find out where Reynolds lived.

Sam thought of what had struck her years ago: the obsessed, unstoppable mind of Daniel Pell.

Dance said, 'Well, I wanted to thank you. The information you gave us saved his life.'

'Us?' Linda asked.

'Yep.' She explained how the observations they'd offered earlier – particularly about Pell's reaction to being laughed at and about disguises – had let her deduce what the killer might be up to.

Rebecca was shaking her head, her expressive lips tight. She said, 'But he *did* get away from you, I noticed.'

Sam was embarrassed at Rebecca's abrasive comment. It always amazed her how people wouldn't hesitate to criticize or insult, even when there was no purpose to it.

'He did,' Dance said, looking the taller woman in the eyes. 'We didn't get there in time.'

'The newscaster said Reynolds tried to capture him himself,' Rebecca said.

'That's right,' Kellogg said.

'So maybe he's the reason Pell got away.'

Dance held her eye easily. Sam was so envious of that ability. Her husband would often say, 'Hey, what's the matter? Look at me.' It seemed that her eighteen-month-old son was the only person in the world she could look in the eye.

Dance now said to Rebecca, 'Possibly. But Pell was at the front door with a gun. Reynolds didn't really have any choice.'

Rebecca shrugged. 'Still. One of him, all of you.'

'Come on,' Linda snapped. 'They're doing the best they can. You know Daniel. He thinks out everything. He's impossible to get ahead of.'

The FBI agent said, 'No, you're right, Rebecca. We have to work harder. We're on the defensive. But we *will* get him, I promise.'

Samantha noticed Kellogg glance at Kathryn Dance and Sam thought: Damn, he's sweet on her, the phrase from one of the hundreds of old-time books she'd spent her summers reading as a girl. As for the policewoman? Hm, could be. Sam couldn't tell. But she didn't waste much time thinking about the romantic life of two people she'd known for one day. They were part of a world she wanted to leave behind as fast as possible.

Rebecca relented. 'Well, if we got you that close last time, maybe we'll get you there five minutes earlier next.'

Dance nodded. 'Thank you for that. And everything. We really appreciate it. Now, a couple of things. Just to reassure you, I've added another deputy outside. There's no reason to believe that Pell has any clue you're here, but I thought it couldn't hurt.'

'Won't say no to that,' Rebecca said.

The agent glanced at the clock. It was 10:15. 'I'm proposing we call it quits for tonight. If you think of anything else about Pell or the case and want to talk about it, I can be here in twenty minutes. Otherwise, we'll reconvene in the morning. You've got to be exhausted.'

Samantha said, 'Reunions have a way of doing that.'

Parking in the back of the Sea View, Jennie shut off the Toyota's engine. Daniel Pell didn't get out. He felt numb and everything seemed surreal, the lights ghostly auras in the fog, the slow-motion sound of the waves piling up on Asilomar Beach.

An alternate world, out of some weird movie the cons would watch in Capitola and talk about for months afterward.

All because of the bizarre incident at the prosecutor's house.

'Are you all right, sweetie?'

He said nothing.

'I don't like it that you're unhappy.' She rested a hand on his thigh. 'I'm sorry things didn't work out for you.'

He was thinking of that instance eight years ago, at the Croyton trial, when he had turned his blue eyes, blue like ice, on prosecutor James Reynolds, to intimidate, to make him lose his concentration. But Reynolds had glanced his way and snickered. Then turned to the jury with a wink and a sour joke.

And they had laughed too.

All his efforts were wasted. The spell was broken. Pell had been convinced that he could will his way to an acquittal, to make the jury believe that Jimmy Newberg was the killer, that Pell was a victim too; all he'd done was act in self-defense.

Reynolds, laughing, like Pell was some kid making faces at adults.

Calling him the Son of Manson . . .

Controlling *me*!

*That* had been the unforgivable sin. Not prosecuting Pell – no, many people had done that. But controlling him. Jerking him about like a puppet, to be laughed at.

And not long after that the jury foreman had read the verdict. He saw his precious mountaintop vanishing, his freedom, his independence, the Family. All gone. His whole life destroyed by a laugh.

And now Reynolds – a threat to Pell as serious as Kathryn Dance – would go underground, be far more difficult to find.

He shivered in rage.

'You okay, baby?'

Now, still feeling like he was in a different dimension, Pell told Jennie the story about Reynolds in court and the danger he represented – a story no one knew.

And, funny, she didn't seem to think it was so odd.

'That's terrible. My mother'd do that, laugh at me in front of other people. And she'd hit me too. I think the laughing was worse. A lot worse.'

He was actually moved by her sympathy.

'Hey, lovely? . . . You held fast tonight.'

She smiled and made fists – as if displaying the tattooed letters, *H-O-L-D F-A-S-T*.

'I'm proud of you. Come on, let's go inside.'

But Jennie didn't move. Her smile slipped away. 'I was thinking about something.'

'What?'

'How did he figure it out?'

'Who?'

'The man tonight, Reynolds.'

'Saw me, I suppose. Recognized me.'

'No, I don't think so. It sounded like the sirens were coming, you know, *before* you knocked on the door.'

'They were?'

'I think so.'

*Kathryn* . . . Eyes as green as mine are blue, short pink nails, red rubber band around her braid, pearl on her finger and a polished shell at her throat. Holes in her lobes but no earrings. He could picture her perfectly. He could almost feel her body next to him. The balloon within him began to expand.

'Well, there's this policewoman. She's a problem.'

'Tell me about her.'

Pell kissed Jennie and slipped his hand down her bony spine, past the strap of her bra, and kept going into the waistband of her slacks, felt the lace. 'Not here. Let's go inside. I'll tell you about her inside.'

# Chapter
# THIRTY-SEVEN

'I've had enough of that,' Linda Whitfield said, nodding toward the TV, where news stories about Pell kept looping over and over.

Samantha agreed.

Linda walked into the kitchen and made decaf coffee and tea, then brought out the cups and milk and sugar, along with some cookies. Rebecca took the coffee but set it down and continued to sip her wine.

Sam said, 'That was nice, what you said at dinner.'

Linda had said grace, apparently improvised, but articulate. Samantha herself wasn't religious but she was touched by Linda's words, intended for the souls of the people Daniel Pell had killed and their families, as well as gratitude for the chance to reunite with her sisters and a plea for a peaceful resolution of this sad situation. Even Rebecca – the steel magnolia among them – had seemed moved.

When she was young, Sam often wished her parents would take her to church. Many of her friends went with their families, and it seemed like something parents and a daughter could do together. But then, she'd have been happy if they'd taken her to grocery shop or for a drive to the airport to watch the planes take off and land while they ate hot dogs from a catering truck parked near the fence, like Ellie and Tim Schwimmer from next door did with their folks.

*Samantha, I'd love to go with you but you know how important the meeting is. The issue isn't just about Walnut Creek. It could affect all of Contra Costa. You can make a sacrifice too. The world's not all about you, dear . . .*

But enough of that, Sam commanded herself.

During dinner the conversation had been superficial: politics, the weather, what they thought of Kathryn Dance. Now Rebecca, who'd had plenty of wine, tried to draw Linda out some, find out what had happened in prison to make her so religious, but the woman might have sensed, as did Sam, that there was something challenging about the questions and deflected them. Rebecca had been the most independent of the three and was still the most blunt.

Linda did, though, explain about her day-to-day life. She ran the church's neighborhood center, which Sam deduced was a soup kitchen, and helped with her brother and sister-in-law's foster children. It was clear from the conversation – not to mention her shabby clothing – that Linda was struggling financially. Still, she claimed she had a 'rich life' in the spiritual sense of the word, a phrase she'd repeated several times.

'You don't talk to your parents at all?' Sam asked.

'No,' Linda said softly. 'My brother does every once in a while. But I don't.' Sam couldn't tell whether the words were defiant or wistful. (Sam recalled that Linda's father had tried to run for some election following Linda's arrest and been defeated – after the opposing candidate ran ads implying that if Lyman Whitfield couldn't maintain law and order in his family he'd hardly be a good public servant.)

The woman added that she was dating a man from her church. 'Nice' was how she described him. 'He works at Macy's.' Linda didn't go into specifics and Samantha wondered if she was actually dating him or they were merely friends.

Rebecca was much more forthcoming about her life. Women's Initiatives was doing well, with a staff of four full-time employees, and she lived in a condo overlooking the water. As for her romantic life, she described her latest boyfriend, a landscape designer, almost fifteen years older but handsome and pretty well off. Rebecca had always wanted to get married but, as she talked about their future, Sam deduced there were stumbling blocks and guessed that his divorce wasn't final (if the papers had even been filed). Rebecca mentioned other boyfriends too.

Which made Sam a bit envious. After prison she'd changed her identity and moved to San Francisco, where she hoped she could get lost in the anonymity of a big city. She'd avoided socializing for fear she'd let slip some fact about her real identity, or that somebody might recognize her, despite the surgery.

Finally the loneliness caught up and she started to go out. Her third date, Ron Starkey, was a Stanford electrical engineer grad. He was sweet and shy and a bit insecure – a classic nerd. He wasn't particularly interested in her past; in fact, he seemed oblivious to just about every-thing except avionics navigation equipment, movies, restaurants and, now, their son.

Not the sort of personality most women would go for, but Samantha decided it was right for her.

Six months later they were married, and Peter was born a year after that. Sam was content. Ron was a good father, a solid man. She only wished she'd met him a few years later, after she'd lived and experienced a bit more of life. She felt that meeting Daniel Pell had resulted in a huge hole in her life, one that could never be filled.

Both Linda and Rebecca tried to get Sam to talk about herself. She demurred. She didn't want anyone, least of all these women, to have any possible clues as to her life as Sarah Starkey. If word got out, Ron would leave her. She knew it. He'd broken up with her for a few months when she'd tearfully 'confessed' about the fake embezzlement; he'd walk right out the door – and take their child with him, she knew – if he learned she'd been involved with Daniel Pell and been lying to him about it for years.

Linda offered the plate of cookies again.

'No, no,' Samantha said. 'I'm full. I haven't eaten that much for dinner in a month.'

Linda sat nearby, ate half a cookie. 'Oh, Sam, before you got here we were telling Kathryn about that Easter dinner. Our last one together. Remember that?'

'Remember it? It was fantastic.'

It *had* been a wonderful day, Sam recalled. They'd sat outside around a driftwood table she and Jimmy Newberg had made. Piles of food, great music from Jimmy's complicated stereo, sprouting wires everywhere. They'd dyed Easter eggs, filling the house with the smell of hot vinegar. Sam tinted all of hers blue. Like Daniel's eyes.

The Family wouldn't survive long after that; six weeks later the Croyton family and Jimmy would be dead, the rest of them in jail.

But that had been a good day.

'That turkey,' Sam said, shaking her head at the memory. 'You smoked it, right?'

Linda nodded. 'About eight hours. In that smoker Daniel made for me.'

'The what?' Rebecca asked.

'That smoker out back. The one he made.'

'I remember. But he didn't make it.'

Linda laughed. 'Yes, he did. I told him I'd always wanted one. My parents had one and my father'd smoke hams and chickens and ducks. I wanted to help but they wouldn't let me. So Daniel made me one.'

Rebecca was confused. 'No, no. He got it from what's-her-name up the street.'

'Up the street?' Linda frowned. 'You're wrong. He borrowed some tools and made it out of an old oil drum. He surprised me with it.'

'Wait, it was . . . Rachel. Yeah, that was her name. Remember her? Not a good look – gray roots with bright red hair.' Rebecca looked perplexed. 'You have to remember her.'

'I remember Rachel.' Linda's response was stiff. 'What's she got to do with anything?'

Rachel was a stoner who'd caused serious disharmony within the Family because Pell had spent a lot of time at her house doing, well, what Daniel Pell loved to do most. Sam hadn't cared – anything to avoid Pell's unpleasantries in the bedroom was fine with her. But Linda had been jealous. Their last Christmas together Rachel had stopped by the Family's house on some pretense when Daniel was away. Linda had thrown the woman out of the house. Pell had heard about it and promised he wouldn't see her anymore.

'He got the smoker from her,' said Rebecca, who'd arrived after the Yuletide blow-out and knew nothing about the jealousy.

'No, he didn't. He *made* it for my birthday.'

Sam foresaw disaster looming. She said quickly, 'Well, whatever, you made a real nice turkey. I think we had sandwiches for two weeks.'

They both ignored her. Rebecca sipped more of the wine. 'Linda, he *gave* it to you on your birthday because he was with her that morning and *she* gave it to him. Some surfer dude made it for her but she didn't cook.'

'He was with her?' Linda whispered. 'On my birthday?'

Pell had told Linda he hadn't seen Rachel since the incident at Christmas. Linda's birthday was in April.

'Yeah. And, like, three times a week or so. You mean you didn't know?'

'It doesn't matter,' Sam said. 'It was a long –'

'Shut up,' Linda snapped. She turned to Rebecca. 'You're wrong.'

'What, you're surprised Daniel lied to you?' Rebecca was laughing. 'He told *you* he had a retarded brother and he told *me* he didn't have a brother. Let's ask the authority. Sam, was Daniel seeing Rachel that spring?'

'I don't know.'

'Wrong answer . . . Yes, you do,' Rebecca announced.

'Oh, come on,' Sam said, 'what difference does it make?'

'Let's play who knows Daniel best. Did he say anything to you about it? He told everything to his Mouse.'

'We don't need to –'

'Answer the question!'

'I don't have any idea. Rebecca, come on. Let it go.'

'Did he?'

Yes, in fact, he had. But Sam said, 'I don't remember.'

'Bullshit.'

'Why would he lie to me?' Linda growled.

'Because you told him that Mommy and Daddy didn't let you play at the cookout. That gave him something to work with. And he used it. And he didn't just buy you one. He claimed he *made* it! What a fucking saint!'

'You're the one who's lying.'

'Why?'

'Because Daniel never made anything for you.'

'Oh, please. Are we back in high school?' Rebecca looked Linda over. 'Oh, I get it. You were jealous of *me*! That's why you were so pissed off then. That's why you're pissed off now.'

This was true too, Sam reflected. When Rebecca joined the Family, Daniel had spent far less time with the other women. Sam could handle it – anything as long as he was happy and didn't want to kick her out of the Family. But Linda, in the role of mother, was stung that Rebecca seemed to supplant her.

Linda denied it now. 'I was not. How could anybody afford to be jealous living in that situation? One man and three women living together?'

'How? Because we're human, that's how. Hell, you were jealous of *Rachel*.'

'That was different. She was a slut. She wasn't one of us, she wasn't part of the Family.'

Sam said, 'Look, we're not here about us. We're here to help the police.'

Rebecca scoffed. 'How could we *not* be here about us? The first time we've been together after eight years? What, you think we'd just show up, write a top-ten list – "Things I remember about Daniel Pell" – and go home? Of course this's about us as much as him.'

Angry too, Linda darted a gaze toward Sam, 'And you don't have to defend me.' A contemptuous nod toward Rebecca. '*She's* not worth it. She wasn't there from the beginning like we were. She wasn't a part of it, and she took over.' Turning to Rebecca. 'I was with him for more than a year. You? A few months.'

'Daniel asked me. I didn't force my way in.'

'We were going along fine, and then *you* show up.'

'"Going along fine"?' Rebecca set down her wine glass and sat forward. 'Are you hearing what you're saying?'

'Rebecca, please,' Sam said. Her heart was pounding. She thought she'd cry as she looked at the two red-faced women, facing each other across a coffee table of varnished yellowing logs. 'Don't.'

The lean woman ignored her. 'Linda, I've been listening to you since I got here. Defending him, saying it wasn't so bad, we didn't steal all that much. Maybe Daniel didn't kill so-and-so . . . Well, that's bullshit. Get real. Yes, the Family was sick, totally sick.'

'Don't say that! It's not true.'

'Goddamn it, it *is* true. And Daniel Pell's a monster. Think about it. Think about what he did to us . . .' Rebecca's eyes were glowing, jaw trembling. 'He looked at you and saw somebody whose parents never gave her an inch of freedom. So what does he do? He tells you what a fine, independent person you are, how you're being stifled. And puts you in charge of the house. He makes you mommy. He gives you power, which you never had before. And he hooks you in with that.'

Tears dotted Linda's eyes. 'It wasn't like that.'

'You're right. It was *worse*. Because *then* look at what happened. The Family breaks up, we go to jail and where do you end up? Right back where you started. With a domineering male figure again – only this time, Daddy's God. If you thought you couldn't say no to your real father, think about your *new* one.'

'Don't say that,' Sam began. 'She's –'

Rebecca turned on her. 'And *you*. Just like the old days. Linda and I go at it, and you play Little Miss United Nations, don't want anybody upset, don't want anybody making waves. Why? Is it because you *care* about us, dear? Or is it because you're terrified we'll self-destruct and you'll be even *more* alone than you already are?'

'You don't have to be like that,' Sam muttered.

'Oh, I think I do. Let's take a look at your story, Mouse. Your parents didn't know you existed. "Go do whatever you want, Sammy. Mommy and Daddy're too busy with Greenpeace or the National Organization for Women or walking for the cure to tuck you in at night." And what does Daniel do for you? He's suddenly the involved parent you never had. He looks out for you, tells you what to do, when to brush your teeth, when to repaint the kitchen, when to get on all fours in bed . . . and you think it means he loves you. So, guess what? *You're* hooked too.

'And now? You're back to square one, just like Linda. You didn't exist to your parents, and now you don't exist to *anyone*. Because you're not Samantha McCoy. You became somebody else.'

'Stop it!' Sam was crying hard now. The harsh words, born from a harsh truth, stung deeply. There were things she could say too – Rebecca's selfishness, her bluntness bordering on cruelty – but she held back. It was impossible for her to be harsh, even in self-defense.

*Mouse* . . .

But Linda didn't have Sam's reticence to fight. 'And what gives you the right to talk? You were just some tramp pretending to be this bohemian artist.' Linda's voice shook with anger, tears streaming down her face. 'Sure, we had some problems, Sam and me, but *we* cared for each other. You were just a whore. And here you are, judging us. You weren't any better!'

Rebecca sat back, her face still. Sam could almost see the anger bleeding away. She looked down at the table, said in a soft voice, 'You're right, Linda. You're absolutely right. I'm no better at all. I fell for it too. He did the same thing to me.'

'You?' the woman snapped. 'You didn't have *any* connection with Daniel! You were just there to fuck.'

'Exactly,' she said with a sad smile on her face, one of the saddest that Samantha McCoy had ever seen.

Sam asked, 'What do you mean, Rebecca?'

More wine. 'How do you think he got *me* hooked?' Another sip of wine. 'I never told you that I hadn't slept with anybody for three years before I met him.'

'You?'

'Funny, huh? Sexy me. The femme fatale of the Central Coast? The truth was a lot different. What did Daniel Pell do for me? He made me feel good about my body. He taught me that sex was good. It wasn't dirty.' She set down the wine glass. 'It wasn't something that happened when my father got home from work.'

'Oh,' Sam whispered.

Linda said nothing.

Downing the last of the wine. 'Two or three times a week. Middle and high school . . . You want to hear what my graduation present was?'

'Rebecca . . . I'm so sorry,' Sam said. 'You never said anything.'

'You mentioned that day in the van, when we met?' Speaking to Linda, whose face was unmoved. 'Yeah, we were there for three hours. You thought we were fucking. But all we did was talk. He was comforting me because I was so freaked-out. Just like so many other times – being with a man who wanted me, and me wanting him, only I couldn't go there. I couldn't let him touch me. A sexy package – with no passion inside. But Daniel? He knew exactly what to say to make me feel comfortable.

'And now look at me – I'm thirty-three and I've dated four different men this year. And, you know, I can't remember the name of the second one. Oh, and every one of them was at least fifteen years older than me . . . No, I'm not any better than you guys. And everything I said to you, I mean it twice for myself.

'But come on, Linda, look at him for who he is and what he did to us. Daniel Pell's the worst thing you can possibly imagine. Yes, it *was* all that bad . . . Sorry, I'm drunk and this's brought up more crap than I was prepared to deal with.'

Linda said nothing. Sam could see the conflict in her face. After a moment she said, 'I'm sorry for your misfortune. I'll pray for you. Now please excuse me, I'm going to bed.'

Clutching her Bible, she went off to the bedroom.

'That didn't go over very well,' Rebecca said. 'Sorry, Mouse.' She leaned back, eyes closed, sighing. 'Funny about trying to escape the past. It's like a dog on a tether. No matter how much he wants to run, he just can't get away.'

# Chapter
# THIRTY-EIGHT

Dance and Kellogg were in her office at CBI headquarters, where they'd briefed Overby, working late for a change, on the events at Reynolds's house – and learned from TJ and Carraneo that there were no new developments. The time was after 11:00 p.m.

She put her computer on standby. 'Okay, that's it,' she said. 'I'm calling it a night.'

'I'm with you there.'

As they walked down the dim hallway, Kellogg said, 'I was thinking, they really are a family.'

'Back there? At the lodge?'

'Right. The three of them. They're not related. They don't even like each other particularly. But they *are* a family.'

He said this in a tone suggesting that he defined the word from the perspective of its absence. The interaction of the three women, which she'd noted clinically and found revealing, even amusing, had touched Kellogg in some way. She didn't know him well enough either to deduce why or to ask. She noted his shoulders lift very slightly and two fingernails of his left hand flicked together, evidence of general stress.

'You going to pick up the children?' he asked.

'No, they'll stay at their grandparents tonight.'

'They're great, they really are.'

'And you never thought about having kids?'

'Not really.' His voice faded. 'We were both working. I was on the road a lot. You know. Professional couples.'

In interrogation and kinesic analysis the content of speech is usually secondary to the tone – the 'verbal quality' – with which the words are delivered. Dance had heard many people tell her they'd never had children, and the resonance of the words explained whether that fact was inconsequential, a comfortable choice, a lingering sorrow.

She'd sensed something significant in Kellogg's statement. She noted more indications of stress, little bursts of body language. Maybe a physical problem on his part or his wife's. Maybe it had been a big issue between them, the source of their breakup.

'Wes has his doubts about me.'

'Ah, he's just sensitive about Mom meeting other men.'

'He'll have to get used to it someday, won't he?'

'Oh, sure. But just now . . .'

'Got it,' Kellogg said. 'Though he seemed to be comfortable when you're with Michael.'

'Oh, that's different. Michael's a friend. And he's married. He's no threat.' Aware of what she'd just said, Dance added quickly, 'It's just, you're the new kid in town. He doesn't know you'.

There was a faint hesitation before Kellogg answered. 'Sure, I can see that.'

Dance glanced at him to find the source of the pause. His face gave nothing away. 'Don't take Wes's reaction personally.'

Another pause. 'Maybe it's a compliment.'

His face remained neutral after this exploratory venture too.

They walked outside. The air was so crisp it would signal impending autumn in any other region. Dance's fingers were quivering from the chill but she liked the sensation. It felt, she decided, like ice numbing an injury.

The mist coalesced into rain. 'I'll drive you to yours,' she said. Kellogg's car was behind the building

They both got into hers and she drove to his rental. Neither of them moved for a minute. She put the transmission into park. Then closed her eyes, stretched and pressed her head back against the rest. It felt good.

She opened her eyes and saw him turning toward her and, leaving one hand on the dash, touched the shoulder closest to him, both firmly, yet somehow tentatively. He was waiting for some signal. She gave him none, but looked into his eyes and remained silent. Both of which, of course, were signals in themselves.

In any case, he didn't hesitate any longer but leaned forward and kissed her, aiming straight for her lips. She tasted mint; he'd subtly dropped a tic tac or Altoid when she wasn't looking. Slick, she thought, laughing to herself. She'd done the same with Brian that day on the beach, in front of the sea otter and seal audience. Kellogg now backed off slightly, regrouping and waiting for intelligence about the first skirmish.

This gave Dance a moment to figure how she was going to handle it.

She made a decision and when he eased in again, she met him halfway, her mouth opened. She kissed back fervently. She slipped her arms up to his shoulders, which were as muscular as she'd thought they'd be. His beard stubble troubled her cheek.

His hand slipped behind her neck, pulling her harder into him. She felt that uncurling within her, heart stepping up its pace. Mindful of the bandaged wound, she pressed her nose and lips against the flesh beneath his ear, the place where, with her husband, she'd rested her face when they'd made love. She liked the smooth plane of skin there, the smell of shave cream and soap, the pulse of blood.

Then Kellogg's hand detached itself from her neck and found her chin, easing her face to him again. Their whole mouths participated now, and breathing came fast. Both of them. His fingers were moving tentatively to her shoulder, locating the satin strap and, using it as a road map, began to move down, outside her blouse. Slowly, ready to divert at the least sign of reluctance.

Her response was to kiss him harder. Her arm was near his lap, and she could feel his erection flirting with her elbow. He shifted away, perhaps so he wouldn't seem too eager, too forward, too much of a teenager.

But Kathryn Dance pulled him closer as she reclined – kinesically, an agreeable, submissive position. Images of her husband came to mind once or twice, but she observed them from a distance. She was completely with Winston Kellogg at this moment.

Then his hand reached the tiny metal hoop where the strap transitioned to the white Victoria's Secret cup.

And he stopped.

The hand retreated, though the evidence near her elbow was undiminished. The kisses became less frequent, like a merry-go-round slowing after the power's shut off.

But this seemed to her exactly right. They'd arrived at the highest pinnacle they could under the circumstances – which included the manhunt for a killer, the short time they'd known each other and the terrible deaths that had recently occurred.

'I think –' he whispered.

'No, it's okay.'

'I –'

She smiled and lightly kissed away any more words.

He sat back and squeezed her hand. She curled against him, feeling her heart rate slow as she found within herself a curious balance: the perfect stasis of reluctance and relief. Rain pelted the windshield. Dance reflected that she always preferred to make love on rainy days.

'But one thing?' he said.

She glanced at him.

Kellogg continued, 'The case won't go on forever.'

From his mouth to God's ear . . .

'If you'd be interested in going out afterward. How does that sound?'

'"Afterward" has a nice ring to it. Real nice.'

A half-hour later Dance was parking in front of her own house.

She went through the standard routine: a check of security, a glass of pinot grigio, two pieces of cold flank steak left over from last night and a handful of mixed nuts enjoyed to the soundtrack of phone messages. Then came canine feeding and their backyard tasks and stowing her Glock – without the kids home she kept the lockbox open, though she still stashed the gun inside, since imprinted memory would guide her hand there automatically no matter how deep a sleep she awoke from. Alarms on.

She opened the window to the guards – about six inches – to let in the cool, fragrant night air. Shower, a clean T-shirt and shorts. She dropped into bed, protecting herself from the mad world by an inch-thick down comforter.

Thinking:

Golly damn, girl, making out in a car – with a bench front seat, no buckets, just made for reclining with the man of the hour. She recalled mint, recalled his hands, the flop of hair, the absence of aftershave.

She also heard her son's voice and saw his eyes earlier that day. Wary, jealous. Dance thought of Linda's comments earlier.

*There's something terrifying about the idea of being kicked out of your family . . .*

Which was ultimately Wes's fear. The concern was unreasonable, of course, but that didn't matter. It was real to him. She'd be more careful this time. Keep Wes and Kellogg separate, not mention the word 'date', sell the idea that, like him, she had friends who were both male and female. Your children are like suspects in an interrogation: It's not smart to lie but you don't need to tell them everything.

A lot of work, a lot of juggling.

*Time and effort . . .*

Or, she wondered, her thoughts spinning fast, was it better just to forget about Kellogg, wait a year or two before she dated? Age thirteen or fourteen is hugely different from twelve. Wes would be better then.

Yet Dance didn't want to. She couldn't forget the complicated memories of his taste and touch. She thought too of his tentativeness about children, the stress he exhibited. She wondered if it was because he was uneasy around youngsters and was now forming a connection with a woman who came with a pair of them. How would he deal with that? Maybe –

But, hold on here, let's not get ahead of ourselves.

You were making out. You enjoyed it. Don't call the caterer yet.

For a long time she lay in bed, listening to the sounds of nature. You were never very far from them around here – throaty sea animals, temperamental birds and the settling bed sheet of surf. Often, loneliness sprang into Kathryn Dance's life, a striking snake, and it was at moments like this – in bed, late, hearing the soundtrack of night – that she was most vulnerable to it. How nice it was to feel your lover's thigh next to yours, to hear the adagio of shallow breath, to awake at dawn to the thumps and rustling of someone's rising: sounds, otherwise insignificant, that were the comforting heartbeats of a life together.

Kathryn Dance supposed longing for these small things revealed weakness, a sign of dependency. But what was so wrong with that? My God, look at us fragile creatures. We *have* to depend. So why not fill that dependency with somebody whose company we enjoy, whose body we can gladly press against late at night, who makes us laugh? . . . Why not just hold on and hope for the best?

Ah, Bill . . . She thought of her late husband. Bill . . .

Distant memories tugged.

But so did fresh ones, with nearly equal gravitation.

*Afterward. How does that sound?*

# THURSDAY

## Chapter
# THIRTY-NINE

In her backyard again.

Her Shire, her Narnia, her Hogwarts, her Secret Garden.

Seventeen-year-old Theresa Croyton Bolling sat in the gray teak Smith and Hawkins glider and read the slim volume in her hand, flipping pages slowly. It was a magnificent day. The air was as sweet as the perfume department at Macy's, and the nearby hills of Napa were as peaceful as ever, covered with a mat of clover and grass, verdant grapevines and pine and gnarly cypress.

Theresa was thinking lyrically because of what she was reading – beautifully crafted, heartfelt, insightful . . .

And totally *boring* poetry.

She sighed loudly, wishing her aunt were around to hear her. The paperback drooped in her hand and she gazed over the backyard once more. A place where she seemed to spend half her life, the green prison, she sometimes called it.

Other times, she loved the place. It was beautiful, a perfect setting to read, or practice her guitar (Theresa wanted to be a pediatrician, a travel writer or, in the best of all worlds, Sharon Isbin, the famous classical guitarist).

She was here, not in school, at the moment because of an unplanned trip she and her aunt and uncle were going to be taking.

*Oh, Tare, we'll have fun. Roger's got this thing he has to do in Manhattan, a speech, or research, I don't really know. Wasn't paying attention. He was going on and on. You know your uncle. But won't it be great, getting away, just on a whim? An adventure.*

Which was why her aunt had taken her out of school at 10:00 a.m.

on Monday. Only, hello, they hadn't left yet, which was a little odd. Her aunt explaining there were some 'logistical difficulties. You know what I mean?'

Theresa was eighth in her class of 257 students at Vallejo Springs High. She said, 'Yes, I do. You mean "logistic".'

But what the girl *didn't* understand was, since they were still not on a fucking airplane to New York, why couldn't she stay in school until the 'difficulties' were taken care of?

Her aunt had pointed out, 'Besides, it's study week. So study.'

Which didn't mean study; what it meant was no TV.

And meant no hanging with Sunny or Travis or Kaitlin.

And meant not going to the big literacy benefit formal in Tiburon that her uncle's company was a sponsor of (she'd even bought a new dress).

Of course, it was all bullshit. There *was* no trip to New York, there were no difficulties, logistic, logistical or otherwise. It was just an excuse to keep her in the green prison.

And why the lies?

Because the man who'd killed her parents and her brother and sister had escaped from prison. Which her aunt actually seemed to believe she could keep secret from Theresa.

Like, please ... The news was the first thing you saw on Yahoo's home page. And *everybody* in California was talking about it on MySpace and Facebook. (Her aunt had disabled the family's wireless router somehow, but Theresa had simply piggybacked through a neighbor's unsecured system.)

The girl tossed the book on the planks of the swing and rocked back and forth as she pulled the scrunchie out of her red-streaked brown hair and rebound the ponytail.

Theresa was certainly grateful for what her aunt had done for her over the years and gave the woman a lot of credit, she really did. After those terrible days in Carmel eight years ago her aunt had taken charge of the girl everybody called the Sleeping Doll. Theresa found herself adopted, relocated, renamed (Theresa *Bolling*; could be worse) and plopped down on the chairs of dozens of therapists, all of whom were clever and sympathetic and who plotted out 'routes to psychological wellness by exploring the grieving process and being particularly mindful of the value of transference with parental figures in the treatment.'

Some shrinks helped, some didn't. But the most important factor – time – worked its patient magic and Theresa became someone other than the Sleeping Doll, survivor of a childhood tragedy. She was a student, friend, occasional girlfriend, veterinary assistant, not bad sprinter in the fifty- and the hundred-yard dash, guitarist who could play Scott Joplin's 'The Entertainer' and do the diminished chord run up the neck without a single squeak on the strings.

Now, though, a setback. The killer was out of jail, true. But that wasn't the real problem. No, it was the way her aunt was handling everything. It was like reversing the clock, sending her back in time, six, seven, oh, God, *eight* years. Theresa felt as if she were the Sleeping Doll once again, all the gains erased.

*Honey, honey, wake up, don't be afraid. I'm a policewoman. See this badge? Why don't you get your clothes and go into your bathroom and get changed.*

Her aunt was now panicked, edgy, paranoid. It was like in that HBO series she'd watched when she was over at Bradley's last year. About a prison. If something bad happened, the guards would lock down the place.

Theresa, the Sleeping Doll, was in lockdown. Stuck here in Hogwarts, in Middle Earth . . . in Oz . . .

The green prison.

Hey, that's sweet, she thought bitterly: Daniel Pell is out of prison and I'm stuck inside one.

Theresa picked up the poetry book again, thinking of her English test. She read two more lines.

*Borrrring.*

Theresa then noticed, through the chain-link fence at the end of the property, a car ease past, braking quickly, it seemed, as the driver looked through the bushes her way. A moment's hesitation and then the car continued on.

Theresa planted her feet and the swinging stopped.

The car could belong to anyone. Neighbors, one of the kids on break from school . . . She wasn't worried – not *too* much. Of course, with her aunt's media blackout she had no idea if Daniel Pell had been rearrested or was last seen heading for Napa. But that was crazy. Thanks to her aunt she was practically in the witness protection program. How could he possibly find her?

Still, she'd go sneak a look at the computer, see what was going on.

A faint twist in her stomach.

Theresa stood and headed for the house.

Okay, we're bugging a little now.

She looked behind her, back at the gap through the bushes at the far end of their property. No car. Nothing.

And turning back to the house, Theresa stopped fast.

The man had scaled the tall fence twenty feet away, between her and the house. He looked up, breathing hard from the effort, from where he landed on his knees beside two thick azaleas. His hand was bleeding, cut on the jagged top of the six-foot chain link.

It was him. It was Daniel Pell!

She gasped.

He *had* come here. He was going to finish the murders of the Croyton family.

A smile on his face, he rose stiffly and began to walk toward her.

Theresa Croyton began to cry.

'No, it's all right,' the man said in a whisper, as he approached, smiling. 'I'm not going to hurt you. Shhhh.'

Theresa tensed. She told herself to run. Now, do it!

But her legs wouldn't move; fear paralyzed her. Besides, there was nowhere to go. He was between her and the house and she knew she couldn't vault the six-foot chain-link fence. She thought of running away from the house, into the backyard, but then he could tackle her and pull her into the bushes, where he'd . . .

No, that was too horrible.

Gasping, actually tasting the fear, Theresa shook her head slowly. Felt her strength ebbing. She looked for a weapon. Nothing: only an edging brick, a bird feeder, *The Collected Poems of Emily Dickinson.*

She looked back at Pell.

'You killed my parents. You . . . don't hurt me!'

A frown. 'No, my God,' the man said, eyes wide. 'Oh, no, I just want to talk to you. I'm not Daniel Pell. I swear. Look.'

He tossed something in her direction, ten feet away. 'Look at it. The back. Turn it over.'

Theresa glanced at the house. The one time she needed her aunt, the woman was nowhere in sight.

'There,' the man said.

The girl stepped forward – and he continued to retreat, giving her plenty of room.

She walked closer and glanced down. It was a book. *A Stranger in the Night,* by Morton Nagle.

'That's me. Look.'

Theresa wouldn't pick it up. With her foot, she eased it over. On the back cover was a picture of a younger version of the man in front of her.

Was it true?

Theresa suddenly realized that she'd seen only a few pictures of Daniel Pell, taken eight years ago. She'd had to sneak a look at a few articles online – her aunt told her she'd be set back years psychologically if she read anything about the murders. But looking at the younger author photo, it was clear that this wasn't the gaunt, scary man she remembered.

Theresa wiped her face. Anger exploded inside her, a popped balloon. 'What're you doing here? You fucking scared me!'

The man pulled his sagging pants up as if planning to walk closer. But evidently he decided not to. 'There was no other way to talk to you. I saw your aunt yesterday when she was shopping. I wanted her to ask you something.'

Theresa glanced at the chain link.

Nagle said, 'The police are on their way, I know. I saw the alarm on the fence. They'll be here in three, four minutes, and they'll arrest me. That's fine. But I have to tell you something. The man who killed your parents has escaped from prison.'

'I know.'

'You do? Your aunt –'

'Just leave me alone!'

'There's a policewoman in Monterey who's trying to catch him but she needs some help. Your aunt wouldn't tell you, and if you were eleven or twelve I'd never do this. But you're old enough to make up your own mind. She wants to talk to you.'

'A policewoman?'

'Please, just call her. She's in Monterey. You can – Oh, God.'

The gunshot from behind Theresa was astonishingly loud, way louder than in the movies. It shook the windows and sent birds streaking into the clear skies.

Theresa cringed at the sound and dropped to her knees, watching Morton Nagle tumble backward onto the wet grass, his arms flailing in the air.

Eyes wide in horror, the girl looked at the deck behind the house.

Weird. She hadn't even known her aunt owned a gun. Much less knew how to shoot it.

\*    \*    \*

TJ Scanlon's extensive canvassing of James Reynolds's neighborhood had yielded no helpful witnesses or evidence.

'No vee-hicles. No nothin'.' He was calling from a street near the prosecutor's house.

Dance, in her office, stretched and her bare feet fiddled with one of the three pairs of shoes under her desk. She badly wanted an ID of Pell's new car, if not a tag number; Reynolds had reported only that it was a dark sedan, and the officer who'd been bashed with the shovel couldn't remember seeing it at all. The MCSO's crime scene team hadn't found any trace or other forensic evidence to give even a hint as to what Pell might be driving now.

She thanked TJ and disconnected, then joined O'Neil and Kellogg in the CBI conference room, where Charles Overby was about to arrive to ask for fodder for the next press conference – and his daily update to Amy Grabe of the FBI and the head of the CBI in Sacramento, both of whom were extremely troubled that Daniel Pell was still free. Unfortunately, though, Overby's briefing this morning would be primarily about the funeral plans for Juan Millar.

Her eyes caught Kellogg's and they both looked away. She hadn't had a chance to talk to the FBI agent about last night in the car.

Then decided: What is there to talk about?

*Afterward. How does that sound?*

It was then that young Rey Carraneo, eyes wide, stuck his perfectly round head into the conference room and said breathlessly, 'Agent Dance, I'm sorry to interrupt.'

'What, Rey?'

'I think . . .' His voice vanished. He'd been sprinting. Sweat dotted his dark face.

'What? What's wrong?'

The skinny agent said, 'The thing is, Agent Dance, I think I've found him.'

'Who?'

'Pell.'

# Chapter
# FORTY

The young agent explained that he'd called the upscale Sea View Motel in Pacific Grove – only a few miles from where Dance lived – and learned that a woman had checked in on Saturday. She was mid-twenties, attractive and blonde, slightly built. On Tuesday night, the desk clerk had seen her and a Latino go into her room.

'The clincher's the car, though,' Carraneo said. 'On the registration she put down Mazda. With a fake tag number – I just ran it. But the manager was sure he saw a turquoise T-bird there for a day or two. It's not there anymore.'

'They're at the motel now?'

'He thinks so. The curtain's drawn but he saw some motion and lights inside.'

'What's her name?'

'Carrie Madison. But there's no credit card info. She paid cash and showed a military ID but it was in a plastic wallet sleeve and scratched. Might've been faked.'

Dance leaned against the edge of the table, staring at the map. 'Occupancy of the motel?'

'No vacancies.'

She grimaced. Plenty of innocents in the place.

Kellogg said, 'Let's plan the takedown.' To Michael: 'You have tactical on alert?'

O'Neil was looking at Dance's troubled face, and Kellogg had to repeat the question. The detective answered, 'We can get teams there in twenty minutes.' He sounded reluctant.

Dance was, as well. 'I'm not sure.'

'About what?' the FBI agent asked.

'We know he's armed and he'll target civilians. And I know the motel. The rooms look out on a parking lot and courtyard. Hardly any cover. He could see us coming. If we try to empty the rooms nearby and across the way, he'd spot us. If we don't, people're going to get hurt. Those walls wouldn't stop a twenty-two.'

Kellogg asked, 'What're you thinking?'

'Surveillance. Get a team around the building, watch it nonstop. When he leaves take him on the street.'

O'Neil nodded. 'I'd vote for that too.'

'Vote for what?' Charles Overby asked, joining them.

Dance explained the situation.

'We've found him? All *right*!' He turned to Kellogg. 'FBI tactical?'

'They can't get here in time. We'll have to go with county SWAT.'

'Michael, you've called them?'

'Not yet. Kathryn and I have some problems with a takedown.'

'What?' Overby asked testily.

She explained the risk. The CBI chief understood but he shook his head. 'Bird in the hand.'

Kellogg too persisted. 'I really don't think we can risk waiting. He's gotten away from us twice now.'

'If he gets any hint we're moving in – and all he has to do is look out the window – he'll go barricade. If there's a door to the adjoining room –'

'There is,' Carraneo said. 'I asked.'

She gave him a nod for his initiative. Then continued, 'Then he could take hostages. I say we get a team on the roof across the way and maybe somebody in a housekeeping uniform. Sit back and watch. When he leaves, we'll tail him. He hits a deserted intersection, block him in and get him in a crossfire. He'll surrender.'

Or be killed in a shootout. Either way . . .

'He's too slippery for that,' Kellogg countered. 'We surprise him in the motel, we move fast, he'll give up.'

Our first spat, Dance thought wryly. 'And go back to Capitola? I don't think so. He'll fight. Tooth and nail. Everything the women have told me about him makes me believe that. He can't stand to be controlled or confined.'

Michael O'Neil said, 'I know the motel too. It could turn barricade real easy. And I don't think Pell's the sort you could have a successful negotiation with.'

Dance was in an odd situation. She had a strong gut feel that moving too fast was a mistake. But with Daniel Pell she was wary of trusting her instinct.

Overby said, 'Here's a thought. If we *do* end up with a barricade, what about the women in the Family? Would they be willing to help talk him out?'

Dance persisted, 'Why would Pell listen to them? They never had any sway over him eight years ago. They sure don't now.'

'But still, they're the closest thing to family that Pell's got.' He stepped toward her phone. 'I'll give them a call.'

The last thing she wanted was Overby scaring them off.

'No, I'll do it.' Dance called and spoke to Samantha and explained the situation to her. The woman begged Dance not to involve her; there was too great a risk her name would appear in the press. Rebecca and Linda, though, said they were willing to do what they could if it came to a barricade.

Dance hung up and related to those in the room what the women had said.

Overby said, 'Well, there's your backup plan. Good.'

Dance wasn't convinced that Pell would be swayed by sympathetic pleas for surrender, even – or maybe especially – from members of his former surrogate family. 'I still say surveillance. He's got to come out eventually.'

O'Neil said firmly, 'I agree.'

Kellogg looked absently at a map on the wall, then turned to Dance. 'If you're really opposed, okay. It's your choice. But remember what I was saying about the cult profile. When he goes out on the street he'll be alert, expecting something to go down. He'll have contingencies planned out. In the motel he won't be as well prepared. He'll be complacent in his castle. All cult leaders are.'

'Didn't work too well in Waco,' O'Neil pointed out.

'Waco was a standoff. Koresh and his people knew the officers were there. Pell won't have a clue we're coming.'

That was true, she reflected.

'It *is* Winston's expertise, Kathryn,' Overby said. 'That's why he's here. I really think we should move.'

Maybe her boss genuinely felt this way, though he could hardly oppose the view of the specialist that *he'd* wanted on board.

*Stash the blame . . .*

She stared at the map of Monterey.

'Kathryn?' Overby asked, voice testy.

Dance debated. 'Okay. We go in.'

O'Neil stiffened. 'We can afford some time here.'

She hesitated again, glancing at Kellogg's confident eyes as he too scanned the map. 'No, I think we should move on it, she said.'

'Good,' Overby said. 'The pro-active approach is the best. Absolutely.'

Pro-active, Dance thought bitterly. A good press-conference word. She hoped the announcement to the media would be the successful arrest of Daniel Pell, and not more casualties.

'Michael?' Overby asked. 'You want to contact your people?'

O'Neil hesitated, then called his office and asked for the MCSO SWAT commander.

Lying in bed in the soft morning light, Daniel Pell was thinking that they'd now have to be particularly careful. The police would know what he looked like in the Latino disguise. He could bleach much of the color out and change his hair again, but they'd be expecting that too.

Still, he couldn't leave yet. He had one more mission on the Peninsula, the whole reason for his remaining here.

Pell made coffee and when he returned to the bed, carrying the two cups, he found Jennie looking at him. Like last night, her expression was different. She seemed more mature than when they'd first met. 'What, lovely?'

'Can I ask you something?'

'Sure.'

'You're not coming with me to my house in Anaheim, are you?'

Her words hit him hard. He hesitated, not sure what to say, then asked, 'Why do you think that?'

'I just feel it.'

Pell set the coffee on the table. He started to lie – deception came so easily to him. And he could have gotten away with it. Instead he said, 'I have other plans for us, lovely. I haven't told you yet.'

'I know.'

'You do?' He was surprised.

'I've known all along. Not exactly *known*. But I had a feeling.'

'After we take care of a few things here, we're going somewhere else.'

'Where?'

'A place I have. It's not near *anything*. There's no one around. It's wonderful, beautiful. We won't be bothered there. It's on a mountain. Do you like the mountains?'

'Sure, I guess.'

That was good. Because Daniel Pell owned one.

Pell's aunt, in Bakersfield, was the only decent person in his family, as far as he was concerned. Aunt Barbara thought her brother, Pell's father, was mad, the chain-smoking failed minister obsessed with doing exactly what the Bible told him, terrified of God, terrified of making decisions on his own as if doing so would offend Him. So the woman tried to divert the Pell boys as best she could. Richard would have nothing to do with her. But she and Daniel spent a lot of time together. She didn't coral him, didn't order him around. She let him come and go as he wished, spent money on him, asked about what he'd done during the days when he visited. She took him places. Pell remembered driving up into the hills for picnics, the zoo, movies – where he sat amid the smell of popcorn and her weighty perfume, mesmerized by the infallible assuredness of Hollywood villains and heroes up on the screen.

His relationship with Aunt Barbara had inspired him to create the Family.

She also shared her views with him. One of which was her belief that there'd be a wildfire of a race war in the country at some point (her vote was the millennium – oops on that one), so she bought some 200 acres of forest in Northern California, a mountaintop near Shasta. Daniel Pell had never been racist but neither was he stupid, and when the aunt ranted about the forthcoming Great War of Black and White, he was with her one hundred percent.

She deeded over the land to her nephew so that he and other 'decent, good, right-thinking people' (defined as 'Caucasian') could escape to it when the shooting started.

Pell hadn't thought much about the place at the time, being young. But then he'd hitchhiked up there and knew instantly it was the place for him. He loved the view and the air, mostly loved the idea that it was so *private*; he'd be unreachable by the government and unwelcome neighbors. (It even had some large caves – and, the balloon within him expanding, he often fantasized about what would go on there.) He did some clearing work himself and built a shack.

He knew that some day this would be his kingdom, the final destination to which the Pied Piper would lead his children and begin the new Family.

Pell had to make sure, though, that the property stayed invisible – not from the rampaging minorities but from law enforcers, given his history and proclivity toward crime. He bought books written by survivalists and the right-wing, anti-government fringe about hiding ownership of property, which was surprisingly easy, provided you made sure the property taxes were paid (a trust and a savings account were all that it took). The arrangement was 'self-perpetuating', a term that Daniel Pell loved; no dependency.

Pell's mountaintop.

Only one glitch had interfered with his plan. After he and a girl he'd met in San Francisco, Alison, had hitched up there, he happened to run into a guy who worked for the county assessor's office, Charles Pickering. He'd heard rumors of building supplies being delivered there. Did that mean improvements? Which in turn would mean a tax hike? That itself wouldn't've been a problem; Pell could have added money to the trust. But, the worst of all coincidences, Pickering had family in Marin County and recognized Pell from a story in the local paper about his arrest for a break-in.

Later that day the man tracked Pell down near his property. 'Hey, I know you,' the assessor said.

Which turned out to be his last words. Out came the knife and Pickering was dead thirty seconds after slumping to the ground in a bloody pile.

Nothing was going to jeopardize his enclave.

He'd escaped that one, though the police had held him for a time – long enough for Alison to decide it was over and head back south. (He'd been searching for her ever since; she'd have to die, of course, since she knew where his property was.)

The mountaintop was what sustained him after he went into the Q and then into Capitola. He dreamed of it constantly. It was what had driven him to study appellate law and craft a solid appeal for the Croyton murders, which he'd believed he'd win, getting the convictions knocked down, maybe even to time served.

But last year the appeal was rejected.

And he'd had to start thinking of escape.

Now he was free, and after doing what he needed to in Monterey he'd get to his mountain as soon as he could. When that idiot of a prison guard had let Pell into the office on Sunday he'd managed to take a look at the place on the website Visual-Earth. He wasn't exactly sure of the coordinates of his property but he'd come close enough. And been thrilled to see that the area appeared as deserted as ever, no structures for miles around – the caves invisible from the prying eye of the satellite.

Lying now in the Sea View Motel, he told Jennie about the place – in general terms, of course. It was against his nature to share too much. He didn't tell her, for instance, that she wouldn't be the only one living there. And he certainly couldn't tell her what he envisioned for them all, living on the mountaintop. Pell realized the mistakes he'd made in Seaside ten years ago. He was too lenient, too slow to use violence.

This time, any threats would be eliminated.

But she was content – even excited – about the few facts he shared. 'I mean it. I'll go wherever you are, sweetie . . .' She took his coffee cup from his hands, set it aside. She lay back. 'Make love to me, Daniel. Please?'

*Make love*, he observed. Not *fuck*.

It was an indication that his student had graduated to another level. This, more than her body, began expanding the bubble within him.

He smoothed a strand of dyed hair off her forehead and kissed her. His hands began that familiar, yet always new, exploration.

Which was interrupted by a jarring ring. He grimaced and picked up the phone, listened to what the caller said, then held his hand over the mouthpiece. 'It's housekeeping. They saw the "Do-not-disturb" sign and want to know when they can make up the room.'

Jennie gave a coy smile. 'Tell her we need at least an hour.'

'I'll tell her two. Just to be sure.'

# Chapter
# FORTY-ONE

The staging area for the assault was in an intersection around the corner from the Sea View Motel.

Dance still wasn't sure about the wisdom of a tactical operation here, but once the decision had been made, certain rules fell automatically into place. And one of those was that she had to take a backseat. This wasn't her expertise and there was little for her to do but be a spectator.

Albert Stemple and TJ would represent the CBI on the takedown teams, which were made up mostly of SWAT deputies from Monterey County and several Highway Patrol officers. The eight men and two women were gathered beside a nondescript truck, which held enough weapons and ammunition to put down a modest riot.

Pell was still inside the room that the woman had rented; the lights were off but a surveillance officer, in the back, clapped a microphone on the wall and reported sounds coming from their room. He couldn't be sure, but it sounded like they were having sex.

That was good news, thought Dance. A naked suspect is a vulnerable suspect.

On the phone with the manager, she asked about the rooms next to Pell's. The one to his left was empty; the guests had just left with fishing tackle, which meant they wouldn't be back until much later. Unfortunately, though, as for the room on the other side, a family appeared to be still inside.

Dance's initial reaction was to call them and tell them to get down on the floor in the back. But they wouldn't do that, of course. They'd flee, flinging open the door, the parents rushing the children outside.

And Pell would know exactly what was going on. He had the instincts of a cat.

Imagining them, the others in the rooms nearby and the housekeeping staff, Kathryn Dance told herself suddenly, Call it off. Do what your gut tells you. You've got the authority. Overby wouldn't like it – that would be a battle – but she could handle him. O'Neil and the MCSO would back her up.

Still, she couldn't trust her instinct at the moment. She didn't know people like Pell; Winston Kellogg did.

He happened to arrive then, walking up to the tactical officers, shaking hands and introducing himself. He'd changed outfits yet again. But there was nothing country club about his new look. He was in black jeans, a black shirt and a thick bulletproof vest, the bandage on his neck visible.

TJ's words came back to her.

*He's a bit of a straight arrow but he's not afraid to get his hands dirty . . .*

In this garb, with his attentive eyes, he reminded her even more of her late husband. Bill had spent most of his time doing routine investigations, but occasionally he'd dressed for tactical ops. She'd seen him once or twice looking like this, confidently holding an elaborate machine gun.

Dance watched Kellogg load and chamber a round in a large silver automatic pistol.

'Now that's some weapon of mass destruction,' TJ said. 'Schweizerische Industrie Gesellschaft.'

'What?' Impatient.

'S-I-G as in SIG-Sauer. It's the new P220. Forty-five.'

'It's forty-five caliber?'

'Yup,' TJ said. 'Apparently the bureau's adopted a let's-make-sure-they're-never-getting-up-ever-ever-again philosophy. One I'm not necessarily opposed to.'

Dance and all the other agents at the CBI carried only 9mm Glocks, concerned that a higher caliber could cause more collateral damage.

Kellogg pulled on a windbreaker advertising him as an FBI agent and joined her and O'Neil, who today was in his khaki chief deputy uniform – body armor too.

Dance briefed them about the rooms next to Pell's. Kellogg said when they did the kick-in, he'd simultaneously have somebody enter the room next door and get the family down, under cover.

Not much, but it was something.

Rey Carraneo radioed in; he was in a surveillance position on the far side of the parking lot, out of sight, behind a Dumpster. The lot was empty of people at the moment – though there were a number of cars – and the housekeepers were going about their business, as Kellogg had instructed. At the last minute, as the tac teams were on their way, other officers would pull them to cover.

In five minutes the officers had finished dressing in armor and checking weapons. They were huddled in a small yard near the main office. They looked at O'Neil and Dance but it was Kellogg who spoke first. 'I want a rolling entry, one team through the door, the second backup, right behind.' He held up a sketch of the room, which the manager had drawn. 'First team, here to the bed. Second, the closets and bathroom. I need some flash-bangs.'

He was referring to the loud, blinding hand grenades used to disorient suspects without causing serious injury. One of the MCSO officers handed him several. He put them in his pocket.

Kellogg said, 'I'll take the first team in. I'm on point.'

Dance wished he wouldn't; there were far younger officers on the Sheriff's Office SWAT team, most of them recent military discharges with combat experience.

The FBI agent continued, 'He'll have that woman with him, and she may appear to be a hostage but she's just as dangerous as he is. Remember, she's the one who lit up the courthouse and the reason Juan Millar's dead.'

Acknowledging nods from them all.

'Now, we'll circle around the side of the building and move in fast along the front. Those going past his window, stay on your *bellies*. Don't crouch. As close to the building as you can get. Assume he's looking out. I want people in armor to pull the housekeepers behind cars. Then we go in. And don't assume there are only two perps in there.'

His words put in mind Dance's conversation with Rebecca Sheffield. *Structure the solution . . .*

He said to Dance. 'That sound okay to you?'

Which wasn't really the question he was asking.

His query was more specific: Do I have authority here?

Kellogg was being generous enough to give her one last chance to pull the plug on the op. She debated only a moment and said, 'It's fine. Do it.' Dance started to say something to O'Neil but couldn't think of any words that conveyed her thoughts – she wasn't sure what those thoughts were, in any case. He didn't look at her, just drew his Glock and, along with TJ and Stemple, moved out with a backup team.

'Let's get into position,' Kellogg said to the tactical officers.

Dance joined Carraneo by the Dumpster and plugged in her headset and stalk mike.

A few minutes later her radio crackled. Kellogg, saying, 'On my five, we move.'

Affirmative responses came in from the leaders of the various teams. 'Let's do it. One . . . two . . .'

Dance wiped her palm on her slacks and closed it around the grip of her weapon.

'. . . three . . . four . . . five, go!'

The men and women dashed around the corner and Dance's eyes flipped back and forth from Kellogg to O'Neil.

Please, she thought. No more deaths . . .

Had they structured it right?

Had they recognized the patterns?

Kellogg got to the door first, giving a nod to the MCSO officer carrying a battering ram. The big man swung the weighty tube into the fancy door and it crashed open. Kellogg pitched in one of the grenades. Two officers rushed into the room beside Pell's and others pulled the maids behind parked cars. When the flash-bang detonated with a stunning explosion, Kellogg's and O'Neil's teams raced inside.

Then: silence.

No gunshots, no screams.

Finally she heard Kellogg's voice, lost in a staticky transmission, ending with ' . . . him.'

'Say again,' Dance transmitted urgently. 'Say again, Win. Do you have him?'

A crackle. 'Negative. He's gone.'

Her Daniel was brilliant, her Daniel knew everything.

As they drove, fast but not over the limit, away from the motel, Jennie Marston looked back.

No squad cars yet, no lights, no sirens.

Angel songs, she recited to herself. Angel songs, protect us.

Her Daniel was a genius.

Twenty minutes ago, as they'd started to make love, he'd frozen, sitting up in bed.

'What, honey?' she'd asked, alarmed.

'Housekeeping. Have they ever called about making up the room?'

'I don't think so.'

'Why would they today? And it's early. They wouldn't call until later. Somebody wanted to see if we were in. The police! Get dressed. Now.'

'You want –'

'Get dressed!'

She leapt from bed.

'Grab what you can. Get your computer and don't leave anything personal.' He'd put a porn movie on TV, looked outside, then walked to the adjoining door, held the gun up and kicked it in, startling two young men inside.

At first she thought he'd kill them but he just told them to stand up and turn around, tied their hands with fishing line and taped washcloths in their mouths. He pulled their wallets out and looked them over. 'I've got your names and addresses. You stay here and be quiet. If you say anything to anybody, your families're dead. Okay?'

They nodded and Daniel closed the adjoining door and blocked it with a chair.

He dumped out the contents of the fishermen's cooler and tackle boxes and put their own bags inside. They dressed in the men's yellow slickers and, wearing baseball caps, they carried the gear and the fishing rods outside.

'Don't look around. Walk right to our car. But slow.' They headed across the parking lot. He spent some minutes loading the car, trying to look casual. They then climbed in and drove away. Jennie, struggling to keep calm. She wanted to cry, she was so nervous.

But excited too, she had to admit. It was a total high. She'd never felt so alive, driving away from the motel. She thought about her husband, the boyfriends, her mother . . . nothing she'd experienced with any of them approached what she felt at this moment.

They passed four police cars speeding toward the motel. No sirens.

*Angel songs* . . .

Her prayer worked. Now, they were miles from the inn and no one was after them.

Finally he laughed and exhaled a long breath. 'How 'bout that, lovely?'

'We did it, sweetie!' She whooped and shook her head wildly as if she were at a rock concert. She pressed her lips against his neck and bit him playfully.

Soon they were pulling into the parking lot of the Butterfly Inn, a small dump of a motel on Lighthouse, the commercial strip in Monterey. Daniel told her, 'Go get a room. We'll be finished up here soon, but it might not be till tomorrow. Get it for a week, though; it'll be less suspicious. In the back again. Maybe that cottage there. Use a different name. Tell the clerk you left your ID in your suitcase and you'll bring it in later.'

Jennie registered and returned to the car. They carried the cooler and boxes inside.

Pell lay on the bed, arms behind his neck. She curled up next to him. 'We're going to have to hide out here. There's a grocery store up the street. Go get some food, would you, lovely?'

'And more hair dye?'

He smiled. 'Not a bad idea.'

'Can I be a redhead?'

'You can be green if you want. I'd love you anyway.'

God, he was perfect . . .

She heard the crackle of the TV coming on as she stepped out of the door, slipping the cap on. A few days ago she'd never have thought she'd be okay with Daniel hurting people, giving up her house in Anaheim, never seeing the hummingbirds and cardinals and sparrows in her backyard again.

Now, it seemed perfectly natural. In fact, wonderful.

Anything for you, Daniel. Anything.

# Chapter
# FORTY-TWO

'And how did he know you were there?' Overby asked, standing in Dance's office. The man was jumpy. Not only had he engineered CBI's taking over the manhunt, but he was now on record as supporting the bad tactical decision at the motel. Paranoid, too. Dance could tell this from his body language and his verbal content as well: his use of 'you', whereas Dance or O'Neil would've said 'we'.

*Stashing the blame . . .*

'Must've sensed something about the hotel was different, maybe the staff were acting strange,' Kellogg replied. 'Like in the restaurant at Moss Landing. He's got the instincts of a cat.'

Echoing Dance's thoughts earlier.

'And I thought your people heard him inside, Michael.'

'Porn,' Dance said.

The detective explained, 'He had porn on pay-per-view. That was what surveillance heard.'

The postmortem was discouraging, if not embarrassing. It turned out that the manager had, without knowing it, seen Pell and the woman leaving – pretending to be the two fishermen in the adjoining room – headed off for squid and salmon in Monterey Bay. The two men, bound and gagged in the next room were reluctant to talk; Dance pried out of them that Pell had gotten their addresses and threatened to kill their families if they called for help.

*Patterns . . . goddamn patterns.*

Winston Kellogg was upset about the escape, but not apologetic. He'd made a judgment call, like Dance's at Moss Landing. His plan could have worked, but fate had intervened, and she respected that he wasn't bitter or whiny about the outcome; he was focused on the next steps.

Overby's assistant joined them. She told her boss he had a call from Sacramento, and the SAC. from San Francisco, Amy Grabe, was holding on two. She wasn't happy.

An angry grunt. The CBI chief turned and followed her back to his office.

Carraneo called to report that the canvass he and several other officers were conducting had so far yielded nothing. A cleaning woman thought she'd seen a dark car driving toward the back of the lot before the raid. No tag number. No one had seen anything else.

Dark sedan. The same useless description they'd gotten at James Reynolds's house. A Monterey Sheriff's deputy arrived with a large packet. He handed it to O'Neil. 'Crime scene, sir.' The detective set out photos and a list of the physical evidence. The fingerprints revealed that the two occupants of the room had indeed been Pell and his accomplice. Clothes, food wrappers, newspapers, personal hygiene items, some cosmetics. Also clothespins, what looked like a whip made out of a coat hanger, dotted with blood, pantyhose that had been tied to the bedposts, dozens of condoms – new and used – and a large tube of K-Y lubricant.

Kellogg said, 'Typical of cult leaders. Jim Jones in Guyana? He had sex three or four times a day.'

'Why is that?' Dance asked.

'Because they *can*. They can do pretty much whatever they want.'

O'Neil's phone rang and he took the call. He listened for a few moments. 'Good. Scan it and send it to Agent Dance's computer. You have her email? . . . Thanks.'

He looked at Dance. 'Crime scene found an email in the pocket of the woman's jeans.'

A few minutes later Dance called up the message on the screen. She printed out the pdf attachment.

From: CentralAdmin2235@Capitolacorrectional.com
To: JMSUNGIRL@Euroserve.co.uk.
Re:

Jennie, my lovely –
Bargained my way into the office to write this. I had to. There's something I want to say. I woke up thinking about you – our plans

to go out to the beach, and the desert, and watching the fireworks every night in your backyard. I was thinking, you're smart and beautiful and romantic – who could ask for anything more in a girl? We've danced around it a lot and haven't said it but I want to now. I love you. There's no doubt in my mind, you're unlike anybody I've ever met. So, there you have it. Have to go now. Hope these words of mine haven't upset you or 'freaked' you out.

Soon, Daniel

So Pell *had* sent emails from Capitola – though prior to Sunday, Dance noted, probably why the tech hadn't found them.

Dance noted that Jennie was her first name. Last or middle initial M. *JMSUNGIRL*.

O'Neil added, 'Our tech department's contacting the ISP now. Foreign servers aren't very cooperative but we'll keep our fingers crossed.'

Dance was staring at the email. 'Look at what he said: beach, desert and fireworks every night. All three near her house. That ought to give us some ideas.'

Kellogg said, 'The car was stolen in Los Angeles ... She's from Southern California somewhere: beach and desert. But fireworks every night?'

'Anaheim,' Dance said.

The other parent present nodded. O'Neil said, 'Disneyland.'

Dance met O'Neil's eye. She said, 'Your idea earlier: the banks and withdrawals of ninety-two hundred dollars. All of L.A. County – okay, maybe that was too much. But Anaheim? Much smaller. And now, we know her first name. And possibly an initial. Can your people handle this one, Win?'

'Sure, that'd be a more manageable number of banks,' he said agreeably. He picked up the phone and called the request in to the L.A. field office.

Dance phoned the women at the Point Lobos Inn. She explained about what had happened at the motel.

'He got away again?' Samantha asked.

'I'm afraid so.' She gave her the details of the email, including the screen name, but none of them could recall anybody with that name or initials.

'We also found evidence of S and M activity.' She described the sexual gear. 'Could that've been Pell, or would it've been the woman's idea?

Might help us narrow down a search, if it was hers. A professional, a dominatrix maybe.'

Samantha was quiet for a moment. Then she said, 'I, ah . . . that would've been Daniel's idea. He was kind of that way.' Embarrassed.

Dance thanked her. 'I know you're anxious to leave. I promise I won't keep you much longer.'

It was only a few minutes later that Winston Kellogg received a call. His eyes flashed in surprise. He looked up. 'They've got an ID. A woman named Jennie Marston withdrew ninety-two-hundred dollars – virtually her whole savings account – from Pacific Trust in Anaheim last week. Cash. We're getting a warrant, and our agents and Orange County deputies're going to raid her house. They'll let us know what they find.'

Sometimes you *do* get a break.

O'Neil grabbed the phone and in five minutes a jpeg image of a young woman's driver's license photo was on Dance's computer. She called TJ into her office.

'Yo?'

She nodded at the screen. 'Do an EFIS image. Make her a brunette, redhead, long hair, short hair. Get it to the Sea View. I want to make sure it's her. And if it is, I want a copy sent to every TV station and newspaper in the area.'

'You bet, boss.' Without sitting, he typed on her keyboard, then hurried out, as if he were trying to beat the picture's arrival to his office.

Charles Overby stepped into the doorway. 'That call from Sacramento is –'

'Hold on, Charles.' Dance briefed him on what had happened and his mood changed instantly.

'Well, a lead. Good. At last . . . anyway, we've got another issue. Sacramento got a call from the Napa County Sheriff's Office.'

'Napa?'

'They've got someone named Morton Nagle in jail.'

Dance nodded slowly. She hadn't told Overby about enlisting the writer's aid to find the Sleeping Doll.

'I talked to the sheriff. And he's not a happy camper.'

'What'd Nagle do?' Kellogg asked, lifting an eyebrow to Dance.

'The Croyton girl? She lives up there somewhere with her aunt and uncle. He apparently wanted to talk her into being interviewed by you.'

'That's right.'

'Oh. I didn't hear about it.' He let that linger for a moment. 'The aunt told him no. But this morning he snuck onto their property and tried to convince the girl in person.'

So much for uninvolved, objective journalism.

'The aunt took a shot at him.'

'*What?*'

'She missed but if the deputies hadn't shown up, the sheriff thinks she would've taken him out on the second try. And nobody seemed very upset about that possibility. They think we had something to do with it. This's a king-size can of worms.'

'I'll handle it,' Dance told him.'

'We *weren't* involved, were we? I told him we weren't.'

'I'll handle it.'

Overby considered this, then gave her the sheriff's number and headed back to his office. Dance called the sheriff and identified herself. She told him the situation.

The man grunted. 'Well, Agent Dance, I appreciate the problem, Pell and all. Made the news up here, I'll tell you. But we can't just release him. Theresa's aunt and uncle went forward with the complaint. And I have to say we all keep a special eye out for that girl around here, knowing what she went through. The magistrate set bail at a hundred thousand and none of our bailbondsmen're interested in handling it.'

'Can I talk to the prosecutor?'

'He's on trial, will be all day.'

Morton Nagle would have to spend a little time in jail. She felt bad for him, and appreciated his change of mind. But there was nothing she could do. 'I'd like to talk to the girl's aunt or uncle.'

'I don't know what good it'd do.'

'It's important.'

A pause. 'Well, now, Agent Dance, I really don't think they'd be inclined. In fact, I can pretty much guarantee it.'

'Will you give me their number? Please?' Direct questions are often the most effective.

But so are direct answers. 'No. Good-bye now, Agent Dance.'

# Chapter
# FORTY-THREE

Dance and O'Neil were alone in her office.

She'd learned from the Orange County Sheriff's Department that Jennie Marston's father was dead and her mother had a history of petty crime, drug abuse and emotional disabilities. There was no record of the mother's whereabouts; she had a few relatives on the East Coast but no one had heard from Jennie in years.

Dance learned that Jennie had gone to a community college for a year, studying food management, then dropped out, apparently to get married. She'd worked for a Hair Cuttery for a year then went into food service – employed by a number of caterers and bakeries in Orange County she was a quiet worker, who would arrive on time, do her job well, then leave. She led a solitary life, and deputies could find no acquaintances, no close friends. Her ex-husband hadn't talked to her in years but said that she deserved whatever happened to her.

Not surprisingly, police records revealed a history of difficult relationships. Deputies had been summoned by hospital workers at least a half-dozen times on suspicion of domestic abuse involving the ex and at least four other partners. Social Services had started several files, but Jennie had never pursued any complaints, let alone sought restraining orders.

Just the sort to fall prey to someone like Daniel Pell.

Dance mentioned this to O'Neil. The detective nodded. He was looking out Dance's window at two pine trees that had grafted themselves to each other over the years, producing a knuckle-like knot at eye level. Dance would often stare at the curious blemish when the facts of a case refused to coalesce into helpful insights.

'So, what's on your mind?' she asked.

'You want to know?'

'I asked, didn't I?' In a tone of good humor.

It wasn't reciprocated. He said testily, 'You were right. He was wrong.'

'Kellogg? At the motel?'

'We should've followed your initial plan. Set up a surveillance perimeter the minute we heard about the motel. Not spent a half-hour assembling tactical. That's how he caught on. Somebody gave something away.'

*Instincts of a cat . . .*

She hated defending herself, especially to someone she was close to. 'A takedown made sense at the time. A lot was going on and it was happening fast.'

'No, it didn't make sense. And you knew it. That's why you hesitated. Even at the end, you weren't sure.'

'Who knows anything in situations like this?'

'Okay, you *felt* it was the wrong approach and what you feel is usually right.'

'It was just bad luck. If we'd moved in earlier, we probably would've had him.' She regretted saying this, afraid he'd take her words as a criticism of the MCSO.

'And people would've died. We're just goddamn lucky nobody was hurt. Kellogg's plan was a prescription for a shootout. We're lucky Pell *wasn't* there. It could've been a bloodbath.' He crossed his arms – a protective gesture, which was ironic because he still had on the bulletproof vest. 'You're giving up control of the operation. *Your* operation.'

'To Winston?'

'Yes, exactly. He's a consultant. And it seems like he's running the case.'

'He's the specialist, Michael. I'm not. You're not.'

'He is? I'm sorry, he talks about the cult mentality, he talks about profiles. But I don't see *him* closing in on Pell. You're the one who's been doing that.'

'Look at his credentials, his background. He's an expert.'

'Okay, he's got some insights. They're helpful. But he wasn't enough of an expert to catch Pell an hour ago.' He lowered his voice. 'Look, at the hotel, Overby backed Winston. Obviously – he's the one who wanted him on board. You got the pressure from the FBI *and* your boss. But we've handled pressure before, the two of us. We could've backed them down.'

'What exactly are you saying? That I'm deferring to him for some other reason?'

Looking away. An aversion gesture. People feel stress not only when they lie; sometimes they feel it when they tell the truth. 'I'm saying you're giving Kellogg too much control over the operation. And, frankly, over yourself.'

In a flinty voice she asked, 'Because he reminds me of my husband? Is that what you're saying?'

'I don't know. You tell me. *Does* he remind you of Bill?'

'This is ridiculous.'

'You brought it up.'

'Well, anything other than professional judgment's none of your business.'

'Fine,' O'Neil said tersely. 'I'll stick to professional judgment. Winston was off base. And you acquiesced to him, knowing he was wrong.'

'Knowing?' she snapped. 'It was fifty-five, forty-five on the tac approach at the motel. I had one opinion at first. I changed it. Any good officer can be swayed.'

'By *reason*. By logical *analysis*.'

'What about your judgment? How objective are you?'

'Me? Why aren't I objective?'

'Because of Juan.'

A faint recognition response in O'Neil's eyes. Dance had hit close to home, and she supposed the detective felt responsible in some way for the young officer's death, thinking perhaps that he hadn't trained Millar enough.

*His protégés . . .*

She regretted her comment.

Dance and O'Neil had fought before; you can't have friendship and a working relationship without wrinkles. But never with an edge this sharp. And why was he slipping over the bounds into her personal life? This was a first.

And the Kinesics read almost as jealousy.

They fell silent. The detective lifted his hands and shrugged. This was an emblem gesture, which translated as: I've said my piece. The tension in the room was as tight as that entwined pine knot, thin fibers woven together into steel.

They resumed their discussion of the next steps: checking with Orange County for more details about Jennie Marston, canvassing for witnesses and following up on the crime scene at the Sea View Motel. They sent

Carraneo to the airport, bus station and rental-car offices, armed with the woman's picture. They kicked around a few other ideas too, but the climate in the office had dropped significantly, summer to fall, and when Winston Kellogg came into the room, O'Neil retreated, explaining that he had to check in with his office and brief the sheriff. He said a perfunctory good-bye that was aimed at neither of them.

His hand throbbing from the cut sustained when he vaulted the Bollings' chain-link fence, Morton Nagle glanced at the guard outside the holding cell of Napa County Men's Detention.

The big Latino reciprocated with a cold gaze.

Apparently Nagle had committed *the* number-one offense in Vallejo Springs – not the technical infractions of trespass and assault (where the hell had they got *that*?) but the far-more-troubling crime of upsetting their local daughter.

'I have a right to make a phone call.'

No response.

He wanted to reassure his wife that he was okay. But mostly he wanted to get word to Kathryn Dance about where Theresa was. He'd changed his mind and had given up on his book, along with journalistic ethics. Goddamn it, he was going to do everything in his power to make sure that Daniel Pell got caught and flung back into Capitola.

Not illuminating evil, but attacking it himself. Like a shark.

But apparently they were going to keep him incommunicado for as long as they possibly could.

'I really would like to make a phone call.'

The guard looked at him as if he'd been caught selling crack to kids outside Sunday school and said nothing.

He stood up and paced. The look from the guard said, Sit down. Nagle sat.

Ten long, long minutes later he heard a door open. Footsteps approached.

'Nagle.'

He gazed at another guard. Bigger than the first one.

'Stand up.' The guard pushed a button and the door opened. 'Hold out your hands.'

It sounded ridiculous, like someone offering a child some candy. He lifted them and watched the cuffs clatter around his wrists.

'This way.' The man took him by the arm, strong fingers closing around his biceps. Nagle smelled garlic and cigarette smoke residue. He almost pulled away but didn't think it would be a smart idea. They walked like this, the chains clinking, for fifty feet down a dim corridor. They continued to Interview Room A.

The guard opened it and gestured Nagle inside.

He paused.

Theresa Croyton, the Sleeping Doll, sat at a table, looking up at him with dark eyes. The guard pushed him forward and he sat down across from her.

'Hello again,' he said.

The girl looked over his arms and face and hands, as if searching for evidence of prisoner abuse. Or maybe hoping for it.

He knew she was only seventeen but there was nothing young about her, except the white delicacy of her skin. She hadn't died in Daniel Pell's attack, Nagle thought. But her childhood had.

The guard stepped back. But he remained close; Nagle could hear his large body absorbing sounds.

'You can leave us alone,' Theresa said.

'I have to be here, Miss. Rules.' He had a moveable smile. Polite to her, hostile to Nagle.

Theresa hesitated, then focused on the writer. 'Tell me what you were going to say in my backyard. About Daniel Pell.'

'He's staying in the Monterey area for some reason. The police can't figure out why.'

'And he tried to kill the prosecutor who sent him to jail?'

'James Reynolds, that's right.'

'Reynolds is okay?'

'Yes. The policewoman I was telling you about saved him.'

'Who are you exactly?' she asked. Direct questions, unemotional.

'Your aunt didn't tell you anything?'

'No.'

'I've been speaking to her for a month now about a book I wanted to write. About you.'

'Me? Like, why would you want to write that? I'm nobody interesting.'

'Oh, I think you are. I want to tell the story of somebody who's been hurt by something bad. How they're hurt. How they were beforehand, how they are after. How their life changes – and how things might've gone without the crime.'

'No, my aunt didn't tell me any of that.'

'Does she know you're here?'

'Yeah, I told her. She drove me here. She won't let me have a driver's license.'

She glanced up at the guard, then back to Nagle. 'They didn't want me to talk to you either, the police here. But there was nothing they could do about it.'

'Why did you come to see me, Theresa?' he asked.

'That policewoman you mentioned?'

Nagle was astonished. 'You mean, it's all right if she comes to see you?'

'No,' the girl said adamantly, shaking her head.

Nagle couldn't blame her. 'I understand. But –'

'I want to go see *her*.'

The writer wasn't sure he'd heard correctly. 'You want to what?'

'I want to go down to Monterey. Meet her in person.'

'Oh, you don't have to do that.'

She nodded firmly. 'Like, yeah, I do.'

'Why?'

'Because.'

Which Nagle thought was as good a response as any.

'I'll have my aunt drive me down there now.'

'She'll do that?'

'Or I'll take the bus. Or hitchhike. You can come with us.'

'Well, there's one problem,' Nagle said.

The girl frowned.

He chuckled. 'I'm in jail.'

She looked toward the guard, surprise in her eyes. 'Didn't you tell him?'

The guard shook his head.

Theresa said, 'I bailed you out.'

'You?'

'My father was worth a lot of money.' She now gave a laugh, a small one, but genuine and from her heart. 'I'm a rich girl.'

# Chapter
# FORTY-FOUR

Footsteps approaching.

The gun was in Daniel Pell's hand instantly.

In the cheap hotel, its aroma air freshener and insecticide, he glanced outside, slipped the pistol back into his waistband, seeing that it was Jennie. He shut off the TV and opened the door. She stepped inside, carrying a heavy shopping bag. He took it from her and set it on the bedside table beside a clock alarm flashing *12:00*.

'How'd it go, lovely? See any police?'

'None.' She pulled her cap off and rubbed her scalp.

Pell kissed her head, smelled sweat and the sour scent of the dye. Another glance out the window. After a long moment Daniel Pell came to a decision. 'Let's get out of here for a bit, lovely.'

'Outside? I thought you didn't think it was a good idea.'

'Oh, I know a place. It'll be safe.'

She kissed him. 'Like we're going on a date.'

'Like a date.'

They put their caps on and walked to the door. Her smile gone, Jennie paused and looked him over. 'You okay, sweetheart?'

*Sweetheart.*

'Sure am, lovely. Just that scare back at the motel. But everything's fine now. Fine as could be.'

They drove along a complicated route of surface streets to a beach on the way to Big Sur, south of Carmel. Wooden walkways wound past rocks and dunes cordoned off with thin wires to protect the fragile environment. Sea otters and seals hovered in the raging surf and, at ebb, the tidal pools displayed whole universes in their salt-water prisms.

It was one of the most beautiful stretches of beach on the Central Coast.

And one of the most dangerous. Every year three or four people died here, wandering out onto the craggy rocks for photos, only to be swept breathlessly into the forty-five-degree water by a surprise wave. Hypothermia could kill, though most didn't last that long. Usually the screaming victims were smashed on the rocks or drowned, tangled in the maze-like kelp beds.

Normally the place would be crowded, but now, with the day's sweeping fog, wind and mist, the area was deserted. Daniel Pell and his lovely walked from the car down to the water. A gray wave exploded on rocks fifty feet away.

'Oh, it's beautiful. But it's cold. Put your arm around me.'

Pell did. Felt her shivering.

'This is amazing. Near my house, the beaches there? They're all flat. It's, like, just sand and surf. Unless you go down to La Jolla. Even then, it's nothing like this. It's very spiritual here. Oh, look at them!' Jennie sounded like a schoolgirl. She was staring at the otters. A large one balanced a rock on his chest and pounded something against it.

'What's he doing?'

'He's breaking open a shell. Abalone or a clam or something.'

'How'd they figure out how to do that?'

'Got hungry, I guess.'

'Where we're going, your mountain? Is it as pretty as this?'

'I think it's prettier. And a lot more deserted. We don't want tourists, do we?'

'Nope.' Her hand went to her nose. Was she sensing that something was wrong? She muttered something, the words lost in the relentless wind.

'What was that?'

'Oh, I said "Angel songs".'

'Lovely, you keep saying that. What do you mean?'

Jennie smiled. 'It's like a prayer, or a mantra. I say it over and over to help me feel better.'

'And "angel songs" is your mantra?'

Jennie laughed. 'When I was little and Mother'd get arrested –'

'For what?'

'Oh, I don't have time to tell you everything.'

Pell looked around again. The area was deserted. 'That bad, huh?'

'You name it, she did it. Shoplifting, menacing, stalking. Assault too. She attacked my father. And boyfriends who were breaking up with her – there were a lot of those. If there was a fight, the police came to our house or wherever we were and a lot of times they'd be in a hurry and use the siren. Whenever I'd hear it, I'd think, Thank God, they're going to take her away for a while. It's like the angels were coming to save me. I got to think of sirens like that. Angel songs.'

'Angel songs. I like that.' Pell nodded.

Suddenly he turned her around and kissed her on the mouth. He leaned back and looked at her face now.

The same face that had been on the motel TV screen a half-hour earlier while she'd been out shopping.

*'There's been a new development in the Daniel Pell escape. His accomplice has been identified as Jennie Ann Marston, twenty-five, from Anaheim, California. She's described as about five foot five, weighing a hundred and ten pounds. Her driver's license picture is in the upper left-hand corner of your screen and the photos to the right and below show what she might look like now, after cutting and dyeing her hair. If you see her, do not attempt to apprehend. Call 911 or the hotline you see at the bottom of your screen.'*

The picture was unsmiling, as if she was upset that the DMV camera would capture her flawed nose and make it more prominent than her eyes, ears and lips.

Apparently Jennie had left something in the Sea View Motel room after all.

He turned her around to face the raging ocean, stood behind her.

'Angel songs,' she whispered.

Pell held her tight for a moment, then kissed her on the cheek.

'Look at that,' he said, gazing at the beach.

'What?'

'That rock there, in the sand.'

He bent down and unearthed a smooth stone, which weighed maybe ten pounds. It was luminescent gray.

'What do you think it looks like, lovely?'

'Oh, when you hold it that way it's like a cat, don't you think? A cat sleeping all curled up. Like my Jasmine.'

'That was your cat?' Pell hefted it in his hand.

'When I was a little girl. My mother loved it. She'd never hurt Jasmine. She'd hurt me, she'd hurt a lot of people. But never Jasmine. Isn't that funny?'

'That's exactly what I was thinking, lovely. It looks just like a cat.'

Dance called O'Neil first with the news.

He didn't pick up, so she left a message about Theresa. It wasn't like him not to answer but she knew he wasn't screening. Even his outburst – well, not outburst, okay – even his *criticism* earlier had been grounded in a law enforcer's desire to run a case most efficiently.

She wondered now, as she occasionally did, what it would be like to live with the cop/book-collector/seafarer. Good and bad, each in large quantities, was her usual conclusion, and she now hung up on that thought at the same time she did the phone.

Dance found Kellogg in the conference room. She said, 'We've got Theresa Croyton. Nagle just called from Napa. Get this. She bailed him out.'

'How 'bout that? Napa, hm? That's where they moved to. Are you going up there to talk to her?'

'No, she's coming here. With her aunt.'

'*Here?* With Pell still loose?'

'She wanted to come. Insisted, in fact. It was the only way she'd agree.'

'Gutsy.'

'I'll say.'

Dance called massive Albert Stemple and arranged for him to take over Theresa's guard detail when they arrived.

She looked up and found Kellogg studying the pictures on her desk – the ones of her children. His face was still. She wondered again if there was something about the fact that she was a mother that touched, or troubled, him. This was an open question between them, she noted, wondering if there were others – or, more likely, what the others would be.

The great, complicated journey of the heart.

She said, 'Theresa won't be here for a while. I'd like to go back to the inn, see our guests again.'

'I'll leave that up to you. I think a male figure's a distraction.'

Dance agreed. The sex of each participant makes a difference in how an interrogator handles a session, and she often adjusted her behavior along the androgyny scale depending on the subject. Since Daniel Pell had been such a powerful force in the women's lives, the presence of a man might skew the dynamics. He'd backed off earlier and let her pursue the questioning, but it would be better for him not to be there at all. She told him this and said she appreciated his understanding.

She started to rise but he surprised her by saying, 'Wait, please.'

Dance sat back. He gave a faint laugh and looked into her eyes.

'I haven't been completely honest with you, Kathryn. And it wouldn't mean anything . . . except for last night.'

What was it? she wondered. An ex who isn't exactly ex? Or a girlfriend who's very much present?

'About children.'

Dance dropped the it's-about-me line of thought, and sat forward, giving him her full attention.

'The fact is my wife and I did have a child.'

The tense of the verb made Kathryn Dance's stomach clench.

'She died in a car accident when she was sixteen.'

'Oh, Win . . .'

He gestured at the picture of Dance and her husband. 'Bit of a parallel. Car crash . . . Anyway, I was a shit about it. I couldn't handle the situation at all. I tried to be there for Jill, but I really wasn't, not the way I should've been. You know what it's like being a cop. The job can fill up as much of your life as you want. And I let too much in. We got divorced and it was a really bad time for a few years. For both of us. We've patched it up and we're friends now, sort of. And she's remarried.

'But I just have to say, the kid thing. It's hard for me to be natural with them. I've cut that out of my life. You're the first woman I've gotten anywhere near close to who has children. All I'm saying is, if I act a little stiff, it's not you or Wes or Maggie. They're wonderful. It's something I'm working on in therapy. So, there.' He lifted his hands, which is usually an emblem gesture, meaning, I've said what I wanted to. Hate me or love me, but there it is . . .

'I'm so sorry, Win.' She took his hand, pressed it. He squeezed back.

'I'm glad you told me. I know it was hard. And I did see something. I wasn't sure what, though.'

'Eagle eye.'

She laughed. 'I overheard Wes one time. He told his friend it sucks to have a mom who's a cop.'

'Especially one who's a walking lie detector.' He smiled too.

'I've got my own issues, because of Bill.'

And because of Wes, she thought, but said nothing about this now.

'We'll take things slow.'

'Slow is good,' she said.

He gripped her forearm, a simple, intimate and appropriate gesture. 'Now I should get back to the Family reunion.'

She walked him to his temporary office, then drove back to the Point Lobos Inn.

As soon as she walked inside, she knew the atmosphere had changed. The kinesics were wholly different from yesterday. The women were restless and edgy. She noted postures and facial expressions that suggested tension, defensiveness and outright hostility. Interviews and interrogations were long-term processes, and it wasn't unusual for a successful day to be followed by one that was a complete waste of time. Dance was discouraged and assessed that it might take long hours, if not days, to get them in a place mentally where they could once again provide helpful information.

Still, she gave it a shot. She ran through what they'd learned about Jennie Marston and asked if the women knew anything about her. They didn't. Dance then tried to resume the conversation of yesterday but today the comments and recollections were superficial.

Linda seemed to be speaking for all of them when she said, 'I just don't know how much more I can add. I'd like go home.'

Dance believed they'd already proved invaluable; they'd saved the life of Reynolds and his family and had given insights into Pell's M.O. and, more important, his goal to retreat to a 'mountaintop' somewhere; with more investigation they might find out where. Still, Dance wanted them to stay until she'd interviewed Theresa Croyton, in the hope that something the girl said might be a springboard to help the women's memories. She didn't want to say anything about the girl's trip here – the risk word might get out was too great – but, at her request, they agreed to wait a few more hours.

As Dance left, Rebecca accompanied her outside. They stood under an awning; a light drizzle was falling. The agent lifted an eyebrow. She was tense, wondering if the woman was going to deliver another lecture on their incompetence.

But the message was different.

'Maybe it's obvious but I thought I should mention something. Sam doesn't appreciate how dangerous Pell is, and Linda thinks he's a poor, misunderstood product of his childhood.'

'Go on.'

'What we were telling you yesterday about him – all that psychological stuff – well, it's true. But I've been through plenty of therapy and I know it's easy to focus on the jargon and the theory and forget about the person behind them. You've managed to stop Pell doing what he wants to, a couple of times, and nearly caught him. Does he know your name?'

A nod. 'But do you think he'd waste time coming after me?'

'Are you immune to him?' Rebecca asked, cocking an eyebrow.

And that answered the question right there. Yes, she was immune to his control. And therefore she was a risk.

*Threats have to be eliminated . . .*

'I have a feeling he's worried. You're a real danger to him and he wants to stop you. And he gets to people through their family.'

'Patterns,' Dance said.

Rebecca nodded. 'You have family in the area, I assume?'

'My parents and children.'

'Are the children with your husband?'

'I'm a widow.'

'Oh, I'm sorry.'

'But they're not at home right now. And I've got a deputy guarding them.'

'Good, but watch *your* back.'

'Thank you . . .' Dance glanced back into the cabin. 'Did something happen last night? Between all of you?'

She laughed. 'I think we've had a little more past than we can handle. We aired some laundry. It should've been aired years ago. But I'm not sure everybody felt that way.'

Rebecca walked back inside and closed and locked the door. Dance glanced in through a gap in the curtain. She saw Linda reading the Bible, Samantha looking at her cell phone, undoubtedly thinking up some lie to tell her husband about her out-of-town conference. Rebecca sat down and began covering her sketch pad with broad, angry strokes.

The legacy of Daniel Pell and his Family.

# Chapter
# FORTY-FIVE

Kathryn Dance had been gone a half-hour when one of the deputies called the cabin to check up on the women.

'Everything's fine,' Sam replied – apart from the broiling tensions inside the suite.

He had her make sure the windows and doors were locked. She checked and confirmed that everything was secure.

Sealed in, nice and tight. She felt a burst of anger that Daniel Pell had them trapped once again, stuck in this little box of a cabin.

'I'm going stir crazy,' Rebecca announced. 'I've got to get outside.'

'Oh, I don't think you should.' Linda looked up. Sam noticed that the tattered Bible had many fingerprints on the page it was open to. She wondered what particular passages had given her so much comfort. She wished she could turn to something so simple for peace of mind.

Rebecca shrugged. 'I'm just going out there a little ways.' She gestured toward Point Lobos State Park.

'Really, I don't think you should.' Linda's voice was brittle.

'I'll be careful. I'll wear my galoshes and look both ways.' The joke fell flat.

'It's stupid but do what you want.'

Rebecca said, 'Look, I'm sorry about last night. I drank too much.'

'Fine,' Linda said distractedly and continued to read her Bible.

Sam said, 'You'll get wet.'

'I'll go to one of the shelters. I want to do some drawing.' Rebecca picked up her pad and pencils, pulled on her leather jacket and stepped outside, pulling the hood up. Sam saw her looking back and could easily read the regret in her face for her vicious words last night. 'Lock it after me.'

Sam went to the door and put the chain on, double-locked it. She watched the woman walking down the path. She wished Rebecca hadn't gone.

But for an entirely different reason than the woman's safety.

She was now alone with Linda.

No more excuses.

Yes or no? Sam continued the internal debate that had begun several days ago, prompted by Kathryn Dance's invitation to come to Monterey and help them.

Come back, Rebecca, she thought.

No, stay away.

'I don't think she should've done that,' Linda muttered.

'Should we tell the guards?'

'What good would it do? She's a big girl.' A grimace. 'She'll tell you so herself.'

Sam said, 'Those things that happened to her, with her father. That's so terrible. I had no idea.'

Linda continued to read. Then looked up. 'They want to kill him, you know.'

'What?'

'Daniel. They're not going to give him a chance.'

Sam didn't respond. She was still hoping Rebecca would return, hoping she wouldn't.

With an edge to her voice Linda said, 'He can be saved. He's not hopeless. But they want to gun him down on sight. Be rid of him.'

Of course they do, Sam thought. As to the question of his redemption, that was unanswerable in her mind.

'That Rebecca . . . Just like I remember her.' Linda grunted.

Sam said, 'What're you reading?'

Linda asked, 'Would you know if I told you the chapter and verse?'

'No.'

'So.' Linda started to read, then looked up from the holy book again. 'She was wrong. What Rebecca said. It wasn't this . . . nest of self-deception.'

Sam was silent. Okay, she told herself. Go ahead. Now's the time. 'I know she was wrong about one thing.'

'What's that?'

Sam exhaled long. 'I wasn't a mouse all the time.'

'Oh, that. Don't take it seriously. I never said you were.'

'I stood up to him once. I told him no.' She gave a laugh. 'Ought to get a T-shirt printed up. "I told Daniel Pell no."'

Linda's lips pressed together. The attempt at humor fell leaden between them.

Walking to the TV, Sam shut it off. Sat down in an armchair, leaning forward.

Linda's voice was wary as she said, 'This is going somewhere. I can tell. But I'm not in the mood to get beat up again.'

'It's about beating me up, not you.'

'What?'

A few deep breaths. 'About the time I said no to Daniel.'

'Sam –'

'Do you know why I came down here?'

A grimace. 'To help capture the evil escapee. To save lives. You felt guilty. You wanted a nice drive in the country. I don't have any idea, Sam. Why *did* you come?'

'I came because Kathryn said you'd be here, and I wanted to see you.'

'You've had eight years. Why now?'

'I thought about tracking you down before. I almost did once. But I couldn't. I needed an excuse, some motivation.'

'You needed Daniel to escape from prison for motivation? What's this all about?' Linda set the Bible down, open. Samantha kept staring at the pencil notes in the margins. They were dense as bees clustered in a hive.

'You remember that time you were in the hospital?'

'Of course.' In a soft voice. The woman was gazing steadily at Sam. Wary.

The spring before the Croyton murders, Pell had told Sam he was serious about retreating to the wilderness. But he wanted to increase the size of the Family first.

'I want a son,' Pell had announced with all the bluntness of a medieval king bent on heirs. A month later Linda was pregnant.

And a month after that she'd miscarried. Their absence of insurance relegated them to a line at a lower-tier hospital in the barrio, frequented by pickers and illegals. The resulting infection led to a hysterectomy. Linda was devastated; she'd always wanted children. She'd told Sam often that she was meant to be a mother and, aware of how badly her parents had raised her, she knew how to excel at the role.

'Why are you bringing this up now?'

Sam picked up a cup filled with tepid tea. 'Because it wasn't supposed to be you who got pregnant. It was supposed to be me.'

'You?'

Sam nodded. 'He came to me first.'

'He did?'

Tears stung Sam's eyes. 'I just couldn't go through with it. I *couldn't* have his baby. If I did he'd have control over me for the rest of my life.' No point in holding back, Sam reflected. She gazed at the table and said, 'So I lied. I said you weren't sure you wanted to stay in the Family. Ever since Rebecca joined, you were thinking about leaving.'

'You what?'

'I know.' She wiped her face. 'I'm sorry. I told him that if you had his baby it'd show how much he wanted you to stay.'

Linda blinked. She looked around the room, picked up and rubbed the cover of the holy book.

Sam continued, 'And now you can't have children at all. I took them away from you. I had to choose between you and me, and I chose me.'

Linda stared at a bad picture in a nice frame. 'Why are you telling me this now?'

'Guilt, I guess. Shame.'

'So this confession then, that's about you too, right?'

'No, it's about us. All of us . . .'

'Us?'

'All right, Rebecca's a bitch.' The word felt alien in her mouth. She couldn't remember the last time she'd used it. 'She doesn't think before she says things. But she *was* right, Linda. None of us're leading normal lives . . . Rebecca should have a gallery and be married to some sexy painter and be flying around the world. But she's jumping from older man to older man – we know why now. And you should have a real life, get married, adopt kids, a ton of 'em and spoil them like crazy. Not spend your time in soup kitchens and caring for children you see for two months and never again. And maybe you could even give your dad and mom a call . . . No, Linda, it *isn't* a rich life you're living. And you're miserable. You know you are. You're hiding behind that.' A nod at the Bible. 'And me?' She laughed. 'Well, I'm hiding even deeper than you are.'

Sam rose and sat next to Linda, who leaned away. 'The escape, Daniel coming back like this . . . it's a chance for us to fix things. Look, here we are! The three of us in a room together again. We can help each other.'

'And what about now?'

Sam wiped her face. 'Now?'

'Do you have children? You haven't told us a thing about your mysterious life.'

A nod. 'I have a son.'

'What's his name?'

'My –?'

'What's his name?'

Sam hesitated. 'Peter.'

'Is he a nice boy?'

'Linda –'

'Is he a nice boy, I asked.'

'Linda, you think it wasn't so bad back then, in the Family. And you're right. But not because of Daniel. Because of *us*. We filled all those gaps in our lives that Rebecca was talking about. We helped each other! And then it fell apart and we're back to where we started. But we can help each other again! Like real sisters.' Sam leaned forward and gripped the Bible. 'You believe in this, right? You think things happen for a purpose. Well, I think we were meant to get back together. To give us this chance to fix our lives.'

'Oh, but mine is perfectly fine,' Linda said evenly, pulling the Bible away from Sam's trembling fingers. 'Work on yours as much as you want.'

Daniel Pell parked the Camry in a deserted lot off Highway 1, near Carmel State River Beach, beside a sign that warned of the dangerous waters here. He was alone in the car.

He caught a whiff of Jennie's perfume.

Slipping his pistol into a pocket of the windbreaker, he climbed out of the car.

That perfume again.

Noticing Jennie Marston's blood in the crescent of his nails, he spat on his fingers and wiped, but couldn't remove all of the crimson stain.

Pell looked around at the meadows, the cypress and pine and oak woods and the rugged outcroppings of granite and Carmelo formation rock. In the gray ocean sea lions, seals and otters swam and played. A half-dozen pelicans flew in perfect formation over the uneasy surface, and two gulls fought relentlessly for a scrap of food washed up on the shore.

Head down, Pell moved south through the thick trees. There was a path nearby but he didn't dare take it, though the park seemed deserted; he couldn't risk being seen as he headed for his destination: the Point Lobos Inn.

The rain had stopped but the overcast was heavy and more sprinkles seemed likely. The air was cold and thick with the scent of pine and eucalyptus. After ten minutes he came to the dozen cabins of the inn. Crouching, he circled to the rear of the place and continued, pausing to get his bearings and look for police. He froze, gripping his gun, when a deputy appeared, surveyed the grounds, then returned to the front of the cabin.

Easy, he told himself. Now's not the time to be careless. Take your time.

He walked for five minutes through the fragrant misty forest. About a hundred yards away, invisible to the cabins and the deputy, was a small clearing, inside which was a shelter. Someone sat at a picnic bench underneath it.

Pell's heart gave an uncharacteristic thud.

The woman was looking out over the ocean. A pad of paper was in her hand, and she was sketching. Whatever she was drawing, he knew it would be good. Rebecca Sheffield was talented. He remembered when they'd met, a cool, clear day by the beach. She squinted up from the low chair in front of her easel near where the Family had a booth at a flea market.

'Hey, how'd you like me to do your portrait?'

'I guess. How much?'

'You'll be able to afford it. Take a seat.'

He looked around once more and, not seeing anyone else, made his way toward the woman, who was oblivious to his approach. Wholly focused on the scenery, on the motion of her pencil.

Pell closed the distance quickly, until he was right behind her. He paused. 'Hello,' he whispered.

She gasped, dropped the pad and stood, turning quickly. 'Jesus.' A moment of silence.

Then Rebecca's face lurched into a smile as she stepped forward. The wind slapped them hard and nearly carried off her words, 'Damn, I missed you.'

'Come here, lovely,' he said and pulled her toward him.

# Chapter
# FORTY-SIX

They'd moved into the grove of trees, so there was no chance of being spotted by anyone at the motel.

'They know about Jennie,' Rebecca said.

'I know. I saw it on the TV.' He grimaced. 'She left something in the room. They tracked her down.'

'And?'

He shrugged. 'She won't be a problem.' Glanced down at the blood in his nails. He kissed Rebecca again, couldn't help but recall that she'd been the hottest of the girls in the Family. The bubble within him began to swell. He whispered. 'Lovely, if you hadn't called, I don't know what would've happened.'

Pell had left a message on Rebecca's voice mail at home, giving her the name of the Sea View motel. The call he'd received at their motel, supposedly from housekeeping, was from Rebecca, telling him in a frantic whisper that the police were on their way – Dance had asked if she and the others would help out in the event Pell took hostages. He hadn't wanted Jennie to know about Rebecca yet so he'd come up with the story about the maids.

'That was lucky,' Rebecca said, wiping a coating of mist from her face. Pell thought she did look pretty good. Jennie was fine in bed, but less of a challenge. Rebecca could keep you going all night. Jennie needed sex to validate herself. Rebecca simply needed sex. He got a twist inside him, the bubble expanding.

'How are my little gals holding up under the pressure?'

'Bickering and driving me fucking crazy. I mean, it's like not a day's gone by. Same as eight years ago. Except Linda's a Bible-thumper and

Sam isn't Sam. Changed her name. She's got boobs too.'

'And they're helping the cops, they're actually doing that?'

'Oh, you bet. I tried to lead things off as best I could. But I couldn't be too obvious about it.'

'And they don't guess anything about you?'

'Nope.'

Pell kissed her again. 'You're the best, baby. I'm free only 'cause of you.'

Jennie Marston had been just a pawn in the escape; it was Rebecca who'd planned everything. After his appeal was finally rejected, Pell had begun thinking about escape. He'd managed some unsupervised phone time in Capitola and spoken to Rebecca. For some time she'd been considering how to break Pell out. But there'd been no opportunities until recently, when Rebecca told him she'd come up with an idea.

She'd read about the unsolved Robert Herron killing and decided to make him the prime suspect so he'd be transferred to a lower-security facility for the indictment and trial. Rebecca had found an old hammer, which she'd had from the days of the Family in Seaside, and slipped it into his aunt's garage in Bakersfield.

Pell had sifted through his fan letters to look for a candidate who'd help. He settled on Jennie Marston, a woman in Southern California who suffered from the disease of bad-boy worship. She seemed wonderfully desperate and vulnerable. Pell had limited access to computers, so Rebecca had set up an untraceable email address and masqueraded as Pell to win Jennie's heart and work out the plan. One reason they'd picked her was that Jennie lived only an hour or so away from Rebecca, who could check her out and learn details of her life to make it seem that she and Pell had some spiritual connection.

*Oh, you're so much like me, honey, it's like we're two sides of the same coin.*

The love of cardinals and hummingbirds, the color green, Mexican comfort food . . . It doesn't take much in this mean world to make somebody like Jennie Marston your soul mate.

Finally Rebecca, as Pell, convinced Jennie that he was innocent of the Croyton killings and got her to agree to help him escape. Rebecca had come up with the idea for the gas bombs after scoping out the Salinas lockup and the delivery-service schedules at the You Mail It franchise. She'd sent the woman instructions: stealing the hammer, making up the fake wallet, planting them in Salinas. And then how to construct the gas bomb and where to buy the fire suit and bag. She'd checked with Jennie, via email, and then, when everything seemed in order, posted the message on the 'Manslaughter' bulletin board that everything was in place.

Pell now asked her, 'That was Sam when I phoned, wasn't it?'

The call – thirty minutes ago – purporting to be the guard checking up on them was Pell. The arrangement he'd made with Rebecca was that he'd ask whoever answered – if she didn't – to check the window locks. That meant he'd be there soon and Rebecca was supposed to go to the shelter and wait for him.

'She didn't catch on. The poor thing's still a little mouse. She just doesn't get it.'

'I want to get out of here as soon as possible, lovely. What's our time like?'

'Won't be long now.'

Pell said, 'I've got her address. Dance's.'

'Oh, one thing you'll want to know. Her kids aren't at home. She didn't say where they are but I found a Stuart Dance – probably her father or brother – in the phone book. I'd guess they're there. Oh, and there's a cop guarding them. There's no husband.'

'A widow, right?'

'How'd you know?'

'Just did. How old are the kids?'

'I don't know. Does it matter?'

'No.'

Rebecca eased back and studied him. 'For an undocumented alien you look pretty damn good. You really do.' Her arms looped him. The nearness of her body, bathed in air fragrant with ripe sea vegetation and pine, added to his already-stoked arousal. He slipped his hand into the small of her back. The pressure growing. He kissed her hungrily, his tongue slipping into her mouth. 'Daniel . . . not now. I have to get back.'

But Pell hardly heard the words. He led her farther into the forest, put his hands on her shoulders and started to push her down. She held up a finger. Then set her sketch pad on the wet ground, cardboard base down. She knelt on it. 'They'd wonder how I got wet knees.' And began to unzip his jeans.

That was Rebecca, he reflected. Always thinking.

\*     \*     \*

Michael O'Neil finally called.

She was glad to hear his voice, though the tone was purely professional, and she knew he didn't want to talk about their fight earlier. He was, she sensed, still angry. Which was odd for him. It bothered her, but there was no time to consider their grievances, given his news.

'Got a call from CHP,' O'Neil said. 'Some hikers halfway to Big Sur found a purse and some personal effects on the beach. Jennie Marston's. No body yet, but there was blood all over the sand. And blood, hairs and scalp tissue on a rock that crime scene found. Pell's prints're on the rock. The Coast Guard has two boats out looking. There wasn't anything helpful in the purse. ID and credit cards. If that's where she kept what's left of the ninety-two hundred dollars, Pell's got it now.'

He killed her . . .

Dance closed her eyes. Pell had seen her picture on TV and knew she'd been identified. She'd become a liability to him.

*A second suspect logarithmically increases the chances for detection and arrest . . .*

'I'm sorry,' O'Neil said. He'd understand what she was thinking – that Dance never would have guessed releasing the woman's picture would result in her death.

I believed it would be just another way to help find this terrible man.

The detective said, 'It was the right call. We had to do it.'

*We*, she noted. Not an Overby *you*.

'How long ago?'

'Crime scene's estimating an hour. We're checking along One and the cross roads, but no witnesses.'

'Thanks, Michael.'

She said nothing more, waiting for him to say something else, something about their earlier discussion, something about Kellogg. Didn't matter what, just some words that would give her a chance to broach the subject. But he said merely, 'I'm making plans for a memorial service for Juan. I'll let you know the details.'

'Thanks.'

'Bye.'

*Click.*

She called Kellogg and Overby with the news. Her boss was debating whether it was good or bad. Someone else had been killed on his watch, but at least it was one of the perps. On the whole, he suggested, the press and public would receive the development as a score for the good guys.

'Don't you think, Kathryn?'

Dance had no chance to formulate an answer, though, because just then the CBI's front desk called on the intercom to tell her the news that Theresa Croyton, the Sleeping Doll, had arrived.

The girl didn't resemble what Kathryn Dance had expected.

In baggy sweats, Theresa Croyton Bolling was tall and slim and wore her light-brown hair long, to the middle of her back. The strands had a reddish sheen. Four metallic dots were in her left ear, five in the other, and the majority of her fingers were encircled by silver rings. Her face, free of makeup, was narrow and pretty and pale.

Morton Nagle ushered the girl and her aunt, a solid woman with short, gray hair, into Dance's office. Mary Bolling was somber and cautious and it was obvious that this was the last place in the world she wanted to be. Hands were shaken and greetings exchanged. The girl's was casual and friendly, if a bit nervous; the aunt's stiff.

Nagle would want to stay, of course – talking to the Sleeping Doll had been his goal even before Pell's escape. But some bargain had apparently been struck that he'd take a backseat for the time being. He now said he'd be at home if anybody needed him.

Dance gave him a sincere 'Thank you.'

'Good-bye, Mr Nagle,' Theresa said.

He nodded a friendly farewell to both of them – the teenager and the woman who'd tried to gun him down (she looked as if she'd like a second opportunity). Nagle gave one of his chuckles, tugged up the saggy pants and left.

'Thank you for coming. You go by "Theresa"?'

'Mostly "Tare".'

Dance said to her aunt, 'Do you mind if I talk to your niece alone?'

'It's okay.' This was from the girl. The aunt hesitated. 'It's okay,' the girl repeated more firmly. A hit of exasperation. Like musicians with their instruments, young people can get an infinite variety of sounds out of their voices.

Dance had arranged a room at a chain motel near CBI headquarters. It was booked under one of the fictional names she sometimes used for witnesses.

TJ escorted the aunt to the office of Albert Stemple, who would take her to the motel and wait with her.

When they were alone, Dance came out from around the desk and closed her door. She didn't know if the girl had hidden memories to be tapped, some facts that could help lead them to Pell. But she was going to try to find out. It would be difficult, though. Despite the girl's strong personality and her gutsy foray here, she'd be doing what every other seventeen-year-old in the universe would do at a time like this: raising subconscious barriers to protect herself from the pain of recollection.

Dance would get nothing from her until those barriers were lowered. In her interrogations and interviews the agent didn't practice classic hypnosis. She did, though, know that subjects who were relaxed and not focused on external stimuli could remember events that otherwise they might not. The agent directed Theresa to the comfortable couch and shut off the bright overhead light, leaving a single yellow desk lamp burning.

'You comfortable?'

'Sure, I guess.' Still, she clasped her hands together, shoulders up, and smiled at Dance with her lips taut. Stress, the agent noted. 'That man, Mr Nagle, said you wanted to ask me about what happened the night my parents and brother and sister were killed.'

'That's right. I know you were asleep at the time, but –'

'What?'

'I know you were asleep during the murders.'

'Who told you that?'

'Well, all the news stories . . . The police.'

'No, no, I was awake.'

Dance blinked in surprise. 'You were?'

The girl's expression was even more surprised. 'Like, yeah. I mean, I thought *that's* why you wanted to see me.'

# Chapter
# FORTY-SEVEN

'Go ahead, Tare.'

Dance felt her heart tapping fast. Was this the portal to an overlooked clue that might lead to Daniel Pell's purpose here?

The girl tugged at her earlobe, the one with five dots of metal in it, and the top of her shoe rose slightly, indicating she was curling her toes. *Stress* . . .

'I was asleep earlier, for a while. Yeah. I wasn't feeling good. But then I woke up. I had a dream. I don't remember what it was, but I think it was scary. I woke myself up with a noise, kind of moaning. You know how that happens?'

'Sure.'

'Or shouting. Only . . .' Her voice faded, she was squeezing her ear again.

'You're not sure it was *you* making the noise? It might've been somebody else?'

The girl swallowed. She'd be thinking that the sound had perhaps come from one of her dying family members. 'Right.'

'Do you remember what time?' The TODs was between 6:30 and 8:00 p.m., Dance recalled.

But Theresa couldn't remember for sure. She guessed around 7:00.

'You stayed in bed?'

'Uh-huh.'

'Did you hear anything after that?'

'Yeah, voices. I couldn't hear them real well. I was, you know, groggy, but I definitely heard them.'

'Who was it?'

'I don't know, men's voices. But definitely not my father or brother. I remember that.'

'Tare, did you tell anybody this back then?'

'Yeah.' She nodded. 'But nobody was interested.'

How on earth had Reynolds missed it?

'Well, tell me now. What did you hear?'

'There were, like, a couple of things. First of all, I heard somebody mention money. Four hundred dollars. I remember that exactly.'

Pell had been found with more than that when he was arrested. Maybe he and Newberg were going through Croyton's wallet and commenting on how much money was inside. Or was the phrase actually 'four hundred thousand'?

'What else?'

'Okay, then somebody – a man, but somebody different – said something about Canada. And somebody else asked a question. About Quebec.'

'And what was the question?'

'He just wanted to know what Quebec was.'

Somebody not knowing about Quebec? Dance wondered if that was Newberg – the women had said that while he was a genius at woodworking, electronics and computers he was pretty damaged otherwise, thanks to drugs.

So, a Canadian connection. Is that where Pell wanted to escape to? A lot easier to get through that border than going south. A lot of mountaintops too.

Dance smiled and sat forward. 'Go on, Tare. You're doing great.'

'Then,' Teresa continued, 'somebody was talking about used cars. Another man. He had a low voice. He talked fast.'

Used-car dealerships were popular venues for money-laundering. Or they might have been talking about getting a car for their escape. And it hadn't been just Pell and Newberg. Somebody *else* was there. A third person.

'Did your father do business in Canada?'

'I don't know. He traveled a lot. But I don't think he ever mentioned Canada . . . I could never figure out why the police back then didn't ask me more about it. But since Pell was in jail, it didn't matter. But now that he's out . . . Ever since Mr Nagle said you needed help finding the killer, I've been trying to make sense out of what I heard. Maybe you can figure it out.'

'I hope I can. Anything else?'

'No, it was about then that I guess I fell back asleep. And the next thing I knew . . .' she swallowed '. . . there was this woman in a uniform there. A policewoman. She had me get dressed and . . . that was it.'

Dance reflected: four hundred dollars, a car dealership, a French Canadian province.

And a third man.

Was Pell intent on heading north now? At the very least she'd call Homeland Security and Immigration; they could keep an eye on the northern border crossings.

Dance tried again, walking the girl through the events of that terrible night. But the efforts were useless. She knew nothing more.

Four hundred dollars . . . Canada . . . What's Quebec? . . . used cars . . . Did they contain the key to the Daniel Pell conspiracy?

And then Dance had a thought that, surprisingly, involved her own family: herself, Wes and Maggie. An idea occurred to her. She ran through the facts of the murder in her mind. Impossible . . . But then the theory grew more likely, though she didn't like the conclusion.

She reluctantly asked, 'Tare, you said this was around seven p.m. or so?'

'Yeah, maybe.'

'Where did your family eat?'

'Where? The den most of the time. We weren't allowed to use the dining room. That was just for, like, formal things.'

'Did you watch TV while you were having dinner?'

'Yeah. A lot. Me and my brother and sister, at least.'

'And was the den near your bedroom?'

'Like, right down the stairs. How did you know?'

'Did you ever watch *Jeopardy!*?'

She frowned. 'Yeah.'

'Tare, I'm wondering if maybe the voices you heard were from the show. Maybe somebody picking the category of geography for four hundred dollars. And the answer was "The French-speaking province of Canada." The question would be "What is Quebec?"'

The girl fell silent. Her eyes were still. 'No,' she said firmly, shaking her head. 'No, that wasn't it. I'm sure.'

'And the voice talking about the dealership – could it have been a commercial? Somebody talking fast in a low voice. Like they do on car ads.'

The girl's face flushed with dismay. Then anger. 'No!'

'But maybe?' Dance asked gently.

Theresa's eyes closed. 'No.' A whisper. Then: 'I don't know.'

That was why Reynolds hadn't pursued the child's testimony. He too had figured out she was talking about a TV show.

Theresa's shoulders slumped forward, collapsing in on themselves. It was a very subtle movement but Dance could clearly read the kinesic signal of defeat and sorrow. The girl had been so certain that she'd remembered something helpful to find the man who'd killed her family. Now, she realized that her courageous trip here, defying her aunt . . . The efforts had been pointless. She was crestfallen. 'I'm sorry . . .' Tears pooled in her eyes.

Kathryn Dance smiled. 'Tare, don't worry. It's nothing.' She gave the girl a Kleenex.

'Nothing? It's terrible! I wanted to help so bad . . .'

Another smile. 'Oh, Tare, believe me, we're just getting warmed up.'

In her seminars Dance told the story of the city slicker stopping in a small town to ask a farmer directions. The stranger looks at the dog sitting at the man's feet and says, 'Your dog bite?' The farmer says no and, when the stranger reaches down to pet the dog, he gets bitten. The man jumps back and angrily says, 'You said your dog didn't bite!' The farmer replies, 'Mine doesn't. This here dog's not mine.'

The art of interviewing isn't only about analyzing the subjects' answers and their body language and demeanor; it's also about asking the right questions.

The facts about the Croytons' murders and every moment afterward had been documented by police and reporters. So Kathryn Dance decided to inquire about the one period of time that apparently no one had ever asked about: *before* the murders.

'Tare, I want to know about what happened earlier.'

'Earlier?'

'Sure. Let's start with earlier that day.'

Theresa frowned. 'Oh, I don't even remember much about it. I mean, what happened that night, it kind of shoved everything else away.'

'Give it a try. Think back. It was May. You were in school then, right?'

'Yeah.'

'What day of the week?'

'Uhm, it was Friday.'

'You remembered that pretty fast.'

'Oh, because on a lot of Fridays Dad'd take us kids places. That day we were going to the carnival rides in Santa Cruz. Only everything got messed up because I got sick.' Theresa thought back, rubbing her eyes. 'Brenda and Steve – my sister and brother – and I were going, and Mom stayed at home because she had a benefit or something on Saturday she had to work on.'

'But plans got changed?'

'Right. We were, like, on our way but . . .' she looked down '. . . I got sick. In the car. So we turned around and went home.'

'What did you have? A cold?'

'Stomach flu.' Theresa winced and touched her belly.

'Oh, I just hate that.'

'Yeah, it sucks.'

'And you got back home about when?'

'Five thirty, maybe.'

'And you went straight to bed.'

'Yeah, that's right.' She looked out the window at the gnarled tree.

'And then you woke up, hearing the TV show.'

The girl twined a brown-red strand of hair around a finger. 'Quebec.' A laughing grimace.

At this point, Kathryn Dance paused. She realized she had a decision to make, an important one.

Because there was no doubt that Theresa was being deceptive.

When she'd been making casual conversation and, later, talking about what Theresa had overheard from the TV room, the girl's kinesic behavior was relaxed and open, though she obviously was experiencing general stress – anyone who's talking to a police officer as part of an investigation, even an innocent victim, experiences this.

But as soon as she started talking about the trip to the Santa Cruz boardwalk she displayed hesitations of speech, she covered parts of her face and ear – negation gestures – and looked out the window, aversion. Trying to appear calm and casual, she revealed the stress she was experiencing by bobbing her foot. Dance sensed deception stress patterns and that the girl was in the denial response state.

Everything Theresa was telling her was presumably consistent with facts that Dance could verify. But deception includes evasion and omission as well as outright lying. There were things Theresa wasn't sharing.

'Tare, something troubling happened on the drive, didn't it?'

'Troubling? No. Really. I swear.'

A triple play there: two denial flag expressions, along with answering a question with a question. Now the girl was flushed and her foot bobbed again, an obvious cluster of stress responses.

'Go on, tell me. It's all right. There's nothing you have to worry about. Tell me.'

'Like, you know. My parents, my brother and sister . . . They were *killed*. Who wouldn't be upset?' A bit of anger now.

Dance nodded sympathetically. 'I mean before that. You've left Carmel, you're driving to Santa Cruz. You're not feeling well. You go home. Other than being sick, what was there about that drive that bothered you?'

'I don't know. I can't remember.'

That sentence, from a person in a denial state, means: I remember perfectly well but I don't want to think about it. The memory's too painful.

'You're driving along and –'

'I –' Theresa began, then she fell silent. And lowered head to hands, breaking into tears. A torrent, accompanied by the soundtrack of breathless sobbing.

'Tare.' Dance rose and handed her a wad of tissues as the girl cried hard, though quietly, the sobs like hiccups.

'It's okay,' the agent said compassionately, gripping her arm. 'Whatever happened, it's fine. Don't worry.'

'I . . .' The girl was paralyzed. Dance could see she was trying to make a decision. Which way would it go? the agent wondered. She'd either spill everything, or stonewall – in which case the interview was now over.

Finally she said, 'Oh, I've wanted to tell somebody. I just couldn't. Not the counselors or friends, my aunt . . .' More sobbing. Collapsed chest, chin down, hands in her lap when not mopping her face. The textbook kinesic signs that Theresa Croyton had moved into the acceptance stage of emotional response. The terrible burden of what she'd been living with was finally going to come out. She was confessing.

'It's my fault. It's all my fault they're dead!'

Now she pressed her head back against the couch. Her face was red, tendons rose, tears stained the front of her sweater.

'Brenda and Steve, Mom and Dad . . . all because of me!'

'Because you got sick?'

'No! Because I *pretended* to be sick!'

'Tell me.'

'I didn't want to go to the boardwalk. I couldn't stand going, I hated it! All I could think of was to pretend to be sick. I remembered about these models who put their fingers down their throats so they throw up and don't get fat. When we were in the car on the highway I did that when nobody was looking. I threw up in the backseat and said I had the flu. It was all gross, and everybody was mad and Dad turned around and drove back home.'

So that was it. The poor girl was convinced it was her fault her family'd been slaughtered because of the lie she told. She'd lived with this terrible burden for eight years.

One truth had been excavated. But at least one more remained. And Kathryn Dance wanted to unearth this one as well.

'Tell me, Tare. Why didn't you want to go to the pier?'

'I just didn't. It wasn't fun.'

Confessing one lie doesn't lead automatically to confessing them all. The girl had now slipped into denial once again.

'Why? You can tell me. Go on.'

'I don't know. It just wasn't fun.'

'Why not?'

'Well, Dad was always busy. So he'd give us money and tell us he'd pick us up later and he'd go off and make phone calls and things. It was boring.'

Her feet tapped again and she squeezed the right-side earrings in a compulsive pattern: top, bottom, then in the middle. The stress was eating her up.

Yet it wasn't only the kinesics that were sending significant deception signals to Kathryn Dance. Children – even a seventeen-year-old high school student – are often hard to analyze kinesically. Most interviewers of youngsters perform a content-based analysis, judging their truth or deception by *what* they say, not *how* they say it.

What Theresa was telling Dance didn't make sense – both in terms of the story she was offering, and in terms of Dance's knowledge of children and the place in question. Wes and Maggie, for instance, loved the Santa Cruz boardwalk, and would have leapt at the chance to spend hours there unsupervised with a pocketful of money. There were hundreds of things for children to do, carnival rides, food, music, games.

And another contradiction Dance noted: Why hadn't Theresa simply said she wanted to stay home with her mother before they left that

Friday and let her father and siblings go without her? It was as if she didn't want them to go to Santa Cruz either.

Dance considered this for a moment.

A to B . . .

'Tare, you were saying your father worked and made phone calls when you and your brother and sister went on the rides?'

She looked down. 'Yeah, I guess.'

'Where would he go to make the calls?'

'I don't know. He had a cell phone. Not a lot of people had them then. But he did.'

'Did he ever meet anybody there?'

'I don't know. Maybe.'

'Tare, who were these other people? The ones he'd be with?'

She shrugged.

'Were they other women?'

'No.'

'You sure?'

Theresa was silent, looking everywhere but at Dance. Finally she said, 'Maybe. Some, yeah.'

'And you think they might've been girlfriends of his?'

A nod. Tears again. Through clenched teeth she began, 'And . . .'

'What, Tare?'

'He said that when we got home, if Mom asked, we were supposed to say he was with us.' Her face was flushed now.

Dance recalled that Reynolds hinted Croyton was a womanizer.

A bitter laugh escaped the girl's trembling lips. 'I saw him. Brenda and me, we were supposed to stay on the boardwalk but we went to an ice cream place across Beach Street. And I saw him. There was this woman getting into his car and he was kissing her. And she wasn't the only one. I saw him later with somebody else, going into her apartment or house by the beach. *That's* why I didn't want him to go there. I wanted him to go back home and be with Mommy and us. I didn't want him to be with anybody else.' She wiped her face. 'And so I lied,' she said simply. 'I pretended I was sick.'

So he'd meet his mistresses in Santa Cruz – and take his own children with him to allay his wife's suspicion, abandoning them till he and his lover were finished.

'And my family got killed. And it was my fault.'

Dance leaned forward and said in a low, compassionate voice, 'No,

Tare. It's not your fault at all. We're pretty sure Daniel Pell *intended* to kill your father. It wasn't random. If he'd come by that night and you weren't there, he would've left and come back when your dad was home.'

She grew quiet. 'Yeah?'

Dance wasn't sure about this at all. But she absolutely couldn't let the girl live with the terrible burden of her guilt. 'Yeah.'

Theresa calmed at this tentative comfort. 'Stupid.' She was embarrassed. 'It's all so stupid. I wanted to come help you catch him. And I haven't done anything except act like a baby.'

'Oh, we're doing fine,' Dance said with a significance in her voice that was reflecting some intriguing thoughts she'd just had.

'We are?'

'Yep . . . In fact, I've just thought of some more questions. I hope you're up for them.' Dance's stomach gave a peculiar, and opportune, growl just at that moment. They both laughed, and the agent added, 'Provided there're two Frappuccinos and a cookie or two in the near future.'

Theresa wiped her eyes. 'I could go for that, yeah.'

Dance called Rey Carraneo and set him on the mission of collaring some sustenance from Starbucks. She then made another call. This one was to TJ, telling him to remain in the office; she believed there'd be a change of plans.

*A* to *B* to *X* . . .

# Chapter
# FORTY-EIGHT

Parked up the road from the Point Lobos Inn, out of sight of the guards, Daniel Pell continued to stare at a space between the cypress trees. 'Come on,' he muttered.

And then, just a few seconds later, there she was, Rebecca, hurrying through the bushes with her backpack. She climbed into the car and kissed him firmly.

She sat back. 'Shitty weather,' she said, grinned and kissed him again. 'Sorry I'm late.'

'Nobody saw you?'

A laugh. 'Climbed out the window. They think I went to bed early.'

He put the car in gear and they started up the highway.

This was Daniel Pell's last night in the Monterey Peninsula – and, in a way, his last night on earth. Later, they'd steal another car – an SUV or truck – and head north, winding along the increasingly narrow and rugged roads of Northern California until they came to Pell's mountain property. He'd be king of the mountain, king of a new Family, not answering to anybody, no one to interfere. No one to challenge him. A dozen young people, two dozen, seduced there by the Pied Piper.

*Heaven* . . .

But first his mission here. He had to make certain his future was guaranteed.

Pell handed her the map of Monterey County. She opened a slip of paper and read the street and number as she studied the map. 'It's not too far. Shouldn't take us more than fifteen minutes.'

\* \* \*

Edie Dance glanced out the window of the front of her house and observed the police car.

It certainly made her feel comfortable, with an escaped killer somewhere in the area, and she appreciated the fact that Katie was looking out for them.

Still, it wasn't Daniel Pell who occupied her thoughts, but Juan Millar.

Edie was tired, the old bones not behaving, and she was grateful she'd decided not to work overtime – it was always available for any nurse who wanted it. Death and taxes weren't the only certain aspects of life; the need for healthcare was a third, and Edie Dance would have a career for as long as she wished, anywhere she wished. She couldn't understand her husband's preference for marine, over human, life. People were so fascinating, helping them, reassuring them, taking away their pain.

*Kill me . . .*

Stuart would be back with the children soon. She loved her grandchildren, of course, but she also truly enjoyed their company. Edie knew how lucky she was that Katie lived nearby; so many of her friends had children hundreds, even thousands, of miles away.

Yes, she was happy Wes and Mags were staying here, but she'd be a lot happier when that terrible man was arrested again and put back in jail. Katie's becoming a CBI agent had always bothered her a lot – Stu actually seemed pleased, which irritated her all the more. Edie Dance would never suggest a woman give up a career – she'd worked all her life – but, my God, carrying around a gun and arresting murderers and drug dealers?

Edie would never say it, but her secret desire was that her daughter would meet another man, remarry and abandon police work. Katie had been a successful jury consultant. Why not go back to that? And she and Martine Christensen had that wonderful website, which actually made a little money. If the women devoted themselves to it full-time, think how successful it could be.

Edie had loved her son-in-law dearly. Bill Swenson was sweet, funny, a great father. And the accident that had taken his life was a true tragedy. But that was several years ago. Now it was time for her daughter to move on.

Too bad Michael O'Neil wasn't available; he and Katie were a perfect match (Edie couldn't see why on earth he was with that prima donna Anne, who seemed to treat her children like Christmas decorations and cared more about her gallery than her home).

Then that FBI agent at Stu's party, Winston Kellogg, seemed pretty nice too. He reminded Edie of Bill. And then there was Brian Gunderson, the man Katie'd dated recently.

Edie never worried about her daughter's good sense when it came to picking partners. Her problem was like the one plaguing Edie's golf swing – the follow-through. And she knew the source. Katie'd told her about Wes, his unhappiness at his mom's dating. Edie had been in nursing for a long time, both pediatric and adult. She'd seen how controlling children can be, how clever and manipulative, even subconsciously. Her daughter *had* to approach the subject. But she simply wouldn't. Her approach was duck and cover . . .

But it wasn't Edie's role to talk to the boy directly. Grandparents have the unqualified joy of children's company, but the price for that is abdicating much of the right to parental intervention. Edie'd said her piece to Katie, who'd agreed but, apparently, ignored her completely by breaking up with Brian and –

The woman cocked her head.

A noise from outside, the backyard.

She glanced up to see if Stu had arrived. No, the carport was empty, except for her Prius. Looking out the front window she saw the police officer was still there.

Then she heard the sound again. The clatter of rocks.

Edie and Stu lived off Ocean, on the long hill descending from downtown to Carmel Beach. Their backyard was a stepped series of gardens, boarded by rock walls. Walking the short path to or from the neighbor's adjoining backyard sometimes set loose a tiny spill of gravel down the face of those walls. That's what the noise sounded like.

She walked to the back deck and opened the door, then stepped outside. She couldn't see anyone and heard nothing else. Probably just a cat or a dog. They weren't supposed to run free; Carmel had strict pet laws. But the town was also animal-friendly (the actress Doris Day owned a wonderful hotel here, where pets were welcome), and several cats and dogs roamed the neighborhood.

She closed the door and, hearing Stu's car pull into the driveway, forgot all about the noise. Edie Dance walked to the refrigerator to find a snack for the children.

The interview with the Sleeping Doll had come to an intriguing conclusion.

Back in her office, Dance called and checked up on the girl and her aunt, both safely ensconced in the motel and protected by a 250-pound monolith of a CBI agent who carried two large weapons. They were fine, Albert Stemple reported, then added, 'The girl's nice. I like her. The aunt you can keep.'

Dance read over the notes she'd taken in the interview. Then read them again. Finally she called TJ.

'Your genie awaits, boss.'

'Bring me what we've got so far on Pell.'

'The whole ball of wax? Whatever that means.'

'All the wax.'

Dance was reviewing James Reynolds's notes from the Croyton murder case when TJ arrived – only three or four minutes later, breathless. Maybe her voice had sounded more urgent than she'd realized.

She took the files he carted and spread them out until they covered her desk an inch thick. In a short time they'd accumulated an astonishing amount of material. She began riffling through the pages.

'The girl, was she helpful?'

'Yep,' the agent replied absently, staring at a particular sheet of paper.

TJ made another comment but she wasn't paying any attention. Flipping through more reports, more pages of handwritten notes, and looking over Reynolds's timeline and his other transcriptions. Then returning to the piece of paper she held.

Finally she said, 'I've got a computer question. You know a lot about them. Go check this out.' She circled some words on the sheet.

He glanced down. 'What about it?'

'It's fishy.'

'Not a computer term I'm familiar with. But I'm on the case, boss. We never sleep.'

'We've got a situation.'

Dance was addressing Charles Overby, Winston Kellogg and TJ. They were in Overby's office and he was playing with a bronze golf ball mounted on a wooden stand, like a gearshift in a sports car. She wished Michael O'Neil were here.

Dance then dropped the bomb. 'Rebecca Sheffield's working with Pell.'

'What?' Overby blurted.

'It gets better. I think she was behind the whole escape.'

Her boss shook his head, the theory troubling him. He was wondering undoubtedly if he'd authorized something he shouldn't have.

But Winston Kellogg encouraged her, 'Interesting. Go on.'

'Theresa Croyton told me a few things that made me suspicious. So I went back and looked over the evidence so far. Remember that email we found in the Sea View? Supposedly Pell sent it to Jennie from prison. But look.' She showed the printout. 'The email address says Capitola Correctional. But it has a dot-com extension. If it was really a Department of Corrections address it would've had dot-ca-gov.'

Kellogg grimaced. 'Hell, yes. Missed that completely.'

'I just had TJ check out the address.'

The young agent explained, 'The company's a service provider in Denver. You can create your own domain, as long as the name's not taken by somebody else. It's an anonymous account. But we're getting a warrant to look at the archives.'

'Anonymous? Then why do you think it was Rebecca?' Overby asked.

'Look at the email. That phrase. "Who could ask for anything more in a girl?" It's not that common. It stuck with me because it echoes a line in an old Gershwin song.'

'Why is that important?'

'Because Rebecca used the exact expression the first time I met her.'

Overby said, 'Still –'

She pushed forward, not in the mood to be obstructed. 'Now, let's look at the facts. Jennie stole the Thunderbird from that restaurant in L.A. on Friday and checked into the Sea View on Saturday. Her phone and credit card records show she was in Orange County all last week. But the woman who checked out the You Mail It office near the courthouse was there on *Wednesday*. We faxed a warrant to Rebecca's credit card companies. She flew from San Diego to Monterey on Tuesday, flew back on Thursday. Rented a car here.'

'Okay,' Overby allowed.

'Now, I'm guessing that in Capitola it wasn't Jennie that Pell was talking to; it was Rebecca. He must've given her Jennie's name and street and email address. Rebecca took over from there. They picked her because she lived near Rebecca, at least close enough to check her out.'

Kellogg added, 'So she knows where Pell is, what he's doing here.'

'Has to.'

Overby said, 'Let's pick her up. You can work your magic, Kathryn.'

'I want her in custody, but I need some more information before I interrogate her. I want to talk to Nagle.'

'The writer?'

She nodded. Then said to Kellogg, 'Can you bring Rebecca in?'

'Sure, if you can get some backup for me.'

Overby said he'd call the MCSO and have another officer meet Kellogg outside the Point Lobos Inn. The agent-in-charge surprised Dance by pointing out something she hadn't thought of: They had no reason to think Rebecca was armed, but since she'd driven from San Diego and not gone through airport security she could have a weapon with her.

Dance said, 'Good, Charles.' Then, a nod at TJ. 'Let's go see Nagle.'

Dance and the younger agent were en route to their destination when her phone rang.

'Hello?'

Winston Kellogg said in an uncharacteristically urgent voice, 'Kathryn, she's gone.'

'Rebecca?'

'Yes.'

'Are the others okay?'

'They're fine. Linda said Rebecca wasn't feeling well, went to lie down. Didn't want to be disturbed. We found her bedroom window open but her car's still at CBI.'

'So Pell picked her up?'

'I'm guessing.'

'How long ago?'

'She went to bed an hour ago. They don't know when she slipped out.'

If Pell and Rebecca had wanted to hurt the other women, she could've done it herself or snuck Pell in through the window. Dance decided they weren't at immediate risk, especially with the guards.

'Where are you now?' she asked Kellogg.

'Going back to CBI. I think Pell and Rebecca are making a run for it. I'll talk to Michael about getting roadblocks set up again.'

When they hung up, she called Morton Nagle.

'Hello?' he answered.

'It's Kathryn. Listen, Rebecca's with Pell.'

'What? He kidnapped her?'

'They're working together. She was behind the escape.'

'No!'

'They might be headed out of town but there's a chance you're in danger.'

'Me?'

'Lock your doors. Don't let anybody in. We're on our way. I'll be there in five minutes.'

It took them closer to ten, even with TJ's aggressive – he called it 'assertive' – driving; the roads were crowded with tourists getting an early start on the weekend. They skidded to a stop in front of the house and walked to the front door. Dance knocked. The writer answered a moment later. He glanced past her at TJ, then scanned the street. The agents stepped inside.

Nagle closed the door. His shoulders slumped. 'I'm sorry.' The writer's voice broke. 'He told me if I gave anything away on the phone, he'd kill my family. I'm so sorry.'

Daniel Pell, standing behind the door, touched the back of her head with a pistol.

# Chapter
# FORTY-NINE

'It's my friend. The cat to my mouse. With the funny name. Kathryn *Dance* . . .'

Nagle continued, 'When you phoned, your number came up on caller ID. He made me tell him who it was. I had to say everything was fine. I didn't want to. But my children. I –'

'It's all right –' she began.

'Shhhhh, Mr Writer and Ms Interrogator. Shush.'

In the bedroom to the left, Dance could see Nagle's family lying belly-down on the floor, their hands on top of their heads. His wife, Joan, and the children – teenage Eric and young, round Sonja. Rebecca was sitting on the bed over them, holding a knife. She gazed at Dance without a fleck of emotion.

The only reason the family weren't dead, Dance knew, was that Pell was controlling Nagle through them.

*Patterns* . . .

'Come on out here, baby, lend a hand.'

Rebecca slid off the bed and joined them.

'Get their guns and phones.' Pell held the gun to Dance's ear while Rebecca took her weapon. Then Pell told her to cuff herself.

She did.

'Not tight enough.' He squeezed the bracelets and Dance winced.

They did the same with TJ and pushed both of them down on the couch.

'Watch it,' TJ muttered.

Pell said to Dance, 'Listen to me. You listening?'

'Yes.'

'Is anybody else coming?'

'I didn't call anyone.'

'That's not what I asked. You, being the ace interrogator, oughta know that.' The essence of calm.

'As far as I know, no. I was coming here to ask Morton some questions.'

Pell set their phones on a coffee table. 'If anybody calls you, tell them that everything's fine. You'll be back at your headquarters in an hour or so. But you can't talk now. We clear on that? If not, I pick one of the kiddies in there and −'

'Clear,' she said.

'Now, no more words from anybody. We've −'

'This is not smart,' TJ said.

No, no, Dance thought. Let him control you! With Daniel Pell you can't be defiant.

Pell stepped up to him and, almost leisurely, touched his gun to the man's throat. 'What did I tell you?'

The young man's flippancy was gone. 'Not to say a word.'

'But you did say something. Why would you do that? What a stupid, stupid thing to do.'

He's going to kill him, Dance thought. Please, no. 'Pell, listen to me −'

'You're talking too,' the killer said, and swung the gun toward her.

'I'm sorry,' TJ whispered.

'That's more words.' Pell turned to Dance. 'I've got a few questions for you and your little friend here. But in a minute. You sit tight, enjoy the scene of domestic bliss.' Then he said to Nagle, 'Keep going.'

Nagle returned to what was apparently the task Dance and TJ had interrupted: It seemed that he was burning all of his notes and research material.

Pell watched the bonfire and added absently, 'And if you miss something and I find it, I will cut your wife's fingers off. Then start on your kids'. And quit crying. It's not dignified. Have some control.'

Ten agonizing minutes of silence passed as Nagle found his notes and tossed them into the fire.

Dance knew that as soon as he finished and heard from her and TJ what he needed to know, they'd be dead.

Nagle's wife was sobbing. She said, 'Leave us alone, please, please, anything . . . I'll do anything. Please . . .'

Dance glanced into the bedroom, where she lay beside Sonja and Eric. The little girl was crying pathetically.

'Quiet there, Mrs Writer.'

Dance glanced at her watch, partly obscured by the cuffs. She imagined what her own children were doing now. The thought was too painful, though, and she forced herself to concentrate on what was happening in the room.

Was there anything she could do?

Bargain with him? But to bargain you need something of value the other person wants.

Resist? But to resist you need weapons.

'Why are you doing this?' Nagle moaned, as the last of the notes went up in flames.

'Hush there.'

Pell rose and stirred the fire with a poker to keep the pages burning. He dusted his hands off. He held up his sooty fingers. 'Makes me feel at home. I've been fingerprinted probably fifty times in my life. I can always tell the new clerks. Their hands shake when they roll your fingers. Okay, then.' He turned to Dance, 'Now, I understand from your call earlier to Mr Writer here you figured out about Rebecca. Which is what I have to talk to you about. What do you know about us? And who else knows it? We've got to make some plans and we need to know what to do next. And understand this, Agent Dance, you're not the only one who can spot liars at fifty paces. I have that gift too. You and me, we're naturals.'

Whether she lied or not didn't matter. They were all dead.

'Oh, and I should say that Rebecca found another address for me. The home of one Stuart Dance.'

Dance felt this news like a slap in the face. She struggled to keep from being sick. A wash of heat, scalding water, enveloped her face and chest.

'You son of a bitch,' TJ raged.

'And if you tell me the truth, your mom and pop and kiddies'll be fine. I was right about your brood, wasn't I? At our first get-together. And no husband. You, a poor widow, Rebecca tells me. Sorry about that. Anyway, I'll bet the kiddies're with the grandfolks right now.'

At that moment Kathryn Dance came to a decision.

It was a gamble, and under other circumstances it would have been a difficult, if not impossible, choice. Now, although the consequences would probably be tragic, one way or the other, there was no option.

No weapons – except words, and her intuition. *A* to *B* to *X* . . .

They would have to do.

Dance shifted so she was facing Pell directly. 'Aren't you curious why we're here?'

'That's a question. I didn't want a question. I wanted an answer.'

Make sure he remains in charge – Daniel Pell's trademark. 'Please, let me go on. I *am* answering your question. Please, let me.'

Pell looked her over with a frown. He didn't object.

'Now think about it. Why would we come here in such a big hurry?'

Normally she would have used a subject's first name. But doing so could be interpreted as an attempt to dominate, and Daniel Pell needed to know he was in control.

He grimaced impatiently. 'Get to the point.'

Rebecca scowled. 'She's stalling. Let's go, baby.'

Dance said, 'Because I had to warn Morton –'

Rebecca whispered, 'Let's just finish up and get going. Jesus, we're wasting –'

'Quiet, lovely.' Pell's bright blue eyes turned back to Dance and he looked her over carefully, just as he'd done in Salinas during their interview on Monday. It seemed like years ago. 'Yeah, you wanted to warn him about me. So?'

'No. I wanted to warn him about Rebecca.'

'What're you talking about?'

Dance held Pell's eyes as she said, 'I wanted to warn him that she was going to use you to kill him. Just like she used you at William Croyton's house eight years ago.'

# Chapter
# FIFTY

Dance saw the flicker in Daniel Pell's other-worldly eyes.

She'd touched something close to the god of control.

*She used you . . .*

'This is such bullshit,' Rebecca snapped.

'Probably,' Pell said.

Dance noted the conditional word, not an absolute one. The agent eased forward. We believe that those who are physically closer to us tell the truth more than those leaning away. 'She set you up, Daniel. And you want to know why? To kill William Croyton's wife.'

He was shaking his head, but he was listening to every word.

'Rebecca was Croyton's lover. And when his wife wouldn't give him a divorce she decided to use you and Jimmy Newberg to kill her.'

Rebecca laughed harshly.

Dance said, 'You remember the Sleeping Doll, Daniel? Theresa Croyton?'

Now Dance was using his first name, which solidified their bond against a shared enemy, a trick interrogators use.

He said nothing. His eyes flicked to Rebecca, then back to Dance, who continued, 'I just talked to the girl.'

Rebecca was shocked. 'You what?'

'We had a long conversation. It was quite revealing.'

Rebecca tried to recover. 'Daniel, she didn't talk to her at all. She's bluffing to save her ass.'

But Dance asked, 'Was *Jeopardy!* on the TV in the den the night you and Newberg broke into the Croytons'? She told me it was. Who else would have known that?'

*What is Quebec? . . .*

The killer blinked. Dance saw she had his complete attention. 'Theresa told me that her father was having affairs. He'd drop the children off at the Santa Cruz boardwalk, then meet his lovers there. One night Croyton spotted Rebecca doing sketches and picked her up. They started an affair. She wanted him to get a divorce but he wouldn't, or couldn't, because of his wife. So Rebecca decided to kill her.'

'Oh, this is ridiculous,' Rebecca raged. 'She doesn't *know* any of this.'

But Dance could see it was posed. The woman was flushed and her hands and feet were flashing subtle but clear affect displays from the stress. There was now no doubt that Dance was on to something.

Dance looked at him with steady eyes. 'The boardwalk . . . Rebecca would've heard about you there, wouldn't she, Daniel? That's where the Family went to sell things at flea markets and to steal and shoplift. Caused kind of a stir, this cult of criminals. Gypsies, they called you. It made the news. She needed a fall guy, a killer. Linda told me you two met on the boardwalk. You thought you seduced her? No, it was the other way around.'

Rebecca's voice remained calm. 'Shut up! She's lying, Dan —'

'Quiet!' Pell snapped.

'She joined your clan when? Not long before the Croyton murders. A few months?' Dance pressed forward relentlessly. 'Rebecca talked her way into the Family. Didn't it seem a little sudden? Didn't you wonder why? She wasn't like the others. Linda and Samantha and Jimmy, they were children. They'd do what you wanted. But Rebecca was different. Independent, aggressive.'

Dance recalled Winston Kellogg's comment about cult leaders.

*Women can be just as effective and as ruthless as men. And often they're more devious . . .*

'Once she was in the Family she saw right away that she could use Jimmy Newberg too. She told him that Croyton had something valuable in his house and he suggested that the two of you break in and steal it. Right?'

Dance saw that she was. 'But Rebecca had made *other* plans with Jimmy. Once you were in the Croytons' house, he was supposed to kill Croyton's wife, then kill *you*. With you gone, he and Rebecca could be in charge. Of course, her idea was to turn Jimmy in after the killings — or maybe even kill him herself. William Croyton would go through a suitable period of mourning and he'd marry her.'

'Honey, no. This is —'

Pell lunged forward and grabbed Rebecca's short hair, pulled her close. 'Don't say another word. Let her talk!'

Moaning in pain, cringing, she slipped to the floor.

With their attention elsewhere, Dance caught TJ's eye. He nodded slowly.

She continued, 'Rebecca thought only Croyton's wife would be home. But the whole family was there because Theresa said she was sick. Whatever happened that night – only you know that, Daniel – whatever happened, everybody ended up dead.

'And when you called the Family to tell them what happened, Rebecca did the only thing she could to save herself: She turned you in. *She's* the one who made the call that got you arrested.'

'That's bullshit,' Rebecca said. 'I'm the one who got him out of jail now!'

Dance laughed coldly. She said to Pell, 'Because she needed to use you again, Daniel. To kill Morton. A few months ago she got a call from him and he told her about the book *The Sleeping Doll*, how he was planning to write about the Croytons' life *before* the murders and Theresa's life afterward. He'd learn about the affairs Croyton had. It was just a matter of time before somebody put the pieces together – that she was behind the plot to murder Croyton's wife.

'So Rebecca came up with the plan to break you out of Capitola.' Dance frowned and looked at Pell. 'One thing I don't know is what she said to you, Daniel, to convince you to murder him.' She glanced angrily at Rebecca, as if she were offended by what the woman had done to her good friend Daniel Pell. 'So what lies *did* you tell him?'

Pell shouted at Rebecca, 'What you told me – is it true or not?' But before she could speak, Pell grabbed Nagle, who cringed. 'That book you're writing! What were you going to say about me?'

'It wasn't about *you*. It was about Theresa and the Croytons and the girls in the Family. That's all. It was about your *victims*, not you.'

Pell pushed the man to the floor. 'No, no! You were going to write about my land!'

'Land?'

'Yes!'

'What're you talking about?'

'My land, my mountaintop. You found out where it was, you were going to write about it in your book!'

Ah, Dance finally understood. Pell's precious mountaintop. Rebecca had convinced him that the only way to keep it secret was to kill Morton Nagle and destroy the notes.

'I don't know anything about that, I swear.' Pell looked him over closely. He believed the writer, Dance could see.

'As soon as you killed Nagle and his family, Daniel, you know what was coming next, don't you? Rebecca was going to murder *you*. Claim you kidnapped her from the inn.' Dance gave a sad laugh. 'Oh, Daniel, how she used you ... All along *she* was the Pied Piper, she was the puppeteer.'

Pell blinked when he heard her use those words. Then he rose and charged toward Rebecca, knocking a table over as he lifted the gun.

The woman cringed but suddenly she too leapt forward, swinging the knife madly, slicing into Pell's arm, grabbing at his gun. The weapon went off, the bullet digging a chunk of rosy brick out of the fireplace.

Instantly Dance and TJ were on their feet.

The young agent kicked Rebecca hard in the ribs and grabbed Pell's gun hand. They wrestled for control of the weapon, sliding to the floor.

'Call nine one one,' Dance shouted to Nagle, who scrabbled for a phone. She started for the guns on the table, recalling: *Check your backdrop, aim, squeeze in bursts, count the rounds, at twelve drop the clip, reload. Check your backdrop* ...

Screaming from Nagle's wife, wailing from his daughter.

'Kathryn,' TJ shouted breathlessly. She saw that Pell was twisting the gun toward her.

It fired.

The bullet streaked past her.

TJ was young and strong, but his wrists were still cuffed and Pell had desperation and adrenaline coursing through him. With his free hand he pounded at TJ's neck and head. Finally the killer broke away, holding the gun, as the young agent rolled desperately for cover under a table.

Dance struggled forward but knew she'd never make it to the weapons in time. TJ was dead ...

Then a huge explosion.

Another.

Dance dropped to her knees and looked behind her.

Morton Nagle had picked up one of their guns and was firing the weapon toward Pell. Clearly unfamiliar with guns, he jerked the trigger and the bullets were wide. Still he stood his ground and kept firing. 'You son of a bitch!'

Crouching, hands up in a futile effort to protect himself, Pell cringed, hesitated a moment, fired one round into Rebecca's belly, then flung the door open and ran outside.

Dance took the gun from Nagle, grabbed TJ's as well and shoved it into his cuffed hands.

The agents got to the half-open door just as a round slammed into the jamb, peppering them with splinters. They jumped back, crouching. She fished the cuff keys from her jacket and undid the bracelets. TJ did the same.

Cautiously they glanced outside at the empty street. A moment later they heard the screech of an accelerating car.

Calling back to Nagle, 'Keep Rebecca alive! We need her,' Dance ran to her car and grabbed the microphone off the dash. It slipped out of her shaking hands. She took a breath, controlled the tremors and called the Monterey Sheriff's Office.

# Chapter
# FIFTY-ONE

An angry man is a man out of control.

But Daniel Pell couldn't staunch the rage as he sped away from Monterey, replaying what had just happened. Kathryn Dance's voice, Rebecca's face.

Replaying the events of eight years ago too.

Jimmy Newberg, the goddamn computer freak, the doper, had said that he had inside information about William Croyton – thanks to a programmer who'd been fired six months earlier. He'd managed to find out Croyton's alarm code and had a key to the back door (though Pell now knew where he'd gotten those – from Rebecca, of course). Jimmy'd said too that the eccentric Croyton kept huge amounts of cash in the house.

Pell would never rob a bank or check-cashing operation, nothing big. But, still, he needed money to expand the Family and to move to his mountaintop. And here was a chance for a once-in-a-lifetime break-in. No one was going to be home, Jimmy said, so there'd be no risk of injuries. They'd walk away with a hundred thousand dollars, and Croyton would make a routine call to the police and the insurance company, then forget the matter.

Just what Kathryn Dance had figured.

The two men had snuck through the backyard and made their way to the house through the sumptuous landscaping. Pell had seen the lights on, but Jimmy told him they were on a timer for security. They slipped into the house through a side utility door.

But something wasn't right. The alarm was off. Pell turned to Jimmy to tell him that somebody must be home after all, but the young man was already hurrying into the kitchen.

Walking right up to the middle-aged woman cooking dinner, her back to them. No! Pell remembered thinking in shock. What was he doing?

Murdering her, it turned out.

Using a paper towel, Jimmy pulled a steak knife from his pocket – one from the Family's house, with Pell's fingerprints on it, he realized – and, gripping the woman around the mouth, stabbed her deeply. She slumped to the floor.

Enraged, Pell whispered, 'What the hell are you doing?'

Newberg turned and hesitated, but his face was telegraphing what was coming. When he lunged, Pell was already leaping aside. He just managed to dodge the vicious blade. Pell swept up a frying pan, smashed it into Newberg's head. He crashed to the floor and, with a butcher knife from the counter, Pell killed him.

A moment later William Croyton hurried into the kitchen, hearing the noise of the struggle. His two older children were behind him, screaming as they stared at their mother's body. Pell pulled his gun out and forced the hysterical family into the pantry. He finally calmed Croyton down and asked about the money, which the businessman said was in the desk in the ground-floor office.

Daniel Pell had found himself looking at the sobbing, terrified family as if he were looking at weeds in a garden or crows or insects. He'd had no intention of killing anyone that night but to stay in control of his life he had no choice. In two minutes they were all dead.

Pell had then wiped what fingerprints he could, taken Jimmy's steak knife and all his ID, then run to the office, where he found, to his shock, that, yes, there was money in the desk, but only a thousand dollars. A fast search of the master bedroom downstairs revealed only pocket change and costume jewelry. He never even got upstairs, where that little girl was in bed, asleep. (He was now glad she'd been up there; ironically, if he'd killed her then, he never would've learned about Rebecca's betrayal.)

And, yes, to the soundtrack of *Jeopardy!* he'd run back to the kitchen, where he pocketed the dead man's wallet and the wife's diamond cocktail ring.

Then outside, to his car. And only a mile later he was pulled over by the police. Rebecca . . .

Thinking back to meeting her for the first time – the 'coincidental' meeting that she had apparently engineered near the boardwalk in Santa Cruz.

Pell remembered how much he loved the boardwalk, the rides. Amusement parks fascinated him, people giving up complete control to somebody else – either risking harm on the roller coasters and parachute drops or becoming mindless laboratory rats on rides like the boardwalk's famous hundred-year-old Looff carousel, round and round . . .

Remembered too Rebecca nine years ago, near that very same merry-go-round, gesturing him over.

*'Hey, how'd you like me to do your portrait?'*

*'I guess. How much?'*

*'You'll be able to afford it. Take a seat.'*

And then after five minutes, with only the basic features of his face sketched in, she'd lowered the charcoal stick, looked him over and asked, challenging, if there was someplace private to go. They'd walked to the van, Linda Whitfield watching them with a solemn, jealous face. Pell hardly noticed her.

And a few minutes later, after kissing frantically, his hands all over her, she'd eased back. 'Wait . . .'

What? he'd wondered. Clap, AIDS?

Breathless, she'd said, 'I . . . have to say something.' She'd paused, looking down.

'Go on.'

'You might not like this, and if not, okay, we'll just call it quits and you get a picture for free. But I feel this connection with you, even after just a little while, and I've got to say . . .'

'Tell me.'

'When it comes to sex, I don't really enjoy it . . . unless you hurt me. I mean, *really* hurt me. A lot of men don't like that. And it's okay . . .'

His response was to roll her over on her taut little belly.

And pull off his belt.

He gave a grim laugh now. It was all bullshit, he realized. Somehow in that ten minutes on the beach and five minutes in the van she'd tipped to his fantasy and played it for all it was worth.

*Svengali and Trilby . . .*

He now continued driving until his right arm began to throb with pain from Rebecca's knife slash at Nagle's house. He pulled over, opened his shirt and looked at it. Not terrible – the bleeding was slowing. But, damn, it hurt.

Nothing like the slash of her betrayal, though.

He was at the edge of the quiet portion of town and would have to continue through populated areas, where the police would be looking for him everywhere.

He made a U-turn and drove through the streets until he found an Infiniti, pausing at a stoplight ahead of him. Only one person inside. No other cars were around. Pell slowed but didn't hit the brakes until he was right on top of the luxury car. The bumpers tapped with a resonant thud. The Infiniti rolled forward a few feet. The driver glared in his rear-view mirror and got out.

Pell, shaking his head, climbed out too. He stood, studying the damage.

'Weren't you looking?' The driver of the Infiniti was a middle-aged Latino man. 'I just bought it last month.' He glanced up from the cars and frowned at the blood on Pell's arm. 'Are you hurt?' His eyes followed the stain down to Pell's hand, where he saw the gun.

But by then it was too late.

# Chapter
# FIFTY-TWO

The first thing Kathryn Dance had done at Nagle's house – while TJ called in the escape – was to phone the deputy guarding her parents and children and have him take them, under guard, to CBI headquarters. She doubted Pell would waste time at this point carrying out his threats, but she wasn't going to take any chances.

She now asked the writer and his wife if Pell had said anything about where he might be fleeing, especially his mountaintop. Nagle had been honest with Pell; he'd never heard anything about an enclave in the wilderness. He, his wife and children could add nothing more. Rebecca was badly wounded and unconscious. O'Neil had sent a deputy with her in the ambulance. The moment she was able to talk, he'd call the detective.

Dance now joined Kellogg and O'Neil, who stood nearby, heads bowed, as they discussed the case. Whatever personal reservations O'Neil had about the FBI man, and vice versa, you couldn't tell it from their posture and gesturing. They were efficiently and quickly coordinating roadblocks and planning a search strategy.

O'Neil took a phone call. He frowned. 'Okay, sure. Call Watsonville . . . I'll handle it.' He hung up and announced, 'Got a lead. Carjacking in Marina. Man fitting Pell's description – and bleeding – snatched a black Infiniti. Had a gun.' He added grimly, 'Witness said he heard a gunshot and, when he looked, Pell was closing the trunk.'

Dance closed her eyes and sighed in disgust. Yet another death.

O'Neil said, 'There's no way he's staying on the Peninsula anymore. He jacked the car in Marina so he's headed north. Probably aiming for the One-oh-one.' He climbed into his car. 'I'll set up a command post in Gilroy. And Watsonville, in case he sticks to the One.'

She watched him drive off.

'Let's get up there too,' Kellogg said, turning to his car.

Following him, Dance heard her phone ring. She took the call. It was James Reynolds. She briefed him on what had just happened, and then the former prosecutor said he'd been through the files from the Croyton murders. He'd found nothing particularly helpful about where Pell might be headed but he had found something curious. Did Dance have a minute now?

'You bet,' she said and held up a hand to Kellogg, signaling him to wait.

Sam and Linda huddled together, watching the news reports about yet another attempted murder by Daniel Pell: the writer, Nagle. Rebecca, described as an accomplice of Pell's, had been badly wounded. And Pell had once again escaped. He was in a stolen car, most likely heading north, the owner of the car another victim.

'Oh, my,' Linda whispered.

'Rebecca was with him all along.' Sam stared at the TV screen, her face a mask of shock. 'But who shot her? The police? Daniel?'

Linda closed her eyes momentarily. Sam didn't know if this was a prayer or a reaction to the exhaustion from the ordeal they'd been through in the past few days. Crosses to bear, Sam couldn't help but think. Which she didn't tell to her Christian friend. Another newscaster devoted a few minutes to describing the woman who'd been shot, Rebecca Sheffield, founder of Women's Initiatives in San Diego, one of the women in the Family eight years ago. She mentioned that Sheffield had been born in Southern California. Her father had died when she was six and she'd been raised by her mother, who had never remarried.

'Six years old,' Linda muttered in a whisper.

Sam blinked. 'She lied. None of that stuff with her father ever happened. Oh, boy, were we taken in.'

The older woman shook her head. 'This is all way too much for me. I'm packing.'

'Linda, wait.'

'I don't want to talk about anything, Sam. I've had it.'

'Just let me say one thing.'

'You've said plenty.'

'I don't think you were really listening.'

'And I wouldn't be listening if you said it again.' She headed toward her bedroom.

Sam jumped when the phone rang. It was Kathryn Dance.

'Oh, we just heard –' she began.

But the agent said, 'Listen to me, Sam. I don't think he's headed north. I think he's coming for you.'

'What?'

'I just heard from James Reynolds. He's been going through his files from the case eight years ago and he found a reference to Alison. It seems that during his interrogation after the Croyton deaths, Pell assaulted him. Reynolds was questioning him about the incident in Redding, the Charles Pickering murder, and was talking about Alison, his girlfriend you mentioned. Pell went crazy and attacked him, or tried to – the same thing that happened to me in Salinas – because he was getting close to something important.

'James thinks he killed Pickering because the man knew about Pell's mountaintop. And that's why he was trying to find Alison. She'd know about it too.'

'But why hurt us?'

'Because Pell told *you* about Alison. Maybe you wouldn't make the connection between her and his property, maybe you wouldn't even remembered. But that place is so important to him – his kingdom – that he's willing to murder anybody who's a risk to it. That means you. Both of you.'

'Linda, come here!'

The woman appeared in the doorway, frowning angrily.

Dance continued 'I've just radioed the officers outside. They're going to take you to CBI headquarters. Agent Kellogg and I are on our way to the inn now. We're going to wait in the cabin and see if Pell shows up.'

Breathlessly Sam said to Linda, 'Kathryn thinks Daniel might be coming this way.'

'No!' The curtains were drawn, but the women instinctively looked toward the windows. Then Sam glanced toward Rebecca's bedroom. Had she remembered to lock the window after finding that the woman had climbed out? Yes, Sam recalled, she had.

There was a knock on the door. 'Ladies, it's Deputy Larkin.'

Sam glanced at Linda. They froze. Then Linda slowly walked to the peephole and looked out. She nodded and opened the door. The MCSO deputy stepped inside. 'I've been asked to take you to CBI. Just leave everything and come with me.' The other deputy was outside, looking around the parking lot.

Sam said into the phone, 'It's the deputy, Kathryn. We're leaving now.' They hung up.

Samantha grabbed her purse. 'Let's go.' Her voice was shaking.

The deputy, hand near his pistol, nodded them forward.

Which was when the bullet struck him in the side of the head. He dropped fast.

Another shot, and the second deputy grabbed his chest and slumped to the ground, crying out. A third bullet struck him as well. The first officer crawled toward his car and collapsed on the sidewalk.

Linda gasped. 'No, no!'

Footsteps were running on the pavement. Daniel Pell was sprinting toward the cabin.

Sam was paralyzed.

Then she leapt forward and slammed the door, managed to get the chain on and step aside just as another bullet snapped through the wood. She lunged for the phone.

Daniel Pell gave two solid kicks. The second one cracked the lock on the door, though the chain held. It opened only a few inches.

'Rebecca's room!' Sam cried. She ran to Linda and grabbed her arm but the woman stood rooted in the doorway.

Sam assumed she was frozen in panic.

But her face didn't look frightened at all.

She pulled away from Sam. 'Daniel,' she called.

'What are you doing?' Sam screamed. 'Come on!'

Pell kicked the door again, but the chain continued to hold. Sam dragged Linda a step or two closer to Rebecca's bedroom but she pulled away. 'Daniel,' Linda repeated. 'Please, listen to me. It's not too late. You can give yourself up. We'll get you a lawyer. I'll make sure you're –'

Pell shot her.

Simply lifted the gun, aimed through the gap in the door and shot Linda in the abdomen as casually as if he were swatting a fly. He tried to shoot again but Sam dragged her into Rebecca's bedroom. Pell kicked the door once more. This time it crashed open, smashing into the wall and shattering a picture of a seashore.

Sam closed and locked Rebecca's door. She whispered fiercely, 'We're going outside, now! We can't wait here.'

Pell tested the bedroom knob. Kicked the panel. But this door opened outward and it held against his blows.

Feeling a horrifying tickle on her back, sure that at any moment he'd shoot through the door and hit her by chance, Sam helped Linda to the windowsill, pushed her out, then tumbled after her onto the damp, fragrant earth. Linda was whimpering in pain and clutching her side.

Sam helped her up and, holding her arm in a bruising grip, guided her, jogging, toward Point Lobos State Park.

'He shot me,' Linda moaned, still astonished. 'It hurts. Look . . . wait, where are we going?'

Sam ignored her. She was thinking only of getting as far away as she could from the cabin. As for their destination, she couldn't say. All she could see ahead of them were acres of trees, formations of harsh rock and, at the end of the world, the explosive, gray ocean.

# Chapter
# FIFTY-THREE

'No,' Kathryn Dance gasped. 'No . . .'

Win Kellogg skidded the car to a stop beside the two deputies, sprawled on the sidewalk in front of the cabin.

'See how they are,' Kellogg told her and pulled out his cell phone to call for backup.

Gun in her sweating hand, Dance knelt beside the deputy, saw he was dead, his blood a huge stain, slightly darker than the dark asphalt that was his deathbed. The other officer as well. She glanced up and mouthed, 'They're gone.'

Kellogg folded up his phone and joined her.

Though they'd had no tactical training together, they approached the cabin like seasoned partners, making sure they offered no easy target and checking out the half-open door and the windows.

'I'm going in,' Kellogg said.

Dance nodded. 'I'm with you.'

'Just back me up. Keep an eye on the doorways inside. Scan. Constantly scan them. He'll lead with the gun. Look for metal. And if there're bodies inside, ignore them until the place is clear.' He touched her arm. 'That's important. Okay? Ignore them even if they're screaming for help. We can't do anything for anyone if we're wounded. Or dead.'

'Got it.'

'Ready?'

No, not the least bit. But she nodded. He squeezed her shoulder. Then took several deep breaths and pushed through the doorway fast, weapon up, swinging it back and forth, covering the inside of the cabin.

Dance was right behind him, remembering to target the doors – and to raise her muzzle when he passed in front of her.

Scan, scan, scan . . .

She glanced behind them from time to time, checking out the open doorway, thinking Pell could easily have circled around and be waiting for them.

Then Kellogg called, 'Clear.'

And inside, thank God, no bodies. Kellogg, though, pointed out bloodstains, fresh ones on the sill of an open window in the bedroom Rebecca had been using. Dance noticed some on the carpet too.

She looked outside, saw more blood and footprints in the dirt beneath it. She told Kellogg this and added, 'Think we have to assume they got away and he's after them.'

The FBI agent said, 'I'll go. Why don't you wait here for the backup?'

'No,' she said automatically; there was no debate. 'The reunion was *my* idea. And I'm not letting them die. I owe that to them.'

He hesitated. 'All right.'

They ran to the back door. Inhaling deeply, she flung it open, and with Kellogg beside her, Dance sprinted outside, expecting at any moment to hear the crack of a gunshot and feel the numbing slap of a bullet.

He hurt me.

My Daniel hurt me.

Why?

The pain in Linda's heart was nearly as bad as the pain in her side. She had forgiven Daniel for the past. She was ready to forgive him for the present.

Yet he *shot* me.

She wanted to lie down. Let Jesus cloak them, let Jesus save them. She whispered this to Sam, but maybe she didn't. Maybe it was in her imagination.

Samantha said nothing. She kept them jogging, Linda in agony, along the twisty paths of the beautiful yet stern park.

Paul, Harry, Lisa . . . the names of the foster-children reeled through her mind.

No, that was last year. They were gone now. She had others.

What were their names?

Why don't I have a family?

Because God our Father has another plan for me, that's why.

Because Samantha betrayed me.

Mad thoughts, rolling through her mind, like the sea nearby cycled over the bony rocks.

'It hurts.'

'Keep going,' was Sam's whisper. 'Kathryn and that FBI agent'll be here any minute.'

'He shot me. Daniel shot me.'

Her vision crinkled. She was going to faint. Then what'll the Mouse do? Lug my 162 pounds over her shoulder?

No, she'll betray me like she did before.

Samantha, my Judas.

Through the sound of the troubled waves, the wind hissing through the slippery pines and cypress, Linda heard Daniel Pell behind them. The snap of a branch, a rustle of leaves. They hurried on. Until the root of a scrub oak caught her foot and she went down hard, her wound burning with pain. She screamed.

'Shhhhh.'

'It hurts.'

Sam's voice, shaking with fear. 'Come on, get up, Linda. Please!'

'I can't.'

More footfalls. He was closer now.

But then it occurred to Linda that maybe the sounds were the police. Kathryn and that cute FBI agent. She winced in agony as she turned to look.

But, no, it wasn't the police. She could see, fifty feet away, Daniel Pell. He spotted them. He slowed, caught his breath and continued forward.

Linda turned to Samantha.

But the woman was no longer there.

Sam had left her yet again, just like she'd done years ago.

Abandoned her to those terrible nights in Daniel Pell's bedroom.

Abandoned then, abandoned now.

# Chapter
# FIFTY-FOUR

'My lovely, my Linda.'

He approached slowly.

She winced at the pain. 'Daniel, listen to me. It's not too late. God will forgive you. Turn yourself in.'

He laughed, as if this were a joke of some sort. 'God,' he repeated. 'God forgives me . . . Rebecca told me you'd gone religious.'

'You're going to kill me.'

'Where's Sam?'

'Please! You don't need to do this. You can change.'

'Change? Oh, Linda, people don't change. Never, never, never. Why, you're still the same person you were when I found you, all red-eyed and lumpy, under that tree in Golden Gate Park, a runaway.'

Linda felt her vision turning to black sand and yellow lights. The pain ebbed as she nearly fainted. When she floated back to the surface, he was leaning forward with his knife. 'I'm sorry, baby. I've got to do it this way.' An absurd but genuine apology. 'But I'll be fast. I know what I'm doing. You won't feel much.'

'Our Father . . .'

He pushed her head to the side so that her neck was exposed. She tried to resist but she couldn't. The fog was burned away completely now and as he moved the blade toward her throat, it flashed with a red glint from the low sun.

'Who art in heaven. Hallowed be —'

Which was when a tree fell.

Or an avalanche of rock crashed onto the path.

Or a flock of gulls, screaming in rage, landed on him.

Daniel Pell grunted and slammed into the rocky ground.

Samantha McCoy leapt off the killer, climbed to her feet and, hysterical, swung the solid tree branch onto his head and arms. Pell seemed astonished to see his little Mouse attacking him, the woman who scurried off to do everything he told her, who never told him no.

Except once . . .

Daniel slashed at her with the knife but she was too fast for him. He grabbed for the gun, which had fallen to the trail. But the rough branch connected hard again and again, bouncing off his head, tearing his ear. He wailed in pain. 'Goddamn.' He struggled to his feet. Lashing out with his fist, he caught her in the knee with a solid blow and she dropped hard.

Daniel dove for the gun, grabbed it. He scrabbled back, rose to his feet once more and swung the pistol muzzle her way. But Samantha rolled to her feet, stood her ground and struck with the branch again, two-handed. It connected with his shoulder. He stepped back, flinching.

Two words from the past came back to Linda, seeing Sam fight. What Daniel used to say when he was proud of someone in the Family: 'You held fast, lovely.'

*Hold fast* . . .

Samantha lunged again, swinging the branch.

But now Daniel had a solid stance. He managed to catch the branch with his left hand. For a moment they stared at each other, three feet apart, the wooden stick connecting them like a live wire. Daniel gave a sad smile and lifted the gun.

'No,' Linda croaked.

Samantha gave a smile too. And she pushed toward him, hard, and let go of the branch. Daniel stepped backwards – into the air. He'd been standing on the edge of a cliff, twenty feet above another nature trail.

He cried out, fell backward and tumbled down the rough rock face.

Whether he survived or not, Linda didn't know. Not at first. But then she supposed he must have. Samantha glanced down with a grimace, then helped Linda to her feet. 'We've got to go. Now.' And led her into the dense woods.

Exhausted, in pain, Samantha McCoy struggled to keep Linda upright.

The woman was pale, but the bleeding wasn't bad. The wound would be excruciating but she could at least walk.

A whisper.

'What?'

'Thought you left me.'

'No way. But he had the gun – I had to trick him.'

'He's going to kill us.' Linda still sounded amazed.

'No, he's not. Don't talk. We have to hide.'

'I can't go on.'

'Down by the water, the beach, there're caves. We can hide in one. Until the police get here. Kathryn's on her way. They'll come after us.'

'No, I can't. It's miles.'

'It's not that far. We can make it.'

They continued for another fifty feet, then Sam felt her start to falter.

'No, no . . . I can't. I'm sorry.'

Sam found some reserve of strength and managed to get Linda another twenty feet. But then she collapsed – at the worst possible place, a clearing visible for a hundred yards from all around. She expected Pell to appear at any moment. He could easily pick them off.

A shallow trough in the rocks was nearby; it would hide them well enough.

Whispers floating from Linda's mouth.

'What?' Sam asked.

She leaned closer. Linda was speaking to Jesus, not her.

'Come on, we've got to go.'

'No, no, you go on. Please. I mean it . . . You don't need to make up for what happened. You just saved my life a minute ago. We're even. I forgive you for what happened back in Seaside. I –'

'Not now, Linda!' Sam snapped.

The wounded woman tried to rise but then collapsed. 'I can't.'

'You have to.'

'Jesus'll take care of me. You go on.'

'Come on!'

Linda closed her eyes and began to whisper a prayer.

'You are not going to die here! Stand up!'

She took a deep breath, nodded and, with Sam's help, climbed to her feet. Together they staggered off the path, stumbling through brush and over roots as they made their way to the shallow ravine.

They were on a promontory about fifty feet above the ocean. The crashing of the surf was nearly constant, a jet engine, not a pulse. Deafening too.

The low sunlight hit them full on in a blinding orange wash. Sam squinted and made out the ravine, very close now. They'd lie down in it, pull brush and leaves over themselves.

'You're doing fine. A few more feet.'

Well, twenty.

But then they closed the distance to ten.

And finally they reached their sanctuary. It was deeper than Sam had thought and would be perfect cover.

She began to ease Linda into it.

Suddenly, with the sound of cracking underbrush, a figure pushed out of the woods, coming right at them.

'No!' Sam cried. Letting Linda slump toward the ground, she grabbed a small rock, a pathetic weapon.

Then, gasping, she barked a hysterical laugh.

Kathryn Dance, crouching, whispered, 'Where is he?'

Her heart slamming, Sam mouthed, 'I don't know.' Then repeated the words louder. 'We saw him about fifty yards back that way. He's hurt. But I saw him walking.'

'He's armed?'

A nod. 'A gun. And a knife.'

Dance scanned the area around them, squinting into the sun. She assessed Linda's condition. 'Get her down there.' Nodding at the ravine. 'Keep her on her back and press something on the wound.'

Together they eased the wounded woman into the depression.

'Please, stay with us,' Sam whispered.

'Don't worry,' Dance said. 'I'm not going anywhere.'

# Chapter
# FIFTY-FIVE

Winston Kellogg was somewhere to the south of them.

After they'd left the Point Lobos Inn, they'd lost track of the foot-prints and blood near a fork in the nature trails. Arbitrarily Dance had gone right, Kellogg left.

She'd moved silently through the brush – staying off the trail – until she saw motion by the edge of a cliff. She'd identified the women and approached them quickly.

She called the FBI agent from her mobile phone. 'Win, I've got Sam and Linda.'

'Where are you?'

'We're about a hundred yards from where we split up. I went due west. We're almost to the cliff. There's a round rock near us, about twenty feet high.'

'Do they know where Pell is?'

'He was near here. Below us and to our left about fifty yards. And he's still armed. Pistol and knife.'

Then she tensed, looking down, saw a man's form on the sand. 'Win, where are you? Are you on the beach?'

'No. I'm on a path. The beach is below me, maybe two, three hundred feet away.'

'Okay, he's there! You see that small island? Seals all over it. And gulls.'

'Got it.'

'The beach in front of that.'

'I can't see it from here. But I'm moving that way.'

'No, Win. There's no cover for your approach. We need tactical. Wait.'

'We don't have time. He's gotten away too many times already. I'm not letting it happen again.'

The gunslinger attitude . . .

It bothered her a lot. Suddenly she really didn't want anything to happen to Winston Kellogg.

*Afterward. How does that sound?*

'Just . . . be careful. I lost sight of him. He was on the beach, but he's in the rocks now. There'd be perfect firing positions from there. He can cover all the approaches.'

Dance stood up, shielding her eyes as she scanned the beach. Where is he?

She found out a second later.

A bullet slammed into the rocks not far from her, and then she heard the crack of Pell's pistol.

Samantha screamed and Dance dropped to cover in the recess, nicking her skin, furious that she'd presented a target.

'Kathryn,' Kellogg called on the radio, 'are you firing?'

'No, that was Pell.'

'You okay?'

'We're fine.'

'Where did it come from?'

'I couldn't see. Had to be the rocks near the beach.'

'You stay down. He's got your position now.'

She asked Samantha, 'Does he know the park?'

'The Family spent a lot of time here. He knows it pretty good, I'd guess.'

'Win, Pell knows Point Lobos. You could walk right into a trap. Really, why don't you wait?'

'Hold on.' Kellogg's voice was a quiet rasp. 'I think I see something. I'll call you back.'

'Wait, Win. Are you there?'

She changed position, moving some distance away so Pell wouldn't be looking for her. She glanced out fast between two rocks. Couldn't see a thing. Then she noticed Winston Kellogg making his way toward the beach. Against the massive rocks, gnarled trees, the expanse of ocean, he seemed so fragile.

Please . . . Dance sent him a silent message to stop, to wait.

But, of course, he kept on moving, her tacit plea as ineffectual as, she reflected, his would have been with her.

\*       \*       \*

Daniel Pell knew more cops were on their way. But he was confident. He knew this area perfectly. He'd robbed plenty of tourists in Point Lobos – many of them stupid to the point of being co-conspirators. They'd leave their valuables in their cars and at the picnic grounds, never thinking that anybody would conceive of robbing fellow humans in such a spiritual setting.

He and the Family had also spent plenty of time just relaxing here, camping out on the way back from Big Sur when they didn't feel like making the drive up to Seaside. He knew routes that would get him to the highway, or to the private residences nearby, invisible routes. He'd steal another car, head east into the back roads of the Central Valley, through Hollister, and work his way north.

To the mountaintop.

But now he had to deal with the immediate pursuers. There were just two or three, he believed. He hadn't seen them clearly. They must've stopped at the cabin, seen the dead deputies, then pursued him on their own. And it seemed that only one was actually nearby.

He closed his eyes momentarily against the pain. He pressed the stab wound, which had opened in the fall down the rocks. His ear hurt worse, throbbing from Sam's blow.

*Mouse . . .*

Goddamn!

He rested his head and shoulder against a cold, wet rock. It seemed to lessen the agony.

He wondered if one of the pursuers was Kathryn Dance. If so, he suspected that, no, it wasn't a coincidence she'd shown up at the cabin. She'd have guessed that he hadn't stolen the Infiniti to go north but to head here.

Well, one way or the other, she wasn't going to be a threat much longer.

But how to handle the immediate situation?

The cop pursuing him was getting close. There were only two approaches to where he was at the moment. Whoever came after him would either have to climb down a twenty-foot-high rockface, completely exposed to Pell below, or – taking the path – would turn a sharp corner from the beach and be a perfect target.

Pell knew that only a tactical officer would try the rock face and that his pursuer probably wouldn't be decked out in rappelling gear. They'd have to come from the beach. He hunkered down behind a cluster of rocks, hidden from above and from the beach, and waited for the officer to get close, resting the gun on a boulder.

He now heard wouldn't shoot to kill. He'd wound. Maybe in the knee. And then, when he was down, Pell would blind him with the knife. He'd leave the radio nearby so the cop, racked by agony, would call for help, screaming and distracting the other officers. Pell could escape into a deserted area of the park.

He now heard someone approaching, trying to be quiet. But Pell had hearing like a wild animal's. He curled his hand around his gun.

The emotion was gone. Rebecca and Jennie and even the hateful Kathryn Dance were far, far from his thoughts.

Daniel Pell was in perfect control.

Dance, in yet another spot on the ridge, hidden by thick pines, looked out fast.

Winston Kellogg was on the beach now, close to where Pell must have been when he'd fired at her. The agent was moving slowly, looking around him, gun in both hands. He looked up at a cliff and seemed to be debating climbing it. But the walls were steep and Kellogg was in street shoes, impractical for the slippery stone. Besides, he'd undoubtedly be an easy target climbing down the other side.

Looking back to the path in front of him he seemed to notice marks in the sand, where she'd seen Pell. He crouched and moved closer to them. He paused at an outcropping.

'What's going on?' Samantha asked.

Dance shook her head. She looked down at Linda. The woman was half-conscious and paler than before. She'd lost a lot of blood. She'd need emergency treatment soon.

Dance called MCSO central and asked for the status of the troops.

'First tac responders in five minutes, boats in fifteen.'

Dance sighed. Why was it taking the cavalry so damn long? She gave them her approximate position and explained how the med techs should approach, to stay out of the line of fire. Dance glanced out again and saw Winston Kellogg ease around the rock, glistening burgundy in the low sun. The agent was heading directly toward the spot where Pell had vanished a few minutes earlier.

A long minute passed. Two.

Where was he? What –

The boom of an explosion.

What the hell was that?

Then a series of gunshots from behind the outcropping, a pause, then several more pistol cracks.

'What happened?' Samantha called.

'I don't know.' Dance pulled the radio out. 'Win. Win! Are you there? Over.'

But the only sounds she heard were the rush of the waves and the edgy cries of the frightened, fleeing gulls.

# Chapter
# FIFTY-SIX

Kathryn Dance hurried along the beach, her Aldo shoes, among her favorites, ruined by the saltwater.

She didn't care.

Behind her, back on the ridge, medical technicians were trundling Linda to the ambulance parked at the Point Lobos Inn, Samantha with her. She nodded to two MCSO officers ringing yellow tape from rock to rock, though the only intruder to trouble the crime scene would be the rising tide. Dance ducked under the plastic tape and turned the corner, continuing to the scene of the death.

Dance paused. Then walked straight up to Winston Kellogg and hugged him. He seemed shaken and kept staring at what lay in front of them: the body of Daniel Pell.

He was on his back, his sand-stained knees in the air, arms out to the sides. His pistol lay nearby where it had flown from his hand. Pell's eyes were partly open, intensely blue no longer, but hazy in death.

Dance realized that her hand remained on Kellogg's back. She dropped it and stepped aside. 'What happened?' she asked.

'I nearly walked right into him. He was hiding there.' He pointed out a stand of rocks. 'But I saw him just in time. I got under cover. I had one of the flash-bangs left from the motel. I pitched it his way and it stunned him. He started shooting. But I was lucky. The sun was behind me. Blinded him, I guess. I returned fire. And . . .' He shrugged.

'You're okay?'

'Oh, sure. Little scraped up from the rocks. Not used to mountain climbing.'

Her phone rang. She answered, glancing at the screen. It was TJ.

'Linda's going to be fine. Lost some blood, but the slug missed the important stuff. Oh, and Samantha's not hurt bad.'

'Samantha?' Dance hadn't noticed the woman was injured. 'What happened?'

'Cuts and bruises is all. Had a boxing match with the deceased, prior to his deceasing, of course. She's hurting but she'll be peachy.'

She'd fought with Pell?

*Mouse . . .*

Monterey County Sheriff's crime scene officers arrived and began working the site. Michael O'Neil, she noticed, wasn't here.

One of the CS officers said to Kellogg, 'Hey, congrats.' He nodded at the body.

The FBI agent smiled noncommittally.

A smile, kinesics experts know, is the most elusive signal that the human face generates. A frown, a perplexed gaze or an amorous glance means only one thing. A smile, though, can telegraph hate, indifference, humor or love.

Dance wasn't sure exactly what this smile meant. But she noticed that an instant later, as he stared at the man he'd just killed, the expression vanished, as if it had never existed.

Kathryn Dance and Samantha McCoy stopped by Monterey Bay Hospital to see Linda Whitfield, who was conscious and doing well. She'd spend the night in the hospital but the doctors said she could go home tomorrow.

Samantha was chauffeured by Rey Carraneo back to a new cabin in the Point Lobos Inn, where she'd decided to spend the night, rather than returning home. Dance asked Samantha to join her for dinner, but the woman said she wanted some 'downtime'.

And who could blame her?

Dance left the hospital and returned to CBI, where she saw Theresa and her aunt standing by their car, apparently awaiting her return to say good-bye. The girl's face brightened when she saw Dance. They greeted each other warmly.

'We heard,' the aunt said, unsmiling. 'He's dead?' As if she couldn't have too much confirmation.

'That's right.'

She gave them the details of the incident at Point Lobos. The aunt seemed impatient, though Theresa was eager to hear exactly what had happened. Dance didn't edit the account.

Theresa nodded and took the news unemotionally.

'We can't thank you enough,' the agent said. 'What you did saved lives.'

The subject didn't come up of what had actually happened on the night her family was killed, Theresa's feigned illness. Dance supposed that would remain a secret between herself and the girl forever. But why not? Sharing with one person was often as cathartic as sharing with the world.

'You're driving back tonight?'

'Yeah,' the girl said with a glance at her aunt. 'But we're making a stop first.'

Dance thinking: seafood dinner, shopping at the cute stores in Los Gatos?

'I want to see the house. My old house.'

Where her parents and siblings had died.

'We're going to meet Mr Nagle. He talked to the family who lives there now and they've agreed to let me see it.'

'Did he suggest that?' Dance was ready to run interference for the girl and knew that Nagle would back down in an instant.

'No, it was my idea,' Theresa said. 'I just, you know, want to. And he's going to come to Napa and interview me. For that book. *The Sleeping Doll*. That's the title. Isn't it weird having a book written about you?'

Mary Bolling didn't say anything, though her body language – slightly lifted shoulders, a shift in the jaw – told Dance instantly that she didn't approve of the evening's detour and that there'd been an argument on the subject.

As often, following significant life incidents – like the Family's reunion or Theresa's journey here to help catch her family's killer – there's a tendency to look for fundamental changes in the participants. But that didn't happen very often and Dance didn't think it had here. She found herself with the same people they'd been earlier: a protective middle-aged woman, blunt but stepping up to the difficult task of becoming a substitute parent, and a typically attitudinal teenage girl who'd impulsively done a brave thing. They'd had a disagreement about how to spend the rest of the evening and, in this case, the girl had won, undoubtedly with concessions.

Maybe, though, the very fact that the disagreement had occurred and been resolved was a step forward. This was, Dance supposed, how people change: incrementally.

She hugged Theresa, shook her aunt's hand and wished them a safe trip.

Five minutes later Dance was back in the GW portion of CBI headquarters, accepting a cup of coffee from Maryellen Kresbach. And, today, an oatmeal cookie.

Walking into her office, she kicked off the damaged Aldos and dug in her closet for a new pair: Joan and David sandals. Then she stretched and sat, sipping the strong coffee and searching through her desk for the remainder of a pack of M&Ms she'd stashed there a few days ago. She ate them quickly, stretched again and enjoyed looking at the pictures of her children.

Photos of her husband too.

How she would have liked to lie in bed next to him tonight and talk about the Pell case.

Ah, Bill . . .

Her phone chirped.

She glanced at the screen and her stomach did a small jump.

'Hi,' she said to Michael O'Neil.

'Hey. Just got the news. You okay? Heard there were rounds exchanged.'

'Pell parked one near me. That's all.'

'How's Linda?'

Dance gave him the details.

'And Rebecca?'

'ICU. She'll live. But she's not getting out any time soon.'

He, in turn, told her about the phony getaway car – Pell's favorite means of diversion and distraction. The Infiniti driver wasn't dead. He had been forced by Pell to call and report his own murder and carjacking. He'd then driven home, put the car in the garage and sat in a dark room until he'd heard the news of Pell's death.

He added that he was sending her the crime-scene reports from the Butterfly Inn, which Pell and Jennie had checked into after they'd escaped from the Sea View, and from Point Lobos.

She'd been glad to hear O'Neil's voice. But something was off. There was still a matter-of-fact tone in his voice. He wasn't angry, but he wasn't overly pleased to be speaking to her. She thought his earlier remarks about Winston Kellogg were out of line but, while she didn't want an apology, she did wish that the rough seas between them would calm.

She asked, 'You all right?' With some people, you had to prime the pump.

'Fine,' he said.

*That* goddamn word, which could mean everything from 'wonderful' to 'I hate you.'

She suggested he come by the Deck that night.

'Can't, sorry. Anne and I have plans.'

Ah. *Plans.*

That's one of those words too.

'Better go. Just wanted to let you know about the Infiniti driver.'

'Sure, take care.'

*Click . . .*

Dance grimaced for the benefit of no one and turned back to a file.

Ten minutes later Winston Kellogg's head appeared in the doorway. She gestured toward the chair and he dropped down into it. He hadn't changed; his clothes were still muddy and sandy. He saw her salt-stained shoes sitting by the door and gestured toward his own. Then laughed, pointing to a dozen pairs in her closet. 'Probably nothing in there that'd work for me.'

'Sorry,' she answered, deadpan. 'They're all a size six.'

'Too bad, that lime-green number has a certain appeal.'

They discussed the reports that needed to be completed and the shooting review board that would have to issue a report on the incident. She'd wondered how long he'd be in the area and realized that whether or not he followed through on asking her out, he'd have to stay for four or five days; a review board could take that long to convene, hear testimony and write the report.

*Afterward. How does that sound? . . .*

Like Dance herself a few minutes ago, Kellogg stretched. His face gave a very faint signal – he was troubled. It would be the shootout, of course. Dance had never even fired her weapon at a suspect, let alone killed anyone. She'd been instrumental in tracking down dangerous perps, some of whom had been killed in the takedown. Others had gone to death row. But that was different from pointing a gun at someone and ending his life.

And here Kellogg had done so twice in a relatively short period of time.

'So what's next for you?' she asked.

'I'm giving a seminar in Washington on religious fundamentalism – it shares a lot with cult mentality. Then some time off. If the real world cooperates, of course.' He slouched and closed his eyes.

In his smudged, casual clothes and with floppy hair and five-o'clock shadow, he was really an appealing man, Dance reflected.

'Sorry,' he said, opening his eyes and laughing. 'Bad form to fall asleep in colleagues' offices.' The smile was genuine and whatever had been troubling him earlier was now gone. 'Oh, one thing. I've got paperwork tonight, but tomorrow, can I hold you to that offer of dinner? It *is* afterward, remember?'

She hesitated, thinking, You know counterinterrogation strategy: anticipate every question the interrogator's going to ask and be ready with an answer.

But even though she'd just been thinking about this very matter, she was caught off guard.

So, what's the answer? she asked herself.

'Tomorrow?' he repeated, sounding shy – curiously, for a man who'd just nailed one of the worst perps in Monterey County history.

You're stalling, she told herself. Her eyes swept the pictures of her children, her dogs, her late husband. She thought of Wes.

She said, 'You know, tomorrow'd be great.'

# Chapter
# FIFTY-SEVEN

'It's over,' she said in a low voice to her mother.

'I heard. Michael briefed us at CBI.'

They were at her parents' house in Carmel. The family was back from the castle keep of headquarters.

'Did the gang hear?'

Meaning the children.

'I put some spin on it. Phrased it like, oh, Mom'll be home at a decent hour tonight because, by the way, that stupid case of hers is over with, they got the bad guy, I don't know the details. That sort of thing. Mags didn't pay any attention – she's working up a new song for piano camp. Wes headed right for the TV but I had Stu drag him outside to play ping-pong. He seems to've forgotten about the story. But the key word is "seems".'

Dance had shared with her parents that she wanted to minimize news about death and violence, particularly as it involved her work. 'I'll keep an eye on him. And thanks.' She cracked open an Anchor Steam beer and divided it into two glasses. Handed one to her mother.

Edie sipped and then, with a frown, asked, 'When did you get Pell?'

Dance gave her the approximate time. 'Why?'

Glancing at the clock, her mother said, 'I was sure I heard somebody in the backyard around four, four-thirty. I didn't think anything of it at first but then I got to wondering if Pell had found out where we lived. Wanting to get even, or something. I was feeling a little bit spooked. Even with the squad car out front.'

Pell wouldn't hesitate to hurt them, of course – he'd planned to do so – but the timing was off. Pell was already at Morton Nagle's house by then, or on the way.

'It probably wasn't him.'

'Must've been a cat. Or the Perkins' dog. They have to learn to keep it inside. I'll talk to them.'

She knew her mother would do just that.

Dance rounded up the children and herded them into the Pathfinder, where the dogs awaited. She hugged her father and they made plans for her to pick her parents up for his birthday party at the Marine Club on Sunday evening. Dance was the designated driver so they could enjoy themselves and drink as much champagne and pinot noir as they wanted. She thought about inviting Winston Kellogg but decided to wait on that one. See how tomorrow's 'afterward' date went.

Dance thought about dinner and could summon up zero desire to cook. 'Can you guys live with pancakes at Bayside?'

'Woo-hoo!' Maggie called. And began debating aloud what kind of syrup she wanted. Wes was happy but more restrained.

When they got to the restaurant and were seated at a booth, she reminded her son it was his job to pick their Sunday afternoon adventure this week before the birthday party. 'So, what's our plan? Movie? Hiking?'

'I don't know yet.' Wes examined the menu for a long time. Maggie wanted a to-go order for the dogs. Dance explained that the pancakes weren't to celebrate the reunion with the canines; it was simply because she wasn't in the mood to cook.

As the large, steaming plates were arriving, Wes asked, 'Oh, you hear about that festival thing? The boats?'

'Boats?'

'Grandpa was telling us about it. It's a boat parade in the bay and a concert. At Cannery Row.'

Dance recalled something about a John Steinbeck festival. 'Is that on Sunday? Is that what you'd like to do?'

'It's tomorrow night,' Wes said. 'It'd be fun. Can we go?'

Dance laughed to herself. There was no way he could've known about her dinner date with Kellogg tomorrow. Or could he? She had intuition when it came to the children; why couldn't it work the other way?

Dance dressed the pancakes with syrup and allowed herself a pat of butter. Stalling. 'Tomorrow? Let me think.'

Her initial reaction, on seeing Wes's unsmiling face, was to call Kellogg and postpone or even cancel the date.

Sometimes it's just easier . . .

She stopped Maggie from drowning her pancakes in a frightening avalanche of blueberry and strawberry syrups, then turned to Wes and said impulsively, 'Oh, that's right, honey, I can't. I have plans.'

'Oh.'

'But I'm sure Grandpa'd want to go with you.'

'What're you going to do? See Connie? Or Martine? Maybe they'd like to come too. We could all go. They could bring the twins.'

'Yeah, the twins, Mom!' Maggie said.

Dance heard her therapist's words.

*'Kathryn, you can't look at the substance of what he's saying. Parents tend to feel that their children raise valid objections about potential step-parents or even casual dates. You can't think that way. What he's upset with is what he sees as your betrayal of his father's memory. It has nothing to do with the partner himself.'*

She made a decision. 'No, I'm going to have dinner with the man I've been working with.'

'Agent Kellogg,' the boy shot back.

'That's right. He has to go back to Washington soon, and I wanted to thank him for all the work he's done for us.'

She felt a bit cheesy for gratuitously suggesting that because he lived so far away Kellogg was no long-term threat. (Though she supposed Wes's sensitive mind could easily jump to the conclusion that Dance was already planning to uproot them from friends and family here on the Peninsula and resettle them in the nation's capital.)

'Okay,' the boy said, cutting up the pancakes, eating a few bites, pensive. Dance was using his appetite as a barometer of his reaction.

'Hey, son of mine, what's the matter?'

'Nothing.'

'Grandpa would love to go to see the boats with you.'

'Sure.'

Then she asked another impulsive question. 'Don't you like Winston?'

'He's okay.'

'You can tell me.' Her own interest in food was flagging.

'I don't know . . . He's not like Michael.'

'No, he's not. But there aren't many people like Michael.' The dear friend who isn't returning my calls at the moment. 'That doesn't mean I can't have dinner with them, does it?'

'I guess.'

They ate for a few minutes. Then Wes blurted, 'Maggie doesn't like him either.'

'I didn't say that! Don't say things I didn't say.'

'Yeah, you did. You said he's got a potbelly.'

'Did not.' Though her blush told Dance that she had.

She smiled, put down her fork. 'Hey, you two, listen up. Whether I have dinner with somebody or not, or even go out to the movies with them, nothing's going to change us. Our house, the dogs, our lives. Nothing. That's a promise. Okay?'

'Okay,' Wes said. It was a bit knee-jerk, but he didn't seem completely unconvinced.

But now Maggie was troubled. 'Aren't you ever going to get married again?'

'Mags, what brought that up?'

'Just wondering.'

'I can't even imagine getting married again.'

'You didn't say no,' Wes muttered.

Dance laughed at the interrogator's perfect response. 'Well, that's my answer. I can't even imagine it.'

'I want to be best woman,' Maggie said.

'Maid of honor,' Dance corrected.

'No, I saw this after-school special. They do it different now.'

'Differently,' her mother corrected again. 'But let's not get distracted. We've got pancakes and iced tea to polish off. And plans to make for Sunday. You've got to do some thinking.'

'I will.' Wes seemed reassured.

Dance ate the rest of her dinner, feeling elated at this victory: being honest with her son and receiving his acquiescence to the date. Oddly, this tiny step did a huge amount to take away the horror of the day's events.

On a whim she gave in to Maggie's final plea on behalf of the dogs and ordered one pancake and a side of sausage for each, minus the syrup. The girl served the food in the back of the Pathfinder. Dylan the shepherd devoured his in several gulps while the ladylike Patsy ate the sausage fastidiously, then carried the pancake to a space between the backseats, impossible to reach, and deposited it there for a rainy day.

At home, Dance spent the next few hours at domestic chores, fielding phone calls, including one from Morton Nagle, thanking her again for what she'd done for his family. Winston Kellogg did not call, which was good (meaning the date was still on).

Michael O'Neil did not call either, which wasn't so good.

Rebecca Sheffield was in a stable condition after extensive surgery. She'd be in the hospital, under guard, for the next six or seven days. More operations were needed.

Dance talked to Martine Christensen for some time about the American Tunes website, then, business disposed of, it was time for dessert: popcorn, which made sense after a sweet dinner. Dance found a Wallace and Gromit claymation tape, cued it up and at the last minute managed to save the Redenbacher kernels from the microwave of mass destruction before she set the bag ablaze, as she had last week.

She was pouring the contents into a bowl when her phone croaked yet again.

'Mom,' Wes said impatiently, 'I'm like starving.' She loved his tone. It meant he'd snapped out of his unhappy mood.

'It's TJ,' she announced, opening up her mobile.

'Say hi,' the boy offered, shoving a handful of popcorn into his mouth. 'Wes says hi.'

'Back at him. Oh, tell him I got to level eight on "Zarg".'

'Is that good?'

'You have no idea.'

Dance relayed the message and Wes's eyes glowed. 'Eight? No way!'

'He's impressed. So what's up?'

'Who's getting all the stuff?'

'And "stuff" would be?'

'Evidence, reports, emails, everything. The ball of wax, remember?'

He meant for the final disposition report. It would be massive in this case, with the multiple felonies and the interagency paperwork. She'd run the case and the CBI had primary jurisdiction.

'Me. Well, I should say *us.*'

'I liked the first answer better, boss. Oh, by the way, remember "Nimue"?'

The mystery word . . .

'What about it?'

'I just found another reference to it. You want me to follow up?'

'Think we better. I don't want to leave any T undotted. So to speak.'

'Is tomorrow okay? It's not much of a date tonight, but Lucretia might be the woman of my dreams.'

'You're going out with somebody named *Lucretia*? You may have to concentrate . . . Tell you what. Bring me all the wax. And the Nimue "stuff". I'll get started on it.'

'Boss, you're the best. You're invited to the wedding.'

## Chapter
# FIFTY-EIGHT

Kathryn Dance, in a black suit and burgundy cotton sweater – was sitting outside at the Bay View Restaurant near Fisherman's Wharf in Monterey.

The place lived up to its name, usually offering a postcard image of the coast all the way up to Santa Cruz, which was, however, invisible at the moment. The morning was a perfect example of June gloom on the Peninsula. Fog like smoke from a damp fire surrounded the wharf. The temperature was fifty-five degrees.

Last night she'd been in an elated mood. Daniel Pell had been stopped, Linda Whitfield would be all right. Nagle and his family had survived. She and Winston Kellogg had made their plans for 'afterward'.

Today, though, things were different. A darkness hung over her; she couldn't shake it, and the mood had nothing to do with the weather. There were many things contributing to it, not the least of which was planning the memorial services and funerals for the guards killed at the courthouse, the deputies at the Point Lobos Inn yesterday and Juan Millar too.

She sipped her coffee. Then blinked in surprise as a hummingbird appeared from nowhere and dipped its beak into the feeder hanging on the side of the restaurant, near a spill of gardenias. Another bird strafed in and drove the first away. They were pretty creatures, jewels, but could be mean as scrapyard dogs.

Then she heard, 'Hello.'

Winston Kellogg came up behind her, slipped his arm around her shoulders and kissed her on the cheek. Not too close to the mouth, not too far away. She smiled and hugged him.

He sat down.

Dance waved to the waitress, who refilled her cup and poured one for Kellogg.

'So, I was doing some research about the area,' Kellogg said. 'I thought we could go down to Big Sur tonight. Some place called Ventana.'

'It's beautiful. I haven't been for years. The restaurant's wonderful. It's a bit of a drive.'

'I'm game. Highway One, right?'

Which would take them right past Point Lobos. She flashed back to the gunshots, the blood, Daniel Pell lying on his back, dull blue eyes staring unseeing at a dark blue sky.

'Thanks for getting up so early,' Dance said.

'Breakfast *and* dinner with you. The pleasure's mine.'

She gave him another smile. 'Here's the situation. TJ finally found the answer to "Nimue", I think.'

Kellogg nodded. 'What Pell was searching for in Capitola.'

'At first I thought it was a screen name, then I was thinking it might have to do with this computer game, "Nimue" with an X, the popular one.'

The agent shook his head.

'Apparently it's hot. I should have consulted the experts – my kids. Anyway, I was toying with the idea that Pell and Jimmy went to the Croytons' to steal some valuable software, and I remembered Reynolds told me that Croyton gave away all this computer research and software to Cal State-Monterey Bay. I thought maybe there was something in the college archives that Pell planned to steal. But, no, it turns out that Nimue's something else.'

'What?'

'We're not exactly sure. That's what I need your help on. TJ found a folder on Jennie Marston's computer. The name was –' Dance found a slip of paper and read. 'Quote "Nimue – cult suicide in L.A."'

'What was inside?'

'That's the problem. He tried to open it. But it's password-protected. We'll have to send it to CBI headquarters in Sacramento to crack, but frankly, that'll take weeks. It might not be important but I'd like to find out what it's all about. I was hoping you'd have somebody in the bureau who could decrypt it faster.'

Kellogg told her he knew of a computer whiz in the FBI's San Jose field office – in the heart of Silicon Valley. 'If anybody can break it, they can. I'll get it to him today.'

She thanked him and handed over the Dell, in a plastic bag and with a chain-of-custody tag attached. He signed the card and set the bag beside him.

Dance waved for the waitress. Toast was about all she could manage this morning, but Kellogg ordered a full breakfast.

He said, 'Now, tell me about Big Sur. It's supposed to be pretty.'

'Breathtaking,' she said. 'One of the most romantic places you'll ever see.'

Kathryn Dance was in her office when Winston Kellogg came to collect her at 5:30 for their date. He was in formal casual. He and Dance came close to matching – brown jackets, light shirts and jeans. His blue, hers black. Ventana was an upscale inn, restaurant and winery but this was, after all, California. You needed a suit and tie only in San Francisco, L.A. and Sacramento.

For funerals too, of course, Dance couldn't help but think.

'First, let's get work out of the way.' He opened his attaché case and handed her the plastic evidence bag containing the computer found in the Butterfly Inn.

'Oh, you've got it already?' she asked. 'The mystery of Nimue is about to be solved.'

He grimaced. 'Afraid not, sorry.'

'Nothing?' she asked.

'The file was either intentionally written as gibberish or it had a wipe bomb on it, the bureau tech guys said.'

'Wipe bomb?'

'Like a digital booby trap. When TJ tried to open it, it got turned to mush. That was their term too, by the way.'

'Mush.'

'Just random characters.'

'No way to reconstruct it?'

'Nope. And, believe me, they're the best in the business.'

'Not that it matters that much, I suppose,' Dance said, shrugging. 'It was just a loose end.'

He smiled. 'I'm the same way. Hate it when there are danglers. That's what I call them.'

'Danglers. I like that.'

'So are you ready to go?'

'Just a second or two.' She rose and walked to the door. Albert Stemple was standing in the hallway. TJ too.

She glanced at them, sighed and nodded.

The massive, shaved-head agent stepped into the office, with TJ right behind him.

Both men drew their weapons – Dance just didn't have the heart – and in a few seconds Winston Kellogg was disarmed, cuffs on his hands.

'What the hell's going on?' he raged.

Dance provided the answer, surprised at how serene her voice sounded as she said, 'Winston Kellogg, you're under arrest for the murder of Daniel Pell.'

# Chapter
# FIFTY-NINE

They were in room 3, one of the interrogation rooms in CBI's Monterey office, and it was Dance's favorite. This was a little bigger than the other (which was room 1, there being no number 2). And the one-way mirror was a little shinier. It also had a small window and, if the curtains were open, you could see a tree outside. Sometimes, during her interrogations, she'd use the view to distract or draw out the interviewees. Today the curtain was closed.

Dance and Kellogg were alone. Behind the sparkling mirror the video camera was set up and running. TJ was there, along with Charles Overby, both unseen, though the mirror, of course, implied observers.

Winston Kellogg had declined an attorney and was willing to talk. Which he did in an eerily calm voice (very much the same tone as Daniel Pell's in his interrogation, she reflected, unsettled at the thought). 'Kathryn, let's just step back here, can we? Is that all right? I don't know what you think is going on but this isn't the way to handle it. Believe me.'

The subtext of these words was arrogance – and the corollary, betrayal. She tried to push the pain away as she replied simply, 'Let's get started.' She slipped her black-framed glasses on, her predator specs.

'Maybe you've gotten some bad information. Why don't you tell me what you *think* the problem is and we'll see what's really going on?'

As if he were talking to a child.

She looked Winston Kellogg over closely. It's an interrogation just like any other, Dance told herself. Though it wasn't, of course. Here was a man she'd felt romantic toward and who had lied to her. Someone who had used her, like Daniel Pell had used . . . well, everyone.

Then she forced aside her own emotion, hard though that was, and concentrated on the task in front of her. She was going to break him. Nothing would stop her.

Because she knew him well by now, the analysis unfolded quickly in her mind.

First, how should he be categorized in the context of the crime? A suspect in a homicide.

Second, does he have a motive to lie? Yes.

Third, what's his personality type? Extroverted, thinking, judging. She could be as tough with him as she needed to be.

Fourth, what is his liar's personality? A High Machiavellian. He's intelligent, has a good memory, is adept at the techniques of deception and will use all those skills to create lies that work to his advantage. He'll give up lying if he's caught, and use other weapons to shift the blame, threaten or attack. He'll demean and patronize, trying to unnerve her and exploit her own emotional responses, a dark mirror image of her own mission as an interrogator. He'll get information to use later against her.

You had to be very careful with High Machs.

The next step in her kinesic analysis would be to determine what stress response state he fell into when lying – anger, denial, depression or bargaining – and to probe his story when she recognized one.

But here was the problem. She was one of the best kinesics analysts in the country, yet she hadn't spotted Kellogg's lies, which he'd dished up right in front of, and to, her. Largely his behavior was not outright lying but evasion – withholding information is the hardest type of deception to detect. Still, Dance was skilled at spotting evasion. More significantly, Kellogg was, she decided, in that rare class of individuals virtually immune to kinesic analysts and polygraph operators: excluded subjects, like the mentally ill and serial killers.

The category also includes zealots.

Which was what she now believed Winston Kellogg was. Not the leader of a cult, but someone just as fanatical and just as dangerous, a man convinced of his own righteousness.

Still, she needed to break him. She needed to get to the truth, and to do that, Dance had to spot stress flags within him to know where to probe.

So she attacked. Hard, fast.

From her purse, Dance took a digital audiotape recorder and set it on the table between them. She hit 'Play'.

The sounds of a phone ringing, then:

'Tech Resource. Rick Adams speaking.'

'My name's Kellogg from Ninth Street. MVCC.'

'Sure, Agent Kellogg. What can I do for you?'

'I'm in the area and have a problem on my computer. I've got a protected file and the guy who sent it to me can't remember the password. It's a Windows XP operating system.'

'Sure. That's a piece of cake. I can handle it.'

'Rather not use you guys for a personal job. They're cracking down on that back at HQ.'

'Well, there's a good outfit in Cupertino we farm stuff out to. They're not cheap.'

'Are they fast?'

'Oh, for that? Sure.'

'Great. Give me their number.'

She shut the recorder off. 'You lied to me. You said the "bureau tech" guys cracked it. They didn't.'

'Winston, Pell didn't write anything about Nimue or suicides. I created that file last night.'

He could only stare at her.

She said, 'Nimue was a red herring. There was nothing on Jennie's computer until I put it there. TJ did find a reference to Nimue but it was a newspaper story about a woman named Alison Sharpe, an interview in a local paper in Montana – 'My Month with Daniel Pell'. something like that. They met in San Francisco about twelve years ago, when she was living in a group like the Family and going by the name Nimue. The leader named everyone after Arthurian characters. She and Pell hitch-hiked around the state but she left him after he was picked up in Redding on that murder charge. Pell probably didn't know her surname and searched the only two names he knew – Alison and Nimue – to find her. And kill her because she knew where his mountaintop was.'

'So you faked this file and asked me to help you crack it. Why the masquerade, Kathryn?'

'I'll tell you why. Body language isn't limited to the living, you know. You can read a lot into a *corpse's* posture too. Last night TJ brought me all the files in the case for the final disposition report. I was looking over the crime-scene pictures from Point Lobos. Something didn't seem right. Pell wasn't hiding behind the rocks. He was out in the open, on his back. His legs were bent and there were water and sand stains on his knees. *Both* knees, not just one. That was curious. People *crouch* when they're fighting, or at least keep one foot planted on the ground. I saw exactly the same posture in the case of a man who'd been killed in a gang hit, forced on his knees to beg before he was shot. Why would Pell leave cover, get down on both knees and shoot at you?'

'I don't know what you're talking about.' No emotion whatsoever.

'And the coroner's report said that from the downward angle of the bullets through his body you were standing full height, not crouching. If it was a real firefight you would've been in a defensive stance, crouching yourself . . . And I remembered the sequence of the sounds. The flash-bang went off and then I heard the shots, after a delay. No, I think that you saw where he was, tossed the flash-bang and moved in fast, disarmed him. Then had him kneel and you tossed your cuffs on the ground for him to put on himself. When he was reaching for them, you shot him.'

'Ridiculous.'

She continued, unfazed. 'And the flash-bang? After the assault at the Sea View you were supposed to check all the ordnance back in. That's standard procedure. Why keep it? Because you were waiting for a chance to move in and kill him. And I checked the timing of your call for backup. You *didn't* make it from the inn, like you pretended. You made it later, to give you a chance to get Pell alone.' She held up a hand, silencing another protest. 'But whether my theory was *ridiculous* or not, his death raised questions. I thought I should check further. I wanted to know more about you. I got your file from a friend of my husband's on Ninth Street. I found some interesting facts. You'd been involved in the shooting deaths of several suspected cult leaders during attempts to apprehend. And two cult leaders died of suicides under suspicious circumstances when you were consulting with local law-enforcement agencies in their investigations.

'The suicide in L.A. was the most troubling. A woman who ran a cult committed suicide by jumping out of her sixth-story window, two days after you arrived to help out the LAPD. But it was curious – no one had ever heard her talk about suicide before that. There was no note and, yes, she was being investigated, but only for civil tax fraud. Curious reason to kill herself.

'So I had to test you, Winston. I wrote the document in that file.'

It was a fake email that suggested a girl with the name of Nimue was in the suicide victim's cult and had information that the woman's death was suspicious.

'I got a tap warrant on your phone, put a simple Windows password on the file and handed over the computer to see what you'd do. If you'd told me you'd read the file and what it contained, that would've been the end of the matter. You and I'd be on our way to Big Sur right now.

'But, no, you made your phone call to the tech, you had the private company crack the code and you read the file. There was no wipe bomb. No mush. You destroyed it yourself. You *had* to, of course. You were afraid we'd catch on to the fact that your life for the past six years has been traveling around the country and murdering people like Daniel Pell.'

Kellogg gave a laugh. Now, faint kinesic deviation; the tone was different. An excluded subject, yes, but he was feeling the stress. She'd touched close to home. 'Please, Kathryn. Why on earth would I do that?'

'Because of your daughter,' she said, not without some sympathy.

And the fact that he gave no response, merely held her eye as if he were in great pain, was an indication – though a tiny one – that she was narrowing in on the truth.

'It takes a lot to fool me, Winston. And you're very, very good. The only variation from your baseline behavior I ever noticed was when it came to children and the family. But I didn't think much of it. At first I supposed that was because of the connection between us, and you weren't comfortable with children and were wrestling with the idea of having them in your life.

'Then I think you saw that I was curious, or suspicious, and you confessed that you'd lied, that you had had a daughter. You told me about her death. Of course, that's a common trick – confession to one lie to cover up another related one. And what was the lie? Your daughter did die in a car accident, yes, but it wasn't exactly how you described it. You apparently destroyed the police report in Seattle – nobody could find it – but TJ and I made some calls and pieced together the story.

'When she was sixteen your daughter ran away from home because you and your wife were getting divorced. She ended up with a group in Seattle – very much like the Family. She was there for about six months. Then she and three other members of the cult died in a suicide pact because the leader told them to leave, they hadn't been loyal enough. They drove their car into Puget Sound.'

*There's something terrifying about the idea of being kicked out of your family . . .*

'And then you joined the MVCC and made it your life's work to stop people like that. Only sometimes the law didn't cooperate. And you had to take it into your own hands. I called a friend in Chicago PD. You were the cult expert on the scene last week, assisting them. Their report said you claimed the perp fired at you, and you had to "neutralize the threat". But I don't think he did shoot. I think you killed him and then wounded yourself.' She tapped her neck, indicating the bandage. 'Which makes that murder too, just like Pell.'

She grew angry. It hit fast, like a flash of hot sunlight as a cloud passed on. Control it, she told herself. Take a lesson from Daniel Pell.

Take a lesson from Winston Kellogg.

'The dead man's family filed a complaint. They claimed he was set up. He had a long rap sheet, sure. Just like Pell. But he *never* touched guns. He was afraid of the deadly-weapon count.'

'He touched one long enough to shoot me.'

A very faint shift of Kellogg's foot. Almost invisible, but it telegraphed stress. So, he wasn't completely immune to her interrogation.

His response was a lie.

'We'll know more after reviewing the files. And we're checking with other jurisdictions too, Winston. Apparently you insisted on helping local police all over the country whenever there was a crime involving a cult.'

Charles Overby had implied that it was his own idea to bring in a federal specialist on cults. Last night, though, she'd begun to suspect that this probably wasn't what happened and she'd asked her boss point-blank how the FBI agent had come to work the Pell case. Overby hemmed and hawed but ultimately admitted that *Kellogg* had told Amy Grabe in the San Francisco field office of the FBI that he was coming to the Peninsula to consult on the manhunt for Pell; it wasn't up for debate. He'd been here as soon as the paperwork in Chicago was cleaned up.

'I looked back at the Pell case. Michael O'Neil was upset that you wanted a takedown at the Sea View, rather than surveillance. And *I* wondered why you wanted to be first through the door. The answer is so that you'd have a clear shot at Pell. And yesterday, at the beach at Point Lobos, you got him on his knees. And then you killed him.'

'That's your evidence that I murdered him? His posture? Really, Kathryn.'

'And MCSO crime scene found the bullet of the slug you fired at me on the ridge.'

He fell silent at this.

'Oh, you weren't shooting to hit me, I understand. You just wanted to keep me where I was, with Samantha and Linda, so that I wouldn't interfere with your chance to kill Pell.'

'It was an accidental discharge,' he said matter-of-factly. 'Careless of me. I should've owned up to it but it was embarrassing. Here I am, a professional.'

Lie . . .

Under her gaze, his shoulders dipped slightly. His lips tightened. Dance knew there'd be no confession – she wasn't even after that – but he did shift into a different stress state. He wasn't a completely emotionless machine, it seemed. She'd hit him hard, and it hurt.

'I don't talk about my past and what happened with my daughter. I should've shared more with you, maybe, but you don't talk about your husband much either, I notice.' He fell silent for a moment. 'Look around us, Kathryn. Look at the world. We're so fragmented, so shattered. The family's a dying breed, and yet we're starving for the comfort of one. Starving . . . And what happens? Along come people like Daniel Pell. And they suck the vulnerable, needy ones right in. The women in Pell's Family – Samantha and Linda. They were good kids, never did anything wrong, not really. And they got seduced by a killer. Why? Because he dangled in front of them the one thing they didn't have: a family.

'It was only a matter of time before they, or Jennie Marston, or somebody else under his spell started killing. Or maybe kidnapping children. Abusing them. Even in prison, Pell had his followers. How many of them went on to do the same thing he'd done, after they were released? . . . These people have to be stopped. I'm aggressive about it, I get results. But I don't cross the line.'

'You don't cross *your* line, Winston. But it's not your own standards you have to apply. That's not how the system works. Daniel Pell never thought he was doing anything wrong either.'

He gave her a smile and a shrug, the emblem gesture, which she took to mean, You see it your way, I see it mine. And we'll never agree on this.

To Dance it was as clear as saying, 'I'm guilty.'

Then the smile faded, as it had at the beach yesterday. 'One thing.

Us? That was real. Whatever else you think about me, that was real.'

Kathryn Dance recalled walking down the hall with him at CBI when he'd made the wistful comment on the Family, implying gaps in his own life: solitude, a job substituting for a failed marriage, his daughter's unspeakably terrible death. Dance didn't doubt that, though he had deceived her about his mission, this lonely man had been trying, genuinely, to make a connection with her.

And as a kinesic analyst she could see that his comment – 'that was real' – was absolutely honest.

But it was also irrelevant to the interrogation and not worth the breath to respond to.

Then a faint V formed between his brows and the faux smile was back. 'Really, Kathryn. This isn't a good idea. It'll be a nightmare running a case like this. For the CBI . . . for you personally too.'

'Me?'

Kellogg pursed his lips for a moment. 'I seem to recall some questions were raised about your conduct in the handling of the interrogation at the courthouse in Salinas. Maybe something was said or done that helped Pell escape. I don't know the details. Maybe it was nothing. But I *did* hear Amy Grabe has a note or two on it.' He shrugged, lifting his palms. The cuffs jingled.

Overby's ass-covering comment to the FBI, coming back to haunt. Dance was seething at Kellogg's threat but she offered no affect displays whatsoever. Her shrug was even more dismissive than his. 'If that issue comes up, I guess we'll just have to look at the facts.'

'I suppose so. I just hope it doesn't affect your career, long term.'

Taking off her glasses, she eased forward into a more personal proxemic zone. 'Winston, I'm curious. Tell me: What did Daniel say to you before you killed him? He'd dropped the gun and he was on his knees, reaching for the cuffs. Then he looked up. And he knew, didn't he? He wasn't a stupid man. He knew he was dead. Did he say anything?'

Kellogg gave an involuntary recognition response, though he said nothing.

Her outburst was inappropriate, of course, and she knew it marked the end of the interrogation. But that didn't matter. She had her answers, she had the truth – or at least an approximation of it. Which, according to the elusive science of kinesic analysis and interrogation, is usually enough.

# Chapter
# SIXTY

Dance and TJ were in Charles Overby's office. The CBI chief sat behind his desk, nodding and looking at a picture of himself and his son catching a salmon. Or, she couldn't tell for sure, looking at his desk clock. It was 8:30 p.m. Two straight nights the agent-in-charge had been working late. A record.

'I saw the whole interview. You got some good stuff. Absolutely. But he was pretty slick. Didn't really admit anything. Hardly a confession.'

'He's a High Mach with an antisocial personality, Charles. He's not the sort to confess. I was just probing to see what his defenses would be and how he'd structure the denials. He destroyed computer files when he thought they implicated him in a suspicious suicide in L.A.? He used unauthorized ordnance? His gun went off "accidentally" in my direction? A jury'd laugh all the way to a guilty verdict. For him, the interrogation was a disaster.'

'Really? He looked pretty confident.'

'He did, and he'll be a good defendant on the stand – *if* he takes the stand. But tactically his case is hopeless.'

'He was arresting an armed killer. And you're claiming that his motive is that his daughter died because of some cult thing? That's not compelling.'

'I never worry too much about motive ... If a man kills his wife, it doesn't really matter to the jury if it was because she served him a burned steak or he wanted her insurance money. Murder's murder. It'll become a lot less soap opera when we link Kellogg to the others who've been killed.'

Dance told him about the other deaths, the suspicious takedown in Chicago last week, and others, in Fort Worth and New York. The suicide in L. A. and one in Oregon. One particularly troubling case was in Florida, where Kellogg had gone to assist Dade County deputies investigating charges of kidnapping earlier in the year. A Miami man had a communal house on the outskirts of the city. The Latino certainly had a devoted following, some of them quite fanatical. Kellogg shot him when he'd apparently lunged for a weapon during a raid. But it was later discovered that the commune also ran a soup kitchen and a respected Bible study group and was raising funds for a day-care center for children of working single parents in the neighborhood. The kidnapping charges turned out to be bogus, leveled by his ex-wife.

The local papers were still questioning the circumstances of his death.

'Interesting, but I'm not sure any of that would be admissible,' her boss offered. 'What about forensics from the beach?'

Dance felt a pang that Michael O'Neil wasn't here to go through the technical side of the case. (Why wasn't he calling back?)

'They found the slug that Kellogg fired at Kathryn,' TJ said. 'It conclusively matches his SIG.'

Overby grunted. 'Accidental discharge . . . Relax, Kathryn, somebody's got to be the devil's advocate here.'

'The shell casings from Pell's gun on the beach were found closer to Kellogg's position than Pell's. Kellogg probably fired Pell's weapon himself to make it look like self-defense. Oh, and the lab found sand in Kellogg's handcuffs. That means Kellogg –'

'Suggests,' Overby corrected.

'*Suggests* that Kellogg disarmed Pell, got him into the open, tossed the cuffs down and, when Pell went to pick them up, killed him.'

Dance said, 'Look, Charles, I'm not saying it'll be a shoe-in, but Sandoval can win it. I can testify that Pell wasn't a threat when he was shot. The pose of the body's clear.'

Overby's eyes scanned his desk and settled on yet another framed fish picture. 'Motive?'

Hadn't he paid attention earlier? Probably not.

'Well, his daughter. He's killing anybody who's connected –'

The CBI chief looked up and his eyes were sharp and probing. 'No, not Kellogg's motive for killing him. Our motive. For bringing the case.'

Ah. Right. He meant, of course, *her* motive. Was it retribution because she'd been betrayed by Kellogg? 'It'll come up, you know. We'll need a response.'

Her boss was on a roll today.

But so was she. 'Because Winston Kellogg murdered someone within our jurisdiction.'

Overby's phone rang. He stared at it for three trills then answered.

TJ whispered, 'That's a good motive. Better than he served you a lousy steak.'

The CBI chief hung up, staring at the picture of the salmon. 'We've got visitors.' He straightened his tie. 'The FBI's here.'

'Charles, Kathryn . . .'

Amy Grabe took the coffee cup that was offered by Overby's assistant and sat. She gave a nod to TJ.

Dance chose an upright chair near the attractive but no-nonsense special-agent-in-charge of the San Francisco field office. Dance didn't go for the more comfortable but lower couch across from the woman; sitting even an inch below someone puts you at a psychological disadvantage. She proceeded to tell the FBI agent the latest details about Kellogg and Nimue.

Grabe knew some, but not all, of the tale. She frowned as she listened, motionless, unlike fidgety Overby. Her right hand rested on the opposite sleeve of her stylish burgundy suit.

Dance made her case. 'He's an active duty agent killing these people, Amy. He lied to us. He staged a dynamic entry when there was no need to. He nearly got a dozen people hurt. Some could've been killed.'

Overby's pen bounced like a drumstick, and TJ's kinesics read: Okay, now, *this* is an awkward moment.

Grabe's eyes, beneath perfect brows, scanned everyone in the room as she said, 'It's all very complicated and difficult. I understand that. But whatever happened, I've gotten a call. They'd like him released.'

'They – Ninth Street?'

She nodded. 'And higher. Kellogg's a star. Great collar record. Saved hundreds of people from these cults. And he's going to be taking on fundamentalist cases. I mean terrorists. Now, if it makes you feel any better, I talked to them, and they'll have an inquiry. Look into the take-downs, see if he used excessive force.'

'The most powerful handgun known to man,' TJ recited, then fell silent under his boss's withering glance.

'Look into it?' Dance asked, her voice incredulous. 'We're talking questionable deaths – fake suicides, Amy. Oh, please. It's a vendetta. Pure and simple. Jesus, even Pell was above revenge. And who knows what else Kellogg's done.'

'Kathryn,' her boss warned.

The FBI agent said, 'The fact is he's a federal agent investigating crimes in which the perps are particularly dangerous and smart. In some instances they've died resisting. Happens all the time.'

'Pell *wasn't* resisting. I can testify to that – as an expert witness. He was murdered.'

Overby was tapping a pencil on his immaculate blotter. The man was a knotted ball of stress.

'Kellogg has arrested – he *has* arrested some, you know – a lot of dangerous individuals. A few have been killed.'

'Fine, Amy, we can go on and on about this for hours. My concern isn't anything other than presenting a single homicide case to Sandy Sandoval, whether Washington likes it or not.'

'Federalism at work,' TJ said.

*Tap, tap* . . . The pencil bounced and Overby cleared his throat.

'It's not even a great case,' the SAC pointed out. She'd apparently read all the details on the trip to the Peninsula.

'It doesn't have to be a slam dunk. Sandy can still win it.'

Grabe put the coffee down. She turned her placid face to Overby and leveled hard eyes at him. 'Charles, they've asked that you don't pursue it.'

Dance wasn't going to let them dump the case. And, all right, some of her goddamn motive *was* because the man who'd asked her out, who'd won a bit of her heart, had betrayed her.

*Afterward . . . How does that sound?*

Overby's eyes took in more pictures and mementos on his desk. 'It's a tough situation . . . You know what Oliver Wendell Holmes said? He said that tough cases make bad law. Or maybe *hard* cases make bad law. I don't remember.'

What does that mean? she wondered.

Grabe said in a soft tone, 'Kathryn, Daniel Pell was a dangerous man. He killed law enforcers, he killed people you know and he killed innocents. You've done a great job in an impossible situation. You stopped a really bad doer. And Kellogg contributed to that. It's a gold star for everybody.'

'Absolutely,' Overby said. He set down the bouncing writing implement. 'You know what this reminds me of, Amy? Jack Ruby killing Kennedy's assassin. Remember? I don't think anybody had a problem with what Ruby did, gunning Oswald down.'

Dance's jaw closed, her teeth pressing together firmly. She flicked her thumb against her forefinger. Just as he'd 'reassured' Grabe of Dance's innocence in contributing to Pell's escape, her boss was going to sell her out again. By declining to submit the case to Sandy Sandoval, Overby wasn't just covering his ass; he was as guilty of murder as Kellogg himself. Dance sat back, her shoulders slumping slightly. She saw TJ's grimace from the corner of her eye.

'Exactly,' Grabe said. 'So –'

Then Overby held up a hand. 'But a funny thing about that case.'

'What case?' the FBI agent asked.

'The Ruby case. Texas *arrested* him for murder. And guess what? Jack Ruby got convicted and sent to jail.' A shrug. 'I'll have to say no, Amy. I'm submitting the Kellogg case to the Monterey County Prosecutor's office. I'm going to recommend indictment for murder. Lesser included offense'll be manslaughter. Oh, and aggravated assault on a CBI agent. Kellogg *did* take a shot at Kathryn, after all.'

Dance felt her heart thud. Had she heard this right? TJ glanced at her with a raised eyebrow.

Overby was looking at Dance. He said, 'And I think we should go for misuse of legal process too, and lying to an investigative agent. What do you think, Kathryn?'

Those hadn't occurred to her. 'Excellent.'

Grabe rubbed her cheek with a short, pink-polished nail. 'Do you really think this is a good idea, Charles?'

'Oh, I do. Absolutely.'

# Chapter
# SIXTY-ONE

Tears pooling in her eyes, a woman lay on the bed of the cheap transient hotel off Del Monte, near Highway 1. Listening to the hiss of traffic, she was staring at the ceiling.

She wished she could stop crying.

But she couldn't.

Because he was dead.

Her Daniel was gone.

Jennie Marston touched her head, under the bandage, which stung furiously. She kept replaying the last few hours of their time together, Thursday. Standing on the beach south of Carmel, as he held the rock in the shape of Jasmine, her mother's cat, the one thing her mother would never hurt.

Recalling her Daniel, gripping the rock, turning it over and over.

'That's exactly what I was thinking, lovely. It looks just like a cat.' Then he'd held her tighter and whispered, 'I was watching the news.'

'Oh, back at the motel?'

'That's right. Lovely, the police found out about you.'

'About –'

'Your name. They know who you are.'

'They do?' She'd whispered in horror.

'Yes.'

'Oh, no . . . Daniel, sweetheart, I'm sorry . . .' She'd started shaking.

'You left something in the room, right?'

Then she remembered. The email. It was in her jeans. In a weak voice she said, 'It was the first one where you said you loved me. I couldn't throw it out. You told me to, but I just couldn't. I'm so sorry. I –'

'It's okay, lovely. But now we have to talk.'

'Sure, sweetheart,' she'd said, resigned to the worst. She caressed her bumpy nose and no silent recitations of *angel songs, angel songs* were going to help.

He was going to leave her. Make her go away.

But things were more complicated than that. It seemed that one of the women in the Family was working with him. Rebecca. They were going to get another Family together and go to his mountaintop, live by themselves.

'You weren't supposed to be part of it, lovely, but when I got to know you I changed my mind. I knew I couldn't live without you. I'll talk to Rebecca. It'll take a little while. She's . . . difficult. But eventually she'll do what I say. You'll become friends.'

'I don't know.'

'You and me, lovely, we'll be the team. She and I never had that connection. It was about something else.'

If he meant they just had sex, that was okay. Jennie wasn't jealous about that, not *too* much. She was jealous about him loving someone else, sharing laughs and stories, someone else being his lovely.

He'd continued, 'But now we have to be careful. The police know you and they'll be able to find you easily. So you've got to disappear.'

'Disappear?'

'For a while. A month or two. Oh, I don't like it either. I'll miss you.'

And she could see that he would.

'Don't worry. Everything'll work out. I won't let you go.'

'Really?'

'We're going to pretend that I killed you. The police will stop looking for you. I'm going to have to cut you a little. We'll put some blood on that rock and purse. They'll think I hit you with the rock and threw you into the ocean. It'll hurt.'

'If it means we can be together.' (Though thinking: not my hair, not again! What would she look like now?)

'I'd rather cut myself, lovely. But there's no way around it.'

'It's okay.'

'Come on over here. Sit down. Hold my leg. Squeeze my leg tight. It'll hurt less that way.'

The pain was terrible. But she bit down on her sleeve and squeezed his leg hard and managed not to scream as the knife cut and the blood flowed.

The bloody purse, the bloody statue of Jasmine . . .

They'd driven to where he'd hidden the blue Ford Focus stolen at Moss Landing, and he gave her the keys. They'd said good-bye and she'd gotten another room, in this cheap hotel. Just as she'd entered the room, and turned on the TV, lying back and cradling the agonizing wound on her head, she'd seen on the news that her Daniel had been shot dead at Point Lobos.

She'd screamed into the pillow. She'd beaten the mattress with her bony hands. Finally she'd sobbed herself into a tortured sleep. Then she'd wakened and lain in bed, staring at the ceiling, her eyes flicking from one corner to the other. Endlessly. The compulsive gazing.

It reminded her of the endless hours lying in the bedroom when she was married, head back, waiting for the nosebleed to stop, the pain to go away.

And Tim's bedroom.

And a dozen others.

Lying on her back, waiting, waiting, waiting . . .

Jennie knew she had to get up, get moving. The police were looking for her – she'd seen her driver's license picture on TV, unsmiling, and her nose huge. Her face burned with horror at the image.

So get off your ass . . .

Yet for the past few hours, as she'd lain on the cheap bed, swayback and with coils ridging through the skimpy cover, she'd felt something curious within her.

A change, like the first frost of autumn. She wondered what the feeling was. Then she understood.

Anger.

This was an emotion rare to Jennie Marston. Oh, she was great at feeling bad, great at being afraid, great at scurrying, great at waiting for the pain to go away.

Or waiting for the pain to begin.

But now she was angry. Her hands shook and her breath came fast. And then, though the fury remained, she found herself completely calm. It was just like making candy – you cook the sugar for a long time until it reaches the hard-boil stage, bubbling and dangerous (it would stick to your skin like burning glue). And then you poured it onto a piece of marble, and it cooled into a brittle sheet.

That's what Jennie felt within her now. Cold anger within her heart.

Hard . . .

Teeth set, heart pounding, she walked into the bathroom and took a shower. She sat at the cheap desk, in front of a mirror, and put on her makeup. She spent nearly a half-hour doing this, then she looked at herself in the mirror. And she liked what she saw.

*Angel songs . . .*

She was thinking back to last Thursday, as they'd stood beside the Ford Focus, Jennie crying, hugging Daniel.

'I'll miss you so much, sweetie,' she said.

Then his voice had lowered. 'Now, lovely, I've got to go take care of something, make sure our mountaintop is safe. But there's one thing you need to do.'

'What, Daniel?'

'Remember that night on the beach? When I needed you to help me? With that woman in the trunk?'

She nodded. 'You . . . you want me to help you do something like that again?'

His blue eyes staring into hers. 'I don't want you to *help*. I need you to do it yourself.'

'Me?'

He'd leaned close and gazed into her eyes. 'Yes. If you don't, we'll never have any peace, we'll never be together.'

She slowly nodded. He'd then handed her the pistol he'd taken from the deputy guarding James Reynolds's house. He showed her how to use it. Jennie was surprised at how easy it was.

Now, feeling the anger within her, splintery as hard candy, Jennie walked to the bed of the cheap motel and shook out the contents of the small shopping bag she was using as a purse: the gun, half of her remaining money, some personal effects and the other thing Daniel had given her: a slip of paper. Jennie now opened the note and stared at what it contained: the names Kathryn Dance, Stuart and Edie Dance, and several addresses.

She heard her lover's voice as he'd slipped the gun into the bag and handed it to her. 'Be patient, lovely. Take your time. And what's the most important thing I've taught you?'

'To stay in control,' she'd recited.

'You get an A-plus, lovely.'

And he delivered what turned out to be their last kiss.

# Chapter
# SIXTY-TWO

Leaving headquarters, Dance headed down to the Point Lobos Inn, to see about transferring the bill from Kellogg's credit card to the CBI's own account.

Charles Overby wasn't happy about the expenditure, of course, but there was an inherent conflict of interest in having a criminal defendant pay for expenses to help out the very institution that had arrested him. So Overby had agreed to swallow the cost of the inn. His shining moment of supporting Kellogg's prosecution didn't extend to other aspects of his personality, though. He whined mightily about the bill. ('*Jordan* cabernet? Who drank the Jordan? And two bottles?')

Dance didn't tell him that she'd volunteered to let Samantha McCoy stay there for an extra few days.

As she was driving she listened to some music by Altan, the Celtic group. 'Green Grow the Rushes O' was the song. The melody was haunting, which seemed appropriate under the circumstances, since she was en route to the location where people had died.

She was thinking of the trip to Southern California next weekend, the kids and dogs in tow. She was going to record a group of Mexican musicians near Ojai. They were fans of the website and had emailed Martine some mp3s of their music. Dance wanted to get some live recordings. The rhythms were fascinating. She was looking forward to the trip.

The roads here weren't crowded; the bad weather had returned. Dance saw only one car behind her on the entire road, a blue sedan trailing behind her a half-mile.

Dance turned off the road and headed to the Point Lobos Inn. She glanced at her phone. Still no message from O'Neil, she was troubled to learn. Dance could call him on the pretense of a case, and he'd call her back immediately. But she couldn't do that. Besides, probably better to keep some distance. It's a fine line when you're friends with a married man.

She turned down the inn's driveway and parked, listened to the end of the elegiac song. Dance recalled her own husband's funeral. It was logical that Bill, with a wife, two children and a home in Pacific Grove, should be buried nearby. His headstrong mother, though, had wanted him buried in San Francisco, a city he'd fled when he was eighteen, returning only on holidays, and not a lot of them. Mrs Swenson had been quite strident when discussing her son's resting place.

Dance had prevailed, though she felt bad to see her mother-in-law's tears and had paid for the victory in small ways for a year afterward. Bill was now on a hillside where you could see plenty of trees, a stretch of Pacific Ocean and a sliver of the ninth hole at Pebble Beach – a gravesite for which thousands of golfers would have paid dearly. She recalled that, though neither she nor her husband played, they'd planned on taking lessons at some point.

'Maybe when we retire,' he'd said.

'Retire. What's that mean again?'

She now parked and walked into the Point Lobos Inn office, then took care of the paperwork.

'We already had some calls,' the clerk said. 'Reporters wanting to get pictures of the cabin. And somebody's planning to give tours of where Pell got shot. That's sick.'

Yep, it was. Morton Nagle would not have approved; perhaps the tactless entrepreneur would appear as a footnote in *The Sleeping Doll*.

As Dance was walking back to the car, she was aware of a woman nearby, looking out into the mists toward the ocean, her jacket fluttering in the breeze. As Dance continued on, the woman turned away from the view and fell into a pace that matched the agent's, not far behind.

She also noticed that a blue car was parked nearby. It was familiar. Was this the driver who'd been behind her? Then she noticed that it was a Ford Focus, and recalled that the vehicle stolen at Moss Landing had never been recovered. It too was blue. Were there any other loose ends that –

At that moment the woman walked up to her quickly and called, a harsh voice over the wind, 'Are you Kathryn Dance?'

Surprised, the agent stopped and turned. 'That's right. Do I know you?'

The woman continued until she was a few feet away.

She took off her sunglasses, revealing a familiar face, though Dance couldn't place it.

'We've never met. But we kind of know each other. I'm Daniel Pell's girlfriend.'

'You're –' Dance gasped.

'Jennie Marston.'

Dance's hand dropped to her pistol.

But before she touched the weapon's grip, Jennie said, 'I want to turn myself in,' and held her wrists out, apparently for the handcuffs. A considerate gesture Dance had never seen in all her years as a law-enforcement agent.


'I was supposed to kill you.'

This news didn't alarm her as much as it might, considering that Pell was dead, Jennie's hands were cuffed and Dance had found no weapons on her or in the car.

'He gave me a gun, but it's back at the motel. Really, I'd never hurt you.'

She didn't seem capable of it, true.

'He said no policeman had ever gotten into his mind like you had. He was afraid of you.'

*Threats have to be eliminated . . .*

'So he faked your death?'

'He cut me.' Jennie displayed a bandage on the back of her head. 'Some skin and hair and blood. Your head bleeds a *lot*. Then gave me your address and your parents'. I was supposed to kill you. He knew you'd never let him get away.'

'You agreed?'

'I didn't really say anything one way or the other.' She shook her head. 'He was so hard to say no to . . . He just assumed I would. Because I'd always done what he wanted. He wanted me to kill you, then I was going to live with him and Rebecca in the woods somewhere. We'd start a new Family.'

'You knew about Rebecca?'

'He told me.' In a wisp of a voice: 'Did she write the emails to me? Pretending to be him?'

'Yes.'

Her lips pressed together tightly. 'They didn't sound like the way he talked. I thought somebody else wrote them. But I didn't want to ask. Sometimes you just don't want to know the truth.'

Amen, thought Kathryn Dance. 'How did you get here? Did you follow me?'

'That's right. I wanted to talk to you in person. I thought if I just turned myself in, they'd take me right to jail. But I had to ask: Were you there when he was shot? Did he say anything?'

'No, I'm sorry.'

'Oh. I was just wondering.' Her lips tightened, a kinesic clue to remorse. Then a glance at Dance. 'I didn't mean to scare you.'

'I've had worse scares lately,' Dance told her. 'Why didn't you run, though? Maybe in a few weeks, when your body didn't wash up on shore, we'd've wondered. But you could've gotten to Mexico or Canada by the time we started searching.'

'I guess I just got out from underneath his spell . . . I thought things'd be different with Daniel. I got to know him first – you know, not just the physical stuff – and we developed this real connection. Or I thought it was. But then I figured that was all a lie. Rebecca probably told him everything about me so he could hook me in, you know. Just like my husband and boyfriends. I used to get picked up in bars or at catering jobs. Daniel did the same thing, only he was just a lot smarter about it.

'All my life I thought I needed a man. I'd have this idea I was like a flashlight and men were the batteries. I couldn't shine without one in my life. But then after Daniel was killed I was in this motel room and all of a sudden I felt different. I got mad. It was weird. I could taste it, I was so mad. That, like, never happened to me before. And I knew I had to do something about it. But not moaning about Daniel, not going out and finding a new man. Which I always'd do in the past. No, I wanted to do something for *me*. And what's the best thing I could do? Get arrested.' She gave a laugh. 'Sounds stupid, but it's all my decision. Nobody else's.'

'I think that's a good one.'

'We'll see. So, I guess that's it.'

It pretty much was, Dance decided.

She escorted Jennie back to the Taurus. As they drove to Salinas, Dance mentally tallied up the charges. Arson, felony murder, conspiracy, harboring a fugitive, several others.

Still, the woman had surrendered voluntarily and appeared as contrite as they came. Dance would interview her later, if she agreed, and if Jennie was as sincere as she seemed, the agent would go to bat for her with Sandoval.

At the lockup in the courthouse Dance processed her into the system.

'Is there anybody you want me to call?' Dance asked.

She started to say something, then stopped and gave a soft laugh. 'No. I think it's best, you know, just to start everything over. I'm fine.'

'They'll get you a lawyer, then maybe you and I could spend some more time talking.'

'Sure.'

And she was led down the very hallway her lover had escaped from almost one week before.

# Chapter
# SIXTY-THREE

It was perhaps a spectacularly bright Saturday afternoon two or three hundred feet up, but the grounds of Monterey Bay Hospital were leached gray by the dense fog.

The mist carried with it the fragrance of pine, eucalyptus and flower – gardenia, Kathryn Dance believed, but wasn't sure. She liked plants but, like meals, she preferred to purchase them fully functional from those in the know, rather than try her own hand and risk destruction.

Standing beside one of the beds, Dance watched Linda Whitfield being wheeled out of the front door by her brother. Roger was a slim, austere man whose age could have been anywhere from thirty-five to fifty-five. He fit Dance's expectations, quiet and conservative, wearing pressed jeans, a dress shirt starched and ironed, and a striped tie, held in place with a bar that had a cross on it. He'd greeted Dance with a very firm handshake and no smile whatsoever.

'I'll get the truck. Excuse me, please.'

'Are you up for the drive?' Dance asked the woman after he'd gone.

'We'll see. We know some people in Mendocino who used to be in our church. Roger called them. We might stop there for the night.'

Linda's eyes were unfocused and she'd been giving giddy laughs at nothing in particular; Dance deduced that the painkiller she'd taken was really, really good.

'I'd vote for stopping. Take it easy. Be coddled.'

'Coddled.' She laughed at the word. 'How's Rebecca? I haven't asked about her.'

'Still in Critical Care.' A nod at the hospital. 'Probably not too far from where you were.'

'Is she going to be okay?'

'They think so.'

'I'll pray for her.' Another laugh. It reminded Dance of Morton Nagle's signature chuckle.

Dance crouched down beside the chair. 'I can't thank you enough for what you did. I know it was hard. And I'm so sorry you were hurt. But we couldn't've stopped him without you.'

'God does His work, life goes on. It's all for the good.'

Dance didn't follow; it was like one of Charles Overby's nonsequiturs.

Linda blinked. 'Where will Daniel be buried?'

'We called his aunt in Bakersfield, but she doesn't even remember her own name. His brother – Richard? He's not interested. He'll be buried here after the autopsy. In Monterey County, for indigent funerals, the body's cremated. There's a public cemetery.'

'Is it consecrated?'

'I don't know. I'd suppose so.'

'If not, could you find a place for him? A proper resting-place. I'll pay.'

The man who'd tried to kill her?

'I'll make sure.'

'Thank you.'

It was then that a dark blue Acura careened recklessly up the driveway and skidded to a stop nearby. The car's arrival was so abrupt that Dance crouched in alarm and her hand dropped to her pistol.

But the agent relaxed immediately, seeing Samantha McCoy emerging from the driver's seat. The woman joined Dance and Linda. She asked the patient, 'How're you feeling?'

'I'm on pills right now. I think I'll be pretty sore tomorrow. Well, probably for the next month.'

'You were leaving without saying good-bye.'

'My, why would you think that? I was going to call.'

The deception was easily spotted by Dance. Probably by Samantha as well.

'You look good.'

Another slurred chuckle was the response.

Silence. Deep silence; the fog swallowed up whole any ambient noise.

With her hands on her hips, Samantha looked down at Linda. 'Strange few days, huh?'

In response: a laugh both groggy and cautious.

'Linda, I want to call you. We could get together.'

'Why? To psychoanalyze me? To save me from the clutches of the church?' Bitterness bled from the words.

'I just want to see you. It doesn't have to be about more than that.'

With some mental effort Linda offered, 'Sam, we were different people eight, nine years ago, you and me. We're even more different now. We have nothing in common.'

'Nothing in common? Well, that's not true. We went through hell together.'

'Yeah, we did. And God helped us through it and then sent us in different directions.'

Samantha crouched and carefully took the woman's arm, mindful of the wound. She was well within Linda's personal proxemic zone. 'Listen to me. You listening?'

'What?' Impatient.

'There was a man once.'

'A man?'

'Listen. This man was in his house and there was a bad flood, really bad. The river filled his first floor and a boat came by to rescue him but he said, "No, go on, God'll save me." He ran to the second floor, but the water rose up there too. Another rescue boat came by but he said, "No, go on, God'll save me." Then the river kept rising and he climbed to the roof and a helicopter came by but he said, "No, go on, God'll save me." And the helicopter flew away.'

Words slurred from the medication, Linda asked, 'What're you talking about?'

Sam continued, unfazed. 'Then the water sweeps him off the roof and he drowns. Next thing he's in heaven and he sees God and he says, "God, why didn't you save me?" And God shakes his head and says, "Funny, I don't understand what went wrong. I sent you two boats and a helicopter."'

Dance chuckled. Linda blinked at the punch line and, the agent thought, wanted to smile but forced herself not to.

'Come on, Linda. We're each other's helicopters.'

The woman said nothing.

Sam thrust a card into the woman's hand. 'Here's my number.'

Linda said nothing for a long moment, staring at the card. 'Sarah Starkey? That's your name?'

Samantha smiled. 'I can't change it back at this point. But I am going to tell my husband. Everything. He's on his way here now with our son. We're going to spend a few days in the area. That's what I'm hoping. But after I tell him, he might just get back in the car and head home.'

Linda gave no response. She flicked the card with her thumb slipped it into her purse and looked up the driveway as a battered silver pickup truck approached. It stopped and Roger Whitfield climbed out.

Samantha introduced herself to Linda's brother, using her original name, not 'Sarah'.

The man greeted her with a raised eyebrow and another formal handshake. Then he and Dance helped Linda into the car, and the agent closed the door.

Samantha stepped up on the running board. 'Linda, remember: helicopters.'

The woman said, 'Good-bye, Sam. I'll pray for you.'

With no other words or gestures, the brother and sister drove off. Samantha and Dance watched them ease down the winding drive as the taillights, glowing orbs in the fog, grew fainter.

After they were gone, Dance asked, 'When's your husband getting here?'

'He left San Jose an hour ago. Pretty soon, I'd guess.' Sam nodded after the pickup truck. 'Think she's going to call me?'

All of Kathryn Dance's skill as an investigator, all of her talent as a reader of body language couldn't answer that question. The best she could come up with was, 'She didn't throw your card away, did she?'

'Not yet,' Samantha said, offered a weak smile and walked back to her car.

The evening sky was clear, the fog busy elsewhere.

Kathryn Dance was on the Deck, alone, though Patsy and Dylan were nearby, roaming the backyard, engaged in dog intrigue. She'd finished the preparations for her father's big birthday party tomorrow night and was sipping a German beer while listening to 'A Prairie Home Companion', Garrison Keillor's variety radio show she'd been a fan of for years. When the program concluded she shut off the stereo and heard in its stead the distant soundtrack of Maggie playing scales and the faint bass of Wes's stereo.

Listening to the boy's music – she thought it was Coldplay – Kathryn Dance debated a moment then impulsively pulled out her cell phone, found a number in the Samsung and pushed 'Send'.

'Well, hi there,' Brian Gunderson said, answering the phone.

Caller ID has created a whole new response mechanism, she thought. He'd've had three full seconds to figure out a game plan for the conversation, tailored specifically to Kathryn Dance.

'Hi,' she responded. 'Hey, sorry I haven't gotten back to you. I know you called a few times.'

Brian gave a laugh and she remembered the times they'd spent together, dinner, walking on the beach. He had a nice laugh. And he kissed well. 'I'd say if anybody has an excuse, it's you. I've been watching the news. Who's Overby?'

'My boss.'

'Oh, the crazy one you told me about?'

'Yep.' Dance wondered how indiscreet she'd been.

'I saw a press conference and he mentioned you. He said you were his assistant in capturing Pell.'

She laughed. If TJ had heard, it was only a matter of time before she got a message for 'Assistant Dance'.

'So you got him.'

'He's got.'

And then some.

'How've you been?' she asked.

'Good. Up in San Fran for a few days, wheedling money out of people who were wheedling money out of other people. And I wheedled a fee. Worked out for everybody.' He added that he'd had a flat tire on the 101, returning home. An amateur barbershop quartet coming back from a gig had stopped, directed traffic and changed the tire for him.

'They sing while they changed it?'

'Sadly, no. But I'm going to one of their shows in Burlingame.'

Was this an invitation? she wondered

'How are the kids?' he asked.

'Fine. Being kids.' She paused, wondering if she should ask him out for drinks first, or go right for dinner. She figured dinner was safe, given that they had a history.

Brian said, 'Anyway, thanks for calling back.'

'Sure.'

'But, never mind.'

Never mind?

'The reason I'd called? A friend and I're going down to La Jolla this week.'

*Friend.* What a marvelously diverse word that is.

'That's great. You going to snorkel? You said you wanted to, I remember.' There was a huge underwater wildlife refuge there. She and Brian had talked about going.

'Oh, yeah. We've got that planned. I just called to see if I could pick up that book I lent you, the one about backpacking trails down near San Diego.'

'Oh, I'm sorry.'

'Not a problem. I bought another one. Keep it. I'm sure you'll get down there some day.'

She gave a laugh – a Morton Nagle chuckle. 'Sure.'

'Everything else going well?'

'Real well, yeah.'

'I'll call you when I'm back in town.'

Kathryn Dance, kinesics analyst and seasoned interrogator, knew that people often lie, expecting – even hoping – that the listener spots the deception. Usually in contexts just like this one.

'That'd be great, Brian.'

She guessed they'd never share another word together in their lives.

Dance folded up the phone and walked into her bedroom. She pushed aside the sea of shoes and found her old Martin 00–18 guitar, with a mahogany back and sides and a spruce top aged the color of taffy.

She carried it out to the Deck, sat down and, with fingers clumsy from the chill – and lack of practice – tuned up and started to play. First, some scales and arpeggios, then the Bob Dylan song 'Tomorrow Is a Long Time'.

Her thoughts were meandering, from Brian Gunderson to the front seat of the CBI Taurus and Winston Kellogg.

Tasting mint, smelling skin and aftershave . . .

As she played, she noticed motion inside the house. Dance saw her son beeline to the refrigerator and cart a cookie and a glass of milk back into his room. The raid took all of thirty seconds.

She found herself thinking that she'd been treating Wes's attitude all along as an aberration, a flaw to be fixed.

*Parents tend to feel that their children raise valid objections about potential stepparents or even casual dates. You can't think that way.*

But now Dance wasn't so sure. Maybe they *do* raise real concerns at times. Maybe we *should* listen to them, as carefully and with as open a mind as if interviewing witnesses in a criminal investigation. Maybe she'd been taking him for granted all along. Sure, Wes was a child, not a partner, but he still should have a vote. Here I am, she thought, a kinesic expert, establishing baselines and looking for deviations as signals that something's not right.

With Winston Kellogg, was I deviating from my own baseline?

Maybe the boy's reaction was a clue that she had.

Something to think about.

Dance was halfway through a Paul Simon song, humming the melody, not sure of the lyrics, when she heard the creak of the gate below the Deck.

The instrument went silent as she glanced over to see Michael O'Neil breach the stairs. He was wearing the gray-and-maroon sweater she'd bought for him when she'd been skiing in Colorado several years ago.

'Hey,' he said. 'Intruding?'

'Never.'

'Anne's got an opening in an hour. But I thought I'd stop by here first, say hi.'

'Glad you did.'

He pulled a beer from the fridge and, when she nodded, got another for her too. He sat down next to her. The Becks snapped open crisply. They both sipped long.

She started playing an instrumental transcribed for guitar, an old Celtic tune by Turlough O'Carolan, the blind, itinerant Irish harpist.

O'Neil said nothing, just drank the beer and nodded with the rhythm. His eyes, she noticed, were turned toward the ocean – though he couldn't see it; the view was obscured by lush pines. She remembered that once, after seeing the old Spencer Tracy movie about Hemingway's obsessed fisherman, Wes had called O'Neil the 'Old Man of the Sea'. He and Dance had laughed hard at that.

When she finished playing, he said, 'There's a problem with the Juan situation. Did you hear?'

'Juan Millar? No, what?'

'The autopsy report came in. The Coroner's Division found secondary causes. Labeled them suspicious. We've got a file started at MCSO.'

'What happened?'

'It wasn't infection or shock he died of, which is usually what happens in a bad burn. It was from an interaction of morphine and diphenhydramine – that's an antihistamine. The morphine drip was open wider than it should've been and none of the doctors had prescribed an anti-histamine. It's dangerous to mix with morphine.'

'Intentional?'

'Most likely. Just wanted to let you know.'

Dance heard her mother's whispered report of Millar's words.

*Kill me . . .*

'Could he have done it himself?'

'No. That's been ruled out.'

She wondered who might've been behind the death, if it was an assisted suicide. Mercy killings were among the most difficult, and emotional, cases to investigate.

Dance shook her head. 'And after all his family's been through. Whatever we can do, let me know.'

They sat in silence for a moment, Dance smelling wood-fire smoke – and another dose of O'Neil's aftershave. She enjoyed the combination. She started to play once again. Elizabeth Cotten's fingerpicking version of 'Freight Train', as infectious a melody as ever existed. It would rattle around in her brain for days.

O'Neil said, 'Heard about Winston Kellogg. Never would've called that one.'

Word travels fast.

'Yep.'

'TJ gave me all the gruesome details.' He shook his head and gestured for Dylan and Patsy. The dogs bounded over to him. He handed out Milk Bones from a cookie jar that sat beside a bottle of dubious tequila. They took the treats and raced off. He said, 'Sounds like it'll be a tough case. Pressure from Washington to drop it, I'll bet.'

'Oh, yeah. Uphill all the way.'

'If you're interested, we might want to make some calls.'

'Chicago, Miami or L.A.?'

O'Neil blinked, then gave a laugh. 'You've been considering it too, hm? What's the strongest?'

Dance replied, 'I'd go with the suspicious suicide in L.A. It's in state, so CBI's got jurisdiction and Kellogg can't claim that the cult leader died during a takedown. And that's the file that Kellogg destroyed. Why else would he do that, if he wasn't guilty?'

She'd decided that if Kellogg got off the hook on the Pell killing, which was a possibility, she wouldn't let the matter rest there. She'd pursue the case against him in other venues.

And apparently she wasn't going to do it alone.

'Good,' O'Neil said. 'Let's get together tomorrow and look over the evidence.'

She nodded.

The detective finished the beer and got another one. 'I don't suppose Overby'd spring for a trip to L.A.'

'Believe it or not, I think he would.'

'Really?'

'If we fly coach.'

'And standby,' O'Neil added.

They laughed.

'Any requests?' She tapped the old Martin, which resounded like a crisp drum.

'Nope.' He leaned back and stretched his scuffed shoes out in front of him. 'Whatever you're in the mood for.'

Kathryn Dance thought for a moment and began to play.

# Author's Note

The California Bureau of Investigation, within the state's Attorney General's Office, does indeed exist, and I hope the dedicated men and women of that fine organization will forgive me for taking the liberty of reorganizing it some, and creating an office on the picturesque Monterey Peninsula. I've tinkered a bit too with the excellent Monterey County Sheriff's Office.

Similarly, I trust the residents of Capitola, near Santa Cruz, will forgive my plopping a fictional superprison down in their midst.

Those interested in the topics of kinesics and interrogation and wishing to read further might enjoy the books I've found extremely helpful and which sit prominently on Kathryn Dance's and my bookshelves: *Principles of Kinesic Interview and Interrogation* and *The Truth about Lying*, Stan B. Walters; *Detecting Lies and Deceit*, Aldert Vrij; *The Language of Confession, Interrogation, and Deception*, Roger W. Shuy; *Practical Aspects of Interview and Interrogation*, David E. Zulawski and Douglas E. Wicklander; *What the Face Reveals*, eds. Paul Ekman and Erika Rosenberg; *Reading People*, Jo-Ellan Dimitrius and Mark Mazzarella; *Introduction to Kinesics: An Annotation System for Analysis of Body Motion and Gestures*, R. L. Birdwhitsell (the dancer turned anthropologist credited with coining the term 'kinesics').

And thanks, as always, to Madelyn, Julie, Jane, Will and Tina.

# About the Author

A former journalist, folksinger and attorney, Jeffery Deaver is an international number one bestselling author. His novels have appeared on a number of bestseller lists around the world, including *The New York Times*, *The Times* of London and *The Los Angeles Times*. His books are sold in 150 countries and translated into 25 languages. The author of twenty-two novels, he's been awarded the Steel Dagger and Short Story Dagger from the British Crime Writers' Association, is a three-time recipient of the Ellery Queen Reader's Award for Best Short Story of the Year and is a winner of the British Thumping Good Read Award. He's been nominated for six Edgar Awards from the Mystery Writers of America, an Anthony Award and a Gumshoe Award. His book *A Maiden's Grave* was made into an HBO movie staring James Garner and Marlee Matlin, and his novel *The Bone Collector* was a feature release from Universal Pictures, starring Denzel Washington and Angelina Jolie. His most recent books are *The Cold Moon*, *The Twelfth Card*, *Garden of Beasts* and *More Twisted: Collected Stories, Volume II*. And, yes, the rumors are true, he did appear as a corrupt reporter on his favorite soap opera, *As The World Turns*. Readers can visit his website at www.jefferydeaver.com.

# Number one bestselling author Jeffery Deaver is back with sixteen award-winning, spine-tingling tales of suspense.

In 'Afraid' a former model and fashion designer thinks she's found the man of her dreams. Until he takes rather too much control over her life . . . Charles Monroe is 'The Commuter' – a man whose train journey to work is interrupted by his wife ringing to tell him another 30-year-old white male has been found dead. Monroe's life, though he doesn't know it, is over from that moment.

And in 'Locard's Principle', the philosophy on which Lincoln Rhyme has based his career is put to the test when a philanthropist is shot dead in his own bed.

### Are you twisted enough?

Jeffery Deaver's first collection of stories is also available from Hodder: 'A mystery hit for those who like their intrigue short and sweet' *New York Times* on *Twisted*

THE NUMBER 1 BESTSELLING AUTHOR
**Jeffery**
**DEAVER**
**MORE**
**TWISTED**
'[A] collection to keep our blood nicely curdled . . . Terrific'
*Guardian on Twisted*

OUT NOW